MISSING
BELIEVED
DEAD

Chris Longmuir

To Frank

Enjoy

Chris Longmuir

B&J

Published by Barker & Jansen

Copyright © Chris Longmuir, 2013

Cover design by Cathy Helms www.avalongraphics.org

ISBN: 978-0-9574153-2-4

This book is dedicated to all my faithful readers who give me support and provide me with the encouragement to keep on writing. Without readers, a writer is nothing.

1

Friday, 9 March

He checked the van for the last time.

He was a few miles from Dundee and would be there in less than half an hour.

The long drive from Manchester had been more exhausting than he had anticipated so he'd pulled off the road and kipped down in the van late last night. But excitement had made sleep impossible and, when he did doze, he'd had glorious wet dreams.

Jade. That's what she called herself. He wondered if it was her real name or her chat room moniker.

It didn't matter. What mattered was she was twelve and eager to meet him.

He tucked the rope out of sight beneath the mattress and tested the iron rings embedded in the floor of the van. The small bottle of chloroform nestled in his jacket pocket along with a gauze pad.

Giving a nod of approval he climbed over the back of the seat into the front of the van.

The engine started when he turned the key.

He always kept the van tuned up, knowing how disastrous it would be if he had a breakdown when he was carrying cargo.

The rain, spotting his windscreen, suddenly turned into a downpour and he switched his wipers to their highest speed.

Lorries rumbled past drenching the van with spray, and tailgaters annoyed by his slow speed, flashed their lights at him.

Oblivious to them all he whistled through his teeth while he drove, imagining her reaction when she found out he was not a fourteen year old boy but a man nearing his fortieth birthday. It wouldn't matter, he would think up a story to con her into coming back to the van with him and the adventure would begin.

They had arranged to meet at the Overgate Centre, the busiest shopping mall in Dundee, and she got there early so she could look him over when he arrived. If he was a fourteen year old boy, she would walk away. But she doubted that. No boy would be willing to come from Manchester to meet a girl. She was convinced he would be a man.

The food court beside the escalators was busy, but she bought a coffee and found a seat against the partition at the back where she would have a clear line of sight to the servery and all the tables.

The coffee scalded her tongue, and the taste and smell turned her stomach. She placed the cup back in the saucer and cradled it in her hands to stop them trembling. Her breathing became forced and she struggled for air. She thought she was going to choke.

Closing her eyes she battled the panic attack and gradually her breathing returned to normal. She could not afford to chicken out now, not after all her preparations. She had rehearsed everything in her mind over and over, and now she did it again. It would work, it had to. Her planning had been impeccable and the time was almost here. But would she be able to follow through? Would she be able to do it?

The multi-storey car park was almost full but he managed to find a secluded corner. Most folks avoided these spaces unless nothing else was available, but he welcomed them. There was less chance of nosey parkers checking him out.

He waited a few minutes while a woman at the other end of the parking level loaded her car and drove off, then he pushed the van door open and got out. A quick look around reassured him it was safe to go and, leaning into the van, he grabbed the Harry Potter book, tucked it under his arm, and headed for the exit leading to the mall.

The lower level was busy with lunch-time shoppers. He hesitated. Crowds made him nervous, but the girls usually picked somewhere like this and he had developed coping mechanisms.

Breathing deeply, he pulled the brim of his baseball cap forward to partially mask his face, focused on a point above the heads of the moving mass of people, and forced himself to join the stream. He ignored the jostling and pushing, the jab of an umbrella, the heel of someone's shoe digging into his foot, and concentrated on what he would say.

'Kyle,' for that was the name he was using, 'tripped getting out of the van and he's hurt his foot.' He could imagine her frown. 'It's OK,' he would say. 'I'm his dad.' The frown would lessen but she might still be reluctant. 'Silly blighter was keen to meet you. He talked me into driving him here. I was going to have a look round Dundee while you two got together, but . . . ' and here he would shrug and look embarrassed, 'I didn't reckon on him being clumsy. What d'you think? D'you want to come to the van to meet him?' He would wait a few minutes while she considered, and add, 'I'll understand if you don't want to, but he'll be disappointed.' Yeah, that should do it. These young girls were gullible. They would believe anything.

He was easy to spot, and she watched him join the cafeteria queue. She guessed he must be in his forties although he dressed younger and was attractive. Thoughts of what he would want from her flooded her brain. Anger surged through her. She was in danger of losing her self control, so she closed her eyes and breathed deeply. Anger wouldn't help when it came to doing what she had to do.

His eyes scanned the tables but she had not produced her Harry Potter book yet. He probably thought she hadn't arrived. She placed her coffee cup on a nearby table and dug the book out of her knapsack when he reached the till.

He finished wrestling with his copy of the book, his wallet and the small tray with teapot, cup, saucer and Danish pastry, and turned to look for a table. She saw his start of recognition when he spotted her book. This was the crucial moment when she would have to convince him she was a young girl. But that was not the only problem. She had to make sure she could not be identified after she completed her task.

CCTV cameras were all over the shopping mall, in the ceiling and high up on the wall. But she had taken precautions. The hoodie she wore masked her face and, as long as she kept it up, the cameras would be unable to show whether she was young or old, male or female.

His tray wobbled as he picked his way through the tables. A tall, thin man with a hesitant smile, wearing grubby jeans and denim jacket, and a cap with its brim pulled low over his eyes.

'Jade?' His voice was pleasant and reassuring.

She pulled her hood closer to her face. 'Go away. I don't know you.'

He placed his tray on the table. 'Kyle sent me.'

'Why would Kyle send you? Why didn't he come himself?'

'He did come. But he had an accident getting out of the van. The silly sod tripped up over his own big feet and he's sprained his ankle.'

'I don't believe you.' It wouldn't do to make it too easy for him or he would suspect something.

'Cross my heart, it's true. I'm his dad, I should know.'

'Why would he bring his dad with him?'

'He couldn't drive himself from Manchester, could he? He's not old enough for a licence.'

'I suppose.' She made her voice sound grudging, as if she was starting to believe him.

He sat down and poured his tea. 'Can I get you something? Coke maybe? And then I'll take you to Kyle.'

'Yeah, OK. Get me a coke.'

'Don't go away,' he said, 'I'll be right back with your coke.'

As soon as he joined the queue at the counter she tipped the pill into his cup then held her breath until she was sure the tea wasn't going to turn blue. But it was all right, it was just as her supplier had said. The pill was one of the older ones produced before they added the blue dye to cut down on date rapes.

'D'you always wear your hood up?' He set the glass of coke in front of her and sat down.

'Some of my mum's pals might be shopping here,' she mumbled. 'If they see me they'll tell my mum I've bunked off school.'

'I see.'

Luckily he did not push it and she knew she was one step nearer her goal. She felt him watching her and she lowered her head, pretending to drink the coke.

'It's a pity Kyle couldn't meet you here. I bet he's sitting in the van feeling sorry for himself.'

'If you say so.' She could not afford to agree to go with him yet. He hadn't drunk his tea.

'He was keen to come here. I couldn't refuse to drive him.' He took a bite of his Danish pastry.

'Yeah,' she mumbled, willing him to drink the tea. She would never be able to do the next bit unless the drug started to work on him. He was too big for her to overpower without it.

'Please say you'll come back to the van with me. Kyle will be disappointed if he has to go home without seeing you.' He lifted the cup and swallowed.

'Sure,' she said, 'but I'd like to finish my coke first.'

Ten minutes would be sufficient, she thought. And by the time they walked to the van he would be more than ready for the final injection.

He smiled at her. She had taken the bait. Pity he couldn't see her face, but once he got her back to the van he would see far more than that. He was euphoric, thinking what he would do to her, the gifts he would give her. She would never be the same again.

He watched her lift her glass and put it on the tray. 'You ready to go now?'

'Yeah,' she said, stuffing the Harry Potter book into her knapsack and slinging it over her shoulder. 'Let's go.'

The crowds in the mall had increased but they did not bother him. He swayed with them, walking on air. He was more relaxed than he had been for a long time.

He was vaguely aware of her holding onto his arm. 'Nice,' he said, patting it. 'Kyle's going to love you.'

He floated out of the mall into the parking garage. It seemed to be shimmering and swaying.

'Where's your van parked?' Her voice came to him from a distance.

'Top level,' he slurred, 'the far corner.'

'We're here,' she said, although he had no recollection of moving.

'Which one?'

He blinked, refocused and pointed.

Her hands searching his pockets sent delicious shivers through him.

'Wow,' he heard her say. 'This is better than I imagined.'

The mattress felt like a cloud, the ropes like silk scarves, and the injection sent him floating to a higher plane.

2

Saturday, 10 March
He laid the girl on the rug he'd spread out on the dirt floor.
She was beautiful. Her blonde hair was tied back in a
ponytail, although a strand had escaped and fallen over her
face.

There had been another girl, a long time ago. He had
loved her. She had been the light of his life, and he had
thought she loved him in return.

He'd brought her here, to his special place, but something
had gone wrong. She'd fought him, pummelling him with
her fists, and he had held her tight. He could still feel her in
his arms.

Then she started screaming, on and on. It tore a hole in
his heart, and he couldn't bear it. He pressed her face into his
chest, and the woolly jacket he wore muffled her screams.
He pressed harder until the sound stopped. They stayed that
way for a long time, the feel of her body in his arms so
comforting he never wanted to let her go.

It was when she went limp he realized what had
happened. He shook her, but she was like a rag doll. He tried
the kiss of life, but there was no life left in her.

He cradled her in his arms, rocking her and crying. Tears
ran down his face, wet and salty, splashing on her lovely
face.

A long time later, he gently dried her face with his
handkerchief. He would have to do something with her body,
but he didn't want to put it in the cold ground where the
worms would get her.

The oak, cabin trunk in the corner, where he stored his
tools would make an ideal resting place. He emptied it,
padded the bottom with pillows he'd taken from his bed and

covered them with a piece of red velvet. Then he laid her out gently, placing her so she looked asleep.

He closed the lid and left, taking one last sad look at the trunk, before closing the door and locking it.

The trunk was still here and he rested his hand on it, closing his eyes and picturing her all over again.

He looked at the girl lying beside it and, reaching out, he stroked the strand of hair behind her ear with a gentle touch. Her face, so lovely, so innocent, reminded him of the girl whom he had loved with all his heart.

'I'm sorry,' he said, binding her wrists in front of her, 'but it wouldn't do if you ran off, and we are going to have such a good time.'

Once her ankles were bound, he placed a bottle of water and a loaf of bread within her reach, and stood up.

'I have to leave you,' he murmured. 'They'll be looking for you and I need to be back home for the time being. But I'll be back before long.'

Megan stirred and opened her eyes. She didn't know where she was, and it was so dark she couldn't make out whether the place was large or small. The rope binding her wrists and ankles bit into her skin, and when she moved it seemed to tighten. Maybe he was here watching her? She held her breath, listening for sounds that would indicate she wasn't alone, but heard nothing. At least she wasn't gagged, although her mouth was so dry she had difficulty swallowing, and her tongue felt too big.

At first when she screamed the sound was slight, but it gained in intensity, and she screamed and screamed, until her throat felt full of razor blades. No one heard her, and she knew that must have been why he didn't gag her.

Her head ached now, and the shivering wouldn't stop. She tried, yet again, to loosen the rope round her wrists, but they were chafed and sore, and she had to give up. Cramps attacked her limbs and the itch on her leg intensified. Maybe it was a spider, she hated spiders. She opened her mouth to scream again, but all that came out was a croak.

The darkness felt oppressive, pressing in on her and bringing with it strange smells of decay and mould. She shifted her foot and it struck something solid. She seemed to be wedged between it and the wall. There was hardly room to move in the confined space, but she managed to pull her knees up. They cramped again and she stretched her legs out on the cold damp floor, squirming to relieve the tightness in her muscles. The floor beneath her felt strange on her legs, it didn't feel like wood or any other floor covering and she strongly suspected it might be bare earth.

She shuddered. If it was earth, that meant there would be creepy crawlies, and she couldn't stand them.

Tears trickled down her cheeks, plopping off her chin onto her neck. She wriggled her shoulders, trying to reach the damp patches, but it was no use and her cheeks and neck remained wet and sticky, contributing to the chill in her body.

She wondered if her ma would miss her. If she would look for her. But she'd run away too many times, maybe her ma wouldn't bother. Maybe she'd shrug her shoulders and expect her to return once she was ready. But she couldn't return this time.

More tears slipped down her cheeks.

She'd been a fool, no doubt about that. It all started after she met Robbie on Facebook. His photo had been dishy, lovely dark hair, and eyes so blue they made her insides all funny. He was eighteen, he'd said, and she'd told him she was seventeen, even if she was only fourteen. He made her laugh with his comments, and he never said anything out of place, so she thought it safe to meet him.

He suggested the entrance to the Eastern Cemetery because it wasn't far from where she lived. She'd thought it a strange place but he said it would be easy for them to recognize each other there, because loads of folk wouldn't be hanging about, and once they'd met up they could go downtown to the city centre. So, she'd gone there, and waited and waited, but he never came.

A car had driven up and she recognized the guy who got out, he lived in the same block. She turned away hoping he hadn't seen her. He leaned into the back of the car and brought out a bunch of flowers before vanishing up one of the paths. Ten minutes later he returned, without the flowers. She saw him hesitate before he got back in the car. He reversed until it was level with the gate then started to drive out. The car stopped when it reached her. He wound down the window and leaned out. 'You're May's lass, aren't you?' he'd said. 'Your mum was looking for you. I think she was annoyed.'

She shivered, her ma could be a dragon when she was in a paddy.

'I could give you a lift if you like . . . it would get you home quicker.'

'OK,' she said, and got in the car.

'There's a bottle of coke on the back seat if you want it.'

She reached over, took a drink of the coke, and that was the last thing she remembered before waking up here in the dark and the cold.

No one came when she screamed. And now she knew no one ever would.

3

Sunday, 11 March

Detective Inspector Kate Rawlings sorted the papers on her desk into a neat pile and deposited them in the out tray which she lifted and placed in a steel filing cupboard. Tomorrow she had to report for duty at Dundee Police HQ, and there was no way she was going to leave a mess behind at the Forfar office for her detective sergeants to clear up.

Removing her spectacles and laying them on the desk, she massaged her eyelids with her fingers. It had been a long day. She shouldn't have been in the office, because this was supposed to be her Sunday off. But there had been so much to sort out and tidy up before she left. Her brow wrinkled into a frown and she worried whether all the loose ends of her team's many cases had been tied up. But everything had been allocated and her team was a good one, well able to work on their own. She shouldn't have any need to worry.

'Seeing you're still here . . . ' Jan came in and laid a folder on her desk. 'I thought you might want a look at this before you go.'

Kate replaced her spectacles, leaned back in her chair, and sighed. 'What is it?'

'The surveillance report on the Asian guys we were watching. We may have a lead on the location of their cannabis factory.'

'Are we ready to raid it?'

'Just about, but we want to make sure first because it's a bungalow in a fairly classy residential area. Don't want to make a mistake and upset the neighbours.'

Kate combed her fingers through her short fair hair. 'These guys always seem to pick the expensive private housing estates to set up their factories. Maybe they think we won't catch them there.'

Jan laughed. 'They should be so lucky.'

'Anything else on the go?'

'Not really, I think you've tied most things up.'

'Let me know when the raid is arranged,' Kate said, closing the folder and handing it back to Jan. 'I want to be in on it.'

'Won't you have your hands full in Dundee?'

'Probably.' Kate shrugged. 'But I don't want to miss this, we've been waiting long enough to catch them.' She stood up, tucked her white shirt into the top of her trousers, buttoned her cardigan, and pulled her jacket on. 'Well, I'd better make tracks if I want to be bright-eyed and bushy-tailed when I meet my Dundee team tomorrow.'

'Time for a last cuppa before you go? The kettle's on in the staff room.'

'Sure, why not?' Kate was finding it increasingly difficult to leave the Forfar office where she had been happy, and this would put her departure off by a few more minutes.

Jan pushed the door of the staff room open and Kate was greeted by a resounding cheer.

Detective Sergeant Adam Strachan stepped forward. 'Just wanted you to know we wish you every success in this new undertaking, and let you know how much you're appreciated here, ma'am.'

'But it's temporary and I'll still have a foot in this camp.' Kate blinked back tears. At least half the people here had been off duty and must have made an effort to come in. It was at times like this she felt appreciated.

'Yes, but it's a great career opportunity and we wanted you to know how we felt.' He smiled at her. 'We think you're the best DI we've ever had.'

'I hope they think the same in Dundee,' Kate said, thinking she didn't want to go and head up the Dundee team.

'You again!' Mad May Fraser stood in the doorway of her flat. She was a large woman with an ample chest and wild red hair. 'You found the little bitch?'

Bill Murphy shook his head. 'Not yet Mrs Fraser, but I've brought Detective Constable Cartwright to have a look at your daughter's computer. You said she was always on it.'

Mad May glared at Jenny. 'She's nowt but a wee bit lass,' she said. 'What's she know about computers?'

'More than I do, that's why I've brought her.'

Mad May grunted and folded her arms.

The wind, gusting down the walkways in front of the flats, was vicious three floors up. Bill reckoned it must be blowing straight in from the River Tay.

'You going to let us in,' Bill said. 'It's freezing out here.'

May grunted again and reluctantly stood aside.

Bill strode up the hallway into the living room. The dog on the sofa growled, showing yellow teeth.

'Don't mind him,' May said. 'He wouldn't harm a fly.'

The teeth, the growl and the red flecked eyes didn't seem to go with that statement, and Bill gave the dog a wide berth.

The small man, lounging in one of the armchairs and watching television on a massive flat screen telly, lowered his beer can to the floor. 'You found her then?'

Bill shook his head. 'Afraid not, Mr Fraser.'

'Fuck'n useless,' the man snorted, 'couldnae find yer ain arse if ye were lookin for it.'

He reached for his beer can and turned back to watching the television.

'Where do you have the computer, Mrs Fraser?' Jenny Cartwright was staying safely behind Bill. He didn't blame her, she probably didn't like the look of the dog either.

'Oh, you've got a tongue, have you? Well, I hope you're more civil than him.' May jerked her head in Bill's direction. 'He's a waste of space. A proper detective would have found my lassie by now. But not him. All he can say is that she's gone out on the randan, and her only fourteen. What the fuck would he know about it?'

'The computer?' Jenny reminded her.

'Here lass, in the bedroom.'

Bill followed Jenny into a bedroom even more

dishevelled than the living room. The bed looked as if it had never been made, clothes everywhere, and Bill could swear his shoes were sticking to the floor.

Jenny crossed the room to the computer desk which was the only comparatively tidy thing in the room. She switched it on, waited for it to power up and then clicked on the internet icon. A page unavailable came up. She frowned. Turning to Mrs Fraser, she said, 'You did say Megan was always on the internet, didn't you?'

'Yes.' May folded her arms across her chest.

'There is no access to the internet on this computer. How does she connect?'

'Oh, that. She has one of those wee dongle things she sticks into it.'

Jenny sighed and looked at Bill. 'I think we'll have to take it in. I need to get access to the sites she's been using.'

'You're no taking that thing out of here.' Mad May's eyes flared and she stood with arms folded in the doorway.

'I'm afraid we have to,' Bill said in the most soothing voice he could manage. 'We'll give you a receipt for it and make sure you get it back.'

'So you say. I know you polis, the biggest set of thieves around.'

Jenny crossed the room and laid her hand on May's arm. 'I'll take good care of it, and it would help us to find Megan. You do want her found, don't you?'

'Damned sure I do.'

'It'll only be for a few days.'

'Aye. OK. But just a few days, mind. And make sure you find my Megan.'

'I'll carry the tower,' Bill said, 'you take the monitor.'

'I won't need the monitor, just the processing unit, and I'm used to humping them around.'

Bill looked at her. Jenny was small and thin with a cap of short brown hair and oversized glasses that gave her an owlish look. She looked more like a schoolgirl than a police officer.

'And what kind of a man would I be if I let you carry it?'

Bill hoisted the tower into his arms. 'Lead on Cartwright. The sooner we get this back to headquarters the sooner we'll have some idea what has happened to Megan.'

4

Diane Carnegie closed her eyes. She wanted to go back to sleep and return to the dream world where Jade was still part of the family. Without a return to sleep, Jade would slip back into the abyss, with only fragments of the dream left to torture her. But no matter how hard she pressed her eyelids shut, sleep wouldn't come.

Diane couldn't remember a time when she'd slept a whole night. Always she woke in the early hours of the morning. And always she felt compelled to get up and do something. That was the only way to get relief from the pain that never left her. The pain that had been with her since Jade walked out the door and never returned.

She opened her eyes again, letting them grow accustomed to the darkness of her bedroom. When the vague outline of shapes appeared, she slipped out of bed and moved her feet over the carpet until she located her shoes. Her skirt and sweater were draped over the back of a chair and she pulled them on in the dark, on top of her nightgown.

The house was silent, and she was careful to make no noise when she opened the door and slipped out into the corridor at the top of the stairs. Emma and Ryan would be sound asleep, but she crept silently past their bedroom doors, just in case. She paused for a moment outside Emma's door, her remaining daughter, and mourned for the missing one, Jade.

Sighing, and with wet cheeks, she crept down the stairs and into the kitchen where she filled a bucket with scalding water and headed to the front door. She would give the doorstep a good scrub before Emma and Ryan awoke.

Water slopped from the bucket when Diane set it down to

pick up the green envelope from the hall carpet. She turned it over and saw it bore no stamp. It was probably a birthday card. Who could have gone out of their way to hand deliver it? Shrugging, she tore it open, wincing when the paper caught the edge of a hack on her reddened fingers.

She pulled the card from the envelope and stared at the picture of red roses on the front. Happy Birthday to a Special Mother, it said. But she already had cards from Ryan and Emma. Her breath caught in the back of her throat. It couldn't be. Not after all this time. She was afraid to open it and read the signature. But she had to. She had to know.

Diane opened the card with shaking fingers, and read the inscription. A low moan gathered in her throat. The signature she wanted to see was there. She stopped breathing, her chest tightened and a wave of dizziness engulfed her.

She hugged the card to her chest, gasping until her breath returned. Maybe she was imagining it. Maybe she was hallucinating. But they had changed her pills when she started seeing things. So it couldn't be that.

She opened the card again, to read the words written inside through eyes blurred with tears. She dashed them away with the back of her hand and looked at the name again to make sure she was not imagining it. But there it was in a clear upright script – Jade.

She took a deep breath that was half sob. She had always known Jade would come back, that she was not gone forever. When everyone else said she shouldn't hope, she knew what they were thinking. They were thinking Jade was dead. But Diane had never believed that, and now she had proof. Jade was alive, and she had sent her mum a birthday card.

It had been over five years since her daughter disappeared. Diane remembered it as if it were yesterday.

On that nightmarish day in February Diane came home late, delayed at the university by one of her students. The girl was struggling to locate a problem in the source code of the computer programme she needed to complete in order to pass the module, and Diane, always reluctant to fail someone with promise, stayed behind to help her.

Jade came rushing down the stairs as Diane dumped her briefcase on the hall table.

'What's the hurry?' Diane said, blocking the bottom of the stairs.

'Aw, Mum, let me past. I'm meeting Julie, and I'm late.'

'Homework done?'

'Course it is.' Jade jiggled her feet. 'C'mon, Mum, let me past, I'm late.'

'Home by nine, mind. You've school tomorrow.'

'Yeah, yeah!' Jade waved a hand and ran down the front path.

And that was the last time Diane ever saw her daughter.

Emma wasn't sure what had wakened her. She turned her head and peered at the illuminated face of her alarm clock – ten-past-five – too early to get up. She closed her eyes, but it was no use, something had wakened her and she had to find out what it was.

She tried not to look at the empty bed next to her own. It was too much of a reminder of her twin sister, but Mum wouldn't hear of her getting rid of it. 'Jade will need it when she comes back,' she always said, and no matter how much Emma and Ryan tried to convince her Jade was not going to come back, Mum just blanked them and refused to believe. It was as if she were living in a time warp and it was yesterday Jade had left, not five years ago.

The cold wind hit her when she opened the bedroom door. The hall light was on and the front door wide open. Mum was probably outside scrubbing the step. Emma sighed and passed a worried hand through her fair hair, her mum's fetish for scrubbing and cleaning seemed to have grown worse over the past few weeks.

She grabbed her dressing gown and shrugged it on, although she was tempted to return to her room and slide under the duvet. But the vision of her mum, down on her knees, scrubbing the step, seared into her mind. Her mum would catch her death out in that wind. She had to do something. Persuade her to stop scrubbing? Hopeless! But maybe she could persuade her the kitchen floor was more in need than the front doorstep.

The stair carpet shifted under her bare feet and the stair-rod on the step below loosened and bounced to the bottom, clanging against the bucket before coming to rest. Emma stopped and grasped the banister. Mum couldn't be scrubbing the step if her bucket of water was sitting in the hall. Where was she?

'Please! Don't let her have done something stupid.' Emma's throat tightened with fear.

Mum had started acting even more strangely than usual after reading a news item, a few weeks ago, in the Dundee Courier about a missing schoolgirl from the Greenfield estate. Her obsessions had intensified, and her anxiety had gone through the roof.

She hadn't needed to remind Emma and Ryan the girl was not much older than Jade when she disappeared, but it was obvious to them what was in her thoughts.

Emma had breathed a sigh of relief when the girl was found a few days later at a friend's house. But that relief had been short-lived because it intensified her mother's belief that Jade would be found.

She was barely conscious of leaping down the last few steps, nor running out the front door until the coldness of the stone chilled her feet.

The street was dark, but there, under a streetlight, was her mum. A slight figure with rumpled hair, wearing a skirt, and sweater with the sleeves rolled up. Emma breathed a deep sigh of relief and ran down the path, through the gate and over to her. Grasping her arm, she said, 'What are you doing out here, Mum?'

'Jade?'

'No, Mum, it's Emma, not Jade. Jade's gone, remember?'

A confused look passed over Diane's face. 'Yes, yes, of course I know it's you, Emma.' She held something out to her daughter. 'But Jade's sent me a birthday card.'

Emma caught her breath. 'That's not possible. You're imagining things again.'

'I am not!' Diane's voice was taut with anger. 'Have a look at it. You'll see.'

Emma took the card, opening it at an angle so the streetlight shone on it. 'It's someone having a sick joke,' she said. 'Let me see the envelope.'

Diane handed it over.

'There's something inside.' Emma shook the envelope, a small object fell into her hand. She stared at it. 'It's . . . it's a green bead. A jade bead.' Her heart thumped. 'But it can't be.'

'Let me see.' Diane snatched it from her hand. 'It's Jade's. It's part of the necklace she got on her eleventh birthday. D'you remember? I gave her a jade one and you a coral one.'

'Of course, I remember.' After Jade disappeared Emma could not bring herself to wear her coral necklace. It reminded her too much of her sister, and now it had been years since she'd last seen it. 'It doesn't mean anything though. Anyone could have got hold of it.'

'But don't you see? She always wore it. She was wearing it when she left.' Diane never used the word 'disappeared'.

Emma's heart stopped thumping. Jade was gone and there was only one person who could have her necklace.

'Mum, it has to be a sick joke. It can't be Jade. I'd know if it was.'

Diane stared at her blankly, and didn't answer.

'But Mum, don't you remember how we used to feel each other's pain even when we were apart. When she broke her arm I couldn't use mine either, and nothing was wrong with it. When she fell and bruised her knee, I felt the pain. When she was in trouble I always knew it. We were always two halves of the same coin.' Emma paused, thinking of the times they had changed places. It was fun when they fooled their teachers.

Diane nodded.

'Well, I haven't felt anything for five years.' Emma was

careful not to mention the intense sensation of suffocation she had felt the day after her twin sister's disappearance. 'There's nothing there. It's just a big void. Believe me, Mum, I've told you so many times, I would know if she were still alive. Now let's go back in the house and get you warm.'

Diane sensed Emma did not believe her, but that wasn't important. As long as she, Diane, believed Jade had sent the card that was all that mattered. Tightening her fingers on the jade bead and pressing the card to her breast, she followed her daughter into the house.

'You're shivering,' Emma said. 'You shouldn't have gone outside without a coat, and I'll bet you haven't eaten anything yet.'

'I'm fine.'

'No you're not. I'll make porridge. Oatmeal's great for building up warmth.'

Diane opened her mouth to protest and closed it again. Emma meant well, and she knew she had this awful habit of putting her daughter down. Emma never said anything but Diane could always tell by her expression she was hurt.

Emma took a clean pot from the cupboard and scoured it, then washed all the utensils before she started to make the porridge. 'See, I know how you like things spotless,' she said, before ladling some into a plate for her mother.

'You were always the thoughtful one.' Diane forced herself to pick up the spoon and eat.

Three hours later, the house had been cleaned, scrubbed and disinfected. Emma had left for university, and Ryan was slopping about in the bathroom.

Diane collapsed onto the stool in the hall. She lifted the phone book and extracted the business card stuck to the back page. She had always known it would be needed someday, so the card had been moved to each new directory. Rubbing the phone with a disinfectant wipe she dialled the number she knew by heart.

'Detective Inspector Michaels, please.'

'I'm sorry. He's not available at the moment,' the voice replied. 'Can you tell me your name and the nature of your call?'

'It's in connection with the investigation into the disappearance of my daughter, Jade. Can you let me speak to the detective inspector? He knows what it's all about.' Diane's chest tightened and she found it difficult to speak.

'I'm afraid Detective Inspector Michaels won't be available for some time. Is there anyone else I can connect you with?'

Diane struggled for breath. 'There's been a development,' she gasped. 'Just get him to call me as soon as he's available.' Dizziness overcame her and, leaning back against the wall, she carefully replaced the phone in its cradle.

5

Bill Murphy teased the paper cup from underneath the coffee machine spout. It required a special technique to get cup to desk without suffering first degree burns, and Bill hadn't mastered it yet. Not to be beaten, he pulled his shirt-tail out of his trousers and used it to protect his fingers.

Coffee slopped onto the desk and his shirt when he laid the cup down. 'Damn it,' he said. It had been one of those days when his reactions had been slow, his limbs did not seem to belong to him, and his head felt as if it would explode.

'What's up?' Sue Rogers closed the file she'd been studying and looked at him.

'I'm knackered. That's what's up,' Bill grumbled. 'I spent most of yesterday with the couple from Hell. Their daughter's gone walkabout again, and they're convinced she's been snatched by a paedo. I've got half the force out searching for her, and she'll turn up, same as she did the last time, after a rave-up with her pals. Bloody waste of time, if you ask me. Then to top it all, that call out last night took forever. Body in a bag, they said. Bloody body indeed! Turned out it was a dog the size of a race horse. I could have been in my bed instead of spending most of the night freezing my balls off on Broughty Ferry beach.'

'You should have taken time off this morning,' Sue said. 'I'd have covered for you.'

'That'll be right.' Bill rubbed his shirt with a grubby paper napkin he'd dug out of a drawer. 'A little birdie told me our new DI is descending on us today. And I'm already in the super's bad books. Damn, I wish Andy was back.'

Andy Michaels was still on sick leave after suffering a heart attack a couple of months ago, and Bill didn't want to admit to himself how much he missed him. But they had known each other from the time they could walk and talk. They had attended school together, belonged to the same gangs and shared most things, even the same girls from time to time. It was Bill's idea to join the police force and Andy had gone along with it. But, after the initial training, Andy was the one who never doubted the wisdom of their choice of career, while Bill was plagued with doubts.

When Andy was promoted to detective inspector, Bill was glad for him. 'Don't envy you the extra responsibility and paperwork,' he'd said. 'Detective sergeant is good enough for me.' But things had not been the same and there were times when he felt pissed off because he was being left behind.

Sue reached for another file. 'Speaking of Andy, I had a phone call from a woman this morning. She wanted to talk to him about an investigation to do with her missing daughter. I tried to tell her Andy wasn't available but she wouldn't listen. There was something strange about her though – couldn't put my finger on it, although I did wonder whether she might be having a panic attack.'

Bill groaned. 'Not Mrs Fraser again? That woman's driving me nuts.'

'Don't know. I asked for her name but she didn't give it. Daughter's name is Jade though, and she said there had been a development. Thought I might find something in these old files.'

'It's probably some nutter.'

'Maybe, but she did ask for Andy by name. By the way, how is Andy? You seen him since he got out of hospital?'

'Saw him at the weekend. He didn't look good, but they say he's making progress. He's not making it quick enough, if you ask me.'

'Takes a bit of getting over – a heart attack.'

'Yeah. I don't suppose we'll see him back for a while. Give you a laugh though – guess who was in the next bed to him when he was in intensive care?'

'Who?'

'Only one of Tony Palmer's thugs, Gus Daniels, that's who.'

Bill had been trying to get something on Tony Palmer for years, but the man was slick and didn't even have a criminal record, despite being the biggest gangster in Dundee.

Sue laughed. 'That must have made Gus's day, being banged up in hospital beside the copper who's been trying to nail you. Pity we weren't able to get anything on him and his partner, Phil Beattie, we could've banged them both up in prison. A couple of pretty boys would have been welcomed with open arms.'

'Luck of the draw, Sue. One thing's for sure, Phil won't be getting his leg over for a while yet. According to Andy, Gus was smashed up pretty bad in that car crash in January, when we were chasing the Templeton Woods' killer.'

'Speaking of Tony, you ever get anything on him for the zoo caper he pulled?'

'Not yet. But sooner or later he'll slip up and when he does I'll get him.'

'You wish. He's a slippery customer, our Tony.' Sue turned her attention back to the heap of files on her desk. 'Are you going to faff about all day, or are you going to help me sort out these files?'

Bill continued scrubbing at his shirt. 'Bloody coffee stain's not coming out.'

The reception area of Dundee Police Headquarters was accessed at the rear of the building, up a flight of steps and through a door into a fairly large vestibule. Opposite the door were the elevators, and to the left of them the glass partition separating officers from those waiting to be seen. At this time of the morning it was empty, except for Detective Inspector Kate Rawlings, pacing the floor.

Kate knew she should stop, sit down and wait patiently for the super to come and collect her, but her nerves were frazzled. First had been the drive into Dundee during the rush hour and a near miss with a lorry running a red light at the Forfar roundabout. Then the lack of a parking place when she arrived outside the large modern building that was police headquarters, which meant she had to park in the multi-storey car park, a dark cavern of a place. And now she'd been kept waiting for almost half an hour, and she suspected the constables behind the glass partition were talking about her. She was ready to spit nails by the time the super appeared.

Kate memorized the number as the super entered it into a keypad on the wall. She knew from experience she would be ridiculed if she had to ask for help because she couldn't open the elevator doors.

'After you.' Superintendent Logan smiled benignly and touched her elbow. 'This office will be larger than you are accustomed to,' he said as the doors closed.

'Yes, sir.' Kate was careful to keep her voice calm and respectful. It was an unfortunate state of affairs, but women in the police force sometimes had to tolerate a sexist attitude from their male colleagues.

This was one of the reasons she hadn't wanted to be pulled away from Forfar to head up the Central CID team. She was respected in Forfar. She wasn't sure she would be respected in Dundee. Earning that respect would be difficult and would be even harder than usual because she was also expected to keep control of Eastern Division, which would mean dividing her time between the two teams. The chief constable had said he was impressed by her organisational abilities and there were no doubts in his mind she would take both teams in her stride. Likewise, there were no doubts in her mind that if she did not, it would be professional suicide.

'I'll introduce you to the team and then let you get on with it,' the super said, striding along the corridor.

'Yes, sir.' She lengthened her stride to keep up with him. She had heard about this bunch of jokers – a bolshie lot by all reports – and she was not looking forward to meeting them.

He stopped with his hand on the door handle. 'They're a hard-working, experienced team used to working on their own initiative. You'll have to exert your authority from day one.' He turned the handle and opened the door.

Kate seethed. It was obvious from his tone he expected her to have a problem. Well, she would show him a woman could run a team of bolshie cops as efficiently as any man.

The office was large and open plan. A cork board and whiteboard covered the wall at one end. Desks filled the rest of the space, but not all of them were occupied. Two men sitting furthest away from the door looked up from their work, while another one, she wasn't sure if it was a man or woman, continued to tinker with a computer. The woman at the desk in front of her appeared engrossed in files. But the thing that caught her eye was the man standing next to her with his shirt tail hanging out.

The auburn-haired woman raised her head, and Kate heard her hiss, 'Bill!'

He looked up with a start, threw something in the bin and quickly stuffed his shirt into his trousers.

Kate narrowed her eyes. That was the one she would have to sort out first. He was a mess of a man, untidy, sloppy and no self control by the look of it. If he was an example of the rest of the team she was going to have her work cut out licking them into shape.

Bill waited until the super and the DI closed the door of Andy's office behind them before pulling his shirt tail back out of his trousers. 'Damned thing's still damp,' he grumbled.

'You certainly made an impression,' Sue said. 'At least put your jacket on in case they come back.'

'Is that what you call it, an impression? Did you see the way she looked at me? It was as if I was something that had crawled out from under a stone.'

'Can't say I blame her, you look like shit.' She turned her attention back to the files.

After a few moments she looked up. 'You know that girl you thought had gone walkabout? How old did you say she was?'

'Fourteen!'

Sue closed the file she'd been studying and laid it beside two others she had set aside. 'Have a look at these. You might find them interesting.'

Bill wandered over to her desk. 'Why's that?'

'Well, over the last six years three other girls, all aged between twelve to fourteen, vanished into thin air.'

'You thinking there might be a connection?'

'Similar circumstances from what I can see. All of the girls had been playing around in the internet chat rooms before they disappeared. This recent girl who's missing, didn't you say her mother complained she was always on the computer?'

'That's why I brought it in and asked Jenny to have a look.' Bill nodded his head in the direction of the young woman working on a computer.

'Bit unorthodox, shouldn't it be sent to forensics?'

'Not if we want a quick result. Jenny's better than any of those geeks in the lab and it can always be sent to them after she's had a good poke around inside. Anyway, I still think this girl's gone walkabout.'

'What makes you so sure?'

'Gut feeling – besides she's done it before, and I've met the family. Seems to me it's similar to that other one three months ago. She turned up at her pal's house in Arbroath.'

'I'm sure that kind of reasoning will go down well with our new DI.'

Bill snorted. 'Yeah, she looks a real tight-arse.'

'It might be better if we cover our backs and not give her anything to complain about.' Sue tossed the files over to Bill's desk. 'I reckon we should have another look at these old cases, don't you? One of them refers to a girl called Jade.'

Bill frowned as he studied the last file – the one concerning Jade Carnegie. The other two had not rung any bells but this one did. He leaned back in the chair and closed his eyes trying to visualize the family.

Slowly the picture took shape in his brain. The mother had been attractive; a slim, honey blonde, with anxious blue eyes. He recalled she had been some sort of teacher. Her husband had looked more like a man of the earth, with his checked work shirt and jeans. His shoulders were rounded and he had a perpetual stoop, which gave the impression he was uncomfortable with his height. Bill recalled he had dirt under his fingernails and remembered the man was a gardener. There had also been two kids. The boy who was about fifteen had been in tears. The girl was younger, a sullen little miss who had watched him with large emotionless eyes.

The couple had been out of their minds with worry, convinced their missing daughter had been abducted. He could remember the mother saying, 'Jade's a good girl, she'd never go off and not tell us.' One of the things Bill remembered most from that first interview was the long uncomfortable silence that followed – a silence broken by the boy's sobs.

For a time the mother had turned up at the office demanding to know what progress the police had made and what they were doing to find Jade. But they never found Jade and she remained on the missing persons list. After a time the mother stopped coming and Bill assumed she'd come to terms with her daughter's disappearance. It had been a relief not to have to face her and make excuses for their failure, although he'd felt responsible for that failure.

He opened his eyes and sifted through the reports in the file hoping to find something they might have missed. But it was as much a mystery today as it had been five years ago.

He pushed the other two files to the side of his desk and retained the one he'd been studying. 'I'll have another look at this one,' he said to Sue. 'I was part of the original investigation into the Carnegie case.'

'What about the others?'

'I'll have a look at them when I come back.'

Sue raised her eyebrows.

'I'm off to see the family.' Bill closed the file and

buttoned his jacket.

'Isn't it early days to be doing that?'

'I suppose so, but you said a woman phoned in and I'd guess it was probably Mrs Carnegie. I'd be interested to know what the new development is, plus check out how things have been for them since I saw them last.' He was not prepared to tell Sue that something in Diane Carnegie's eyes had got to him.

The DI was clattering about in her office when he passed it, but she hadn't opened the venetian blinds yet. She wouldn't see him leave. He hunched his shoulders and quickened his pace. He was not in the mood to explain his actions to a new team leader. In his hurry he forgot to sign himself out on the staff movements' board.

6

A faint smell of alcohol and sweat hung in the air as Diane carried her bucket of hot water and a waste sack through the disco-bar area of the club.

She pushed the swing door with her shoulder and set the bucket down on the tiled floor while she fumbled for the light switch. Wrinkling her nose in disgust at the smell of urine mingled with the odour from a pool of vomit in front of the last sink, she wondered why it was women's toilets were no better than the men's.

She mopped up the vomit with paper towels and disposed of them in the waste sack, dropped to her knees and started to scrub. The hot water burned her hands but the scrubbing motion that ground the soapy suds into the tiles was something that satisfied her need to get rid of everything soiled, filthy and dirty.

Sometimes the scrubbing helped and sometimes it did not, and today was one of those days when it did not. Dropping the brush into the bucket of hot water she sat back on her heels. Tears dribbled down her cheeks. It had been five years, three weeks and two days since Jade had disappeared, and she had shed tears on every single one of those days. She thrust her hands into the water, swirling it round until she found the cloth. Wringing it out, she wiped up the suds on the soapy floor.

'Ah, there you are. I've been looking all over for you. Bella's reported in sick. I need you to clean the upstairs club and Tony's office when you're finished here. I'll see you get paid for the extra time. Is that OK?'

'No problem,' she said.

She hadn't heard Marlene come in and was uncomfortably aware of her wet cheeks, so she kept her head down, allowing her shoulder length hair to flop over her face.

'Why don't you use the mop?' Marlene sounded puzzled.

'I prefer the old-fashioned way,' she mumbled.

How could she tell her it was the hard physical action of scrubbing and cleaning that kept the pain inside her under control.

Marlene squatted down beside her. 'Look at your hands,' she said, taking one of Diane's hands in her own. 'You soon won't have any skin on them.'

'So!' She snatched her hand back. But Marlene was right. They were red and scaly from too much water. She remembered a time when she'd had nice hands. But that had been in another life. A life when she'd had ambition and a career. A life when she did not have this awful feeling that everything was dirty.

After it happened, the thing that turned her world upside down, she had gone a bit crazy and eventually Paul left her. 'You need to get help,' he'd said when he walked out. Ryan had wanted to go with him, but his father shook his head and said he would send for him once he was settled, but he never did.

It was when she thought she was going to lose the kids, she gave in and saw a psychiatrist. 'You have to stop punishing yourself,' he'd said, 'it's not your fault,' and he had prescribed the pills. They had been her salvation, although they did not stop her thinking it was her fault. She had been too tied up in her own life to keep an eye on what Jade was doing. If she'd looked after her better, Jade would still be here.

'I'll order more gloves,' Marlene said, standing up.

'I still have the gloves you ordered last time.' Diane bent over and mopped the floor. 'I prefer to work without them.'

Marlene shrugged and walked away. 'Well, if you need anything, just ask.'

The floor was spotless but Diane continued to scrub, and the tears continued to flow. Maybe by the time she finished she would be all cried out and she could return to Emma and

Ryan with the false smile on her face. The smile that said, 'Look I've recovered. I'm fine now.'

Ryan Carnegie stood up and stretched, flexing his legs so they wouldn't cramp. He was past his twentieth birthday and small for a man, barely five feet two, slim and gangly, appearing to be all arms and legs. His dark brown hair was tied back in a ponytail, but sometimes he let it hang in loose waves that brushed his shoulders. The stud in his left ear glittered like a diamond, although it was only a cubic zircona.

He walked to the window and parted the curtains to look out. It was a miserable day, tree branches whipped in the wind and the overcast sky gave the impression it was about to rain, or maybe snow. In Dundee it wasn't unknown for there to be snow showers in March, and it was cold enough for it.

The computer monitor blinked away at the other side of the room, reminding him he should be working. Sighing, he returned to his chair and started to key in the last of the code for Tony Palmer's website for his night club, Teasers. It was where his mother worked as a cleaner, and his sister, Emma, was a part-time barmaid. That was probably the reason Tony had asked him to do the website. Ryan was starting to wish he hadn't, and that he'd never come into contact with Tony. Everyone said the man was a gangster and Ryan had no reason to disbelieve this. It made him uncomfortable though.

This was the second set of mock-up web pages he had completed for Tony. He was still smarting from the man's reaction to the first lot, and hoped this would suit better.

'That the best you can do?' Tony had snapped. 'I should have got a professional company to do it.'

'Just because I work from home doesn't mean I'm not professional,' he'd retorted.

Tony glared at him, and Ryan knew it had been a mistake to answer back. Damn, what had possessed him to agree to put up a web site for this man. He had more than enough clients on his books and didn't need the extra work. But Tony had a reputation and was not someone you could safely say no to.

He rose from the chair, stretched and wandered downstairs to the kitchen. Mum was at work and Emma had lectures today, it would be hours before they came back, and he was restless.

Holding the kettle under the tap, he filled it and switched it on. But he didn't really want tea or coffee.

Turning his back on the hissing kettle he walked upstairs to Emma's bedroom, the one she had shared with Jade, and quietly let himself in. He could feel the spirit of Jade in here. It was where he felt closest to her. If he closed his eyes he could see her, sitting in the corner at her computer. 'Come here,' she'd demand. 'Come and help me think of something smart to say to this geek.'

'You shouldn't be talking to anyone on the computer,' he'd say. 'It could be a weirdo.'

Her laughter was as fresh in his mind as if she were sitting there. 'I'm not daft. I'm just stringing him along, having a bit of fun with him.'

Jade's side of the room had not changed. Her computer, an antique beige monstrosity, sat on the corner desk at the other side of her bed – the bed that was still there, waiting for her return. But she would never return. She was dead, he was sure of it. He blinked hard.

'I wish you'd listened to me,' he whispered. 'I miss you.'

Walking over to the bed, he fingered the tiny teddy bears pinned to her headboard. She had collected them and he could remember her excitement when she found one she did not already have. 'Buy it for me,' she'd say, and he always would, even though he didn't get much more pocket money than she did. It was worth it to see the expression on her face and watch her jumping up and down with excitement.

Unclipping one, he held it to his cheek. It still held a faint smell of perfume mingled with dust. He smiled, remembering how she used to nick Mum's perfume, 'Shh, don't tell,' she'd say, as she squirted it all over her neck.

Funny how the smell lingered when only a memory of Jade remained.

Sighing, he walked over to the dressing table and sat on the stool. The silk scarf draped over the mirror, hid the framed photograph he knew was there. Gently he removed the scarf. It smelled of flowers. He held it to his face, feeling the silk caress his skin. Then he draped it round his neck.

He had seen the photo many times before but he never tired looking at it – Jade and Emma with their arms around each other, twins, identical in dress and face, but with two very different personalities. Jade always had a sparkle in her eyes. She was bouncy and full of life, while Emma was the opposite, such a serious and quiet child. Even now, he did not know what Emma had felt at the time. She had gone into a catatonic phase and had not cried or shown much emotion. But Mum had done enough crying for all of them.

After Jade's disappearance, it took him a long time to face going into her room, and he found it perplexing Emma would still want to use it. But she refused to sleep anywhere else. 'It's my room too,' she'd said, setting her jaw in that unmistakable stubborn way that was so familiar.

He cradled the tiny bear against his cheek, thinking, not for the first time, it was a pity it had been Jade who had gone. Emma would not have been such a loss.

Emma Carnegie switched off from Mandy's voice shortly after she entered the library. She had no interest in Mandy's latest love affair. Last week it had been Steven who was enrolled in the new Ethical Hacking course. The week before it was Mark studying Computer Games Technology. Who on earth would want to get tied up with someone who was into games playing as a career? Not that Mandy was in any danger of getting tied up with one guy, when there were so many to choose from.

'Next!' The librarian sounded as weary as Emma felt. Maybe she didn't want to be here either.

She handed over her library card and books, while

Mandy's voice continued to rattle on behind her. Emma wondered whether she'd made a mistake enrolling for the Computing and Networks undergraduate course. She didn't seem to fit in with the student life going on all around her.

The librarian date-stamped and slid the books across the counter. Emma pushed her blonde hair back from her eyes, gathered the books up and stuffed them into her haversack. 'I'll see you later,' she said to Mandy, cutting her off in mid-stream, 'I'm off home to study.'

'A bunch of us are going for lunch. You sure you don't want to tag along?'

Emma paused in the doorway and shook her head. She couldn't put up with any more of the chatter. 'I'll give it a miss. I wouldn't have come in at all this morning if I'd known the prof's lecture was going to be cancelled.' Lectures were the part of her course she liked the least. She had thought a computer science course would have been more hands-on. At least at home she would have access to a computer and she would not have to wait for a library one to come free.

Outside she shivered in the biting March wind, buried her chin in her scarf, pulled the zip of her jacket as high as it would go, and hurried to the bus stop.

The house was quiet when she let herself in. Mum would still be at work, and she never knew what Ryan was up to. She slung her jacket over the banister and went into the kitchen. The kettle was hot. She flipped the switch, waited until the water boiled, and made a cup of coffee.

Cradling the cup in her hands, she headed for her study at the back of the house, switched on the computer and waited for it to fire up. That was when she heard the footsteps in the room overhead – her bedroom.

She stared at the ceiling for a moment. Then, setting her cup down, she tiptoed out of the study and up the stairs.

Ryan dashed tears from his eyes with the back of his hand. The movement sent the fragrance of flowers wafting up from the silk scarf round his neck. Holding it to his face, he breathed in the smell and luxuriated in the softness of the fabric against his skin.

It aroused him. The urge to cover his body with silk was irresistible. He slid open a drawer, plunged his hands inside and closed his eyes, enjoying the sensuous feel of silk running through his fingers.

'What do you think you're doing?' Emma's voice, harsh with annoyance, cut into his reverie.

He snatched his hands out of the drawer and slammed it shut. 'I was thinking about Jade and wanted to see her photo again.' She was not convinced. He could see it in her eyes.

'You were rummaging in my undie drawer,' she spat. 'You had no right.'

He squirmed. 'I thought there might be more photos in there.'

'Likely story.'

'It's the honest truth.'

She strode towards him and grabbed the silk scarf from his neck. 'You'll be wearing my panties next.'

Heat rose from his neck to burn his cheeks. 'Don't talk crap!'

'Weirdo!'

'I'm not a weirdo. I miss Jade.'

'And you think I don't?'

'You're a cold fish. You don't miss her the way I do.'

He held his breath. Emma's eyes widened, and he found the look on her face difficult to decipher. Getting up he pushed past her and rushed from the room.

She staggered, pulled herself together and ran after him. He reached his own room and tried to slam the door, but he was too late. Emma pushed in after him. Anger suffused her face and he backed away from her. He had never seen her like this before and he was suddenly afraid of what she might do to him.

'I'm sorry,' he stammered, hoping to appease her.

'You're sorry,' she blazed. 'Damn well stay out of my room and keep your hands off my things.' She raised a hand to strike him.

The doorbell rang, and her hand dropped to her side. Breathing heavily, she muttered, 'Don't think I'm going to forget this,' before backing out of the room.

7

After the super left, Kate took stock of her office. It was smaller than the one she had at Forfar, but the desk and chair were nowhere near as dilapidated as she was accustomed to. It reflected the priority level the Tayside force gave to Eastern division, which came lower in the pecking order than Central.

She sank into the leather swivel chair and twirled back and forth. This definitely was a lot more comfortable than her saggy old one. Pulling out the top right desk drawer, she frowned when she saw it was full of reports. Security evidently had not been a priority with the previous DI, and if he was sloppy about security it would reflect back on the team. Things here would have to change.

She lifted the reports out of the desk drawer and riffled through them. Nothing seemed to be urgent or pending so she got up to lock them safely away in the filing cabinet, snorting softly to herself when she discovered the cabinet wasn't even locked. She pulled out the top drawer. It was full. She tried the rest of them until she found space in the bottom one. Placing the reports in it she slammed the drawer shut with her foot.

A wave of despondency overtook her and she slumped back into the chair. What had she got herself into? It would take forever to sort out this mess of paperwork, never mind whip the team into shape. She stared at the closed Venetian blinds on the window separating her room from the main office and willed herself to get up and open them. If the team thought she was watching them maybe they would buck themselves up.

She was halfway across the room when her mobile rang. Fishing it out of her pocket she flipped it open and frowned.

Her finger hovered on the accept button for a moment but then she closed the screen and rammed the phone back into her pocket. It was probably another of those silent phone calls she'd been getting lately. She should report it and get a trace put on it but that would send out the wrong signal to whoever was making the calls, and she didn't want to give them the pleasure of knowing they irritated her. Better to ignore them and the caller would eventually give up.

Pulling the cord to open the venetians she stared with angry eyes into the team room. DS Rogers, the auburn-haired woman, was rummaging in a filing cabinet drawer. The desk next to her was now empty. DC Cartwright was hunched over a computer, while the other DC, whose name she couldn't remember, had his head down studying a file.

Her lips tightened when she noted no sign of DS Murphy. The venetians swung when she let go of the cord to open the office door. Marching into the main office she approached DS Rogers who was now shrugging her coat on.

'I'd like a word about procedures.' Kate found it difficult to suppress her annoyance, but Rogers had done nothing to warrant it.

Sue smiled apologetically. 'Can it wait, ma'am. The super asked me to represent him at a meeting at Tayside House and I don't want to be late.'

'See me when you get back.' Kate turned away in an attempt to hide her anger. The super knew she would be starting today. Why hadn't he asked her?

She took several deep breaths until she felt calmer, walked over to the water cooler where she filled a paper cup and gulped its contents. That was better, her heart had stopped racing and she felt more in charge of her emotions.

'Ma'am!'

She had been deep in thought and had not heard the constable approaching. 'Yes?' She smiled. 'It's DC Cartwright, isn't it?' The girl seemed hardly old enough to be a constable let alone a detective.

'Yes, ma'am. I've found some interesting chat room stuff on the computer and we need to check it out with Mrs

Fraser.'

Kate frowned, concentrating on what the super had told her about ongoing cases. 'Is that the family whose daughter is missing?'

'Yes, ma'am.'

'You've met the family?'

'Yes, ma'am. I went with Bill – I mean DS Murphy, on the initial investigation.'

'I see. I suppose we could wait for DS Murphy to come back. Do we know when that will be?'

'No, ma'am.' The young woman seemed embarrassed. 'Should I wait for him?'

'No, no!' Kate nodded towards the detective constable at the other desk. 'Take him with you.'

'Yes, ma'am.'

A few minutes later Kate prowled round the empty room, thinking it was amazing what you could deduce from a person's desk and working space. When she came to DS Murphy's, she tutted with exasperation and lifted the three files sitting on his desk. He needed a lesson on data security. She would make sure his name was put forward for the next training course.

The phone in her office rang, breaking the silence. She walked briskly there, dropped the files on her desk, and lifted the receiver. 'DI Rawlings!'

She listened with rising excitement, scribbling the details on a writing pad. Replacing the pencil on the desk, she said, 'Find DS Murphy, wherever he is, and instruct him to meet me at the Overgate multi-storey car park.' She listened for a moment. 'I don't care what he's involved in. This is a suspicious death and I'll accept no excuses from him.'

Bill drew into the kerb in front of the house in Johnston Avenue. It was one of a row of two-storey, semi-detached villas set back from the street with a small area of garden in front. He sat for a moment thinking what he was going to say, but when he finally got out of the car he was still undecided.

The iron gate hung open and he strolled up the garden path and rang the bell.

The sound of raised voices coming from inside the house stopped. He stood back to get a better view of the windows, waited a moment and rang the bell again. When there was no response he pressed it yet again and this time he kept his finger on it.

Muted voices, the sound of scuffling and someone running downstairs, preceded the door opening.

'OK, OK.'

The slight young man who opened it looked flustered. A strand of hair had escaped his ponytail and flopped over his face.

'You must be Ryan,' Bill said, doing mental arithmetic. The boy was fifteen at the time of the initial investigation. He must be twenty now, although he looked younger – maybe because he was small.

'Yeah!' He frowned as if trying to remember who Bill was.

'You don't remember me?' Bill rummaged in his wallet for his ID card. Finding it he held it up. 'I was involved in the investigation of your sister's disappearance.'

'That was a long time ago.'

'Yes,' Bill said, 'we're having another look at it. D'you think I could talk to your parents?'

'Mum's at work. She won't be back until after four.'

'What about your father?'

'He's not here anymore.' Ryan shuffled his feet and looked away.

'And good riddance too – he was a waste of space.' The girl coming down the stairs was slim with the same honey blonde hair he remembered her mother having, although hers was shorter and worn in a straight style that covered her ears and partly hung over her face almost masking one eye.

'You must be Emma?' Bill reckoned she would be eighteen now, although her unsmiling face, which reflected a mixture of maturity and vulnerability, made it difficult to tell.

'Must I?' she mocked, looking at him with serious eyes.

He changed his mind about the vulnerability. This was a girl who would be able to hold her own.

Bill considered for a moment before saying, 'Can I come in and talk to you?'

'What's there to talk about? You weren't able to help at the time. What's different now?' Emma tilted her chin and glared her defiance. 'Besides it'll upset Mum all over again. She'll think you've found her.'

Ryan fingered the earring in his left ear. 'Maybe we should listen to what he has to say. It can't hurt.'

Emma turned on her brother. 'You want Mum to have another breakdown?' she demanded furiously. 'You know what she was like the last time.' She seemed to remember Bill was there, and added, 'She's never been the same since Jade disappeared but at least she's stabilized now and this will set her off again.'

It was obvious they were unaware their mother had phoned the department so all he said was, 'I'm sorry if it will upset your mother but we do have to take another look at the circumstances around Jade's disappearance. It could help because there have been others.'

'D'you think we don't know that? We read the newspapers, and it hasn't helped Mum. It's only stirred things up again.'

'Maybe it might help her if she knows we're reinvestigating Jade's disappearance. At least she'll know we haven't given up on finding her.'

'Emma's right, what good is false hope going to do her? Jade's not going to come back now.' Ryan's voice was flat and Bill thought he saw tears in the young man's eyes before he turned away.

Bill reckoned nothing could be gained by interviewing Ryan and Emma while they were in this state. 'I'll come back when your mother's at home,' he said, before turning to walk back to the car. The door slammed behind him.

His mobile rang while he was inserting his car key into

the door. Sliding into the driving seat he lifted the phone to his ear. 'On my way,' he said, put the car into gear and headed for the Overgate multi-storey car park.

8

After the door slammed shut, Emma and Ryan stood silent, deep in thought. Ryan was the first to speak.

'D'you suppose after all this time she is still alive?'

Emma desperately wanted Jade to be alive, to walk in the door as if nothing had happened, and for a moment she almost believed it was possible. In her heart she wanted it to be so, but her head told her otherwise.

'Of course she's not,' she grated. 'She would have come home long before now if she had been.'

Ryan blinked hard and Emma thought she saw the glint of a tear.

'Why d'you think the cops are interested in Jade after all this time?' He turned his back on her and walked down the hall to the lounge.

Emma followed him. 'It's not about Jade. It's about all the other girls who have disappeared. They think if they reopen her case it will look good in the papers. It'll look as if they're doing something.'

'I suppose.' Ryan sounded doubtful. 'It'll upset Mum though.'

Emma flopped into an armchair, leaned back and closed her eyes. She remembered only too well how Jade's disappearance had affected her mother. Overnight she had changed from a confident career woman into a neurotic wreck with an obsession for cleanliness. Her father had been no use, he had lapsed into an alcoholic haze, while Ryan couldn't stop crying long enough to offer any support. It had been down to Emma. She'd had to grow up fast, and at thirteen she had said goodbye to her childhood.

'I have to go to the club with the mock-up for Tony's website. I'll see Mum there and let her know what's happening.'

'Yeah, you do that,' Emma said.

It was time Ryan started to pull his weight. She hoped he wouldn't botch it and upset Mum even more.

Diane lugged the vacuum cleaner up the stairs. The hose kept getting in the way of her feet, and her arms and shoulders ached. Stopping at the top she clutched her breast and waited for her breathing to become calmer, before pushing open the door into the night club. This was where many of Tony's customers, mostly men, gathered to watch the pole dancers and strippers while they paid exorbitant prices for their drinks.

The night club was fancier than the downstairs disco, with its plush red chairs, and glass topped tables edged with mahogany. A circular glass stage, with several silvery poles reaching to the ceiling, dominated the middle of the room, and she thought it must be here the dancers performed. However the carpet and chairs were grubby and the whole room had a tawdry look, which no doubt wouldn't be noticed when the entertainment was at its height.

Diane plugged the cleaner into a wall socket and lapsed into a semi-aware state, listening to the buzz of the motor as she pushed the machine over the red carpet, which in her opinion could have done with a deeper clean.

Feeling less than satisfied with the job she'd done, she pulled back the red velvet curtain on the back wall. Marlene had left the door open for her and she passed through it, lugging the vacuum cleaner up another flight of stairs.

Compared to the disco toilets, Tony's en suite bathroom wasn't difficult to clean, although the marble tops and gold fittings made her eyes widen.

Likewise, the huge mahogany desk and the leather armchairs positioned in front of a large one-way glass wall, and the deep pile carpet, provided a feeling of luxury that was absent from the club area.

'You're not the usual cleaner.'

Tony's voice made Diane jump. 'No, sir,' she said, switching off the vacuum cleaner. 'Bella's off sick and Marlene asked me to clean up here.' She pulled the electric plug out and started to reel in the cable. 'I usually clean downstairs.'

'Ah,' he said, looking at her appraisingly.

Heat suffused Diane's body and she turned away to avoid the penetrating stare of his eyes. It had been a long time since a man had looked at her in that way and she found it embarrassing.

'Don't mind me,' he said. 'I won't get in your way.'

'It's all right,' she mumbled. 'I'm finished here anyway. I only have the nightclub toilets to clean and then I'm done.' She picked up the vacuum cleaner and left the office as fast as possible. Anything to get away from those eyes.

Downstairs once more, she stashed the machine beside the others at the back of the small room at the end of the back lobby, which was known as the cleaners' cupboard. Each cleaner had her own equipment as well as her own area of responsibility. Bella, when she was not off sick, cleaned the upstairs nightclub and Tony's office; Diane cleaned the entrance hallway as well as the downstairs disco and bar, while wee Lizzie cleaned the lounge bar and the Members Only area in the small room behind it.

'They watch porn movies in there,' she had whispered to Diane one day, 'but I'm not supposed to know.'

At the time, Diane had shrugged. It made no difference to her what went on, but she had warned Emma to stay clear of that part of the club when her daughter had landed the temporary barmaid job.

Grabbing a bucket she filled it with scalding water. The nightclub had a better class of customer so the upstairs toilets shouldn't be as bad as the disco ones, but they would still need a good scrub.

It was the good-looking blond one who admitted Ryan to the club. 'Come to see the boss, have you?'

Ryan looked up into the man's face and nodded, not trusting himself to speak.

'The name's Phil,' he said, holding out his hand.

Ryan took it. The warmth sent a shiver down his spine.

Phil smiled. 'I expect we'll be seeing a lot more of each other.' He was still holding Ryan's hand.

A door opened and the moment was lost. Phil let go of his hand and said, 'Follow me.' He led the way up the corridor, hesitated a moment at the bottom of the stairs, and turned to look back at Ryan. 'Come on, if you're coming.' There was a hint of suggestion in his voice.

Heat spread from Ryan's neck into his face and he tightened his grasp on the briefcase. The fingers of his other hand were tingling from the contact with Phil, and he wondered what was happening to him. After all, he was a normal guy, wasn't he? He should not be having these feelings. Pulling himself together he strode towards Phil. 'I was just checking I had everything,' he mumbled.

Phil laughed. 'Sure,' he said. The note of suggestion was still in his voice.

Ryan's knees suddenly felt weak but he followed Phil up the stairs to the nightclub. They had just pushed through the door when he spotted his mother coming towards them.

'Ryan?' she said placing the bucket of water on the floor.

'I'm seeing Tony about his website,' Ryan explained. 'I shouldn't be long, wait for me and I'll drive you home.'

Diane nodded and picked up her bucket. 'I'll wait for you in the cleaners' room off the back lobby.'

Phil laid his hand on Ryan's arm. 'Are you coming, or what? Tony doesn't like to be kept waiting,' he said.

Ryan nodded and followed him through the deserted night club which looked a lot different from the last time he had been in it. Then, the glitter-ball had spun shafts of light over the dancing girls below, writhing round the silver poles on the uplighted glass stage, and the men sitting at the tables, watching. He remembered his disgust when a man at a nearby table inserted a note into the g-string of the girl lap dancing in front of him and how the man's finger lingered and caressed her skin. Rage had swamped him, catching him unawares, reflecting his hatred of men who took advantage of women.

Phil pushed aside the red velvet curtain covering the wall and tapped a number into the keypad of the door behind it. Ryan followed him up the stairs and into the office.

Tony moved away from the one-way mirrored wall which overlooked the club, strode to the door and grasped Ryan's hand in a firm handshake. 'You've got something for me?' He seemed in a better mood than the last time Ryan had been here.

'Yes,' Ryan said. 'I think you'll like it this time.'

'Let me see what you've got.'

Ryan walked over to the desk, opened his briefcase and laid out sheets of paper. 'These are mock-ups but the finished thing will have animations. You see the banner here? I thought we could have spotlights sweeping over the name of the club which will have a glitterball circling behind it and sending out facets of light.' He paused to gauge the effect on Tony, before continuing. 'A midnight blue background should set the lights off to perfection and I thought the name should be in gold lettering.'

'That sounds good.' Tony picked up one of the sheets of paper. 'The photographs down the side, will they be animated as well?'

'Yes.' Ryan could hardly contain his excitement. 'The photos of the club will be in a slide show that cycles through all the different areas of the club, and below that I'll put a framed programme of events.'

'I see.'

'In the middle will be a list of facilities with icon logos that can be clicked on to give more details. And the left side will have all the links to the different pages of your site.'

Tony tapped the page. 'Remember what we discussed about having one of the dancers featured on the site?'

'Once you approve the general layout I'll come back with my video camera and get that done.'

'Right, I'll phone you as soon as I've set it up. We'll use

Angel. She's my best dancer.' Tony handed the sheet of paper back to Ryan. 'See him out, Phil.'

Ryan scooped up the other papers and snapped his briefcase shut. 'Thank you, sir,' he said, but Tony had turned away.

Diane washed her bucket, tidied the cleaning stuff away, and waited for Ryan. But she couldn't settle and, taking a polishing cloth, she started to wipe down the shelves.

She had finished cleaning the shelves, mopped the floor and polished her bucket before she heard footsteps in the lobby. Opening the door, she peered out. 'Ryan,' she said as her son approached, 'I'm in here.'

Ryan hugged her. She relaxed, winding her arms round his wiry body. He had never been big and as a child had been bullied because he was smaller than the others, but that had never mattered to her. 'Good things come in small parcels,' she had always said.

'Mum.' His voice sounded anxious.

'Yes?'

'We had a visit from that policeman today. You know, the one who came when Jade disappeared.'

Diane froze. Time stopped. She struggled to breathe. 'They've found her! Thank God! I knew they would . . . '

'No Mum, they haven't found her. But the cop said they're looking into it again.'

Diane's heart missed a beat and she struggled to overcome her disappointment. 'But don't you see,' she said, 'that must mean they have new information and they'll find her.'

Ryan's eyes were troubled.

'They will find her. I know they'll find her.' Diane wrapped her arms more tightly round her son's waist. 'They will find her,' she repeated.

9

Kate held her ID up to the constable, lifted the blue tape and ducked under it. Grasping her hands behind her back, she surveyed the top storey of the car park.

The place was large, gloomy, and smelled of fumes. She could hear rustling noises and footsteps and even the sound of her own breathing. It was the kind of place where even the smallest sound would bounce off the bare walls. She looked up to the ceiling to check out the CCTV cameras, and made a mental note to acquire the tapes.

Most of the cars were gone, although the ones nearest to the shadowy corner, where the dirty white van was parked, were still there. The van's rear doors were open and a white-clad scene of the crime officer was busy working on them.

Outside the tape, in the opposite corner, two boys were guarded by a WPC. One of them was crying.

She hesitated before going any further and, turning back to the policeman, said, 'What's the story?'

The constable pointed to the two boys. 'Those two kids found the body, ma'am. They'd been going through the car park looking for unlocked cars and they opened the back doors of the van.' The policeman grinned, although his eyes remained cold. 'The brats got more than they bargained for though, and they were about to scarper. But they didn't know they'd been spotted on CCTV and they ran right into me.'

'I see. Who else is here?'

'The SOCOs are here, ma'am, one of them is inside the van with the doc, and the other is dusting for fingerprints. They reckon there's been too much coming and going in the car park to find any trace evidence outside the area where the van is parked, but they still wanted this level sealed off.

Constables Hastie and Douglas are standing guard down below and Adams is over at the lift. It's causing havoc with the folks who've parked here. Some of them are pretty annoyed. Then there's myself and Constable Burns. She's the one looking after the kids until someone from the Child and Family Support Unit turns up.'

'And you are?'

'PC Corbett, ma'am.'

'Well, Corbett, I was expecting Detective Sergeant Murphy to join me. I don't suppose he's arrived yet?'

'No, ma'am.'

Kate compressed her lips and walked to the rear of the van where the SOCO was dabbing powder on the doors with a brush that reminded Kate of the one she used to apply make-up. He stopped and looked at her. Kate held up her ID and he nodded before turning back to the task in hand.

'Any prints coming up?'

'Lots,' he said. 'Whether they'll be any use though is another matter.'

A man reversed out of the van. Kate stepped back but was not quick enough and he stood on her toe.

'Sorry,' he said, 'didn't see you.' He pushed back the hood on his white paper suit to reveal a bald coffee-coloured head.

'I hope you were careful not to contaminate the crime scene when you were in there,' the SOCO said without looking up.

'Of course, I was careful,' the man replied testily. 'But it's just as important to ensure the victim's dead as it is to gather evidence.'

The SOCO laughed. 'I could have saved you the trouble and done your job for you, because I never saw anyone more dead than the guy in there.'

Kate's toe throbbed and her annoyance at being ignored showed in her sharp tone when she said, 'Just when you're finished.'

The man glowered at the SOCO, and turned to Kate. 'I'm Doctor Malik, and you are?'

'Detective Inspector Rawlings.' Kate held her ID up. 'What do you have for me?'

He wrenched the front of the paper suit open and shrugged one arm out of it before he answered her. 'Well he's certainly dead, but we won't know what he died of until after the autopsy. There's a syringe stuck in his arm though, I suppose it could be an overdose.'

'Accidental?'

'I doubt it, considering he's tied to the floor of the van. Oh, and something's been pushed into his eyes. I doubt he would have done that himself.'

'His eyes?' She moved towards the open doors.

The SOCO put a hand on her arm. 'You'll have to wait until the crime scene's been processed.'

Kate shook the hand off and turned back to the doctor. 'What's in his eyes?'

'How do I know? I'm not doing the autopsy I'm only confirming death.'

Kate clenched her hands so hard her fingernails dug into the palms. 'What about time of death?'

Malik laughed. 'Impossible to say with any certainty, but the autopsy might be able to pin it down.'

'Would you care to hazard a guess?' The ice in her tone was wasted on him.

'Not really.' He turned his back on her and started to peel off the paper suit. 'But I think you're looking at days rather than hours.'

Bill snorted with disgust. 'For fuck's sake. What am I supposed to do with the blasted car if you won't let me drive up to the next level?'

'Sorry, sir. I have my instructions.'

Bill turned off the ignition. 'Well, I'm leaving it right here and if it's in the way that's too bad.'

He got out of the car, slammed the door, and strode up the ramp. His bad mood did not improve when he spotted the new DI talking to Doc Malik at the back of a van. He groaned inwardly. Why did it have to be her? Why couldn't it have been Sue?

'You've arrived,' she said.

Bill did not have to hear her say, 'At last,' but he was damned sure that was what she was thinking.

'Sorry, ma'am, I was in the middle of an interview when the call came.'

'Well, now you're here, you can get the CCTV tapes for the past week. As soon as I'm finished here I'm going to talk to the boys.'

'Wouldn't it be better to wait until they have a parent or responsible adult present?'

Kate made a noise that sounded suspiciously like a snort. 'I'm perfectly aware of procedures,' she said, 'besides, if I'm not mistaken the officer from the Child and Family Support Unit has arrived.'

Bill glanced over to the boys. His heart did a back-flip when he saw Louise. He had thought she was still off on sick leave after her experience in Templeton Woods in January.

'Yes, ma'am. That's WPC Walker. She worked with CID on our last big murder case,' he said.

Resisting the urge to go over and talk to Louise, he turned back to look at Kate who had said something to the doctor while he was slipping off his plastic overshoes.

'That's it,' Malik said, straightening up. 'I'll arrange for the body to be taken to the mortuary, and once the autopsy's been completed there should be more information about time and cause of death.'

Bill saw Kate's frustrated look as she watched the doctor walk away. 'I'm afraid that's Malik for you,' he said. 'He's never very forthcoming.'

Without waiting for her reply he stepped to the side so he could see into the van. The SOCO in the front seat was leaning over it, and snapping photos.

The body of a man was spread-eagled on a mattress on the floor of the van. His clothing, which had been removed, was piled neatly beside him, and his hands were secured to bolts in the floor.

'What d'you make of it, Colin?' Bill asked the SOCO with the camera.

'I'll be damned if I know? If he hadn't been tied up I'd have said he was a druggie who'd taken an overdose. But I don't see how he could have got that needle in his arm when he's stuck to the floor – looks like he's been crucified.'

Colin laid the camera on the front seat and slid over its back into the rear of the van. 'Make yourself useful, mate, and get me some evidence bags from the boot of my car so I can get finished up.' He counted the garments in the pile beside the body. 'About six should do it.'

Bill returned with the bags and Colin started to put an article of clothing into each one.

'Is there a wallet?'

Colin didn't look up. 'Nope. No sign of one.'

'Anything else to identify him?'

'Not a thing. The only thing we found was a bottle of chloroform in his pocket.'

'Interesting. Wonder what he planned to use it for?'

Colin backed out of the van and stood beside Bill. 'Yeah, I thought that was weird, but there's something that's even weirder, and that's the green beads stuck in his eyes. At a guess I would say they were jade, but we won't know for sure until we get them out to examine, and that'll be after the post mortem.'

10

Emma closed the document and shut down the computer in the time it took for the front door to open and slam shut again. Hurrying out of the study she was concerned to see the look of distress on her mother's face. Emma looked at Ryan and raised her eyebrows in an unspoken question, but he shrugged and refused to meet her eyes.

'Mum,' she said tentatively. 'Are you all right?'

Diane handed her coat to Ryan. 'Of course I am. Why wouldn't I be all right?'

'It's just that you looked a bit . . . ' Emma couldn't find the word to describe what she saw.

A fleeting look of something indescribable passed across Diane's face. 'Ryan told me about the policeman. I think they may have news of Jade.'

'I've told her it's to do with a reinvestigation, but she's convinced they've found her.'

Emma felt sorry for Ryan when she saw his misery, but that could not quell her annoyance with him.

'Jade's not coming home,' she said. 'She's not coming home ever again.'

'I know you think she's dead,' Diane snapped. 'Everybody thinks she's dead Well she's not. She can't be.'

'For goodness sake, Mum! Face up to it. Jade's dead. D'you hear me, she's dead.'

'She must be alive. She has to be. How could she send me a birthday card if she wasn't alive?'

Emma shrugged. Why wouldn't her mother accept what was so obvious to everyone else?

'I told you before, it's someone playing tricks on you.' She avoided looking at Ryan. He hadn't known about the card. 'You have to accept it. After all this time Jade must be dead.'

'I'll never believe that. Never. Not until you show me her body.' Diane raised reddened hands to her face and ran sobbing into the living room.

'Now look what you've done.' Ryan ran after his mother and Emma heard his voice soothing and reassuring her.

Emma sat on the bottom step of the stairs and buried her face in her hands. She wanted to help her mother but how could she when Diane refused to face up to facts? In her mind she cursed Jade for putting them all in this position, but she couldn't deny the empty space in her heart where her twin should be.

After a time Emma went into the living room determined to apologize. However, she knew this would feed into her mother's fantasy that Jade would come home. But, before she could say anything, Diane vanished into the kitchen, leaving Emma frustrated.

The smell of spices filled the house. Diane always made curry when she was most upset, even though, or maybe because, it gave her the most horrible indigestion. Emma was convinced her mother was intent on punishing herself for Jade's disappearance.

She tried to talk to her mother while they ate the chicken korma but Diane ignored her, eating quickly and returning to the kitchen to scrub the pots and dishes. It was always like this. It was as if her mother resented her because she was not Jade.

It was a relief when she left the house to go to work in the club. At least she would have pleasant company who would not look at her with accusing eyes.

Ryan watched Emma go. Her shoulders were slumped and an air of despondency surrounded her. It made him feel miserable as well.

'You need to talk to Emma,' he said to Diane. 'She's hurting too.'

'Since when did you care what Emma feels. The pair of

you are always fighting.'

Ryan didn't respond because his mother was right, and only he knew how much he wished it had been Emma who had gone instead of Jade. But nothing could change what had happened and Emma was still his sister.

Diane sighed and wiped her hands on a towel. 'I'll maybe talk to her when she comes home,' she said, 'I'll see how I feel.'

Ryan nodded. 'I have to go to the club to take photos for the web site. I'll have a word with her when I get there.'

'Don't tell her I'm going to talk to her,' Diane said. 'I might change my mind.'

The disco was crowded when Ryan got to the club, and Emma was busy behind the bar. He waited until she had a moment free and beckoned her over.

'How's Mum,' she said, pulling him a pint.

'Not good. When I left her she was scrubbing out the bathroom. She's got a thing about toilets, always wanting to clean them even when they're already clean.'

'I think she's been getting worse over the past few months.'

Ryan sipped his lager. 'You two need to speak to each other.'

'I know, but it's difficult. When she looks at me, she sees Jade.'

'Probably,' Ryan gulped the rest of the lager. 'I've got photos I need to take, but after I'm finished I'll wait around and drive you home.'

'OK,' Emma said, turning to hurry along the bar to serve a bunch of clamouring students.

Upstairs had a different atmosphere. Most of the customers were engrossed watching the girls dancing on the glass stage in the middle of the room. The girls wound their bodies round silver poles in a series of sinuous movements, and caressed the poles as if they were lovers. Later they would come off the stage to lap dance in close proximity to any man who could pay the price. Ryan found the whole thing decidedly sleazy.

'You've come back.'

Ryan turned to find Phil bending over him. The man's breath wafted hotly over his neck.

'Don't be shy,' Phil murmured, 'you're such an attractive little thing.'

He was so close Ryan could smell his aftershave and the mint chewing gum Phil was never without. Ryan's stomach turned over and he was surprised to find himself wanting Phil to reach out and touch him. But it was a momentary urge and he shook it off, turning his face away from Phil's hypnotic gaze, knowing if he kept up the eye contact, he would be lost.

'Which one is Angel? Tony wants me to video her for his web site.' He hoped his voice was not shaking.

Phil straightened. 'The blonde one,' he said, gesturing towards the stage. 'But I'm sure your tastes don't run in that direction. I know a potential queen when I see one.' He laughed. 'I'll be here when you're ready.'

The evening passed quickly for both Ryan and Emma, and when they got home Diane was scrubbing the kitchen floor. Ryan went into the kitchen while Emma ran upstairs to put her coat away.

'It's time to stop, Mum.' Ryan put his arm round Diane's shoulders and helped her to her feet. 'It's after midnight, you must be tired.'

'Not really,' she said, 'but I have to keep busy.'

'I know, but you have to stop sometime. Besides, you were going to have a word with Emma.'

'Not now. In the morning. I'll talk to her in the morning.' Diane's voice was heavy with exhaustion.

'OK. You go to bed and I'll bring you a mug of Horlicks.'

'I won't sleep. I'm too wired.'

'Take a pill, Mum. It'll help.'

'I don't want a pill. They make me heavy the next day.'

'It would help.'

'You're a good lad, Ryan. Just bring me the Horlicks.'

Emma's bedroom door slammed and he could hear her

descending the stairs.

'Goodnight, Ryan,' Diane said, shuffling out of the kitchen. 'I'm not in the mood just now,' he heard her say to Emma, 'but we'll talk in the morning.'

'What was that all about?' Emma said when she came into the kitchen.

'I was trying to persuade Mum to take one of her sleeping pills but she was resistant. I'll slip one into her Horlicks. She'll never know.'

Ryan set out three mugs. 'The milk's on the boil. I'll take mine upstairs.'

'Sounds a good idea.' Emma watched as he poured the milk. 'I'm beat, I'll be glad to get to bed.'

Ryan mixed the Horlicks and dropped a pill into his mother's mug. 'Not a word, mind,' he said, and lifting two of the mugs he climbed the stairs.

He tapped on his mother's bedroom door. 'Here you are,' he said, 'drink it while it's hot.'

Emma was on the landing when he came out and, after saying, 'Goodnight,' he went into his room and shut the door. He laid the mug on his bedside table, went to his wardrobe and rummaged for the carrier bag at the back. The one he kept hidden from his mum and Emma. Pulling out the sheer, cream silk pyjamas embroidered with roses he held them up to his face, feeling the luxury of the material caress his skin. He shed his clothes and put them on. Pure bliss. At times like this he could imagine he was the girl he was meant to be.

She had found the ideal hiding place, and had perfected the art of stillness when all she moved were her eyes. None of them suspected she was here. It was better they did not know. But now the house was wrapped in silence, brooding and dark, Jade decided it was safe enough to surface.

She stared into the darkness – a darkness as deep as the one inside her – trying to remember who had taken her and what they had done. But the memories were dormant, pushed into the depths of her subconscious. The only thing left was the sense of horror.

Moving first a finger, next her arm, then her legs, she stood up, and cat-like slid from her hiding place. She stretched. It was good to be out in the open, although the time was not yet right to reveal herself.

Inside the house she moved silently on the landing, tempted to open their bedroom doors and look at them. But she had waited so long before her return she could not risk giving herself away now.

Tiptoeing through the darkness she collected the laptop, glided down the stairs – carefully missing the creaking one near the bottom, picked up her mother's car keys from the hall table, and quietly left the house.

She drove down Brantwood Avenue, turned left at the junction with Byron Road, followed it until she came to Derby Street, where she turned to access the quiet parking area behind the multis. There was always sure to be an unprotected wireless hotspot where there were lots of houses. It did not take her long and she was soon online in a private chat room, reeling in her next mark.

When she was done she drove to the club and, using Diane's keys, let herself in the back door. It wouldn't do for either the family or the police to find the laptop. She had to hide it and she knew the perfect place.

11

Kate tightened her lips as Bill moved to peer into the van. The man was insufferable, not only had he tried to advise her about procedure but he had brushed off Malik's treatment of her with a flip remark. Well, a few days of watching CCTV footage would soon sort him out.

Crossing to the far side of the car park she approached the two policewomen guarding the boys. 'DI Rawlings,' she said, brandishing her ID card. 'And you are?'

'WPC Amanda Burns, ma'am.'

'WPC Louise Walker, ma'am.'

'And which of you two boys found the body?' Kate eyed them speculatively. 'Well, speak up lads,' she said, 'we don't have all day.'

'Excuse me, ma'am, but their parents are on the way to the office and I was about to take them there for questioning.'

Kate frowned at Louise. 'I want to know how the body was found. After that you can take them in for questioning.'

A smile of grim satisfaction pulled at the corners of her mouth as she watched Walker's face redden.

'Well lads,' she said, 'which one of you has a tongue in his head?'

'It was me, miss. I was the one as saw the body first.'

'And your name is?'

'Ross, miss. Ross Duncan.'

'Well, Ross. How about telling me what you were doing when you found him.'

'We weren't doing nothing, miss. We was just walking past the van when the door swung open. We couldn't miss seeing him, miss. He were lying there all horrible like.'

Kate's mouth twisted into a grim smile. She wondered

whether his story would change once he knew they'd been spotted on CCTV. She was tempted to tell him but knew if she did, it would contaminate the evidence.

'I see. And what about you?' Kate swung round to face the other boy who immediately burst into tears.

'I think that's enough,' Louise said. 'I don't think we should question them further without their parents present.'

'When I want your opinion I'll ask for it,' Kate snapped. But she knew the policewoman was right, which made it even more aggravating.

'Oops, here comes your boss. I'm off to pack up my kit before she nobbles me.' Colin scuttled to the front of the van and started to gather up his gear.

Bill followed him and tapped his shoulder. 'What's the matter, mate. You got something against women cops?'

'Not particularly, but that is one formidable lady. Besides, I heard the way she talked to the doc and I'm not in the mood for that kind of treatment.'

Bill suppressed a laugh. 'Go on then. I'll keep her occupied.'

He watched Kate's approach, and was forced to agree with Colin's assessment of her as she strode purposefully towards them with a ferocious expression on her face. Beyond her, Louise and WPC Burns were ushering the two boys into a car. He willed Louise to turn and look towards him, maybe send him some signal, Bill was disappointed when she didn't.

He turned back to Colin. 'I expect the DI's going to want to see inside the van,' Bill said. 'Is it clear for that yet?'

'Sure.' Colin grabbed his bag and headed for the SOCO van. 'We're finished but the guys from the mortuary will be here any minute. You'd better be quick.'

'What's happening?' Kate's voice was sharp.

'The SOCOs are finished, ma'am. We can have a closer look at the body now.'

'About time,' she muttered. 'They say anything?'

'They think it's an overdose. He's got a needle stuck in his arm, but he's also tied to the floor of the van. They don't think it was accidental. Oh, and he's got green beads stuck in his eyes.'

Kate scrambled into the van for a closer look. 'You think it might be a weird sexual game gone wrong?'

'Could be,' Bill said. The uncomfortable feeling at the pit of his stomach led him to think it was something more. However, he did not think Kate would be open to anything intuitive. She would be more into facts and evidence than gut feelings.

She reversed out of the van. 'Have a look and see what you think,' she said, 'and write a report. I'll want it on my desk before the briefing meeting tomorrow morning.'

'Yes, ma'am.'

'Stay here and wait for the body to be removed. The meeting will be at 8.30am sharp. Be there.' She strode off in the direction of the lower level where the police cars were parked.

Bill thrust his clenched hands into his pockets to prevent himself from thumping the back of the van. Bloody woman. What made it all right for her to instruct him when she was skiving off? She was the senior officer. She was the one who should have stayed at the crime scene. He struck the side of his thighs repeatedly with his clenched fists until he cooled down, and then turned to inspect what was inside the van.

It was just as Colin had described. The man was on his back on a mattress, his arms and legs spread out and bound by rope which was attached to iron rings embedded in the van's floor. His skin was hairless and pale, apart from the reddened area on the parts of his body resting on the mattress. Bill knew it signified livor mortis, where gravity had ensured the blood pooled in the region of his back. The eyes were open and would have been staring vacantly upwards if it were not for the objects pressed into them. Bill leaned forward for a closer look. He could see intricate carvings on the beads and, like Colin, thought they were jade.

The expression on the man's face gave no indication of any suffering. His lips were curved into a smile and, apart from the beads in his eyes, Bill considered he looked peaceful. It didn't make any sense and he wondered what kind of person could do such a thing.

Pulling his notebook and a pencil from his pocket he made a rough sketch of the interior of the van. It might come in handy later. Then, shivering, he backed out of it relieved this part of the job was complete.

This level of the car park was now deserted and a gust of wind whistled eerily across the empty space, drifting round his ankles, making his feet even colder than they already were. He walked over to the down ramp and leaned over the parapet at the top.

'You still there, constable?' he shouted.

A disembodied voice answered him. 'Yes, sir, I have to wait until they come for the van before I can go.'

Bill nodded and returned to the van. He leaned against the side of it and chewed on the end of his pencil. It was at times like these he missed the fags and the cool feel of smoke being drawn into his lungs. But up to now he had always resisted, although he was not sure how much longer he could hold out. Spitting out the wood splinters on his tongue he dug his hands in his pockets and crossed to the edge of the car park to look out into the darkness of the night.

By the time the mortuary van turned up an hour later, Bill was so cold he could hardly feel his hands or feet. Two men got out. The taller one glared at Bill and said, 'You in charge, mate? Where's this body, then?'

Bill gestured towards the dirty white van and the other man disappeared inside it. Seconds later he stuck his head out and complained, 'How we supposed to shift him when the bleeder's tied to the floor?'

Bill swore under his breath. Colin should have seen to that before he left. 'Sorry, lads.' He looked around to see if he could find anything sharp to cut the ropes. Drawing a blank in the front of the van, he said, 'Don't suppose you lads have a knife or a pair of scissors, do you?'

'It's against the law to carry a knife,' the bigger and more aggressive man said, 'but lucky for you I might happen to have something in the motor.'

Bill's eyes widened when he produced a box and opened it to reveal a large carving knife.

'Before you say anything,' he said, 'it's a present for the missus. Her carver's knackered and I do like a bit of roast beef. Anyway, it's a damn silly law, how're you supposed to get these things home after you've bought them?'

Bill was too cold to argue. He took the knife and cut the ropes, preserving the knots in case they were needed for evidence.

The men produced a long oblong box and after loading the body inside, drove off.

Shortly afterwards the white van was collected by a low-loader and removed to the police compound, and it was only then he felt free to leave the crime scene.

When he arrived back at headquarters Bill was relieved to find the CID room empty. It had been a long day, he was cold and tired, and not in the mood for company. He just wanted to get finished for the night.

He sat at his desk and switched on the computer to write his report and get it out of the way. But he couldn't get the thought of the body in the van out of his mind. Something about those jade beads niggled him. He knew he had read something recently about jade beads or a jade necklace and he couldn't think what it was.

The computer blinked and made a noise as if to say it was ready and why didn't he get on with it. But Bill's mind was far away. He stared blankly at the top of his desk. Something was different about it. It was too tidy. The files he had left were no longer there. He needed those files. They might contain something to trigger his memory.

Sighing, he turned to his filing cabinet. Sue must have tidied up for him. But the files were not there either. Nor were they in his desk drawers, Sue's desk drawers, or her filing cabinet.

He swore loudly and vociferously. The new DI must have been snooping around. He could lay bets she had taken the files. Stamping to her office he searched her desk before turning to the filing cabinet. It was locked. He searched for the keys in all the places office staff usually hid them, but came up a blank.

'Bugger it,' he shouted, thumping the filing cabinet with his fist. That meant he would have to ask her for the files in the morning, and he could guess what she would say to him. Well, let her do her worst, 'It's not as if I care anyway,' Bill thought, with a touch of bravado. 'Damn her.'

Forgetting all about his report Bill left the office. He had better things to do with his life than worry about a here today, gone tomorrow, DI.

12

Kate was still seething when she drove into Forfar.

She'd seen the look on Murphy's face when she left, and knew he thought she was skiving off and leaving him to wait at the crime scene for everything to be concluded. But she was his DI. He would have to learn she meant business and he would have to follow her orders whether he liked them or not.

One parking place was left at Forfar HQ, and she reversed into it faster than she usually did, flung the door open and got out.

'Whoa, you're in an almighty hurry.' DS Adam Strachan opened his car door.

'Good job I waited or you'd have winged me.' He grinned at her. 'Your first day not so good?'

'It wasn't too bad,' Kate said. 'The team seem to be on the ball, apart from one bolshie character who got right up my nose.'

'There's always one.'

'I'm not sure how they see me, though. They've never had a woman DI before.'

'They'll get used to it. We did.'

'I suppose. The Forfar team's a dawdle though, compared to the Dundee one. Anyway, down to business. Are we ready for this raid, or what?'

'Yeah, the team's already been briefed and raring to go, and I've got a bunch of uniforms waiting for the signal.'

'Let's do it.'

Kate travelled to the site of the planned raid with Strachan. The rest of the team followed in unmarked cars, with two police vans following them. The vans parked round the corner out of sight of the cannabis factory which looked like every other bungalow in the street.

Uniformed police exited the vans, taking care not to slam the doors or make a noise. Several of them jumped a fence and headed for the rear of the bungalows where they would move from garden to garden until they reached the rear of the factory. The others bent double, scuttled round the corner in single file, and up the street.

When they reached the bungalow the first man in the line hefted the bull bar onto his shoulder and, at a signal from Kate, ran up the path with the other officers following close behind.

Reaching the door he pounded it with the bar, shouting, 'Police, police!'

It took several hard thumps with the bull bar before the door caved in. Yelling, 'Police, police,' they surged in, followed by Kate and Adam Strachan.

The heat engulfed Kate. The only time she'd encountered anything like it before was when she walked off a plane in Cyprus during a heatwave. She blinked and wiped the sweat from her eyes. The light was blinding, the smell of the plants overwhelming, and there was so much greenery the pots holding the plants couldn't be seen. Every wall inside the house had been demolished leaving one large room filled with thousands of plants, electric wires, duct pipes encased in silver foil, fans and heat lamps.

The two Asian boys cowering in a corner couldn't have been any older than fourteen. They looked blankly at the officer questioning them.

'Are these boys the only ones here?' Kate frowned. The intelligence had been that six men had entered the house late in the afternoon.

DC Jim Morgan nodded. 'They don't seem to speak English and I can't find out what happened to the others,' he said. 'The boys we've detained are gardeners. It's common for gangs to use kids they've brought in to the country to tend the crops.'

'Bring them in anyway. Maybe they can tell us something if we get a translator.'

'They probably don't know much. These gangs are clever.'

'It's worth a try.'

Bill's stomach growled, reminding him he hadn't eaten anything since midday, and that had only been a sandwich. Sue was always saying he'd get an ulcer because he didn't look after himself. Maybe she was right, it was the bane of many a policeman's life, one of the occupational hazards of the job.

The wind caught him as he left the centrally heated police headquarters for the cold of a typical March night in Dundee. He stopped, buttoned his jacket, turned his collar up, and ran down the steps to where he'd left his car in one of the disabled parking spaces. It started at the first turn of the ignition, something of a miracle considering the trouble he'd been having lately, then he drove in the direction of Perth Road and the Deep Sea fish restaurant. A fish and chip supper would go down nicely.

The fish restaurant was a popular place with the students from the university, and workers on their way home, and the queues were usually long, but Bill hit a quiet period and was soon outside again clutching his paper-wrapped supper. He drove the car to Riverside Drive where he found a parking place facing the river. Grabbing the parcel from the front passenger seat he unwrapped it and ate, relishing the taste of fish and chips liberally sprinkled with vinegar. The car would stink for days but he didn't care, he was enjoying it. Finished, he screwed the paper wrapping into a ball and heaved it into the passenger footwell, wiped his hands on a duster he used to clean his windscreen, leaned back in the seat and closed his eyes.

He woke with a start thinking of Evie. He hadn't meant to fall asleep and the dream of his ex-wife was unwelcome. Usually he pushed thoughts of her to the back of his mind, but now he remembered the time before everything became intolerable. Evie, with her long blonde hair streaming behind her in the wind as they walked along the esplanade, her waist soft beneath his hand. They stopped to kiss in front of where he was parked now. He had thought he was lucky having someone like Evie in love with him, and he had been besotted with her. He hadn't recognized the danger signals. The one drink too many, the way her eyes lit up when an attractive man entered the room, the way she flirted with his pals. The wedding had been ostentatious. She'd wanted to be married in white, and she'd wanted everyone to see her special day. It had almost bankrupted Bill, but he hadn't cared because he'd been so much in love. He would have given her anything.

However, Evie had been more in love with the idea of being married than she was with him. She craved excitement. Sometimes she got that from the bottle, but there were the men as well. At first Bill tried to ignore it, but the lying and cheating got to him and he became more and more depressed. If he'd been able to face her with her infidelities it would have been better, but he couldn't bring himself to do that. Eventually things came to a head and she ran off with one of his best mates, Craig, a sergeant in the drug squad.

Bill shook his head. He had to stop thinking of Evie, it made him depressed all over again. Grabbing the greasy wrapping paper from the footwell, he got out of the car, strode to a nearby rubbish bin and tossed it in. He turned to face the river, dark and tumultuous, with waves battering against the wall. Spray stung his skin and the wind battered his body. Faraway lights from Newport-on-Tay, at the other side of the river, gleamed in the darkness. The river beckoned him, but he didn't have the guts to do anything that would end his misery.

Pushing Evie out of his mind, his thoughts turned to what he remembered of Diane Carnegie. She'd seemed vulnerable at the time, and her agony had struck a chord with him. He'd wanted to reach out and wrap his arms round her, protect her, keep her safe. But he couldn't do that because she was part of his work. And now that old case of a missing child had become entangled in the murder case he was currently investigating.

Sighing, he turned back to the car, got in the driving seat, and drove home.

The ground floor flat in the Victorian villa was cold, dark and unwelcoming. It hadn't always been like that. Evie may have had her faults but she'd made the flat a home. That was before she'd run off with Craig. Some mate Craig had been, sneaking about with Evie when Bill's back was turned. But that was ancient history now, and it was time he moved on.

Bill flicked a light switch, nothing happened. Either he'd forgotten to pay the bill or it was a power cut. He felt his way into the kitchen, and fumbled for the torch on the welsh dresser. A cup, dislodged from its hook, shattered on the floor before Bill's hand found what he sought. He shone the torch on the fragments, picked them up and deposited them in the bin under the worktop.

At times like this Bill regretted his bachelor existence, but he didn't seem to have much luck with women. First, Evie who had left before their first anniversary. She hadn't stuck with Craig either, served him right. Then Julie had come into his life, that hadn't worked out, and she'd returned to Edinburgh. And he'd never got beyond first base with Louise, although it had been looking hopeful before that fiasco in Templeton Woods.

He shone the torch round his kitchen, the beam flickering over the pile of dirty dishes in the sink, the newspapers piled on the chair, the littered table. What a mess he'd got himself into. 'Oh, shit,' he muttered, 'can't do anything in the dark, and turning round he left the flat. At least the pub would be bright and warm.

Megan had never been as scared in her life as she was now. To begin with she'd struggled against her bonds, twisting this way and that, but to no avail. It only left her with bruised wrists and ankles which ached worse than toothache. Then she'd screamed until she became hoarse, after that she'd cried for her mum. Nothing helped.

At least he'd left her bread and water which initially she'd ignored, but hunger made her desperate, and now she'd become practised in eating and drinking, even though her wrists were bound.

It was dark outside again. The tiny window with the wire mesh over it that let in faint daylight helped her to assess how long it had been since he'd brought her here. Megan reckoned it must be two nights and days. She'd given up screaming because no one came, and she reckoned if he'd thought her screams would be heard, he wouldn't have left her without a gag.

The dark hours were the worst. She imagined all kinds of bogeymen outside, and sometimes she thought she heard snuffling noises at the door, which conjured up images of wild beasts. She also played out scenarios of what he would do to her when he came back.

However, he hadn't returned yet, and she was terrified he would leave her here until she died. But he'd left her bread and water which meant he would return. She shivered. Whatever way she looked at it, her fate was sealed, and it was terrifying.

Megan reached for the bottle of water. Her lips and throat were parched. She eased herself into a different position, smelling urine when she moved. She tried not to think of that because, despite trying to hang on, she'd wet herself several times.

She closed her eyes and tried not to listen to the strange noises outside.

13

Tuesday, 13 March

Kate groaned when the alarm clanged in her ear. Gavin had his arm slung over her, and she had to disengage herself before she was able to press the button to silence it. He hadn't wakened though, simply stirred in his sleep and mumbled something indistinguishable. He looked younger when asleep with the worry lines smoothed out and his face relaxed. He looked like the young man she had married twenty-five years ago on her twentieth birthday. 'Far too young,' her mother had said, but they'd been happy, well, happy most of the time, she supposed.

Ignoring the temptation to snuggle up to his back, she leaned over to plant the lightest of kisses on his forehead before swinging her feet out of the bed. No way could she go into the office late when she had a new team to manage at Central Division. It was obvious they were not going to accept her without a struggle, and she would have to exert her authority in a way that wasn't necessary with the Forfar team.

She had seen the look on DS Murphy's face when she left the car park last night, and knew Murphy thought she was skiving off. But she was damned if she was going to explain to him or anybody else, that she had been called back to Forfar to oversee a raid on a cannabis factory in one of the town's suburbs. After all, she was the boss and she was not going to undermine her position by justifying her actions, besides, she was damned if she was going to give that bolshie lot the satisfaction of thinking she was not up to the job. That was the problem with having to run two teams; you could get pulled in different directions.

The raid, which was the third in as many weeks, had been

a success though, and this time they had a lead on the Chinese gang operating the factories. But after it was all over, she was still on a high and had slept badly.

Cold water stung her skin when she stepped into the shower which wasn't anything out of the usual. It meant the boiler was playing up again. She would have to make time to get it seen to. Her skin was a rosy pink when she finished, and she scrubbed it madly with a dry towel to get the blood flowing again.

She inserted contact lenses into her eyes. Then she dithered over which trouser suit to wear, eventually deciding she would go to the office in uniform. It would assert her authority in an unspoken way. She needed its support.

Breakfast was a luxury she did not have time for but, conscious of how many police officers developed stomach ulcers, she quickly made a slice of toast, slathered it with butter, took a bite, grabbed her car keys and stepped outside. The bitterly cold March wind blew a large dollop of soft butter off the toast and onto her trousers. Not a good start to the day, she thought, ramming the rest of it into her mouth.

Bill parked his car in a designated parking space, the problem was, it wasn't his space, but he was already late. Jumping out, he raced into the building, frantically hoping the team meeting had been delayed. It hadn't.

The DI glared at him when he crept in.

'Glad you could join us, DS Murphy.'

'Sarky bitch,' Bill thought, but he nodded and sat down.

'I've been filling the team in on the car park incident while we've been waiting for you and now all we need is the report. I imagine you've brought it with you?'

Bill swallowed the lump in his throat. Shit, he had forgotten about the damned report.

'You do have it?'

'Actually,' Bill said, 'I was waiting for SOCO to get back to me with information I needed before I could complete it. But I couldn't raise them last night.'

'I see.' It was obvious from her tone she didn't believe him. 'In that case you will have the report on my desk within the hour.' She paused before continuing, 'I'm sure they'll be on duty now.'

'Yes, ma'am.' Bill slid down in his chair in a useless attempt to hide his face.

'Right, back to where we were before we were so rudely interrupted.'

'The post mortem is scheduled for 8 am tomorrow morning. Can I rely on you, DS Murphy, to be there? It's not too early for you, I hope?'

'Yes, ma'am – I mean no, ma'am.' By this time Bill wasn't sure what he meant. But there was one thing he was certain of, the DI had her knife in him.

The meeting droned on and by the time it finished Bill had managed to become responsible for watching the CCTV tapes, finding out the result of the interviews with the two boys, going out with DC Cartwright to see the Fraser family again, and ensuring HOLMES, the computer database, was updated with the information from the murder case. Although how he was expected to update the computer when he didn't even have a name for the victim, was beyond him.

He slid behind his desk with a groan.

Sue slung some files on her desk and said, 'What's up with you? You look like something the dog dragged in.'

'It's going to be one of those days. I can feel it in my bones.' He leaned forward and planted his elbows on the desk. 'Did you hear how many tasks she's allotted to me? And I still have to get in touch with SOCO, and have my report to her within the hour. The rest of you got off lightly. So why me?'

Sue shrugged. 'Maybe she's sussed you out.'

'What d'you mean by that?'

'Well, you always were a deadbeat.'

'No more than anybody else.'

Sue laughed. 'No need to go into a sulk. I was joking.'

Bill glared at her. 'There are jokes and jokes,' he mumbled, 'and that one wasn't funny.'

'I'll get you a coffee,' she said, 'that'll maybe get you in a better frame of mind.'

Bill watched her stroll up the room to the coffee machine. He wasn't used to being told what to do, so maybe he was touchy. Andy had always let him share the decisions and most times he had pleased himself how he organized his investigations. But this new DI was out to impose her authority on him and he didn't like it.

'There you are,' Sue said, placing the cup in front of him. 'Get that down you and join the land of the living again. And to put you out of some of your misery I'll check the result of the kids' interviews.'

Bill traced his finger round the rim of the paper cup. 'I don't suppose you've seen those files I was looking at yesterday?'

'Which ones d'you mean?'

'The cold case ones. You remember – you passed them to me.'

'The last time I saw them, they were on your desk. Didn't you put them away?'

'I forgot.'

'You checked your filing cabinet?'

'Yeah, and my desk drawers, and yours too.'

'What made you think they'd be in mine?'

'Don't know, I was just checking.'

'This what you're looking for?' Kate heaved the three files onto Bill's desk.

Bill looked up, startled. He hadn't heard the DI approach.

Kate pulled at the bottom of her uniform jacket. 'Files should always be locked up when you are out of the office.'

'Yes, ma'am.'

'It's time this team gave more thought to security so I'll be looking into basic training on these issues. Training, I might add, that should be unnecessary at your level of service.'

'Phew,' Bill said after Kate was out of earshot. 'Speak about being shot down in flames.'

'She had a point.' Sue slid into her chair and started to

organize the files on her desk. 'At least it's better than not knowing where they went to.'

'I suppose you're right.' Bill was already rustling through the Carnegie file. Lifting out a photograph of Jade, he studied it, rose and walked over to Jenny Cartwright's desk.

'D'you think you could scan this photo into your computer and enhance it so I can get a closer look at that necklace she's wearing.'

'Sure,' Jenny said. 'Why d'you want it?'

'It's just a hunch I have.'

14

There was a glimmer of daylight in the sky when Diane woke. She lay for a moment listening to the noise of the aerial wire scraping back and forth on the slates. It always did that when the wind blew in a certain direction. Jade used to say it sounded like birds scrabbling about on the roof, and she would rush outside to try and see them. Diane remembered laughing and agreeing with her daughter, because it was nicer than having to tell her it was a silly old wire not properly fixed down.

Jade had always been fascinated by animals and birds, and some of their happiest times had been when they visited animal parks and sanctuaries. Jade would run ahead, full of life and excitement, while Emma stayed behind, like a shadow. For as long as Diane could remember Emma had been Jade's shadow, following in her footsteps, trying to be like her sister but never succeeding.

Diane turned over in the bed and sighed. No point trying to go back to sleep now when her brain was active with thoughts of Jade. She rose quietly and padded to the bathroom. The water was scalding, the sponge rough but not rough enough, so she took the scrubbing brush to her body and only left the shower after she was red and raw.

She pulled on her clothes, flinching as they touched her skin. Then, fearful of waking them, she crept past Emma and Ryan's closed bedroom doors and tiptoed down the stairs.

The car keys were on the hall table where Ryan had left them last night. She picked them up and silently let herself out of the house.

Camperdown Park was quiet when she got there and she left the car in an empty space near the big house. She got out and walked over the grass, retracing the steps she had often taken with Jade. Over to the left, in among the trees was a small adventure playground which had been a favourite, while in front of her was the larger children's play area, the boating pond and the Wild Life Centre.

The ground sloped gently in front of her and in the distance a woman bent to pick something up, probably a deposit left by the dog she was walking. They used to have a dog, a collie. But she had got rid of it after Jade vanished. Her eyes misted over as she remembered Jade running with the dog. Jade was never still, she always ran and screamed and laughed, while Emma sat quietly on the grass, reading a book.

And suddenly, Jade was gone and with her had gone Diane's zest for living. There had been a search but when nothing was found it was as if everyone lost interest.

'Accept it,' they had said. 'She's gone for good.' What they meant though was that she was dead. But Diane had never believed that and now the unexpected birthday card and the detective coming back into their lives, was all the confirmation she needed. Jade was alive.

Bill groaned. He had been studying the CCTV tapes for half an hour and already he was in brain death. When reception phoned to say Mrs Carnegie was there and wanted to talk to him, he grabbed the opportunity to escape from his present purgatory.

He looked around the room to see who was available to take over and grinned when he spotted DC Armstrong. The constable was young, keen, and with an eye for promotion. He would do nicely.

'Blair,' he called. 'Will you take over here while I interview Mrs Carnegie?'

'Sure thing,' the constable said, but Bill could tell by his expression he wished someone else had been asked.

'Keep working backwards,' Bill said, 'until you spot when the white van arrived in the car park. That'll let us know which tapes to concentrate on.'

On the way out he had to pass the DI, standing at the door of her office. 'I thought I asked you to check the tapes. And, I'm still waiting for that report.'

'Sorry, ma'am, there's someone in reception I need to see.'

'Can't someone else do it?'

'Not really, ma'am. It's connected to a case I'm involved with and she's asked for me. DC Armstrong has kindly offered to check the tapes in my absence so we shouldn't lose any time.'

Bill stared her out until she finally nodded.

'If that's all, ma'am, I'd better not keep Mrs Carnegie waiting.'

He resisted the temptation to slam the office door, but once in the lift he thumped his fist on the wall and swore. The damned woman couldn't leave him alone and he didn't know what he'd done to deserve it.

By the time he reached the ground floor he had calmed down.

'Mrs Carnegie! Where is she?' he asked, peering through the window that formed a division between the officers and the reception area.

One of the officers on duty shrugged his shoulders. 'She seemed agitated and left a couple of minutes ago.' He leafed through a sheaf of papers separating some out to put in different trays. 'Queer one, she was. Couldn't sit still and I could swear she was muttering to herself at one point.'

Bill nodded his thanks, left the office through the security door, walked across the reception area and through the outer glass doors of the building. A gust of wind caught him and he stood for a moment at the top of the steps, buttoning his jacket. Looking down he could see Diane Carnegie pacing back and forth on the pavement like an animal escaped from captivity.

He ran down the steps and grasped her arm to stop her pacing. She turned to face him with wild, confused eyes, and for a moment he thought she might wrench her arm free and run from him.

He let go and smiled at her. 'You asked to see me?'

She looked at him blankly.

'Detective Sergeant Murphy,' he prompted.

'I couldn't stay in there,' she said. 'It reminded me too much of the terrible days after Jade was taken.'

'We don't have to go inside,' he said. 'We can sit in the car; at least it'll get us out of the wind.'

She nodded.

'Over here.' He cupped her elbow in his hand, noting the lack of flesh on her arms. She seemed to have shrunk since the last time he'd seen her. Back then she'd seemed to have a spark about her, even though it was tinged with despair. Now her eyes were dull, her body hunched, and her walk listless.

Bill did not often feel protective of women but Diane's posture and demeanour pulled at something inside him and he wanted to comfort her.

He opened the car door and waited until she settled in the front passenger seat, before walking round the bonnet to get in the other side.

They sat in silence for a time until Bill could stand it no longer. 'You phoned the other day and said there had been developments.'

'I know she's alive . . . I've got proof.' She twisted her hands in her lap, rubbing them so the inflamed skin reddened even more. 'You've got to find her.'

'Proof?'

She nodded and handed him a green envelope. 'It's a birthday card,' she said, 'from Jade.'

Bill studied the card, then carefully placed it back into the green envelope.

'You're sure it's from her?'

'Emma thinks it's someone playing a sick joke on me. But I know it's from Jade.'

Diane's misery seemed to fill the car, and Bill resisted the urge to reach out to her, put his arm round her shoulders, and comfort her. He was convinced Diane was deluding herself but wasn't sure how to handle it. All he knew was, he couldn't let her continue in this fantasy about Jade's return.

'Emma could be right, you know. Some people do have a sick sense of humour.'

Diane hunched further down in the seat. 'You don't believe me either, but it's from Jade. I know it is.'

She kneaded the material of her skirt between her fingers, twisting and pulling at it, until Bill was sure it would tear. She turned her head and looked at him, her pale blue eyes misty with tears. 'Besides, there was something else in the envelope.'

She dug her hand into her pocket, bringing out a bead – a green jade bead – which she pressed into his hand. 'That's from Jade's necklace, I gave it to her on her eleventh birthday, and she always wore it. She was wearing it when she left that day.'

Bill stared at the bead. His stomach churned and he wanted to be sick.

'I've always known she wasn't dead and now, you see, this is proof she can't be.'

Bill fought to control his nausea, and said the first thing that came into his head. 'But wouldn't she have come home if she was alive?'

Tears trembled on her eyelashes and she stared at her hands. 'Maybe she lost her memory or something.'

'I think, somehow, a thirteen year old girl who had lost her memory would have come to our attention.' Her despair touched something in Bill and his voice was gentle.

Tears trickled down her cheeks. 'You read about these men who keep girls locked up in cellars and things. But I try not to think about that. All I know is something must have stopped her from coming home.'

'But if she's able to send you a card, surely she can't be imprisoned in a cellar.'

'I don't know. Maybe she's with her father. He wouldn't want her to come home.'

'What makes you think that?'

'He always favoured her,' she mumbled.

Something in her tone troubled Bill. 'Why was that?'

She looked up and met his eyes with a glare.

'He just did.'

Bill was silent, mulling over the implications of what she had said, and what was left unsaid.

'Where can I find him?'

'Who?'

'Her father.'

'I don't know. He dropped off the face of the earth when he left.' She rubbed her hands over the rough fabric of her skirt. 'Maybe the Witch of the North would know.'

'Witch of the North?'

She twisted her hands and rubbed them even more fiercely, before she answered in a voice that dripped hate. 'His mother – the witch woman – she'll know.'

Sitting up, her body tensed and her fingers hooked into claws. She no longer seemed to be the vulnerable woman who had sat beside him a moment ago. Bill looked at her with fresh eyes and couldn't help wondering if she was capable of murder.

Diane lapsed into an awkward silence, the tension left her body and she was vulnerable again, awash with despair as she rubbed and kneaded her hands. Bill felt ashamed of his doubts; he didn't think this woman capable of murder. He wanted to put his arm round her, take her red hands into his, and comfort her. He wanted to tell her he would find Jade, but knew that would be a mistake. Too much time had elapsed since Jade's disappearance. It would be a miracle if she were still alive. And yet, Diane believed it. The best he could do for her would be to check it out.

'D'you know where his mother lives?' As soon as he spoke Bill knew it was a mistake. He was committing himself to a reinvestigation of Jade's disappearance, and he shuddered to think how his DI would react.

Diane grimaced. 'Where she's always lived, about a mile north of Drumsturdy Road. It's a big house on the road to Newbigging.' She thrust a piece of paper into his hand. 'I've written the address down for you.'

She opened the car door, but before she got out she

leaned over and pecked a kiss onto his cheek. And she was gone, leaving Bill sitting in the car wondering what he was getting involved in.

15

Emma woke to the noisy clanking of bottles and tins being thrown into the recycling lorry.

She lay for a few moments, luxuriating in the warmth of the bed, reluctant to face the day, but the light, filtering through the gap in the curtains, reminded her she should be up and about. So she pushed down the side of her pillow to enable her to see the clock on her bedside table.

'Shit!' She sprang out of bed. It was ten-past-nine, she'd slept in, and she would be late for her first lecture.

Her shower was quick and functional, no time to enjoy the hot water cascading over her body, she was late, late, late. The large white towel was rough against her skin, the softness long gone through too much laundering, but she wrapped it round her body and darted back to her bedroom. That was when it dawned on her the house was too quiet. That was what had been bothering her. That was the reason she had slept in.

It was then she realized she hadn't heard the slam of the door as her mother went out to collect the green recycling box, and looking out the window she could see the box lying on its side on the pavement. She frowned, thinking it strange, because by now Diane would have been scrubbing the box ready for its next intake of bottles and tins. She would never leave it outside.

Thoughts of her lateness or the lecture she would miss, paled into insignificance, swamped by her worries. She pulled on yesterday's clothes which were still draped over a chair – she didn't have time to look for fresh ones – and hurried downstairs. The kitchen was empty, as were all the other rooms. Running back upstairs, she checked her mother's room. It was empty.

Emma tried to suppress the churning in her stomach, the fluttering in her chest, and the choking sensation that restricted her breathing. But it was no use and she was panting for breath by the time she burst into Ryan's bedroom.

Placing both hands on Ryan's sleeping body she shook him until he reluctantly opened his eyes.

'What's up?'

He blinked and rubbed his eyes.

'It's Mum! She's gone!'

'Whoa, calm down.'

'But it's Mum.' Emma wanted to scream at him but the words came out in a gasp.

'What's wrong with Mum?' Ryan raised his head off the pillow.

'She's gone, she's not here.'

'What d'you mean – not here?' Ryan mumbled, his eyes bleary from sleep.

'She's not in the house.'

Ryan sat up. 'But she's always in the house in the morning.'

'That's what I mean. She's not here, and she's been acting real strange lately. Something must be up.'

'You don't think she's gone out searching for Jade like she used to do?'

'That's exactly what I'm afraid of.' Emma groaned. 'If she's anything like she was when Jade disappeared, I don't know what we'll do.'

'Maybe we should ask the doctor to get her into treatment again.'

'No way will she agree to that. You know as well as I do how she feels about psychiatrists. The reason she agreed to treatment the last time was because she thought she'd lose us if she didn't. But now we're older that argument won't cut any ice with her.'

'What will we do then?'

Emma sank onto the edge of the bed.

'I don't know.'

Her shoulders slumped. This fixation, that Jade had returned, was consuming her mother, and Emma didn't know how to help, because nothing she said or did ever made any difference to Diane.

Bill sat in the car deep in thought after Diane left, and he didn't like the way his thoughts were going.

She had refused to let him keep the card or the jade bead, but he knew without a doubt in his mind that Diane's jade bead and the ones found pressed into the John Doe's eyes, were a match. That meant either the person who sent Diane the card, or Diane herself, was involved in the murder.

The other option was that Diane was right, and Jade had returned, and if she had, was she responsible for the John Doe's death?

Either way, Bill thought, the Carnegie family were mixed up in this.

Eventually Bill returned to the team room. DI Rawlings was in her office, giving Bill the chance to nobble Sue.

'You've got to tell the DI,' Sue said, after listening to Bill's spiel.

Bill knew she was right and if it had been Andy there would have been no problem, but this new DI didn't like him and seemed determined to undermine him at every opportunity.

He shrugged his shoulders. 'I suppose you're right, but d'you think she'll listen?'

'Why wouldn't she?'

'You've seen how she is anytime I'm near her. She seems to think I'm some kind of numpty.'

'Well, you are, but that shouldn't stop you reporting to her and the longer you put it off the bigger a numpty she'll think you are.'

'I suppose.'

'Oh, for goodness sake, d'you want me to come and hold your hand?'

'That won't be necessary.' Bill straightened his tie and

braced himself.

The sooner he got it over with the better.

The meeting with the detective left Diane with conflicting emotions. She was convinced he wanted to help her find Jade, but was not sure whether he believed Jade was alive. She had done her best to convince him and wasn't sure what else she could do.

The answer was obvious, of course, she would look for Jade, find her, and prove to everyone Jade had come back. That was why she was now sitting on one of the leather couches on the upper floor of the Overgate Shopping Mall watching the crowds passing by. This had been one of Jade's favourite places in the city centre. Sooner or later she would come here and when she did, Diane would be waiting.

'Mum! Thank goodness I've found you.'

Diane didn't want to look up and spoil the daydream at the point where Jade had come home and was reaching out her arms for a hug.

'Mum!'

The voice was louder and she felt a hand on her arm. She stared up at the girl leaning over her.

'Jade – you've come back. I knew you would.' Diane reached out for her.

'No, Mum, it's Emma. We've been worried about you and we've been hunting everywhere.'

'Oh.' Diane couldn't mask the disappointment in her voice, and she saw Emma wince.

'Come on, Mum. Let's go home.'

'But Jade, if she comes and I'm not here . . . ' Diane's voice trailed off.

'She's not coming back. It's time you faced up to it – there's only you, me and Ryan now. We're all the family that is left.'

Diane looked over the railing to the lower level of the mall, hoping Jade would miraculously appear, but all she saw was Ryan hurrying to the escalator, soon he would join them, and the family would be together. But she didn't really believe that, because she felt deep down within herself Jade was alive and therefore the family would never be complete until she returned.

Kate had her head down trying to make sense of the travel forms in front of her. She never liked authorizing things blind, and as she hadn't been based in Dundee last month she had no way of knowing whether they were accurate. From what she could see the team had run up a lot of mileage, and she didn't know if this was the norm.

A tap at the door interrupted her deliberations and she looked up to see Bill hesitating in the entry. She raised her eyebrows in an unspoken question.

'Have you a moment, ma'am?'

She suppressed her initial feeling of irritation, he did look reasonably tidy, his shirt was clean and tucked in, his tie was straight, his suit jacket buttoned, and his hair had been smoothed back, although still a bit long for her taste. She supposed she'd better give him credit for making an effort.

'What is it, Murphy?'

'I've just interviewed Mrs Carnegie and I think there might be a connection with the murder investigation.'

He sounded awkward, as if he were searching for the right words, and Kate didn't want to make it easy for him so she kept him standing.

'In what way?'

Bill strode across the office and leaned his hands on her desk. 'It's little things, nothing I can put my finger on, but I think there's definitely a connection.'

Kate had to lean back in her chair to look up at him. She should have asked him to sit down. But whatever he had to tell her was obviously more important to him than any psychological advantage his height gave him.

'Take a seat,' she said, more abruptly than she meant to, 'and explain.'

'It's an old case.'

Bill hesitated, obviously expecting her to comment, but she wasn't going to give him that pleasure.

'It was a missing child case. Jade Carnegie, a thirteen year old girl left home one day five years ago and never returned. We did all the usual things but never found any trace of her.'

'So, it's been in limbo ever since. But what has this got to do with the current murder investigation?'

'I'm coming to that. Mrs Carnegie recently phoned, convinced her daughter has come back, although no one has actually seen Jade. But here's the interesting stuff! She got a birthday card, apparently from Jade, with a jade bead in the envelope.'

'And the connection is?'

'The bead Mrs Carnegie says she received from Jade, is identical to the beads found in our John Doe's eyes.'

'I see.' Kate stared at the ceiling, thinking over what Bill had told her.

She leaned forward. 'It's circumstantial, even if they are identical, there could still be other beads the same floating around.'

'I suppose it's possible, but the carvings on these beads made them distinctive. And Mrs Carnegie said the beads were a present to Jade on her eleventh birthday.'

'OK, get me the file and I'll have a look at it. Then we need to see where we'll take it.'

'One thing,' Bill said. 'Mrs Carnegie is mentally vulnerable. I believe she had a breakdown after her daughter disappeared, and she doesn't seem stable at the moment.'

'Well, it seems to me your suspicions are based on gut feelings, but we can't ignore it. However, we'd better tread carefully.'

'What d'you want me to do?'

Kate thought hard. What did she want him to do? Making a sudden decision, she said, 'Write it up for me, I'll need a report and then we'll look at reopening the case. If Mrs Carnegie's daughter has returned we need to know about it, and if she hasn't we also need to know. Either way we could get closure on it. We also need to know what involvement the family have, if any, with this current murder investigation, and if the connection to this case is proved that'll be a bonus.'

Bill got up to leave the office.

'Don't forget the report,' Kate said with a grim smile on her lips. 'And that will be two you owe me now.'

16

'We've come to take you home, Mum.'

Diane wasn't ready to leave and she wished Emma hadn't come. She loved her daughter, but sometimes it seemed as if Emma was the mother and she was the child. The love and concern Emma had for her was suffocating in its intensity.

'But I don't want to go home yet. I have to stay.' Even as Diane said it she knew Emma wouldn't pay any attention. The girl was too stubborn to take account of her desperate need to find Jade.

Emma looked up and beckoned to Ryan who was hurrying to join them. 'Tell her she needs to come home with us, she won't listen to me.'

Ryan sank down on the sofa beside Diane and gently prised her fingers away from her skirt. 'You can't sit here all day, Mum. You need to come home now.'

Diane's eyes brimmed with tears. 'You don't understand – nobody understands – but I know Jade is here somewhere. I have to be here for her.'

'Jade's not coming back, and the sooner you accept it the better it will be.' Ryan gripped her hand, and for a moment Diane felt sorry for him because she could see the misery on his face. He genuinely believed what he'd said but she couldn't ignore it.

'Better for who? Not for me.'

Emma put her arm round her mother's shoulder. Diane did not resist but took no comfort from it.

'You have to stop tormenting yourself.' Emma's voice was low and her arm tightened round Diane's shoulders.

'But I need to find her . . . '

'You know as well as I do she's not coming back.'

'That's not true, she's already come back.'

'If she had, she would have come home.'

'She sent a card.'

Emma was silent for a moment, then with a breaking voice, she said, 'That wasn't her.'

'You don't know that.' Diane wrenched her hand out of Ryan's grasp and tried to shake off Emma's encircling arm. But her daughter increased the pressure and she was unable to break free.

'And you don't know she's still alive.' Anger flared in Emma's eyes. 'Don't you see, if she was alive and had come back, she would never stay away from you.' Emma's fingers dug into Diane's shoulder.

'Maybe she has a reason.'

'Well, if that's the case you'll have to wait until she's ready.'

Diane sighed, the defiance subsided and her body slackened. She didn't have the energy to fight Emma, particularly when Ryan backed her up.

'But what if Jade comes and I'm not here,' she muttered, before allowing them to lead her away.

'Well!' Sue said when Bill emerged from Kate's office. 'What did the DI say?'

'She thinks it's worth following up.' Bill sat in his chair and twirled it round to face Sue. 'Problem is, she wants a report before she'll consider reopening the Carnegie case.'

'That was to be expected.'

'I suppose, but I prefer to be doing things, not sitting banging a keyboard.'

'How else is she, or anybody else for that matter, to know how a case is progressing if no one writes anything up? Then there's the little matter of evidence, of course.'

'OK, you've made your point.' Bill twirled his chair to face the desk and pulled the keyboard towards him. 'Oh, for the days when we had typists to do this for us,' he muttered as his fingers went to work.

Fifteen minutes later he clicked the print command.

'There,' he said, 'that's it done.'

Sue looked up from the file she was studying. 'Good. Now I can tell you, Blair has been giving you the evil eye for the last ten minutes.'

'Oh, shit,' Bill said. 'I forgot I left him checking the CCTV footage.' He stood up, collected the sheets of paper from the printer and strode across the room to Kate's office. Kate looked up as he entered.

'Report on the Carnegie interview,' Bill said, placing it on her desk.

Without looking up, she said, 'Oh, and Murphy . . . '

'Yes, ma'am?'

'That will be one outstanding report now.'

'Didn't even say thanks,' Bill muttered to Sue, before he crossed the room to where Blair was studying the images on a monitor.

'Sorry,' he said, 'the big white chief wanted an urgent report. Found anything yet?'

'I've been tracking the van . . . '

'What day are you working on?'

'Saturday. I've followed it back from when the kids found it on Monday, but it's just sitting there.'

Bill pulled a chair over so he could see the screen better.

'Ah, there we go, movement.'

'Naw, it's only a guy collecting his car. That was it driving off before we got to this bit.'

Blair kept his finger on the fast button and scrolled backwards, stopping occasionally when he spotted signs of movement. Saturday afternoon passed, Saturday morning, Friday night, and the van still sat, immobile.

They were on Friday afternoon when Bill said, 'Hang on a minute. Stop there. Someone's on the down ramp. OK, start it again, but slower this time.'

Blair rolled the image back, tracking the figure walking backwards until it vanished behind the van.

'D'you think it could be him?'

Bill shrugged. 'Hard to tell, but if you roll the recording back to the time when the van arrives we could track it from there. This watching everything happening backwards is doing my head in.'

The image of the white van whizzed back in time until it was no longer there. Blair stopped the recording and started to play it forwards.

'Here it comes, up the ramp.' Bill watched as the van parked and a figure got out. 'What's he carrying?'

'Looks like a book.'

They watched as he vanished into the elevator.

'Fast forward until he returns.'

The recording sped up, with Blair stopping it each time someone returned to their car. But this time, as Bill watched the elevator doors slide open, he knew it was them.

He leaned forward. 'There's two of them.'

'Is it the John Doe?' Blair's voice trembled with excitement.

'Yes,' Bill said, hitting the desk with his fist. 'That's him. He's not steady on his feet, though. He looks drunk.'

'Or drugged.'

'Yeah. Can we get a look at the other one?'

Blair froze the screen, before moving the recording forward in increments. 'Nope, no such luck, that hoodie's masking his face. I think he knows where the cameras are. He's not big though.'

'D'you think it could be a woman?'

'It's possible. Or someone young.'

Bill lapsed into silence. He couldn't give voice to the suspicions he had about Diane, but he couldn't get her out of his mind either.

Diane slumped into the back of the car. Emma sat beside her and put her arm round her shoulders. Diane knew her daughter meant well but took no comfort from the contact. Her thoughts were still with Jade. She was certain Jade was out there, lost and lonely, but she had failed to convince her other children and they thought she had lost her mind.

But she hadn't lost her mind. It was real. It wasn't a

fantasy. Jade had come back and she would need her mother. In the meantime, Diane would have to go along with Emma and Ryan, because if she didn't they would bring the psychiatrist back and she didn't want that. She didn't need someone trying to worm into her brain, or giving her those damned pills, the ones that made the world all fuzzy and blunted her emotions. If she wanted to cry and scream no one had the right to take that away from her.

At least she had the detective on her side. He would find Jade.

17

Ryan was reluctant to leave his mother. He was afraid for her. Afraid she was lapsing into the state she'd been in when Jade disappeared. They had all feared for her sanity at that time, and it was only Dr Murdoch's intervention that saved her. Maybe they needed to call her in again, even though Diane was set against it.

'I have to go, Mum,' he said. 'Tony set up a special meeting with one of his dancers for the photo shoot. He won't be pleased if I'm late.'

'Don't worry about me. I'll be fine.' She patted his hand.

But she didn't look fine. The vacant look in her eyes worried him. If Emma had been there it wouldn't have mattered, but his sister had already left for the university and Diane would be alone. He hesitated, worry niggling at the back of his brain, he shouldn't leave her while she was in this state, but what choice did he have.

'If you're sure . . . '

'I'm sure. You'd better go. You don't want to get on the wrong side of Tony.'

Ryan nodded. He regretted agreeing to provide a web site for Tony, but it would have been a bigger mistake to refuse. Tony wasn't someone you could say no to.

Ryan drove past the front of Teasers, and into the alley at the side which led to the car park. It was too early for many cars to be parked there, and he slid his car into a space beside a clapped out Ford Ka. Turning the engine off he got out and looked around for the back door he had been instructed to use.

The door was opened by a smallish girl with magenta streaked brown hair. But even though she was small, she still topped him by about an inch.

'Tony asked me to come,' he said, unsure of himself.

She looked him up and down. 'You'll be the Carnegie guy, I take it. Follow me.'

The door swung shut behind him. 'I'm here for the photoshoot. Are you one of the dancers?'

She laughed. 'Me, a showgirl? You've got to be joking. No, it's Angel who's been set up for the shoot. I'm Kara.'

'Sorry,' he said, 'I just thought . . . '

'Don't think. Tony won't pay you extra for that. What's your first name, by the way?'

'Ryan.'

He followed her up the dark corridor and out into the main entrance hall. Daylight filtered in from window slits above the closed front doors, making the whole place look dingy.

She led him upstairs to the night club. It looked just as shabby, and a far cry from the evening glamour. The place was empty except for a bored looking girl, wearing only a g-string, sitting on the edge of the glass stage.

'That's Angel.' Kara walked towards the stage, followed by Ryan.

The girl looked up at their approach, flicking her long blonde hair away from her face so it cascaded down her back. Her makeup was perfect. Large blue eyes made larger by the eyeliner she wore, pink lipstick with the slightest sheen, and a complexion that looked natural until seen up close.

Ryan wanted to ask her what she used and how she achieved such a perfect result, but didn't dare.

As if she sensed his interest, she leaned backwards, placing her hands flat on the stage and arching her back so her breasts jutted forward.

Ryan shuffled his feet, and felt the heat rise from his neck into his face. He had never been near a woman who was almost naked. To mask his embarrassment, he slung his knapsack onto a table and started to assemble his camera, screwing the extra lenses into place.

The girl rose and walked over to him, studying what he

was doing. He felt her breast brush against his arm, and he almost choked.

'I'll be over at the bar, checking stock, if you need me.' Kara's voice had a strangled sound and he knew she was suppressing a giggle. She walked off and he was left alone with Angel.

'What d'you want me to do?' Angel removed a piece of chewing gum from her mouth and stuck it under a table top.

'I'll need you to dance, like you do at night.' Ryan tried to keep his voice steady. 'But, for the video, it might be better if you wore something on top.'

'You mean a bra?'

'Yes.'

'OK, give me a minute.'

She returned wearing a black bra that barely covered her breasts. 'This do?'

Ryan nodded. 'What about music, what do we do about that? And lighting?'

'Phil, where the fuck are you?' Angel shouted into the gloom of the club.

The tall blond guy Ryan remembered from previous visits appeared.

'Ah, look who we have here,' he said. 'I knew you'd come back.'

A tremble shivered through Ryan's body. His limbs felt like jelly, while the heat rose upwards into his neck and face. Why did this man have such an effect on him?

'I need the stage set up for the photo shoot, lighting and music,' he mumbled. 'The video has to replicate the type of show you have in the evening, plus I want some action photos.'

Phil strode to the end of the room. First the up-lighting under the stage snapped on, and then the glitter-ball started to spin. When the music started, Angel got on the stage and began to dance. 'Now fuck off, Phil,' she shouted as she writhed round the silver pole, and turning her head towards Ryan, she said, 'anytime you're ready, darling.'

The photoshoot didn't take long, and Ryan was packing

up after it when Kara came over to him. 'Everything go
OK?'

'Yes. I think I've got enough photos and video to add to
the web site.'

'D'you mind if I say something?'

Ryan looked up. 'No, what is it?'

She looked embarrassed. 'I saw the way Phil looked at
you,' she said. 'I wanted to warn you, he can be dangerous.
You don't want to get involved with him.'

'Oh!' He didn't know what to say. His stomach was still
churning because of the effect Phil had on him.

'Just saying,' she said. 'Now if you're ready to leave I'll
show you out.'

He followed her down the stairs and, after thanking her,
he turned towards the corridor leading to the car park.

The guy patrolling the corridor reached for the bunch of
keys dangling from his belt. 'You'd be better going out the
front, mate, cos your car ain't there. The old bird who took it
said to let you know.'

Kate finished reading Bill's report and slotted it into the file
on the John Doe's murder. It had given her a lot to think
about and, while she thought Diane Carnegie could be
involved, she was by no means certain. However, it was a
strand of the investigation that could not be ignored,
although it would have to be handled delicately. DS Murphy
was already involved with the family so, despite her
reservations about him, he was the logical choice of officer
to follow it up.

She walked over to the window that looked into the team
room. DS Murphy and DC Blair Armstrong were huddled
together at the end of the room, and she observed them
pointing to the computer screen. Their body language was
animated and she felt her own excitement rise. They'd found
something.

It only took Kate a moment to leave the office, and cross
the team room. 'What is it? What have you found?'

'We've got a time for the van arriving, plus a sighting of the victim and his killer.'

'Good, that will give us something to work with.' Kate peered over their shoulders. 'Can you see enough to get a description?'

'Only of the victim, ma'am, the killer's face is obscured by a hoodie. I think he knows where the cameras are.'

'Have you looked at CCTV from inside the mall?'

'We've done the garage, so far. We still have to view the other images.'

'Well, get on with it. No not you, Murphy, I've something else for you to do. Armstrong can continue with this.'

Kate did not miss the expression of panic in the constable's eyes. 'You do know how to access the other CCTV files, I trust?'

DC Armstrong froze, reminding Kate of a rabbit paralysed by headlights.

'Oh, for heaven's sake, get Cartwright to help you locate them and you do the inspection of the footage.'

'Yes, ma'am,' his relief was obvious.

'Murphy, we are going out to interview Mrs Carnegie's mother-in-law. We need to find out Mr Carnegie's whereabouts.'

'Yes, ma'am.'

18

Jade stepped out the front door pausing to inhale all the aromas bombarding her senses. The scent of next door's cat, a whiff of smoke from someone's chimney, the faintest of fragrances from the spring flowers, even the smell of petrol fumes. She savoured them all.

It was good to be out in the fresh air after such a long time in the dark place.

The sharp wind made her pull her jacket closer to her body, and she clutched the edge of the hood to prevent it from blowing back and revealing her face. She didn't want the neighbours to see her. It was important to keep her presence hidden.

With that in mind, she walked to a bus stop three streets away from the house. Several people waited in the queue in front of her, which was useful, because she copied them when it was time for her to pay. So much had changed since she was last here and she didn't want to draw attention to herself.

Leaving the bus at Primark in the city centre, she wandered past Samuel, the jewellery shop, and on into the High Street. Marks and Spencer hadn't changed much, but the Woolworths store opposite had gone. She used to love wandering round Woolworths with Emma. That's where they spent their Saturday money, and occasionally pocketed some of the smaller items, for the fun of it.

She turned her face resolutely to the top of the street. It was time she was at the Wellgate Centre, she wanted to arrive before her target did, and she couldn't afford to spend any more time thinking of how things used to be.

When she left the dark place to return to Dundee, it had been with a specific purpose in mind, and she couldn't lose sight of that.

The downstairs part of the mall was busy which suited her fine. Pulling her hood closer to her face she joined the crowds. Thinking back to when she had been here before, she remembered the restaurants and cafes were on an upper level so she headed for the escalators. It wasn't as busy on this level and she wandered along it, stopping now and then to study shop windows, but always alert to the people around her. It was a pity she hadn't come here before arranging to meet her new mark, Simon he said his name was, because the Wellgate she remembered had been much busier.

Once more she scanned the scattering of people roaming the mall, but couldn't see anyone carrying a Harry Potter book. Maybe he'd decided to check the place out before making himself known; maybe he'd kept his book hidden until he was sure it wasn't a police trap.

Jade preferred to see her mark first so she had the advantage, but this time it looked as if she'd have to make the first move. Sighing, she pulled the Harry Potter book out of her knapsack and tucked it under her arm.

The café area was behind her and off to her right. It sat in the centre with shops flanking it on all sides, and was surrounded by a wooden partition that resembled a garden fence. It was too open. The cafes and restaurants she remembered from years before had been much more private. Here, there was nowhere to hide. It had been a bad choice for a meet.

She sauntered over and leaned her elbows on the partition, surveying the afternoon coffee drinkers, but no one seemed to resemble her mark. She frowned, trying to decide whether to join them or give up. But she'd come this far and she was reluctant to lose a mark she'd carefully set up, so she entered the cafeteria area and bought a cup of tea taking it to a seat beside the barrier separating the tables from the shoppers.

She sipped her tea and sized up the other customers, but no one matched her idea of what the mark would look like. He was late, maybe he wasn't coming.

She placed the Harry Potter book on the table beside her. She would give him another fifteen minutes, then she would go.

Bill hadn't got over his surprise at the DI's decision to partner him on the interview because, since she arrived, she'd been trying to undermine him. When she indicated they take his car and he should drive, he was even more surprised.

The traffic wasn't too bad and he drove in silence, while the DI sat beside him deep in thought. He sneaked a look at her trying to suss out what was in her mind, but she was giving nothing away. They were almost at the address Diane Carnegie had given them and he hadn't a clue how Kate intended to handle the interview, or what she wanted him to do. Maybe this was another ploy to cut him down to size. He tightened his lips and decided he would follow her lead.

He turned off the road, drove through a pair of ornamental iron gates, and followed the tree-lined drive until they reached a fairly large three-storey house. 'We're here, ma'am,' he said, slowing to a stop outside the front entrance.

'You have your notebook with you?'

Bill patted his pocket to make sure he hadn't forgotten it. 'Yes, ma'am,' he said with a sigh of relief, glad to have escaped getting the sharp side of her tongue, although he would much prefer to be the one interviewing rather than the note-taker. But it looked like the DI would be in charge and he'd be the patsy taking the notes.

By the time he got out of the car the DI was ringing the doorbell. A curtain twitched at the window on his left, and a few minutes later the door opened.

The woman standing in the doorway was slim and attractive, and appeared younger than the one they were looking for. Her black dress hugged her figure and, although she was small in stature, her five inch heels made her look taller. She seemed familiar, and Bill wondered if he'd met her before, but then realized she reminded him of Joan

Collins. As he got nearer, he realized she wasn't as young as she appeared, and under the makeup she was as old as the ageing film star. Her hair, long and dark, brushed her shoulders in a mass of curls. Was it a wig? Bill found it impossible to tell.

'Can I help you?' The woman's face showed no emotion.

Kate produced her warrant card. 'I'm Detective Inspector Rawlings, and this is Detective Sergeant Murphy. We're looking for Mrs Carnegie?'

'You've found her. What can I do for you?' She looked at them with a lack of curiosity showing in her face, which still showed no movement. Bill moved closer trying to see any tell tale scars indicating she might have had a facelift, but her hair covered her neck and ears. Of course, it might be botox. That would explain the lack of expression.

'We'd like to ask you a few questions about your son, Paul Carnegie.' Kate's voice sounded stiff and unnatural.

'Oh my! Is he in trouble?' The woman placed a hand on her chest in a theatrical gesture.

'May we come in? It would be better than discussing this on the doorstep.' Kate took a step forward.

'Of course.' Mrs Carnegie led them into a large sitting room furnished with a white leather sofa and armchairs, a drinks cabinet in the corner of the room, and a glass coffee table. A large painting of Mrs Carnegie, looking considerably younger, hung above an ornate marble fireplace.

She gestured for them to sit. Kate chose an armchair while Bill perched on the edge of a sofa.

'Can I get you something? A drink perhaps, or a coffee?'

She moved closer to Bill. Her eyes were deep violet, edged with dark eyeliner, and lids shaded a deeper colour of purple. It gave the impression they were large and glowing, and they were focused on him.

He reached into his pocket for his notebook trying, unsuccessfully, to avoid her stare.

'No thank you.' There was an edge to Kate's voice. 'If you don't mind we'll get on with the interview and then we can leave you in peace.'

'Interview? Is that what this is? I thought you wanted to know about Paul.'

'Yes, but we also wanted to check what you remember about your granddaughter's disappearance.'

'That was a long time ago.'

Bill thought he detected a fleeting expression of alarm in her eyes, but he might have been mistaken.

Kate leaned forward in her chair. 'The case has been reopened.'

'What's the point of that after all this time?'

'I would have thought you would have been pleased.'

Mrs Carnegie shrugged her shoulders. 'Why should I be? Paul was far better off once he got rid of that set of leeches.'

Kate seemed momentarily speechless, and Bill leaned forward in his seat to say, 'That's a strange way to refer to your grandchildren.'

Mrs Carnegie ignored him and it was as if she were speaking to herself. 'He should never have married that bitch. He was far better off living with me. I gave him everything and he left me for her.' She strode to the fireplace and reached a hand up to finger the portrait. 'I gave up my career for him and his father.' She turned to face them. 'I was a famous actress, you know, and I gave it all up for them. And how do they repay me? My husband ups and dies, and my son leaves me for her.' She was panting and her eyes had a wild look. 'It was a good day when Jade,' she spat the name, 'disappeared. It brought my son back to me.'

'I see,' Kate said in a measured tone. 'Well, if you can tell us where we can find Mr Carnegie, we'll leave you in peace.'

19

He had been watching her ever since she sat down in the café. At first he wasn't sure but she brought out the book and laid it on the table. All doubts left his mind. It was her. He circled the café, trying to see her face but it was well hidden by the hood on her jacket, and he hesitated to approach her. After a narrow call last month when he'd almost fallen into a police honey trap, he'd been ultra-cautious.

He slipped into a shop doorway and continued to watch her. He saw the frequent looks at her watch, the impatient tap of her feet, and the resigned shrug of her shoulders when she decided he wasn't coming.

She rose, tucked the book into her knapsack, slung it over her shoulder, and left the café. He followed and was close behind her when she reached the escalator. His fingers itched, now was the time to find out whether she was genuine.

He descended a step, stretched out a hand and yanked the hood away from her face. His eyes widened and he found it difficult to breathe. Panic beat a tattoo in his chest. The face was not one he wanted to see, for this was no child who had been waiting for him. The escalator continued downward but already he was running, pushing past the others who were in his way. He leapt off the end of it and didn't stop running until he was well clear of the Wellgate centre.

He was forced to stop when his legs were on the point of collapsing beneath him and he could hardly breathe, each gasp racking his chest with unbearable pain. He slid into an entryway between two shops and bent over, clasping his knees, gulping air. Gradually his breathing returned to normal and he straightened, but the panic hadn't left him. He waited, listening for shouts and the clatter of pursuing feet.

When he didn't hear them he ventured a look into the street, but saw only the usual Tuesday crowds milling about.

Bloody coppers' trap that's what it had been. He'd have to be more careful in the future. Turning his collar up, he joined the crowd of shoppers and walked down the street.

The Greenfield estate was about three miles from Patricia Carnegie's secluded house, but it seemed another universe. It was the dividing line between country and city. Fields lined the road at one side, and ugly housing blocks at the other. The access roads into the estate were named Crescents, because the housing blocks followed the crescent shape of the roads. Opposite the houses were large low-walled parking areas fringed by patchy grass, and scrubby bushes festooned with flapping plastic carrier bags, paper and various other items of rubbish. It was difficult to imagine this estate had won awards when it was built, but now it was an area where only the bold ventured after dark. This was where Paul Carnegie lived.

Kate sat quietly in the passenger seat while Bill drove to the address Patricia Carnegie had supplied. He tried to focus on driving but the interview had left him unsettled, and he wondered if his boss had been as stunned as he was at the woman's outburst, which left him understanding why Diane Carnegie described her mother-in-law as the Witch of the North. He couldn't prevent a shudder as he remembered the venom in the woman's voice when she spoke of her son's family.

'This is it.' Bill parked the car in front of the stairs accessing the upper levels. He wasn't going to risk his car in the car park at the other side of the road, although he wasn't sure how much safer it would be here.

Kate didn't move. 'The interview – what did you make of it?'

Bill noticed the frown on her face.

'Weird. She's one strange lady if you ask me.'

'Yes, that's what I thought, but it left me wondering if

she knew more about her granddaughter's disappearance than she let on.' Kate got out of the car, then leaned back in to collect her bag. She slung it over her shoulder, and said, 'Well, come on, don't just sit there. We have an interview to conduct with her son.'

'Yes, ma'am.' A slight smile twitched at the corners of Bill's mouth. That was more like it, she was back to her officious self. He supposed she couldn't help it.

She was halfway up the first set of stairs by the time Bill caught up with her. 'I wouldn't touch the handrail if I were you, ma'am.'

She kept climbing. 'Why not?'

'Never know what the yobs have smeared on it.' Bill stifled a smile as she removed her hand from the rail.

Wind whistled along the walkway. It was windier here on the third floor than it had been at street level, and Paul Carnegie's flat was at the end of the walkway. Rubbish had blown into the corner and partly over his doorstep. Bill kicked a lager can out of his way and rapped on the door. No response. He rapped again, louder this time. Still no response. It was then Bill spotted the woman with the mess of wild red hair, plodding along the walkway towards them. That was all he needed, Mad May Fraser. He should have remembered she lived in this block.

'You found my Megan yet?'

Kate took a step backwards. Bill couldn't blame her, for May had a ferocious look on her face and looked as if she meant business.

'We're working on it Mrs Fraser,' Bill said.

'Not working hard enough if you ask me.'

'We've highlighted it in the press and had officers doing doorstep enquiries. I'm sure you'll have noticed.'

'Fat lot of good they've been. Who's the bint?'

'This is Detective Inspector Rawlings, and she's pulling out all stops to find your Megan.'

'Hmph! I'll believe that when the cows come home. Anyway, he's not home, went out this morning and hasn't come back yet. What you want with him anyway?'

'Now, now, Mrs Fraser. You know better than to ask that.'

'Hmph!' Hair blowing wildly in the wind she stomped away from them along the walkway. Stopping when she reached the stairwell, she turned and shouted, 'You find my Megan or there'll be trouble.'

Kate had a bemused look on her face. 'Megan, that's the fourteen year old who's missing, right?'

'Yes, ma'am. But it's not the first time she's gone off. We picked her up in Arbroath the last time, and the time before that it was Glasgow.'

'Not sure if you want to go up there, mate. There's two pigs waiting for you.' May Fraser's voice, echoing up the stairwell, had a hollow sound.

Bill suppressed a smile. 'I reckon that's Mr Carnegie on his way up. I'll pop along and meet him.' With that, he strode along the walkway. He'd almost reached the next landing when he caught up with a man in a hooded jacket, retreating down the stairs.

'Paul Carnegie?'

He turned to face Bill, his face in shadow. 'Who wants to know?'

'Police, mate. I'm Detective Sergeant Murphy. My gaffer, Detective Inspector Rawlings, is waiting upstairs. We'd like a word.'

'What about?'

'Better if we discussed that in your flat, we don't want the whole block to know.' Bill nodded his head in May Fraser's direction.

Paul glared at the woman. 'I suppose that would be best,' he said, with a sigh of resignation.

'After you,' Bill said, making sure he remained behind Paul Carnegie in case he changed his mind about the interview.

20

Paul Carnegie led them along a dark hallway and into a sparsely furnished room. It contained one leather armchair that had seen better days, a formica-topped table strewn with newspapers and magazines, a two-bar electric fire, a computer chair, and a corner desk unit dominated by a state of the art computer. He stood for a moment, shifting from foot to foot, as if unsure what to do next. Bill guessed he didn't get many visitors.

'What is it you want?' Paul's voice was soft and high-pitched with a note of anxiety he seemed unable to conceal.

'We wanted to ask you about your daughter, Jade.'

'Jade has been missing for five years, and your lot haven't done much to find her.'

'Then I'm sure you'll be pleased to know we've reopened the case.' Kate's voice was steady, but Bill could tell she wasn't at ease. Maybe it was because Paul Carnegie still had his hood up, or maybe it was because of the accusatory tone of his voice.

'Why would you do that?'

'Let's just say there have been developments.'

Paul was silent, seemingly mulling over what Kate had said.

'Why don't you take your coat off and sit down, and you can tell us what you remember about the day she disappeared.'

Kate leaned against the desk and smiled at him. Bill guessed she was trying to strike a non-threatening pose, so he perched himself on the arm of the leather chair.

Paul sat in the computer chair, loosened the toggle buttons on his coat and pushed back the hood. He kept the coat on his shoulders, but underneath he wore a checked shirt and grubby jeans. His spectacles were held together at the bridge by a piece of sticking plaster, and he looked unkempt. He passed a hand over his partially bald head and smoothed the hair down at the back. His eyes were bright behind his spectacles and Bill wasn't sure if he had tears in them. His chin was dark with stubble which was either a fashion statement or indicated a reluctance to shave.

'It's so long ago, it seems like another life.'

'In your own time,' Kate said.

Bill took out his notebook and rummaged in his pocket for a pencil.

'She's been gone now for five years. It was a day something like it is today. Cold and windy, but it was a month earlier. February it was. As if I'd ever forget.' He paused, lost in thought, before continuing. 'The last time I saw her was at breakfast. When I came home from work she was gone and I never saw her again.'

Paul looked away and lapsed into silence.

'How was she at breakfast time?'

'Same as usual. Giggly, in a hurry. Diane was nagging her to eat before she left for school.'

'And when you came back?'

'I was late that night. I'd been held back at the depot. We'd had a load of spring bulbs delivered earlier in the day and they needed to be stored properly ready for planting.'

'You were a gardener . . . '

'Yes, with the council. I enjoy working with the earth, couldn't abide an indoor job. I haven't worked much since Jade disappeared though. Didn't have the heart for it.'

'You're unemployed?'

'That's right. I do jobbing gardening from time to time, and I keep my mother's grounds tidy. There's lots to do there.'

'Let's get back to the day Jade disappeared,' Kate said.

'As I said, when I came home she'd already gone. Off to visit a friend, Diane said, but she didn't return. It's upsetting remembering that day.' He fumbled with his spectacles. 'D'you mind if I get a drink of water?'

Kate nodded her agreement.

Paul got up and went into the kitchen. When he returned he was carrying a glass which he laid on the desk. Water splashed out and formed a small puddle on the surface. He stared at it for a moment before continuing.

'It destroyed our family, you know. Diane wouldn't stay home. She was always out looking for Jade. We found her on the Tay Bridge one time, getting ready to jump. And Emma, she lapsed into a catatonic state, she was like that for months and when she recovered she didn't even know it had happened. She still thinks she was the one who supported the family through it all, when it was actually me.'

'What about Ryan. You don't mention him.'

'Ryan seemed OK. He was sad, of course, and I caught him crying several times. I thought that was a natural reaction, although he seemed to think it was shameful.'

'And you, how did it affect you?'

'That was the problem. I was busy supporting my family it didn't leave any room for me to grieve, and it all got too much for me. That's why I left.' He looked up. 'I loved Jade, you know. Loved her more than any of them, and when she disappeared there seemed to be nothing left for me.' He lifted the glass and gulped water. 'You said there had been developments. What are they?' He adjusted his spectacles and looked at Kate.

'It's tentative and we're not sure what it means, but your wife has had contact from someone purporting to be Jade.'

'After all this time, how can that be?'

'As I said, we're not sure what it means but we have to investigate it.'

'I see.' He appeared thoughtful. 'It's probably one of Diane's fantasies, she never believed Jade might be dead.' He wiped his eyes with the back of his hands, and, without looking up, said, 'Will you keep me informed?'

'Of course.' Kate fished a business card out of her shoulder bag. 'If you remember anything that might help us. Or if the person claiming to be Jade gets in contact, you can reach me on this number.'

21

Diane emptied the bucket of water down the drain at the back door rather than contaminate her kitchen sink.

She straightened, aware of the ache in her back and the rawness of her knees, but she wasn't finished yet. She still had the aluminium bucket to scrub until it shone. Emma gave her plastic buckets in an attempt to wean her off the aluminium ones, but Diane rejected them because you were never sure they were clean enough.

After Ryan left for his appointment at Tony's club, Diane had been at a loss. She was sure if they'd left her alone she would have found Jade. But Emma and Ryan had interfered and brought her home, so she did what she always did and started cleaning.

The sink, shower unit and bath were spotless but she scoured them anyway, then she bleached the toilet. After that she scrubbed the bathroom and kitchen floors as well as the front step.

Memories of Jade surfaced, bombarding her brain with their immediacy.

She sank onto the stone step outside the kitchen door and closed her eyes, the bucket forgotten in her anguish. Her reddened hands twisted the fabric of her skirt, round and round her fingers until they became numb. Her mind was in turmoil but one thought kept surfacing – she had to find Jade.

She stood up so suddenly she almost overbalanced. The one person Jade might have contacted was Paul. But it had been years since he'd walked out on the family, and she didn't know where he was. However, one person would know, his mother. She shivered. The woman was evil, and when Paul left she'd hoped never to see her again, but if it meant finding Jade she had no option.

Diane, leaving the bucket outside, stumbled into the kitchen and through to the hall, forgetting to close the back door in her hurry. Her hands, no longer numb, tingled with the returning feeling and she had difficulty opening the front door. She paused on the doorstep. There was something she should have done, but the thought eluded her. Then she remembered, she needed a coat. Turning back she grabbed it and, slinging it round her shoulders, ran down the street.

The wind whipped the edges of her coat and skirt whirling them round her knees. A sudden blast forced the coat from her shoulders and she grabbed the cloth edge to prevent it landing in the gutter. Stopping, she thrust her arms into the sleeves, something she should have done when she left the house. She was still buttoning the coat when a bus rumbled past. She watched it with dazed eyes, and that was when it hit her. She had no idea how to get to her mother-in-law's house, which bus to take, and even if there was a bus service. Ryan had gone off with the car and it was too far to walk.

Ryan had said he was going to Tony's night club which was a lot nearer than Patricia Carnegie's house. She walked to the club most days when she was going to work. And her car keys were in her coat pocket. Her mind made up, she turned in the direction of the night club. She needed the car more than Ryan did.

When she reached Teasers' car park it only took a moment before she was sitting in the front seat ready to drive off. She edged the car forward, then stopped. Ryan would wonder where the car was. He might think it stolen. And he might report it to the police. She could do without that hassle, but she didn't want to speak to Ryan either. He would stop her and take her home again, and that was the last thing she wanted.

'Damn,' she muttered. But she got out of the car and entered the club through the rear entrance. It only took a moment to find the security man who was on duty. 'Will you tell Ryan Carnegie I've taken the car,' she said.

'Ryan who?'

'Carnegie. He's here to take photos for Tony.'

'Oh, you mean the guy upstairs videoing Angel.'

'Yes,' she muttered. 'Will you tell him?'

'Sure thing, babe. I'll see to it.'

Diane hurried back to the car, bemused at being called babe.

It didn't take her long to drive to the other side of the town. But when she turned in the gates and drove up the tree-lined drive, she started to have doubts. Patricia hated Diane, just as much as Diane hated her. How the heck was she going to handle it. She stiffened in the driving seat. She'd make the old bitch tell her where Paul was. Jade deserved as much.

Screeching the car to a halt outside the front of the house, she leaped out and battered on the front door. When her knock wasn't answered she hammered on it again.

The door opened a fraction, then started to close again. But Diane was ready and stuck her foot in the opening. 'I want to talk to you.'

'Go away, I don't want to talk or see you. I thought I made that plain when Paul left you and came home to me.'

Diane pushed the door. She was stronger than Patricia, and it opened.

'You have no right barging in here. I'll call the police and get you removed.'

'Maybe so, but not before I've got what I came for.'

'And what would that be? There's nothing here for you and you have no right to barge in.' Patricia retreated down the hallway.

'Paul's address.'

Patricia laughed. 'It'll be a cold day in hell before I give you that.'

'You'd know more about hell than I do, but I can soon arrange for you to find out more.' Diane advanced towards Patricia who retreated further.

'You!' Patricia laughed again, it wasn't a pleasant sound. 'What could you do? Look at you. You look like a washerwoman with your out-of-date coat and your ugly red hands. And your hair hasn't seen a stylist for years. What on earth my Paul ever saw in you, I'll never know.'

'Is that so?' Diane's voice was quiet in contrast to the rage pounding in her brain, making it difficult for her to focus and sending waves of heat through her body.

Patricia laughed again. 'Get out of my house you poor excuse for a woman.'

Unable to contain herself any longer, Diane slapped Patricia, and before the woman could recover slapped her again across the other cheek. Her hands stung from the contact and she hoped Patricia's cheeks were stinging as well. She advanced and grabbed Patricia's shoulder in a tight grip. 'Paul's address, I want it now.'

Patricia tried to shake her off but Diane tightened her grasp. 'Now!'

'You can't make me give it to you. No matter what you do.'

'I haven't even started yet.' Diane dug her fingers into Patricia's hair and yanked.

Patricia grabbed her head and moaned.

'I knew it was a wig, Patty.' Diane knew Patricia hated being called Patty. 'And I'm not going to give it back.'

'I'll call the police.'

'You do that, Patty, but the wig will be long gone by then.'

Patricia reached out and tried to wrench the wig from Diane, but Diane danced away from her.

'I have scissors in my pocket, or maybe a lighter would be better. I wonder how it would burn. Would it flare up or smoulder? Why don't I try to find out?'

Patricia seemed to have shrunk. 'You wouldn't dare,' she said.

'Oh, I would dare all right. But I tell you what, write down Paul's address for me and I'll give back the wig.' Diane grabbed a notepad and pen from the telephone stand behind Patricia.

'Paul won't speak to you.'

'What have you got to lose then. Write his address down and I'll give you the wig and get out of your way.'

'Oh, what the heck, you win.' Patricia scribbled the address on a page of the notepad, tore it out and handed it to Diane.

'Thanks, Patty. I'll be off.' Diane strode out the front door.

'My wig! You said you'd give me back my wig.'

'Oh, yes.' Diane looked at it and was tempted to keep it, but she raised her arm and threw it into the nearest tree. 'There you go, Patty. I always keep my promises, but you'll have to climb for it.'

Diane was smiling when she drove out the gates and onto the main road.

The house was empty when Ryan got back from the photoshoot. Emma was still at university. She'd said she had lectures today, and there was no sign of Diane.

'Mum,' he shouted, but there was no response. Where was she? The worry he'd been feeling about her earlier returned, making his stomach churn and his chest ache. He was sure he was going to be sick.

He checked the lounge and the kitchen ran up the stairs and peered into every bedroom. He even looked in the bathroom. But Diane was nowhere to be seen.

At last he checked the hall cupboard. Her coat wasn't there. She must have gone out again.

He dithered at the front door. Maybe he should go and look for her. But where would he start? He didn't know what to do. Diane's obsession with Jade was affecting them all.

Five years ago the whole family had been in turmoil, every single one of them had been on the point of a breakdown, and Ryan didn't want to go there again.

22

Tears blurred his vision and, although Paul stared at the business card, he was unable to read what was on it. The policewoman's words whirled round his brain but they didn't make any sense. Jade couldn't be back. It was impossible. It had been too long.

He removed his spectacles and scrubbed his eyes with a dirty handkerchief. Jade had been the love of his life and he would give anything to have her back. A faint hope fluttered in his chest, perhaps by some miracle Jade had returned. Fresh tears gathered in his eyes and he rested his head on the computer desk, remembering the good times they'd had together and how she could wind him round her little finger.

'Who do you love most of all?' He always asked the question because he wanted to hear her reply.

'You, Daddy. I love you most of all.'

The edge of the desk bit into his cheek and he sat back in the chair remembering that last morning, when Jade had left the house giggling and happy. They'd argued the night before, a silly argument about a boy, and he wanted to resolve things with her, so he followed her out. Emma had gone on ahead and Jade was alone. When he caught up with her she'd said, 'Not now, Daddy. I'm late for school.' He'd insisted she stay and listen to him but she'd shaken his hand off her arm and run off.

Maybe if they hadn't argued she would still be here, but he knew the flicker of hope that fluttered briefly in his chest was wishful thinking. He, more than anyone, knew Jade would never return.

However, something was going on, he wasn't sure what, but it all centred round Diane. When he'd left, her mental state hadn't been good. Maybe she'd flipped and was imagining it, or maybe someone was playing a trick on her. The urge to find out was overpowering and he hurriedly left the flat.

Wind whistled along the walkway whipping open his unbuttoned coat. He scurried along to the shelter of the stairwell before buttoning it and pulling the hood over his head.

'You seen my Megan?'

Paul jerked round. He hadn't heard Mrs Fraser coming up behind him. She was remarkably silent for such a big woman. Her hair fanned out round her face, whipped by the wind into a flaming halo.

'Why would I have seen your Megan?' he muttered, turning away from her. He pulled the hood closer to his face and scurried down the stairs. Stupid woman always seemed to be watching him.

'I'm keeping my eye on you,' she shouted after him, her voice echoing eerily in the stairwell.

The housing estate was vastly different to the area where Diane lived. To her it was a different universe. Despair seemed to be etched into the stonework of the buildings, while the rubbish-strewn concrete walkways gave the appearance of barriers, rather than access, to the dismal looking flats. Everything stank of poverty and dereliction. At the end of the street a gathering of youths huddled together, their outlines forming a menacing backdrop to the unprepossessing scene.

Diane drove into the car park in front of the block where Paul had his flat. It was deserted and dark, and the cars parked in it were dilapidated and dirty, while over in one corner was the burnt out shell of a van. She took one look and drove back out onto the street, parking at the kerb. Luckily the youths had moved further down the street and appeared to be making their way to an assignation elsewhere.

All the same, she didn't feel safe here and didn't want to

get out of the car. However, she braced herself and, clutching her handbag in vice-like fingers, she got out, turning to make sure the car doors were locked before entering the dark cavern of the stairwell.

Reaching the top of the stairs, she hesitated, then turned to her left. But the numbers were going the wrong way. She retraced her steps and found Paul's flat at the end of the walkway.

When no answer came to her knock, she knocked again and tried the handle, but the door was locked.

'He's out. You've just missed him.'

The voice made Diane jump. She hadn't heard anyone come up behind her and her nerves were raw simply being here. She half-turned towards the woman and, pulling her hood closer round her face, sidled past her. She couldn't avoid seeing the woman's eyes staring at her, though, they seemed to pierce the hood and see right through her.

'I'll come back later,' she muttered, scuttling along the walkway to the stairs.

'You want me to tell him you were here?'

'No.' Diane's voice echoed up the stairwell as she hurried down to the safety of her car.

By the time the bus deposited Paul in Strathmore Avenue, he was frozen. He dug his hands into his pockets, hunched his shoulders and hurried round the corner into Johnston Avenue.

The house was unchanged. It even had the same curtains and he had the odd sensation of having stepped back in time. He stood at the opposite side of the street, reluctant to cross and enter the house he had left five years ago. How would Diane react? Would she be pleased to see him, or would she scream at him? Anything but screaming. He couldn't tolerate that.

Diane had screamed at him when he left. 'You're a useless piece of shit. No good for anything.'

He'd kept walking, anything to get away from her voice.

'What about the kids,' she'd shouted after him. 'They're your kids as well.'

But he'd had enough of Diane's moods, Emma's sullenness and Ryan's tears. There was a limit to what he could stand and he'd passed that limit some time ago. He had to get out.

'Don't think you can come back when you feel like it,' she'd screamed after him, 'because once you've gone, that's it, there's no coming back.'

'No coming back!' All these years later the words still echoed through his brain.

He leaned against a lamp post, remembering, and knew there was no way he could cross that road and knock on the door. But still he stood staring at the house, hypnotized by the light in the window of an upstairs room, sending a welcoming glow into the street.

How long he stood he had no way of knowing. It was as if time had frozen and he was encased in a bubble, remembering the past and dreading the future.

The sound of a car reversing up the drive woke him from his reverie, and he pulled his hood closer to his face so Diane wouldn't see him. He watched her get out of the car and enter the house. When the door closed he released the breath he hadn't been aware he was holding, and with a sigh of regret he walked down the street in the direction of the bus stop.

'Where have you been, Mum?' Ryan clattered down the stairs from his room. Emma stood at the top watching.

Diane shrugged her coat off and draped it over the banister. 'I went looking for your father.'

'Why would you do that?' Emma descended the stairs. 'He opted out of this family a long time ago. We don't want him back now.'

'Nor do I.' Diane smiled at her daughter. 'You don't have to worry on that score.'

'But why?'

'Because I thought he might know where Jade was.'

'And did he?' Ryan sounded concerned.

Diane wanted to pull them both to her and hug them, but they were adults now and they had never been a tactile family. 'He wasn't at home. I didn't see him.'

'Thank goodness for that. God only knows what would have come out of it. Promise me you won't go back.'

'Don't frown, Emma, and don't worry about me.'

'But I do worry and you haven't promised you won't go back.'

'And I don't intend to promise anything. Don't you see I have to find out where Jade is.'

'Jade is nowhere. We keep telling you she's gone. She's not coming back.'

'But the card, and the bead.'

'Tell her Ryan. She won't listen to me. Tell her Jade's never going to come back.'

'Emma's right, Mum.' Ryan's voice was softer and more compassionate than his sister's. 'How did you know where to find him anyway?'

Diane rummaged in the pocket of her coat for the piece of paper. 'I got his address from your gran. I went to see her because I knew she'd still be in touch with him. He'll never be able to escape from that old bat.'

'Gran?' Emma's voice was incredulous. 'You went to see Gran?'

'But you don't get on.' Ryan stared at her with disbelief. 'You almost tore each other's hair out the last time you saw her.'

'Well I succeeded this time.' Diane laughed. 'Her hair was swinging from the branch of a tree when I left her.'

Diane slipped the piece of paper inside the telephone directory on the hall table, planked her car keys beside it and turned towards the kitchen. 'We'll eat in about half an hour,' she said, 'and tomorrow I'll go back to see your father.'

23

'Any developments?' Kate shrugged her coat off and threw it into her office.

Sue looked up from tidying her desk. 'We've narrowed down the CCTV, but I'm afraid it's inconclusive. We can't get a clear look at the face of the person accompanying our John Doe. But we've had a stroke of luck. The forensic guys examining the van found a laptop in a hidden compartment in the floor and it's being examined. Hopefully by tomorrow we'll be able to get an identity for him.' She stuck files in a filing cabinet and turned the key. 'Oh, and Jenny has enhanced that photo of the jade necklace for Bill to have a look at.'

'Where is it?' Bill asked.

'It's on your desk. If you hadn't come back I would have put it in your filing cabinet.'

Kate wondered if that comment was aimed at her, in recognition of her run in with Bill about security.

Bill sat down and grabbed the photos. 'They're a match,' he said to Kate. 'Look.'

Kate looked at the photos of the jade necklace, trying to remember what the beads in the John Doe's eyes had looked like. 'I think you might be right,' she said. 'We'll need to follow that up tomorrow.'

'I could do it now.'

'No! We have to cut back on overtime. Orders from above.' She raised her voice. 'Team meeting at nine tomorrow. Don't be late.'

Kate was last to leave the office. She looked round the room and realized she was starting to feel a sense of belonging.

After struggling through the rush hour traffic, home was

an oasis of peace. Her spirits lifted when she saw Gavin's car parked in front of the house. He hadn't said he would be finished early today, but she was glad he was.

Gavin was in the kitchen, bending over the cooker. The oven door was open and the smell of goulash was irresistible. 'I defrosted a casserole from the freezer,' he said, without looking up. 'Hope that's OK.'

'Smells good.' She hung her shoulder bag on the doorknob and unbuttoned her coat. 'Thank goodness I'm finished,' she said.

'Bad day?' He closed the oven door and straightened up.

'Actually, it wasn't too bad. I took DS Murphy out on a couple of interviews and it went all right. I think the team might be starting to accept me.'

Gavin grinned at her. 'You cut him a bit of slack then?'

'I suppose you could call it that.'

'I told you that would work. After all the guy must have experience or he wouldn't be in that team. He'd be plodding the beat somewhere.'

'You didn't have to say, I told you so.'

'As if,' he said, wrapping his arms round her. 'Come here you. We haven't had much time for each other lately.'

'The casserole!'

'It can wait.'

'I could easily have followed up on that jade bead. Might still do it,' Bill said, as he and Sue waited in the corridor.

'Are you really determined to annoy the DI?' Sue pinged the lift button again. 'Where is that damned lift?'

'She wasn't so bad today. At least she involved me in the interviews instead of making me watch the CCTV footage.'

'So, you reward her by defying her orders?'

Bill shuffled his feet. 'It's the overtime she's worried about. If I did it in my own time surely she'd understand.'

'I doubt it. I think she'd see it as defiance.'

'Maybe you're right.'

'At last,' Sue said, when the lift arrived. 'I was beginning to think we'd be here all night.'

'You didn't tell me Louise was back,' Bill said, following her in.

'How did you find out?'

'She was at the crime scene yesterday, but I didn't get a chance to talk to her.'

The vestibule was empty and the officers on duty behind the glassed in reception didn't look up. 'Why didn't you tell me she was back?'

The staccato click of Sue's high-heeled boots on the tiles quickened, and when she reached the doors she hurried through into the chill March air. 'She didn't want me to.' The words were snatched away by the wind, seeming to float in space before impacting on Bill's ears.

He grabbed her arm and swung her round to face him. 'Why?'

Sue sighed. 'The Templeton Woods fiasco, that's why. It took a lot out of her, although she didn't show it at the time. She's still having nightmares about it.' She shrugged her shoulders. 'If you want my opinion I don't even think she should be back on duty, but she's stubborn. She said that when she thinks of you it reminds her of that terrible night.'

'What if I went to see her?'

'Don't. Give her time. Maybe she'll feel differently in a few months.' Sue prised his fingers off her arm. 'Take care, Bill.' Her voice was gentle, and she patted his arm before turning and hurrying in the direction of her car.

Bill watched her go, glad in a way, because if she'd stayed she would have seen the tears in his eyes. He dashed them away with his sleeve and hurried down the steps towards his own Ford banger. His life was deteriorating at a fast rate and he wasn't sure what to do about it.

Turning the key in the ignition, he drove to his flat, a place that had lost its soul and no longer felt like home.

Paul had been standing at the bus stop when the call came. 'Calm down,' he said, 'I'll come and see you.' He stuck the phone in his pocket and took the bus to the city centre where he hailed a taxi.

'What's happened to you?' He stared at his mother. She looked small and shrivelled, not the confident, glamorous woman he was used to.

'Oh, Paul! I'm so glad you've come.' She threw her arms round his neck, tucked her head into his shoulder, and sobbed.

'Shh, shh.' Paul stroked her head which was covered by a silk scarf. He pulled his fingers back when he realized there was no hair under the scarf. 'What's happened to your hair?'

'It's up in that tree.' Patricia pulled away from him and pointed. 'That horrible woman you married threw it up there.'

'Diane's been here?' He couldn't keep the astonishment out of his voice.

'Yes, she's been here, and she was horrible to me. But you're here now and you'll look after me.' She snuggled back into his arms.

'Of course I will. You know I'm always here for you.'

Paul kept his arms tight round her but looked up at the wig fluttering from a tree branch. 'It's not too high up,' he said. 'I'm sure I could get it down and then you'd look respectable again.'

'Would you? I hate you seeing me like this.'

'Wait here, I've got a ladder in the potting shed. I'm sure it'll reach.'

Once he left the garden and entered the wood the darkness closed around him, but he didn't need a light to find his way to the potting shed. Patricia had insisted he build it out of sight of the house. 'I don't want to look out at that ugly thing,' she'd said, although how she knew what it would look like was beyond him. But the shed suited him being here, it was a place where he could relax, where he could keep his tools and where no one interfered with him.

He fished the keys out of his pocket and unlocked the padlock. The inside of the shed was pitch black and smelled of earth mixed with a tinge of ammonia. But he was an organized man, and knew exactly where everything was inside, so he knew the ladder was leaning on the wall to the right of the door. He reached in and grasped the metal frame which creaked when he pulled it from its resting place. A slight rustling and faint whisper over in the far corner broke the silence. He stared into the darkness for a moment, but then closed the shed door and padlocked it again. He would come back tomorrow and deal with the source of the noise.

Patricia was waiting in the doorway and when he appeared with the ladder she walked over to him. 'You were a long time, I was beginning to worry,' she said.

He extended the ladder and propped it against the tree. 'I know you don't like going into the woods, but you don't need to worry about me. I'm used to them.'

'But there's a fox. It raids my bins and I've seen it in the garden after dark.'

He started to climb the ladder. 'I'll come back tomorrow and lay traps, but you'll have to stay clear of the wooded areas. I don't want you getting caught in them.'

Easing himself off the end of the ladder onto the branch, he inched along it until he could see the wig. Strands of hair fluttered in the breeze. His fingers closed over the hair but the wind whipped it out of his grasp. The branch swayed under his weight and for a moment he thought it might break, but a gust blew the wig back towards him and he grasped it before the wind changed direction again. Holding the wig, he wriggled back to safety.

Patricia vanished inside the house clutching the wig. Paul followed, poured himself a brandy from the crystal decanter in the drinks cabinet, and made himself comfortable on the white leather sofa. He sipped, savouring the flavour of the drink, and studied the painting of his mother. Patricia had been beautiful in her heyday. She never stopped telling him about her stage career and what she had given up for his father. Then, after his father's death, how she had made the ultimate sacrifice for her Paul. He often wondered if she would have been able to make a comeback, but he accepted her sacrifice as his due.

She returned to the lounge and slipped onto the sofa beside him. 'I feel a lot better now.' She patted her hair. 'It's windblown but better than nothing.' She scowled. 'That odious woman, promise me you'll have nothing more to do with her.'

'You haven't told me what Diane came to see you about?'

'She wanted your address. I wasn't going to give it to her, but she got violent, and I had to.'

'Why would she want my address? We haven't been in touch for years and the last time I saw her she was adamant she wanted no contact.'

'Something to do with Jade. I don't know. Promise me you won't take up with her again.'

'Of course I won't. You're the only woman for me now.'

Patricia placed her hand on his thigh. 'You'll stay the night?'

'Not tonight, Patricia.'

She had been Patricia to him for as long as he could remember, mother had been a taboo word. When he was a child she'd insisted he tell everyone she was his sister, and when he got older, his girl friend.

She pouted. 'I don't want to be alone tonight.'

He pulled her close to him and kissed her on the lips. 'Tomorrow,' he whispered. 'I'll come back tomorrow.' He eased himself out of her embrace. 'Can I borrow the car? It'll save me getting a taxi and I'll have it back to you first thing tomorrow.'

She nodded her assent, but he could see the tears welling in her eyes. 'Tomorrow,' he whispered, kissed her forehead and left.

The scrape of a key in the lock woke Megan out of her stupor.

She'd thought he would never return, but he was there, a dark shape standing in the doorway. The time had come and she wasn't sure whether to dread what was going to happen to her, or be glad, because it would all be over and maybe he would let her go.

A cold breeze wafted round her legs, and her shivering increased. That awful shivering that never seemed to stop.

She wished he would say or do something to put her out of her misery, but all he did was stand, look and listen.

'Please,' she whispered through cracked lips. Her tongue felt swollen and her vocal chords weren't working as well as they should.

But he turned away from her, grasped something that clanked, and went out, shutting and locking the door behind him.

She was alone in the dark again.

24

It was dark when Jade returned.

She stood on the top landing, listening, but everything was quiet and the house slumbered, along with its occupants. She descended the stairs in her bare feet, being careful to avoid the creaking step, and once she was in the hallway, she put her shoes on.

The slip of paper was still where Diane had put it, in the telephone directory. She slipped it out, grabbed the car keys and silently left the house.

The drive was on a slight slope. She turned the ignition key to the first notch, released the hand brake and allowed the car to slip out onto the road before she felt safe enough to turn the ignition on fully and drive off.

The roads were quiet and she was soon driving into the Greenfield estate where she planned to confront Paul.

She left the car in the parking area opposite the flats, manoeuvring it out of sight into a space beside a dirty white van and a clapped out Volvo. It wouldn't do if someone noted the number.

Glass crunched under her feet, and the smell of beer mixed with all sorts of other unsavoury aromas, nauseated her. A car trundled along the road and she stepped back into the shadows. After it vanished round a corner she hurried over to the stairwell and climbed to the third floor.

A cat hissed at her when she emerged onto the walkway, and she sideswiped it with her foot, sending it yowling into the stairwell. The walkway was deserted but she made sure the hood obscured her face as she walked towards Paul's flat.

It was in darkness, and the door was locked. She'd thought he would be at home and had been practising what she was going to say. But this was even better. Now she could surprise him.

It only took her five minutes to return to the car, take a screwdriver from the toolkit, and return to Paul's door. After that it was easy to prise the lock open and enter the flat. She would wait for him inside. Surprise him.

The door swung open at his touch. That was strange. He was sure he'd locked it. He flicked the light switch, nothing happened. Damned fuses must have blown. He felt his way along the hallway to the cupboard containing the breaker box, there was a torch in there and he'd soon have the electric on again.

Something moved in the darkness at the end of the corridor. He stopped, alert to the smallest sound.

Something rustled, and the shadows moved again.

'Who's there?'

'Hello, Daddy. Have you missed me?'

The voice reminded him of something or someone. Childlike, and at the same time, seductive. It was a voice he hadn't heard for five years. A voice he'd never expected to hear again.

'Jade?'

Time shifted, and he returned to the day his daughter had vanished without trace.

'Yes, Daddy.'

'Oh, how I've missed you. I knew you didn't mean it when you said you never wanted to see me again, I knew you would come back to me. We loved each other too much for you to stay away for ever.'

In the silence that followed he could hear her breathing.

'Let me sort the lights so I can look at you.'

'No, Daddy. I've been in the dark so long, I like it.'

Past and present collided. It was impossible. He knew it was impossible, but he wanted to believe it was her, wanted to believe it so much he convinced himself it could be her. He fumbled in his pocket for his lighter. He had to see her.

His hand found the lighter and he flicked it on.

'But you're . . . ' The stab of the needle in his neck, cut him short.

The lighter flicked off and he slapped his other hand on the spot where she had stabbed him.

'What have you done, Jade?' He had trouble enunciating the words, and he felt peculiar. His vision blurred and his bones felt heavy. It was as if they'd melted into his feet. He leaned against the wall. It swayed at his touch and he slid down until he was unable to slide any further. The weight of his body made him topple sideways until he was lying flat. Cotton wool encased him in a warm glow and he was back in the past again. Back when he and Jade had been happy. He reached out to stroke her cheek. 'My baby,' he said, and then he floated away.

The mixture of heroin and GHB in the syringe was massive, and it only took a moment for Paul to succumb to the effects of the drug in his bloodstream.

Jade watched him slide into a stupor; it had been easy. She sat back on her heels and stroked his face. 'Poor Daddy,' she murmured. 'You always told me I loved you. All the time you were doing those things. Proving our love, you used to say. But I never loved you, Daddy. I just said I did.'

Paul's lips formed a lopsided smile and his eyes had difficulty focusing.

'Maybe a little more,' Jade murmured.

She stood up and felt her way to the cupboard where she had turned off the electric. When she flicked the master switch the lights came back on. 'That's better I can see what I'm doing now.' Bending down she removed the lighter from Paul's grasp and patted his head. 'I'll be back in a minute.'

The kitchen was a mess, dirty dishes in the sink, mouldy food in the saucepans, the sound of a mouse scarpering back to its home in the skirting board.

'Tut, tut, Daddy. How can you live like this?'

She pulled open a drawer in the sink unit, then another

one, and at last found what she was looking for. Picking a spoon out of the drawer she looked for someplace to put it down, but there didn't seem to be a clear space anywhere. With a sigh, she picked up a cup and plate and tossed them onto the mountain of dishes in the sink. She laid the spoon on the small area she'd cleared and rummaged in her pocket for the packet of powder. It was the pure stuff, lovely and white, not that nasty brown stuff the dealers peddled. After sprinkling it in the spoon and adding a drop of water, she lifted it up and flicked the lighter on, holding the flame beneath the spoon until the mixture bubbled and melted. Laying the spoon back on the table she took the syringe and syphoned the liquid into it.

'Here we go, Daddy,' she said when she returned to his side. 'This will make you feel good and your worries will all be over.'

She plunged the syringe into his neck. 'Goodnight, Daddy. Sleep tight.'

Jade watched him slide deeper into a comatose state. When she was satisfied he was beyond help, she grabbed his heels and pulled him through to the lounge.

She laid him out on the floor, crossing his arms across his chest, and carefully placed the jade beads in his eyes. 'To remind you of me,' she said.

She turned her attention to his computer. 'Let's have a nice picture show. I'm sure you'll have some lovely photos on here.'

It didn't take her long to crack his password and find his hidden files.

'Ah, yes,' she murmured, combining all his photos into one file and setting them to appear on the monitor in a slide show. 'I'm sure the police will find these interesting.'

She turned off all the lights and let herself out as quietly as she'd entered, leaving the door ajar.

25

Wednesday, 14 March

It was still dark outside when Diane woke. Jade had come to her during the night and told her she was happy and everything was going to be all right, and her mother's worries and distress were over and she should get on with her life again.

'Will you come home?' Diane had asked.

Jade hadn't answered, simply told her she would always live on in Diane's heart and she shouldn't worry about her, and she shouldn't try to find her.

'I came back to do what I had to do,' she said, 'but now it's done I can rest again.'

A puff of wind seeped through the window which was opened an inch at the bottom causing the curtains to flutter. Even in the coldest weather Diane needed fresh air in her bedroom, and now she snuggled further down in the bed, pulling the duvet round her neck.

She lay, luxuriating in the warmth, while the need to rise and punish herself, diminished. The need to scrub and clean was in abeyance and she was able to think about Jade without tormenting herself. She knew her daughter was safe, and was convinced she would return when she was ready.

Daylight was sneaking into the room when Emma tapped and opened her door. 'I wondered where you were,' she said. 'I'm used to you being up before me.'

Diane patted the bed. 'Come sit beside me.'

Emma walked over and perched on the edge. She frowned. 'You're different,' she said.

Diane grasped her hand. 'Jade came to me last night. She said I wasn't to worry any more and she was safe.'

'You mean you saw her?'

Diane nodded.

'It must have been a dream.' Emma's frown deepened.

'I don't think so. She was as real as you are now.'

'But that's impossible.'

'No, Emma. It was real.'

Emma withdrew her hand from Diane's grasp. 'I'll go and put the kettle on. You'll feel better after a cup of tea.'

Diane swung her legs out of the bed after Emma left the room, but she could hear her whispering to Ryan outside her bedroom door.

Well, let them whisper all they liked. She knew what she had seen.

'What's up?' Ryan had been waiting for Emma on the landing when she came out of Diane's bedroom. 'Has something happened to Mum?'

'You could say that.' Emma kept her voice low. 'She thinks she's seen Jade.'

'What?'

'Speak quietly, she'll hear.' Emma glanced at the closed bedroom door. 'She says Jade came to her during the night.'

'She must have been dreaming.'

'I said that, but she's convinced it was real.' Emma grabbed his arm. 'I'm worried about her. I think she's going round the twist. She's become convinced Jade has come back, and now she's started seeing her. D'you think we should get on to the GP for a referral to her psychiatrist?'

'She won't like that. You know how she is.'

Emma's brain whirled. She didn't know what to do about her mother. She loved her so much it hurt, and she wanted to protect her from harm. But what could she do when Diane was set on a course that could only lead to disaster? If she did nothing, her mother's mental state might deteriorate further. And if she had her referred to a psychiatrist it would mean the pills again, and they almost destroyed her the last time. Emma wasn't sure she could allow that. What to do, what to do?

'Maybe we should leave it for now and see how things develop.' Ryan's voice cut into her thoughts.

'I don't know.' Emma let go of Ryan's arm. 'Maybe you're right. But we need to keep an eye on her, make sure she's safe.'

'You don't think she's suicidal again, do you?' Panic made Ryan's voice shrill.

'No, not as long as she believes Jade is alive. The problem will be when she realizes it's all wishful thinking on her part, and Jade is never coming back. I think she might be suicidal then.'

Emma glanced at her mother's bedroom door again. She could hear movement behind it. 'Come on, I said I'd make her a pot of tea. Maybe we'll all feel differently once we've had breakfast.'

The kettle was on the boil when Diane entered the kitchen.

'Tea's almost made.'

Emma's voice was bright and cheery. Too bright and cheery for Diane's liking. She looked at Ryan, and he grinned at her.

'What are you two up to?' Diane grabbed three mugs from the worktop and planked them on the table.

'Why should we be up to something?' Emma poured tea into the mugs. 'We're trying to be helpful.'

Diane snorted. 'Helpful? When have you ever been up early enough to make me tea in the morning? You're up to something. I can sense it.'

Ryan studied his cup. Diane thought he looked as if he'd rather be anywhere else but here in the kitchen, listening to his mother and Emma narking at each other.

'Nonsense,' Emma said. 'We aren't up any earlier than usual, it's you who is later. Anyway, why don't you drink the tea I made you.' She slumped into a chair. 'I was trying to be nice, that's what, and that's all the thanks I get.'

Diane felt a sudden pang of remorse. Why was it she could never appreciate anything Emma did for her? She knew her daughter would do anything to please her, but nothing Emma did made any difference to her feelings. And she knew why that was. It was because she wasn't Jade. Emma was the mirror image of Jade, but she could never be her. Jade was bubbly and full of life, while Emma was quiet and introvert, lacking in self esteem and prone to depression.

'Thank you for making the tea,' Diane said, but it was too late, she'd ruined Emma's attempt to please her.

26

Bill woke early, a scream hovering on his lips, while the nightmare hid in the recesses of his brain.

He stared into the darkness, reluctant to get out of bed, but knew if he slept again the nightmare would return. He untangled the sheet wrapping his body in a stranglehold, while the duvet, supposed to keep him warm, lay in a heap on the floor. Leaning over, he flicked on the bedside lamp, relieved it worked. He'd thought the previous night's electricity blackout in the flat was due to an unpaid bill, but the answer was simpler. The hallway bulb had blown causing the breaker box to turn everything off. There was still no light in the hallway, but at least there were lights everywhere else.

When he looked at the black mould on the walls, the heap of unwashed clothes on the floor, and the general disarray of the room, he thought maybe it would have been better if the lights had stayed off.

He swung his legs out of bed and padded out of the room for a quick shower. Returning, he rummaged among the piles of clothes for clean socks, grabbed a shirt from the back of a chair, and got dressed. He'd long ago given up putting his clothes in the wardrobe because they always came out smelling of damp.

Satisfied he looked reasonably presentable he went to the kitchen, but in the fridge he found only the usual cheese with its layer of penicillin, an egg that had been there forever, and some curdled milk. It would have to be a bacon buttie from the sandwich shop.

There had been frost overnight and the car was reluctant to start, but eventually it roared into life and Bill joined the early morning traffic. His first task for today was watching

John Doe's post mortem. Just the thing to start the day off with a bang, he thought, watching someone being sliced and diced.

The new mortuary sat to the side and rear of Dundee Police Headquarters and was a short walk away from where Bill usually parked his car. He knew by the time he returned to HQ there would be no parking spaces left, so he left his car in its usual place.

An uneasy silence cloaked the deserted alley leading to the mortuary. It was a tunnel muting everything around it, even the birds were quiet here.

The clatter of Bill's footsteps on the stone slabs breaking that silence, seemed unusually loud. Officers rarely traversed this alley unless they had to, not even to use the large car park in front of the mortuary. The nondescript stone building at the end was long and low, with a corrugated roof, and no windows. It reminded Bill of storage sheds rather than the high tech facility it was.

The roll up door where the bodies were taken in was closed, and the door beside it had a keypad. He pressed a button and a voice said, 'Yes?'

'Detective Sergeant Murphy.' The door clicked and he pushed it open.

'Dr Armstrong's started the autopsy.' The gangly youth peered at Bill through spectacles perched on the end of his nose, he pushed them upwards but they immediately slipped down again. 'She said for you to go along.'

Bill nodded, and the youth disappeared into a side room, leaving Bill to find his own way into the autopsy suite.

'I started without you.' Rose Armstrong's voice filtered through the intercom system.

She snipped a sample of hair and placed it in a small phial which she handed to the second pathologist to seal and label. Bill didn't recognize him, but that was hardly surprising, considering his body was swathed in a gown that covered his scrubs and the only things showing above the face shield and below the cap, were his eyes. Bill wasn't even sure whether it was a man. It could easily be a woman.

'I'll be opening him up in a minute.' She looked over at Bill through the glass screen. Bill could swear she was smiling because her eyes crinkled at the edges.

Bill groaned. 'You know that's the bit I don't like.'

She shrugged. 'It's got to be done.'

'What about the beads in his eyes?'

'I've got them out and they're in one of the specimen bags.'

'Think you could photograph them for me?'

'Already done. I'll get Ralph to courier the photos across to the office.'

Bill reckoned Ralph must be the gangly youth.

The door behind Bill opened and closed, and a woman in a smoke grey tailored suit walked into the viewing gallery. Bill looked at her curiously, guessing she must be the new procurator fiscal. He'd been at Steve Mulholland's retirement do a week ago, and the word then was the new PF was a woman.

'Detective Sergeant Bill Murphy,' he said holding out his hand.

'Astrid Christensen.' Her handshake was firm and businesslike. 'I'm the fiscal.'

Bill noticed she didn't say 'new', and wasn't sure whether that meant she was asserting her authority, or whether she was unsure of herself.

Rose Armstrong looked up from washing the body, and nodded to the newcomer. The washing completed, she selected a dissecting knife from the trolley at her side, and proceeded to carve an incision from neck to groin. Bill had seen enough of her autopsies to know Rose rarely made a V-shaped incision at the top of the trunk, unless there was a suspicion of strangulation.

Bill's earlier bacon buttie turned in his stomach, and he regretted eating it. 'I think I'll head back to the office,' he said into the intercom. 'There are several new developments that need followed up.'

Rose looked up and her eyes crinkled at the edges again. 'I'll send the report over as soon as we've finished.'

'Thanks.'

Neither of the women responded. Rose was engrossed in the task at hand, while Astrid watched her with a fascination Bill thought verged on the unhealthy.

27

Kate arrived early, keen to get the team meeting underway, but Jenny Cartwright, the computer buff, was already there, studying a laptop computer that was open in front of her.

'Have you found anything?' Kate leaned over to look at the screen, although she wasn't sure what she should be looking for. Computers had never been her strong point.

'Lots of porn, adults and kiddies, really nasty stuff.' Jenny's voice was matter of fact. 'I've got a name as well, but it'll have to be checked out, and I've accessed the chat rooms he used. Seems to be chatting up a lot of kids and young folk. Now I'm trying to access his deleted stuff. These guys all think once you've deleted something it's gone for good. Idiots!'

'Good work, Cartwright. Jot the names down and you can feed it into the team meeting.'

Kate collected a coffee from the machine and carried it into her office. Laying the paper cup on her desk, she sucked her burning fingers and swore softly under her breath, before turning to the filing cabinet to retrieve the file on the murder victim. At least he would no longer be John Doe, he would have a name they could track. The files were so tightly packed the file next to it came out as well, and Kate had a sudden memory of the slovenly woman with the flaming red hair who had accosted her outside Paul Carnegie's flat the previous day. She frowned, thinking of what Jenny had said about porn. This woman's daughter, Megan, was fourteen, and it was an uncomfortable thought.

She walked back out of her office and over to Jenny. 'Remember I sent you out to see Mrs Fraser about her missing daughter?'

'Yes,' Jenny said, 'I took DC Armstrong with me. We

checked up on her computer contacts, and I talked to one or two of the boys she'd been chatting with online. But they were schoolmates and they didn't know where she'd gone. They did mention a couple of places she sometimes goes when she takes off, and I've fed the addresses to the local forces to check out. Apparently she's often run off in the past and it seems to be the same this time. It's simply a question of finding her.'

The team were clustered around the whiteboard at the far end of the room when Bill sidled in. He grabbed his chair from behind his desk and plonked it at the back of the group. He hadn't been sure whether Kate would remember he was attending the post mortem this morning and was ready for her displeasure, but she only looked up and nodded.

'Go on,' she said to Blair.

'That's about it, ma'am. We've isolated all the CCTV images that are relevant so we can plot out the time frame, but although we get a clear view of the victim there are no clear views of the perpetrator because a hood covers the face.'

'We definitely know the victim was killed between midday and 2pm on Friday.' Kate picked up a marker and wrote on the board. 'Rogers, you contacted the Child and Family Support Team, I understand.'

'Yes, ma'am. I talked to Constable Louise Walker,' Sue glanced at Bill. 'She said the boys didn't see anything apart from the body in the van. They'd been going through the multi-storey car park checking for unlocked vehicles when they opened the van's doors. I understand both boys have been referred to a Children's Hearing.'

Sue's mention of Louise felt like a punch to Bill's stomach, and he tried not to squirm when he felt Kate looking at him. The DI's eyes were sharp and she hadn't missed the glance nor Bill's reaction.

'You wanted to add something, Murphy?'

'No, ma'am.'

Kate replaced the marker in the groove at the bottom of the whiteboard, then faced the team.

'Cartwright has been examining the laptop found in a cavity in the van's floor, and I believe we may have a name for the victim.'

Jenny adjusted her spectacles. 'The laptop apparently belongs to a John Gregson, although his chat room persona is Kyle.'

'That ties up with what I found out from DVLA,' Sue cut in. 'The van is registered to John Gregson, with an address in Manchester.'

'Good work.' Kate scribbled the name on the board. 'Tell them what else you found, Cartwright.'

'He frequents a lot of chat rooms and children's sites, and he's been chatting to several girls over the past three weeks.'

'Do we have any names?'

'I'd have to check with the ISPs, but the names they were using are Heather123, Clare21, Jade12, Emma452 . . . '

'There's a Jade he's been talking to? That's too much of a coincidence.' Bill looked over at Kate wondering if she'd seen the connection, and knew by her expression she had.

'Murphy and I went out yesterday to interview Paul Carnegie, the father of a certain Jade Carnegie who was reported missing five years ago, when she was thirteen. It had been assumed Jade was dead, however certain recent events have thrown doubt on that. Whatever the facts are, there is certainly a connection between the Carnegie family and John Gregson's murder. Murphy, I believe you were involved, what can you tell us about the rest of the family?'

Bill stood up and faced the team. What could he tell them about the Carnegies? That Diane was a vulnerable woman who needed protecting? That Emma had been a sullen child and was now a sullen teenager? That Ryan was effeminate and a bit peculiar? However the DI was right, there was a connection between the Carnegie family and the guy who was currently being sliced and diced in the mortuary.

He closed his eyes, hoping to banish the memory of Diane sitting in his car, twisting the material of her skirt round and round her fingers, and pleading with him to find Jade. He had made Diane a promise but keeping it might break her heart.

Opening his eyes, he started to speak. 'The family have changed since I first met them, so it's difficult to describe them now without knowing what they were like before. Five years ago, we were called in to investigate the disappearance of Jade Carnegie, a thirteen year old schoolgirl. Detective Inspector Michaels, who was still a sergeant at the time, was the investigating officer and I was his partner. We didn't get anywhere with the investigation and the child seemed to have vanished into thin air.'

Bill walked to the water cooler and filled a paper cup. Taking a sip, he continued, 'Jade's father, Paul Carnegie, was a landscape gardener, her mother, Diane, was a university lecturer in computing. They had two other children, Ryan who was fifteen, and Emma, who was Jade's twin sister. The family took Jade's disappearance badly. The father started to drink. The mother fell to pieces and had to receive psychiatric help, Ryan seemed to spend most of his time crying, while Emma lapsed into a catatonic state that lasted for several months.'

Bill sipped some more water, lost for a moment in his memories of a family falling apart.

'For most of the first year after Jade's disappearance, her mother turned up regularly at the office demanding to know what we were doing to find her daughter . . . but that gradually tailed off until a few days ago when she contacted us again. Apparently she believed her daughter had returned. This was because she'd received a birthday card signed Jade, but enclosed with the card was a jade bead. That jade bead matches the ones we found pressed into our victim's eyes.'

Bill paused and sipped again.

'Mrs Carnegie came to see me and I was surprised to see the change in her. Physically she seems to have shrunk and her personal care has deteriorated. Five years ago she was a smart, intelligent woman. Now she's working as a cleaner, and seems to be suffering from OCD.'

Bill noticed one of the team fidgeting on his seat. 'You wanted to say something, Blair?'

The constable looked embarrassed. 'Not sure what OCD is,' he mumbled.

'Obsessional compulsive disorder,' Bill suppressed a smile. 'That's where the person has a compulsion to do things over and over again. In Mrs Carnegie's case, it's a compulsion to clean, so I suppose her current job as a cleaner makes sense.'

'You say Mrs Carnegie thinks Jade has returned,' Sue interrupted. 'Do the rest of the family think the same?'

'As far as I'm aware they think their mother is fantasizing. They think her mental health is deteriorating.'

'Do we know what the rest of the family are like now?'

'I've met them once, and that was briefly. Emma seems sensible but wasn't welcoming when I went round to see their mother on Monday. I wasn't sure about Ryan, he's twenty but small for his age.' Bill hesitated. 'He seemed effeminate, and I thought he had a trace of lipstick on his lips. As for their father, the DI interviewed him yesterday at his flat. He's separated from the family now, but gave the impression Mrs Carnegie was mentally disturbed and must be imagining it.'

'Thank you, Murphy.' Kate picked up the marker and added more information to the board. 'Sue, I want you to follow up the Manchester lead. Talk to the force. They might know this John Gregson.'

'Yes, ma'am.'

'Murphy, you and I will go out and interview Mrs Carnegie.' Kate laid down the marker, pulled at the edges of her shirt sleeves and strode off in the direction of her office. 'I'll get my jacket and bag.'

Bill was thoughtful as he picked up his chair and replaced it behind his desk. He'd noticed Kate was now addressing Sue by her first name, while he was still Murphy. He glanced over at Sue, meaning to ask her how she'd managed to weasel her way into the DI's good books, but she was already busy on the phone. It would have to wait until later.

'You ready, Murphy?' Kate reappeared at her office door.

'Yes, ma'am.' Bill buttoned his jacket and accompanied her out of the office.

The Carnegie home was a ten minute drive from police headquarters, and Bill was soon pulling into the pavement outside the house. The iron gate was stiff, and squealed when he opened it.

The front door opened, and Diane peered out at them. 'I heard you coming.'

Bill turned to pull the gate closed after him.

'Don't bother closing it,' Diane said. 'We never close it because it's such a pain to open.'

'Oh,' Bill said, 'I thought . . . '

Diane shrugged. 'It's the paper delivery boy, he always closes it. I must remember to tell him not to.'

Bill and Kate followed Diane into the house.

He noted she seemed less agitated, and she hadn't asked if they had found Jade which seemed out of character, and made him wonder what had happened to effect the change.

Diane gestured towards the sofa, and once they were settled, she said, 'Can I get you a coffee or tea?'

'No thanks,' Kate said.

Bill shook his head.

Diane sat in an armchair, and at once her fingers started teasing at the piping on the edge of its arm. 'You've found Jade,' she said, in a matter of fact tone.

'I'm sorry, but no.' Kate's voice was gentle.

'Oh!' The disappointment was evident in Diane's voice. 'I was sure that was why you'd come.'

'We wanted to ask you about Jade's necklace, and the green bead she sent you.' Kate shifted in her seat. 'DS Murphy, perhaps you would like to continue.'

Bill leaned forward. 'You remember you showed me a green jade bead? Do you still have it?'

'Of course. Jade sent it to me. I'll always treasure it.'

'Can we see it, please?'

Diane reached behind her neck and undid the clasp of her gold chain. 'I threaded it onto the chain so I wouldn't lose it,' she said, handing it over.

'You're sure this was a bead from Jade's necklace, it couldn't be another bead from somewhere else.'

'I'd know that bead anywhere. It's unique. The necklace was passed down in my family from my great grandmother. She spent time in India when she was first married and brought it back with her. I gave it to Jade on her eleventh birthday. We didn't have anything to pass on to Emma, so we bought her a coral necklace at the same time.'

Bill passed the bead to Kate. After looking at it, she said, 'We're going to have to take the bead in as evidence. We'll give you a receipt for it though.'

Diane stood up, and tried to grab the bead back from Kate. 'You can't. It's Jade's. She sent it to me.'

'I'm sorry,' Kate said, 'but we do have to take it.'

Tears slipped down Diane's face. 'You can't.'

'We'll look after it, I promise you, and it will be returned when it's no longer needed for evidence.'

Bill stood up and grasped Diane's arms. He led her to the seat and gently pushed her into it.

'It will be all right,' he said. 'I'll make sure you get it back, but we do need to take it for the time being.' He felt Kate looking at him and he released his hold on Diane and returned to his seat.

'Tell me,' he said. 'Have you heard anything more from Jade?'

'She came to me last night. I woke up and she was leaning over me. She told me not to worry about her, that she was safe, and I wasn't to look for her. She would come to me when she was ready.'

'You mean she was here?'

'Yes.' Diane smiled at him. 'I always knew she would come back.'

28

Jenny Cartwright crossed the room and stood in front of Sue's desk. She fidgeted from foot to foot while Sue continued to talk on the phone to Inspector Hargreaves of the Manchester force. The younger woman's agitation was eroding Sue's concentration and she gestured for her to sit down, pointing at the phone as she did so.

Sue scribbled on the pad in front of her. 'Thank you, sir. I will ensure fingerprints and photographic evidence are sent in order for you to check this is the same John Gregson you've got on your radar, and it would be helpful if you could keep us informed of the progress of your enquiries.' She replaced the phone in its cradle and looked up smiling. 'Manchester police have been investigating a paedophile ring and John Gregson is one of the names they had on their list. We're making progress.'

Jenny shifted in her seat. Her eyes sparkled behind her spectacles. 'I've been digging into the computer and I've found a snippet of chat between Gregson and Jade12. It was an arrangement to meet at the Overgate Centre, in Dundee, on Friday. It looks as if Jade12 is the person we're looking for.'

'Good work, Jenny.'

'That's not all. I traced the IP address and got onto the ISP responsible and,' she waved a piece of paper under Sue's nose, 'I've got a name and address for the person posting as Jade12.'

'How on earth did you manage that?' Jenny was prone to use computer talk in her speech, but at least Sue knew what an ISP was. 'I thought you needed a court order to pry names and addresses out of them,' Sue said.

Jenny's face reddened. 'I conned them into giving it to

me. I said they'd be charged with aiding and abetting a murder if they didn't. Did I do wrong?'

'No, you did OK.' Sue smiled at her. She stood up. 'Anyone know when the DI will be back?'

There was no response, apart from a few shakes of the head and shrugs of the shoulders.

'OK, Jenny,' Sue said. 'You'd better write this up, you know what the DI is like for paperwork, and you don't need to mention the conning bit, just say you acquired the name and address from the ISP.'

Sue gathered up the files she'd been working on and locked them in the filing cabinet. This was an exciting development and it needed to be followed up, but she wasn't sure how the DI would respond if she went out without consulting her. If Andy had still been in charge, there would have been no problem, he liked the team to act on their own initiative. But from what she had already seen, DI Rawlings liked things done by the book. She might not take kindly to Sue diving off and doing her own thing. However, it seemed fairly certain Jade12 was the person they were seeking, so if they had an address the only option was to raid it.

Decision made, she lifted the phone. 'I need officers for a raid,' she said into the receiver. 'At least six . . . well I suppose four will have to do. I'll be downstairs immediately, have them ready.' Clattering the phone down, she looked round the room. 'Blair, Jenny, Sid. Grab your jackets.'

'What's up?' Blair had one arm in the sleeve of his jacket and was struggling to find the other sleeve.

'We've got an address for Jade, thanks to Jenny. We'll need to bring the occupants in for questioning, and confiscate any computer equipment. I've acquired four uniforms to go out with us in case we run into trouble.'

It didn't take them long to get to the Derby Street multis. Two massive buildings, Butterburn Court and Bucklemaker Court, rising above the surrounding houses like sentinels watching over them. They drove into the parking area at the rear and tucked the vehicles, two cars and two police vans behind the entry ramp wall of Bucklemaker Court, which was high enough to mask them from view. Sue checked the address again, it was on the third floor. They wouldn't have to go all the way to the top.

Sue steadied her breathing. Raids always gave her an adrenalin rush and she was never sure if the buzz she got was out of fear or pleasure. Turning to Jenny, who was sitting beside her, she said, 'Let the uniforms go in first and you follow on behind. Your job is to locate the computer equipment and instruct them what to take.'

Jenny nodded. If anything, her eyes looked even bigger behind her spectacles and Sue wondered if she was anxious.

'OK, let's go.' Sue got out of the car and strode to where the uniformed officers were gathered. 'Everyone ready? The flat's on the third floor, and we'll try to gain entry before using the bull bar. It'll save a lot of hassle if we don't need it.'

The constable carrying the bull bar shifted it from one shoulder to the other, and Sue couldn't help noticing the look of disappointment on his face.

They turned the corner and hurried up the concrete ramp to the back entrance of the building. Two elderly ladies, one with a zimmer frame, stopped in their slow progress down the ramp and looked at them with startled eyes. The officers streamed past them and Sue nodded to Blair, he was good with older people. He would reassure them.

The entry hall was empty. Sue pinged the lift button and prayed they weren't out of order. The wait seemed interminable but she could hear the groaning and clanking of the lift as it descended, and when the lift doors creaked open they all crammed in; four detectives, four constables and one bull bar. Luckily, when the Dundee multis were built they ensured the lifts were large enough to take a coffin, so eight living bodies was no problem.

The third floor corridor had seen better days, grubby walls, graffiti, and a floor that hadn't seen a brush for many years. The front door to the flat wasn't any better, the original brown paintwork, dingy and peeling.

Sue rang the bell and pounded on the door with the side

of her fist. The detectives and constables stood at the ready at each side, and the constable with the bull bar gave the impression he was itching to use it.

'Who is it?'

'Police!' Sue said. 'Open up.'

The sound of a key turned in the lock and the door opened a crack, obviously on a door chain.

'You got identification?'

Sue held her warrant card up to the opening, and gestured for one of the uniformed constables to step forward.

'Wait a minute.'

The door closed and opened again. 'Can't be too careful,' the woman said. 'There's a lot of yobbos round here. What d'you want anyway?'

'I think it would be better if we discussed this inside.' Sue appraised the woman in front of her. She looked in her early thirties, dressed in jeans and a red sweatshirt, her hair short with red streaks through it. However, she was too tall and well built to be the person in the CCTV video.

The woman nodded and held the door open.

'Wait here,' Sue instructed the constables. 'Blair, Sid, Jenny, come with me.' The four detectives entered the flat.

'Who is it Bren?' Another woman appeared at the inner door. She was of similar age, but had long fair hair that brushed her shoulders.

'It's the police.'

'What do they want? And why are there so many of them?' She had a cultured voice, out of keeping with where they were living.

This was unlike any raid Sue had been on. The women seemed mystified as to why they were there, and they didn't seem to be the type that would have had much dealings with the police in the past. But this was where Jade had been working from. They must know something.

'We need you to help with our enquiries,' Sue said in a formal voice. 'You are Brenda Sinclair, I assume.'

'Yes.'

'And you are?'

'Julie Baird.'

'Ms Sinclair, your name has been supplied to us by your ISP.'

'What's an ISP?'

'Don't be daft, Bren. They're the ones who provide our broadband. I told you not to download those films.'

A look of panic crossed Bren's face. 'I didn't think I was doing any harm.'

'Depending on the films, downloading them could be illegal, but that's not why we've come.' Sue felt as if she'd entered some parallel universe, they all seemed to be talking at cross purposes. 'We're here because Jade Carnegie has been contacting people from your IP address.'

'Who is Jade Carnegie?' Julie's voice cut in. 'Have you been seeing someone else, Bren?'

'I don't know any Jade Carnegie.' Bren's voice sounded desperate. 'You know there's no one else, Jules.'

'Are you saying neither of you know Jade Carnegie, or someone claiming to be Jade Carnegie?'

'I've never heard of her.'

'Me neither.'

Sue was feeling more uncertain than ever, mainly because neither of these two women matched the figure they'd all watched on CCTV, both of them were too tall. The person they were looking for was small and slim. 'But you must know her because she's been using your wireless connection.'

'We're the only ones here.' Bren's face had a look of confusion that seemed genuine.

'And there's no one else,' Jules interjected. 'The folk round here aren't friendly.'

'It's possible their wireless connection has been compromised.' Jenny's voice cut into the discussion, 'but I won't be able to tell unless I have a look at their computers.'

'Right.' Sue turned back to the two women. 'In order to eliminate you from our enquiries we'll need to examine your computers. Now you can give us permission to take them, or we can go and get a court order. If we do the latter I'll have to take you in for questioning until the court order comes through.'

'How long before we get them back?'

'That depends on what we find and whether they need to be kept as evidence.'

'I don't think we have an option, Bren. They're going to take them anyway so better now than later.'

'OK, the desktop is in the bedroom and the laptop's on the kitchen table.'

Sue opened the door and beckoned a policeman in. 'Jenny, show him what to take and then you get the laptop.'

'Remember, we need them back again.' Bren's voice echoed behind them as they left the flat.

29

Hammers pounded in May Fraser's head. She sat up and groaned. Memories of the nightmares flooded back, and she swore.

It was all the fault of that wee slag Megan. She hadn't had a good night's sleep since she failed to come home on Saturday, and the bloody police weren't doing anything about it. All they said was she'd gone walkabout before and she would come back when she was ready. But this time was different, she could feel it in her water. Besides, she was her mother, and a mother always knew.

It was something to do with that perv along the landing. She'd seen the way he looked at Megan, and the silly wee slag had laughed, enjoying the attention. She knew, she just knew, he had something to do with it. Him with his sidelong looks, and the way he avoided her eyes. Maybe the wee slag was shacked up with him. She wouldn't put it past her.

Well, they weren't going to get off with it, she'd go along right now and confront them, and if Megan wasn't there she'd make him tell her where she was. Bloody perv should never have been housed beside decent folks anyway.

She heaved herself out of the bed, struggled into the skirt she'd been wearing for the past month, pulled her tee shirt on, rammed her feet into a pair of fleecy slippers, and charged out of the flat. The wind on the landing whipped at her red hair, but it was already a tousled mess so it didn't make much difference.

The door to the perv's flat hung open. May thumped on it but when she got no answer she walked in. The kitchen was a mess, a mountain of dirty dishes in the sink, more dishes and pots and pans cluttering every surface, rubbish spilling out of a waste bin. May tutted and turned her back on it. A faint sound of music filtered through the living room door. Without hesitation she gave it a shove. 'Where's my bloody Megan?' she roared when it swung open.

The music continued to play, but the body on the floor looked very dead.

Kate threw her jacket over the back of her chair, stuffed her shoulder bag under the desk, and returned to the team room. She looked round at the empty desks and flickering computer screens, before walking over to Bill at the coffee machine.

'Where is everybody?'

Bill shrugged. 'You know as much as I do. Want a coffee?'

Kate peered at the brown liquid in Bill's paper cup. 'Think I'll give it a pass.'

She marched over to the whiteboard and studied it. 'What did you make of Mrs Carnegie?'

'She seemed calmer today. I'm not sure if that's a good sign or a bad one.'

'Mmm, she seems convinced Jade has come back. D'you think it's possible?'

Bill shrugged. 'It leaves a lot of unanswered questions if she has.'

'I'm not sure Mrs Carnegie would have opened up as much if you hadn't been present.'

'Why would you think that?' Bill wondered what Kate was thinking, but her face gave nothing away.

'I don't know, she seemed to relate to you.'

'Maybe it's because I was part of the original investigation, and I'm the one she's had contact with about this question of Jade's return.'

'Mmm, whatever. It could prove useful though, provided you don't get drawn in.'

'Yes, ma'am.' Bill resisted the urge to run his finger around his collar. He didn't want Kate to know how much she had unsettled him.

A waft of air signalled the door opening. Kate turned. 'Ah, the wanderers have come back.'

Sue dumped her bag on the desk and strode over to join them.

'There's been a development, ma'am. DC Cartwright acquired information about Jade's contact with Gregson and she persuaded the ISP to give us a physical address for the contact. We went out to investigate and have confiscated the computers.'

'You found Jade?'

'No, ma'am. The occupants were obviously nothing like the person we're looking for, but I think we should keep them on our radar. We'll know more once Jenny has plumbed the depths of the computers.'

The gold chain slid through Diane's fingers onto the table. Without the bead, the chain was nothing, the policewoman should have taken it as well, but she hadn't. Instead, she'd slipped Jade's bead into a small polythene bag and left the chain behind.

Emma burst through the door. 'I saw the police driving off. What did they want?'

'They should have taken the chain,' Diane said.

'What?'

Diane looked up at the daughter who was not Jade, and could never take her sister's place. 'They took Jade's bead but they left the chain.'

'Why did they want the bead?' Emma sank to her knees in front of Diane's armchair and grasped her mother's hand.

'They said it was for evidence.'

'Evidence of what?'

'I don't know, they just said evidence. Maybe they've got a lead on Jade. Maybe it'll help them find her.'

Emma's grip on Diane's hand, tightened. 'I doubt it. They must have another reason but for the life of me I can't think what.'

'They will find her. I'm sure of it. Bill Murphy, he's the

sergeant, he promised me he would find her.'

'That's impossible. You must know in your heart Jade's never coming back. How could she? She's been gone too long.'

'He said he would find her, and I trust him.' Diane snatched her hand from Emma's grasp. 'I sometimes think you don't want her to return.'

'What's going on down here.' Ryan appeared in the doorway. 'I heard raised voices . . . '

'Nothing,' Diane said. 'Are you finished working on your computer?'

'Yes, that's Tony's website finished. I just need him to approve it, before I upload it to the web. You working today, Mum?'

Diane nodded.

'I'll drive you in after lunch.'

Emma scrambled to her feet. 'I'm off. I came home to collect a folder I forgot this morning.' She ran upstairs and back down again with the folder in her hand, and left the house without a backward glance.

Diane leaned back in her chair and closed her eyes. She must try to be nicer to Emma, now Jade was coming back.

30

'You ready to go, Mum?' Ryan adjusted the strap cutting into his shoulder. His laptop was a hefty one, a powerful beast built for work, unlike many of the flashier ones meant for play.

Diane emerged from the kitchen. 'I was cleaning the sink, can't leave it in a mess.'

Ryan smiled and kissed her on the cheek. 'When was there ever a time you left anything in a mess? Let's go.' He opened the front door, escorted her down the path and helped her into the car.

'You're becoming quite the gentleman,' Diane said.

Ryan shrugged, got in the driving seat and drove off.

The drive to the club was a silent one, and Ryan kept sneaking looks at his mother who seemed to be lost in her own thoughts. Even her hands, normally active, picking and twisting at anything she was wearing, were clasped loosely in her lap. She wasn't herself and it worried him. Maybe she was planning to go off again, on her futile hunt for Jade.

There was plenty of room in the car park behind Teasers, too early in the day for the punters to be fighting over spaces. But he noticed Tony's flash BMW, and a couple of other cars, one of which he thought was Phil's. A shiver crept down his spine. Phil had a strange effect on him, something about the man's eyes, hypnotic and compelling. This strange attraction was combined, oddly enough, with repulsion, and he didn't trust himself to stay away.

Suppressing the sinking feeling in his stomach, he helped his mother out of the car. Diane seemed more fragile than usual, her thoughts far away. He wanted to reach out to her, wrap her in his arms, but they were not a demonstrative family and the moment passed.

By the time he fished his laptop bag out of the car she was already putting her key into the lock on the back door. He hurried over and followed her into the club and along the corridor to the cleaners' cupboard where she would leave her coat and gather her equipment, ready to start work. But she still hadn't spoken, and seemed to be in a world of her own.

'I'll wait for you after I've finished with Tony, and take you home.' His words sounded loud in the empty corridor.

Diane nodded.

Ryan hesitated, reluctant to leave her, afraid she wouldn't be there when he got back. Afraid she'd go off looking for Jade again. But Tony would be waiting for him, and Tony wasn't a man you kept waiting, so he hurried along the corridor and through the door into the public area of the club.

The foyer was deserted, although a buzzing sound came from behind one of the doors. As there was no sign of the doorman, he opened the door and looked in, but it was one of the other cleaners vacuuming a bar area.

'I was looking for the doorman,' he said. 'I've got a meeting with Mr Palmer.'

She switched the machine off and tucked a lock of hair under the scarf she wore on her head. 'You're Diane's boy. I've seen you here before.'

Ryan nodded. He'd made a mistake following his mother in the back door instead of coming to the front entrance. Too late to rectify that now, though. 'There's usually someone here to meet me,' he said.

'You'll find someone upstairs.' She bent and switched on the machine. 'I've got to get this finished and I'm all behind.'

Ryan took his hand off the door and let it swing shut. The stairs were in front of him, a dark chasm leading upwards, to the lap dancing club, and Tony's office, and Phil.

May Fraser stared at the body with horrified fascination. She'd seen a dead dog before, but never a human body. He looked peaceful, lying with his arms crossed over his chest, but there was something funny about his eyes. It looked as if something was in them. She leaned over for a closer look.

She flopped into the armchair. What sick bugger would want to shove beads in the dead sod's eyes. OK, so he was a perv, she'd seen the way he watched the young girls on the estate, hanging round near the school gates when they were all going home. But that was no reason to mutilate his body. Kill the bugger, sure, but that should be enough.

'What you done with my Megan then?' She stared at the body on the floor.

A flickering red light caught her eye. It was coming from the computer on the desk. Megan's computer used to do that when she hadn't been on it for a while, and she'd seen her daughter twiddle the mouse to wake it up.

Curiosity got the better of her and she heaved herself out of the chair, stepped over the body, and moved the mouse. The monitor sprang into life and May watched fascinated while pictures of schoolgirls flashed over the screen in a relentless slideshow of photographs. Some were everyday photographs of girls, but others verged on the pornographic.

'I knew you were a bloody perv.' She poked the body with her foot. 'You got photos of my Megan in there, do you?' She sat down to watch.

She wasn't sure how long she'd been watching the slideshow before she saw Megan, but there she was, in the street, on the landing, coming out of school, down the shops. The bugger must have been stalking her.

May stood up, maybe Megan was in the flat. She went from room to room, but Megan wasn't there. That was when she decided she'd have to call the cops. But she'd need a phone to do that.

She looked around, but couldn't find a phone in the flat. If he had a mobile it would be in his pocket.

The computer was still running the slideshow, although it wasn't Megan now. The body lay at her feet and she stared at it, considering what to do.

She knelt on the floor. The bugger was dead, he wouldn't

mind if she went through his pockets, but she'd have to touch him, and that gave her the willies.

Steeling herself, she put her hand in one of his pockets, and then another one. The phone was in the third pocket she tried, along with a tenner. She extracted both, stuffed the tenner in her pocket – he wouldn't need money where he was going – and phoned the police.

After she switched the phone off she placed it into her pocket. It was a nice iPhone, and she'd never had one of those before, pity to waste it.

The cops had said to leave the flat, but May Fraser settled down in the armchair and continued to watch the monitor, hoping to see Megan again.

'There's a Mrs Fraser on the line for you, Bill.' Blair waved the phone receiver at him.

Bill scowled. 'Can't you tell her we don't have any fresh news about her daughter?'

'No can do. Says she's found a body, and you're the one she wants to talk to.'

Swearing under his breath he hurried over to take the phone from Blair. Damn, a body, probably Megan. That was all he needed. The DI would blame him for messing up the investigation and she'd never be off his back now.

He lifted the receiver. 'What can I do for you, Mrs Fraser?'

'You can get off your fat arse and come out here.'

Bill held the phone away from his ear.

'That bloody perv along the landing's been topped, and I can see my Megan on his computer screen. What you going to do about it?'

'What d'you mean, he's been topped?'

'Just what I said. He's been bloody topped.'

'You mean he's dead?'

'Isn't that what I just said? He's as dead as a bloody doornail, couldn't be any deader. And he's got queer green beads in his eyes. Weird, that's what it is.'

'Where are you, Mrs Fraser?' Bill pulled a paper pad in front of him and got ready to scribble.

'I'm in the bloody perv's flat, that's where I am.'

'Where is this flat?'

'Along the landing from me. I already told you.'

Bill sighed. 'Which end of the landing?'

'You should bloody know, it's the one I saw you going to yesterday.'

Bill's hand tightened on the pencil and the point snapped when it dug into the paper. 'Paul Carnegie's flat?'

'Yeah, I think that's his name.'

'Are you in the flat now?'

'Yeah, that's what I told you, and my Megan's on his computer screen.'

'What you need to do, Mrs Fraser, is to leave the flat now. Don't touch anything. Go and wait in your own flat until we arrive.'

Bill scribbled the address onto a piece of paper before hurrying over to Blair's desk. 'We've got a body, get the police surgeon and the SOCOs there pronto. I'll let the DI know, she's going to want to check it out.'

Bill grabbed his jacket from the back of the chair and hurried over to where Kate and Sue were deep in discussion.

'We've got a situation. Paul Carnegie's body has just been found by Mrs Fraser. She says he's been topped. It seems genuine because she also says he's got green beads in his eyes.'

Kate turned to face him. 'Right, first thing we need to do is alert the scene of the crime officers, and the police surgeon, of course.'

'It's in hand, ma'am. Blair's onto them now.'

She nodded her approval. 'Well, what are you waiting for? We'll need to get out there.'

'Yes, ma'am.'

31

Kate was silent during the drive to the Greenfield estate. This was the biggest case of her career.

It wasn't her first murder case, but the others had been clearer cut. Domestic violence that had spun out of control, a Saturday night brawl with unintended tragic consequences, or a revenge killing. All of them relatively easy to solve. But this was something entirely different, and she felt out of her depth. However, it would be a mistake to allow the team to see this, when they were starting to gel.

'We're here, ma'am,' Bill said, parking at the kerb in front of the stairs up to Paul Carnegie's flat.

'I thought the SOCOs would have arrived by now.'

'They won't be long. D'you want to wait for them?'

Kate pushed the car door open. 'No, we'll go up and check out the scene.'

She wasn't sure whether that was the right thing to do, but she was anxious to get a handle on this murder before the scene of the crime officers came and restricted their access.

Sensing Bill's hesitation, she said, 'Come on. What are you waiting for?'

'Yes, ma'am.'

Kate led the way up the stairs, the sound of her feet clacking on the stone steps echoing back with an eeriness that made her shiver. On the upper flight she stepped round a patch of dried vomit and almost grabbed the hand rail, pulling her hand back at the last minute. No knowing what might be smeared on it. The top landing was bare but the door at the end hung open and she could hear the faint sound of music.

Kate stood at the door for a moment questioning the wisdom of entering the flat before the SOCOs arrived, but her need to know overcame any doubts she might have. Sticking her hands in her pockets so she wouldn't be tempted to touch anything, she entered the flat.

A light shone from the room directly ahead. The door hung ajar. She pushed it with her elbow, hearing Bill's sharp intake of breath at the same time as she saw the woman sitting on the sofa.

'Mrs Fraser, I told you to leave the flat.' Bill's voice was harsh.

The woman didn't move, her eyes remained fixed on the computer screen. 'I saw my Megan on here. I was waiting to see her again.'

Kate turned her attention to the flickering monitor, where image succeeded image in a never ending slide show of young girls.

The body of Paul Carnegie lay on the floor between May Fraser and the computer desk.

'I told you a perv had taken my Megan, but you didn't believe me.'

She rose from the sofa and glared at Bill, her hands clenched into fists. Her body gave the appearance of increasing in size as she tensed her muscles in a display of anger. The shuddering of her body, the quivering of her fists, and the sight of her dyed red hair waving madly about on top of her head, like the flames of some hellish fire, revealed the level of her distress. 'If you'd looked harder you'd have found him before somebody topped him.' She kicked the body.

'Mrs Fraser, I must ask you to leave and wait in your own flat. We'll come to speak to you shortly.' Kate's voice was calmer than she felt, but she didn't want to arouse the woman into an even greater emotional outburst. After all, the woman's daughter was still missing.

The woman raised her foot to aim another kick, but Bill grabbed her arm and pulled her away from the body.

'I'll have you for assault.' Her eyes were wild.

'And I'll arrest you for obstruction and contamination of a crime scene if you don't leave now.'

For a moment they both glared at each other, then her body seemed to deflate and she shrugged. 'I need you to find my Megan.'

Kate rested a hand on her shoulder. 'We'll find your Megan,' she said. 'We'll take the computer in to examine. I'm sure we'll be able to figure something out from the information we obtain from it.'

The woman shambled out of the door into the hallway. 'You promise,' she said, before leaving the flat.

'I promise,' Kate said, but May Fraser was gone.

May Fraser stumbled along the landing. The wind whipped through her flimsy tee shirt, and the cold penetrated the fleece of her slippers, but her mind was far away, thinking of the images she'd seen on the perv's computer screen.

Bloody filth. If they'd done their job her Megan would be home by now. But it was always the same, just because she lived on the estate and survived on benefits, other folks thought she wasn't worth anything. Thought she was scum. But May knew she wasn't scum. OK, maybe she didn't live like they did, maybe her house wasn't as clean as it should be. But what incentive did she have to clean when she lived in a clapped out flat on a sink estate. If she had a nice house like they had, she'd clean it, well, maybe not every day, but she'd keep it nice.

Her eyes filled with tears. OK, maybe she wasn't as good as them with their fancy houses and fancy cars, but what right did they have to judge her and her family. What right did they have to make the assumption Megan had gone walkabout. May conveniently forgot Megan had done this in the past, so the assumption was a logical one to make.

'Bloody filth,' she muttered, opening the door to her flat.

'Where you been?'

'What's it to you?' May glared at her husband. What the heck had she ever seen in him. A scruffy wee nyaff with dirty grey hair straggling down his neck.

'I was needing my bloody dinner, you lazy cow.'

'Don't you bloody lazy cow me.' May put her hands on her hips and stared him out. 'Get off your lazy arse and get it yourself.'

'It's a good belting you're needing,' Fred Fraser muttered.

'Yeah! You and whose army?' May stumped into the living room and threw herself into an armchair to wait for the police to arrive.

Diane stood in the cleaners' room and listened to Ryan's footsteps echoing up the corridor. The door into the main part of the club clicked shut behind him, but still she stood there. Ryan was a good son. He worried about her, but he didn't understand her. Nor could he understand how her thoughts about Jade were tearing her apart.

She slumped onto a chair and bent down to change her shoes for the old pair she kept here for working in, but her hand hesitated. How could she concentrate on work when Jade was out there? She'd promised Jade she wouldn't look for her, promised to wait until Jade was ready to come home. But deep within she knew Jade was in trouble and needed her help. She had to go and look for her, find her and help her. There was no other way.

Work forgotten, Diane stood, buttoned her coat and headed for the back door. Outside, she turned her back on the car and hurried to the street. She would leave the car for Ryan and get a bus.

A spattering of hail stung Diane's cheeks as she stood at the bus stop, but she was beyond feeling anything physical. She boarded the first bus that stopped and huddled in a back seat. She didn't know where it was heading, nor did she care. When she got off she started to walk, following a noisy group of teenagers, stopping when they stopped and walking when they did.

At last one of the youths turned and glared at her. 'You want something, missus?'

Diane stopped. She couldn't think straight, her mind was

a jumble of questions about Jade. She wasn't even sure why she had been following them. But they might know Jade.

'Oh,' she spluttered, 'I thought you might know where Jade was. Do you?'

Several kids in the group sniggered and one of them made a circular motion with his finger to his forehead.

The youth shrugged his shoulders. 'Don't know no Jade, Missus.' He followed the others who were already walking away.

Diane stood and watched them go, aware she'd made a fool of herself. What on earth was she doing here? She didn't even know where here was. But her mind was fogged and she couldn't think of any answers to the questions buzzing round her brain, nor could she marshal her thoughts sufficiently to find out where she was.

The street was quiet now the teenagers were gone, but Diane continued to walk until she emerged at the river front. To her left she could see a castle-like building jutting out into the water. She walked towards it, passing rows of houses on her left while the river flowed on her right.

She passed an old-fashioned red telephone box and a pole with a lifebelt attached. Rows of cars were parked angle on, facing the river; and in the distance, at the other side of the water, a small town. Tayport or Newport, she wasn't sure which. Beyond the cars was a bench facing the river. She sat for a while looking out at the turbulent waves, before she rose and walked to the building that looked like a castle.

When she got to the castle she walked onto the pier beside it, and stared into the river. It seemed to beckon and she wondered how it would feel to submerge herself in it. Would it be pleasant or painful? Would she see her life passing before her eyes? Was her family right when they said Jade was dead, and was this the only way she would ever be able to join her?

32

Bill hunkered down to get a better look at the body. He hadn't been able to shake off the feeling Paul Carnegie's death was related to the murder of the John Doe in the Overgate car park, and he wanted to check something out. Now, looking at the green jade beads pressed into Paul's eye sockets, he was sure.

'Same signature.' He stood up and looked over to Kate. 'He's got green beads stuck in his eyes.'

'You didn't touch anything, I hope.'

'No, ma'am. I just looked.' Bill suppressed his irritation. What the heck did she think he was? An amateur?

'What about this computer? Mrs Fraser seemed to think she saw images of her daughter on the monitor.' Kate frowned. 'We'll need to take it in for a better look.'

Bill took a paper handkerchief out of his pocket and nudged the mouse. Immediately the slide show started.

'You contaminating my crime scene?'

Bill looked up. Colin, one of the SOCOs was standing in the doorway.

'Damn, you might whistle when you come in. Those blasted bootees you wear don't give any warning.'

'Speaking of bootees, you should be wearing them as well. I hate to think how much contamination you've introduced to the scene, and I bet that mouse has your fingerprints all over it.'

'Not guilty, I nudged it with this.' Bill flapped the paper hankie in front of Colin. 'Besides, you'll find May Fraser's prints all over it, she was watching the screen display when we arrived.'

Colin raised his eyebrows. 'May Fraser?'

'Yes, the woman who discovered the body.'

171

Colin groaned. 'Is there anybody who hasn't been in here before me?' He stood back. 'You'll have to leave now and let me get on with my job.'

Bill shrugged and glanced at Kate who was out of Colin's line of vision. She nodded, and with a bemused smile, emerged from behind the door.

'Sorry, ma'am. I didn't know you were here as well.'

'I'll need that computer sent to headquarters.' Her voice was brisk, daring him to argue.

'Sorry, ma'am. Anything we take from here goes for forensic examination.'

'Oh, yes, and in the meantime a child dies while we wait for the lab boys to get their fingers out. I need that computer today. No arguments.'

Colin looked stunned. 'But procedure . . . '

'Procedure be damned. Today. I want it today. And if it's not at headquarters within the hour I'll want to know the reason why.' Kate turned her back on him and stalked out of the flat.

'Phew! She's a force to be reckoned with, I don't envy you,' he whispered to Bill.

Bill shrugged his shoulders and followed Kate outside. His respect for her had increased enormously following her treatment of Colin.

The wind gusted along the walkway, and he hurried to catch up with Kate who was leaning against the wall at the top of the stairwell. When he drew nearer she nodded to him, but continued to talk into her iPhone. 'As soon as possible and take one of the constables with you,' she said, 'we need to get there before the press do.' She lowered the phone and slipped it into her pocket.

'I've instructed Sue to inform Mrs Carnegie of her son's death, and now we'd better speak to Mrs Fraser,' she said, as he joined her. 'Find out exactly what she saw on that computer.'

Kate strode along the walkway, hands buried in her pockets.

Bill hurried to keep up with her. 'What about his wife and

family? I know they're separated but they'll need to know as well.'

'It's best you do that.'

'Yes, ma'am.'

'But first, there's Mrs Fraser.' She stopped at a door and raised her hand to knock.

'It's the next one, ma'am.'

'Oh!' She drew her hand back before her knuckles made contact with the wood. Walking further along the walkway she halted outside the next door. 'You sure this is the right one?'

'Yes, ma'am. I've been here before.'

The door opened before Kate had time to knock.

'I was watching for you,' May Fraser said. 'You better come in.'

The man watching the flat screen television ignored them, concentrating on an episode of Doctors and the can of beer in his hand. The dog on the sofa raised its head and growled. Bill could have sworn its fangs had grown and were even more yellow than the last time he'd been here. He noticed Kate giving it an anxious look.

'D'you mind putting the dog in another room, Mrs Fraser.'

'No need, he's a big soft lump, he'll no bother ye.'

Bill doubted that. He didn't like the mean look in the dog's eyes. 'It's not that,' he said, hoping his mistrust of the dog wasn't affecting his body language. Dogs were good at sensing fear. 'It's just that we need to concentrate on anything you have to tell us, and he's a distraction.'

The man in the armchair snorted, but didn't take his eyes off the television screen.

'Aye, OK.' May grabbed the dog's collar and heaved him off the sofa.

The dog snarled.

'Come on, Satan, into the kitchen with ye and get your dinner.' She pulled him out of the room.

'It would be helpful if you could turn the television off as well,' Kate said.

The small man in the chair glared at her. 'It's my hoose and I'll no have some jumped up wee wumman telling me what to do.'

Kate glared back. 'If you want us to find your daughter you'll do as I say.'

The man was the first to turn his eyes away. He mumbled, 'Bloody pigs, it's my hoose.'

'Oh, for fuck's sake, turn the bloody box off.' May strode into the room like a Valkyrie prepared for battle.

The man wilted at the force of her voice. 'Aye, OK, love. Whatever you say.'

May turned back to Kate. 'You said you'd find Megan.'

'Yes, we're working on that now, but first I need you to tell me how you found Paul Carnegie, and what you saw on his computer.'

'I saw my Megan, that's what I saw.'

'Yes, but let's start at the beginning. You found the body. Why did you go to his flat?'

'I thought Megan might be there. He'd been giving her looks. I knew he liked her, and the silly wee besom lapped it up. I got it into my head she might be taking up with him, and I went along the landing to his flat to ask him. Well, when I got there his door was open. I thumped on it but nobody came, but I heard music so I went in. That's when I found him lying on the floor. I knew he was dead. But I had a look around the flat in case my Megan was hiding, but she wasn't.'

'What did you do next?'

'Well, I saw the red light on his computer flickering, and I knew if I moved that mouse thing it would come on. So I did that.' May took a deep breath. 'That's when I saw the photos of these girls, one after the other, and then I saw my Megan among them. Some of them didn't have any clothes on, and some of them were doing awful things. Things no kid should know about, never mind do.'

'Megan.' Kate prompted. 'What were her photos like.'

'Shots of her taken in her school clothes, and some when she was all dressed up, but the one that bothered me was where she was tied up in some kind of shed or cellar.' A tear slipped down May's cheek. 'You've got to find her. She's a good girl, she doesn't deserve this.'

'We'll find her.' Kate's voice was grim. 'We're taking the computer in for examination so we can find out where she is.'

Bill nodded in agreement, although he had doubts about how much they might find out.

'Is there anything else you can tell us?' Kate placed her hand on May's shoulder as the woman's body shook with sobs.

'I did see someone going up to his flat yesterday about teatime, but she didn't get him in.'

'Can you describe her?'

'She was wearing a hoodie. I didn't get a clear look.'

'Try to remember, anything would be a help.'

'Couldn't see the colour of her hair but she was definitely a woman.'

'Young? Old?'

'Maybe about my age, slim, nice looking. That's about it.'

Bill glanced at Kate wondering if she'd made the connection. But how could she miss it? A middle-aged woman, looking for Paul Carnegie. It could only have been Diane.

33

Ryan's heart beat faster with each reluctant step he took. He wanted to see Phil again and yet dreaded it, knowing he would finally have to make a decision one way or the other.

Phil had an effect on him like no other he had ever experienced. The man's eyes and touch made his skin quiver, although he wasn't sure why.

The bag containing the laptop was heavy and the strap bit into his shoulder, so he was glad of the opportunity to stop midway up the stairs to adjust it. He stood for a moment, gripping the handrail and looking upwards. The stairs seemed endless and the gloom didn't help. It seemed to gather round him like a poisonous mist, increasing his feeling of unease. He had an urge to turn back, run down the stairs, get in the car and drive home. His hand tightened on the rail. But running away wasn't an option because Tony was waiting to give him the go ahead to upload the new website, and as soon as that was done he would get paid. With a bit of luck this would be the last time he would have to come to the club.

The door at the top of the stairs opened and a beam of light split the gloom. Ryan's heart lurched. Silhouetted in the doorway, was Phil. He climbed up to meet him. It would be now or never.

'You're late, Tony's waiting.' Phil remained where he was until Ryan reached him. 'And so am I.' He reached out his hand and stroked Ryan's cheek with his finger.

Ryan closed his eyes. Phil's touch was gentle, welcoming and abhorrent at the same time. Ryan fought against the confusion in his mind, unable to determine whether he wanted to embrace Phil or flee from him.

'I'll be waiting for you when the meeting's over.' Phil

stood aside.

Ryan nodded, waiting for Phil to move a bit further because there was insufficient room to pass without coming into contact with him. However, Phil didn't move, but stood looking at him with an indecipherable expression on his face. Ryan closed his eyes and pushed past, feeling body heat through the finely tailored suit Phil wore. It was enough to send shivers through him.

Kara was waiting for him at the end of the room. 'Problems with Phil?' She raised an eyebrow.

'No, not really,' Ryan mumbled, still not sure whether Phil was a problem.

'You want to be careful with that one,' she said. 'He can be a nasty piece of work.'

'I'm fine.' But he didn't feel fine. He was too busy trying to come to terms with his warring feelings.

'If you're sure,' she said, emerging from behind the cocktail bar to open the door behind the velvet curtain and lead him up the short flight of stairs to Tony's office.

Tony turned at their entrance. He had been standing observing the clubroom through the one-way glass-mirrored wall.

'This is how I keep track of everything going on in the club,' he said. 'Not much goes past me.'

Ryan stood beside him and looked through the glass. He could see Phil standing where he'd left him, but he was no longer alone. The man he was talking to looked a younger, less groomed, version of Phil, and as Ryan watched them Phil put his arm round the other man's shoulder and laughed.

'They think I don't know about them,' Tony said, watching the two men closely.

Curiosity got the better of Ryan. 'Who is the other man? I haven't seen him in the club before.'

'That's Gus.' Tony's voice was so soft Ryan could hardly hear him. 'He's been in the hospital, got out today.' He turned away from the window. 'I don't want any trouble between them. You understand me? I like a smooth ship.'

Ryan's neck grew hot and he wondered whether he was

blushing. Did Tony mean what he thought he meant? Or was it his imagination? Surely he couldn't know Phil was hitting on him. However, Tony had indicated nothing went on in the club he didn't know about.

'I brought the final version of the website for your approval,' he said, in an attempt to mask his reactions.

'Good, let's get down to it. Let me see how it looks.'

Ryan turned his back on the glass wall and snapped his laptop open. 'I've done everything you wanted, and I'm hoping you'll like it.'

It was two hours later before Ryan left Tony's office. Teasers' website was now operational, and Tony's money nestled in his pocket. He'd never carried much money before and hadn't been sure about accepting cash but Tony had insisted. He patted his pocket as he passed through the door and let the velvet curtain fall in front of it.

'Ah, there you are.' Phil rose from the high stool he'd been sitting on in front of the bar. 'I have something for you. It's a surprise.'

Kara was behind the bar, engrossed in paperwork, but she looked up and shook her head behind Phil's back.

'Can we do this later? I have to collect my mum and take her home.' Ryan's heart felt as if it was trying to break out from the confines of his chest.

'No, no. We need to do it now.' Phil grasped his arm. 'It won't take long.'

Ryan shot a panicked look at Kara. 'I really do have to go.'

'I won't take no for an answer. You'll like this, I promise you.'

When Phil pushed him through the door of the gents' toilet, Ryan's fear hit its peak. He knew now what he was afraid of, what he had always avoided, why he had never formed relationships. It was simple, it was the sex act. It didn't matter whether it involved a man or a woman, he was terrified of the intimacy. It repulsed him.

'I don't want this.' His voice was shrill with terror.

Phil pushed him and he sprawled on the floor, the bag

holding his laptop hitting it with a resounding bang.

'You there, Gus? I promised you a coming home present, and here it is.'

The other man emerged from a cubicle. His hair was longer than Phil's, blond at the tips, and brown nearer the roots. His complexion wasn't as smooth, nor was he as pretty as Phil. But he had the same look in his eyes Phil had.

Ryan curled himself into a ball on the floor and covered his face with his arms. His nightmare was about to begin.

Sue rammed a notebook into her shoulder bag. 'The boss wants us to break the news of the vic's death to his mother. Who's with me?' She looked round the team room but everyone seemed to have found something to do, and their eyes remained focused on their work. It wasn't surprising, because nobody liked having to break the news of a death to a grieving relative.

'Someone? Anyone?'

'I'll come with you.' Jenny emerged from behind her computer screen. 'This can wait.'

'Thanks for the offer, Jenny, but the boss is bringing in the vic's computer and she wants you to look at it as a matter of urgency. And seeing none of you brave lads intends to volunteer, I'll take you with me, Blair.'

'But . . . '

'No excuses, you're coming with me. Grab your jacket and we'll be off.'

Blair glowered at her but did what he was told. When he got into Sue's car he hunched his shoulders and turned his face to look out the window. He reminded her of a sulky little boy who hadn't got his own way. Sometimes men could be childish.

'We're here.' Sue broke the silence when they reached the Carnegie house. 'Are you going to sit there all day, or are you coming in with me to do your job.' She got out of the car and waited for Blair to join her before walking to the front door.

'Detective Sergeant Rogers, and Detective Constable Armstrong.' Sue held up her warrant card. 'Can we come in?'

'It's about time someone came.' Patricia Carnegie's eyes were red, as if she'd been crying. Her hair was a mess and looked as if it hadn't seen a brush for some considerable time, but her white pants suit was immaculate, sculpted to her body, one a younger woman would have been proud of.

Someone must have broken the news to her already, Sue thought, as she followed Patricia into the lounge. Blair lagged behind. Typical, he was going to leave it all to her.

'I'm sorry for your loss.' Sue injected the correct note of sympathy into her voice.

'Loss? What the hell are you talking about?'

'You were expecting us, I thought you knew.'

'Of course I expected you. Paul said he'd report it. I've been waiting for you to get in touch since yesterday.'

'What was he going to report?' Sue glanced at Blair and caught him smirking. She glared, making a mental note to deal with him later.

'That damn woman came here and assaulted me. She wouldn't leave until I gave her Paul's address. She's mad. She's always been mad. Thank goodness Paul left her when he did.'

Sue knew she should tell Patricia Carnegie about her son's death, but she needed to get the details of the woman's complaint first because it might have a bearing on the murder.

'OK, let's start at the beginning and I'll note everything down.' She pulled the notebook from her shoulder bag. 'Who assaulted you?'

'Paul's ex-wife, that's who. It was a great day when he got rid of her, I'll tell you.'

'When did the assault take place?'

'That would be yesterday, round about 4 o'clock.'

Sue wrote Tuesday 13 March, 4pm, in her notebook. 'What happened when she arrived.'

'She assaulted me. I told you.'

'Why did she assault you?'

'She wanted Paul's address and I wouldn't give it to her.'

'So what exactly happened? What did she do to assault you?'

'She forced her way into my house. I asked her to leave but she became aggressive. She shook me and punched me and grabbed my hair.' Patricia paused for breath. 'Then she threatened to set light to my hair, so I had to give her the address to get rid of her. I thought she'd give my hair back but she threw it into a tree and I had to get Paul to come and get it back for me.'

Sue looked up from her notebook. 'Your hair?'

'Yes.' Patricia patted it. 'I wear a wig you see, and now she's ruined it.' Tears streamed down her face. 'I want her punished. She can't do things like that and get away with it.'

'I see.' Sue closed her notebook and placed it in her bag. 'That wasn't why we came to see you, but I'm glad you've told us about this assault, and I'll certainly look into it for you.'

Patricia scrubbed her wet cheeks with the back of her hand. 'What did you come to see me about?'

'I'm afraid it's bad news,' Sue said, hesitating before she continued, 'and I'm afraid there's no easy way to say it, but your son's body was found today, and I'm afraid he's dead.'

'I knew that mad bitch was up to something,' Patricia Carnegie screamed. 'She's murdered my son, my lovely Paul.'

'We're sorry for your loss,' Sue said, but Mrs Carnegie was too busy screaming to listen.

'Is there anyone we can ask to come and be with you?'

'No! Get out and leave me be.'

34

Bill followed Kate out of the flat. They'd got as much information as they could out of May Fraser before they left with a promise the search for Megan would take priority.

Kate turned to him as soon as the door slammed shut. 'Looks as if Diane Carnegie has some explaining to do.' She fastened her top button before thrusting her hands into her pockets.

'Seems like it.'

'Is that all you're going to say? I'd like to know what you're thinking. Is Diane Carnegie our killer?'

'It certainly looks as if things are pointing that way, but somehow I can't quite see it.'

'You said she was mentally unstable.'

Bill shrugged. 'Yes, but it's more in the nature of a fragility rather than a full blown mental condition.'

'Whatever, we still need to bring her in for an interview.' Kate strode off down the walkway until she reached the blue police tape.

'I'm sorry, ma'am, but I have instructions not to let anyone pass.' The young constable shuffled his feet, his uncertainty showing in his posture.

'You know who I am?' Kate snapped.

'Yes, ma'am, but I have instructions . . . '

'Rubbish,' she said. 'Give me a pair of those bootee things so I can go inside.' She grabbed them from him, lifted the tape and ducked under it, then vanished out of sight into Paul Carnegie's flat.

Bill stared after her. He felt sorry for the guy, but the constable had been no match for Kate. She was a strong, determined woman and Bill wasn't even sure he was a match for her. However, he was starting to respect her, because of the competent way she handled things. He just wished she wasn't so black and white in her outlook.

She seemed convinced Diane was responsible for the murder but, despite his earlier suspicions, Bill wasn't sure. He thought about how Diane had presented, and all he saw was a vulnerable woman grieving so much for her missing daughter it had affected her mental state. What he couldn't see was Diane lifting her hands to hurt anyone. She was more of a victim than a perpetrator. Taking her in for questioning would only increase her anxiety levels and might flip her over the edge into a deeper depression. He would have preferred the questioning to take place sympathetically and in a place where Diane would feel safe. Or at the very least prepare her for the ordeal ahead. But he doubted Kate would agree to that course of action.

Kate rejoined him after a few minutes. 'Nothing for us to do here until the SOCOs are finished.' She peeled the bootees off her feet and handed them to the constable.

'What about the computer? We promised Mrs Fraser the search for Megan would be our top priority.'

'It's taken care of. Colin sent it to Headquarters as soon as he'd taken his photos and dusted it for prints.'

Bill noted Kate's use of the chief crime investigator's first name with interest. It hadn't taken Kate long to build that bridge. He wondered if she'd ever get round to using his first name, or whether he was fated to be Murphy forever.

'I've alerted Jenny to start looking for Megan among the girls in his photo collection, and to pinpoint where the photos might have been taken. After that we can look at the other photos in his file and see if we can identify any of them.' Kate headed for the stairwell. 'Come on, we need to get back.'

Sue hesitated with her hand on the car door handle and turned to look back at the house. 'Well, that was interesting,' she said.

'She's weird.' Blair walked round the bonnet of the car,

opened the door and subsided into the passenger seat.

'Oh, I see you've found your tongue. I'd begun to think I'd brought along a puppet.'

'No need to be sarky,' Blair muttered, fastening his seat belt. 'You were doing so well, I didn't want to butt in and maybe shut her up.'

'OK, what did you think?'

'Weird. I wouldn't want her for my mother.'

'Apart from that. What did you think about her assault complaint?'

'She didn't appear to have any bruises, seemed more concerned about her wig. But it does indicate that the victim's ex-wife was looking for him. I suppose we should be looking to see if she had a motive to kill him.'

Sue started the engine, made a three point turn, and drove down the drive. 'Better get back to the office, and start looking for that motive.'

She screeched out of the drive onto the main road, grinning when she noticed Blair bracing himself and clutching the edge of his seat.

Jenny was already hard at work studying the photo files on Paul's computer when Bill and Kate got back to the office. 'Nothing yet,' she said without looking up.

'D'you know what you're looking for?' Bill placed his hands on her desk and leaned over to see the screen.

'I got a photo of Megan from the file.'

'I'll get you a photo of Jade Carnegie as well, in case she's on there.'

'Is she the one from the old case you've been looking at?' Jenny continued to concentrate on the screen.

'Yes, Jade's been missing for a long time, but I have a feeling it links to our murder case.' Bill cast a final look at the monitor before straightening and crossing the room to his own desk. He rummaged in the top drawer for the filing cabinet key, unlocked it and pulled out the Carnegie file. Removing the photograph of Jade he took it to Jenny and placed it on her desk beside the photo of Megan.

Kate joined them, she was in her shirt sleeves, and looked as fresh as she had first thing in the morning. She studied the two photographs. 'You really think there's a connection to Jade Carnegie?'

'I think the whole case hangs on her,' Bill replied. 'If we get the answer to Jade's disappearance, I think we can crack both murders.'

'All right, but we'll need to assess where we're at, and make a plan of action,' Kate said. 'Do we know when DS Rogers will be back?'

DC Sid Nolan looked up from the file he'd been studying. 'She phoned in, they're on their way.'

'Keep searching the computer, Jenny. Murphy you can get started on a report of the interview with Mrs Fraser, while we're waiting for the others to arrive, then we'll see where we're at and draw up a plan of action.'

'Yes, ma'am,' Bill said. He walked over to his desk, but as soon as Kate vanished into her office, he grabbed his jacket.

'Going somewhere?' Jenny kept her eyes on the computer screen.

'I've got something to do. I won't be long.' Bill thrust his arms into his jacket and left the office.

It was dark again, and cramp gripped one of her legs in a painful spasm. Megan shifted her position, trying to ease it, but that made it worse. She'd lost track of time and how long it had been since she'd woken here. It seemed like an eternity.

There had been that moment when he'd returned, and she'd thought he would set her free.

'Please,' she'd said, her voice no more than a croak, but he'd ignored her. It was as if he hadn't heard. 'Please,' she'd said again, raising her voice, but it had no effect, although he seemed to hesitate for a moment and she'd felt, rather than saw his eyes looking at her.

He left. There was the rasping sound of a key, the thump of a lock hitting the wooden door, and she was alone again. Alone in the dark with spiders and insects for company.

So much time had passed since then, and she'd waited for him to come back. She rehearsed in her mind what she would say and what she would do. She would beg him to let her go, tell him she would keep his secret, that she wouldn't go to the police. Who would believe her anyway? He'd want something in return, of course, and she'd decided whatever he asked for she would give him, provided he untied her and allowed her to go home afterwards.

A tear dribbled down her cheeks onto her neck, wetting the collar of her blouse which was already damp and cold.

But time passed and he didn't come back. Maybe he wasn't going to return. Maybe he was going to leave her here to die, in the dark and the cold. She closed her eyes and willed sleep to come. If she could sleep she wouldn't have to think about the spiders and creepy-crawlies sharing her prison.

When she opened her eyes again there seemed to be a sliver of light in the area where she guessed the door to be. She watched it, willing the door to open, but it remained closed, and the only sounds breaking the silence, were the swishing of wind and the patter of rain. She would give anything to be outside to feel the rain on her face and the wind blowing through her hair.

She'd heard it said your life flashes in front of your eyes when you're dying, and now she couldn't get the image of her mother out of her mind. She wasn't the best mother in the world, and it had been a long time since she'd given her any thought, thinking she didn't need her now she was growing up. But she was her mother, the only one she had, and she desperately needed her now.

The sliver of light had vanished and she thought she must have dozed, because she was back in the dark, and the cramp in her leg was excruciating.

35

'He's in a hurry.' Sue pulled hard on the steering wheel to avoid a collision with Bill who didn't even seem to notice she was there. 'Where d'you think he's going?'

Blair shrugged. 'How should I know? He's always off doing his own thing, never thinks to keep anyone else informed.'

Sue reversed into the space Bill had vacated. What Blair had said was true, but she detected a note of disapproval in his voice. 'You don't like Bill much, do you?'

'I never said that.' He got out of the car and slammed the door with more effort than was required.

She joined him on the pavement. 'OK, keep your hair on.' But she reckoned she was right and Bill would have to watch his back when Blair was around.

Blair strode out in front of her, leading the way into headquarters. The smell of his aftershave was overpowering in the confined space of the lift and Sue was glad when they exited into the corridor.

Kate was studying the whiteboard when they walked into the team room. 'How did you get on with Mrs Carnegie?' She didn't look round.

Sue flung her coat and bag on the chair and joined her. 'She's some weird lady,' she said, 'and she seems to think her daughter-in-law, Paul's ex-wife, killed him.'

'That was to be expected, she certainly has no love for his wife and family.'

'It's more than that. Apparently Diane Carnegie went to see her and there was a brawl which resulted in Patricia Carnegie handing over Paul's address to Diane. Mrs Carnegie wants to press charges.'

Kate tapped the pen she held against her teeth.

'Everything seems to lead back to the Carnegie family. I think we need to pull Diane Carnegie in for questioning. See if you can find Murphy, and the pair of you go and bring her in.' She looked round the team room. 'Where is Murphy, anyway? He's never here when you want him.'

Jenny looked up from the computer screen. 'He left a short time ago, said he'd something he had to do.'

Sue looked away, it was evident Kate was annoyed. But she said nothing, although Sue would have laid bets she wanted to.

'Saw him driving out of the car park as we arrived.' Blair had a self satisfied smile on his face.

Sue glared at him. The man was a prick.

'He's probably following up a lead.' Sue knew she should have stayed quiet.

'Then he should have shared it.' Kate's response was swift.

'It'll be something he's not sure about and he's checking it out first.'

'Your loyalty is admirable, but perhaps misplaced.'

Sue bit her tongue. She wanted to tell Kate that Bill was one of the best investigators on the team, even though he often went out on a limb because he was focused on the investigation. But she knew Kate wouldn't be receptive, and it would probably make things worse for him. Instead, she said, 'What's our next plan of action.'

'We bring Diane Carnegie in for questioning. As Murphy isn't here, it'll have to be you and Armstrong again.'

'Yes, ma'am.' Sue would rather have had Bill with her than Blair Armstrong, but Bill wasn't here and she was stuck with Blair.

Jade lay on her bed, relishing the emptiness of the house where not even the tick of a clock broke the silence. It was at times like this when the family were gone she felt at her most free.

She swung her legs over the side of the bed and stood up.

The room hadn't changed much since she'd slept there as a child. Her fingers brushed the tiny teddy bears pinned to the headboard, and she smiled at the memories they invoked. Emma's bed looked different though, with the more up to date duvet covering it while hers still had the candlewick bedspread, pink with embroidered roses. She'd always thought it looked prettier than Emma's yellow one. When it was time to reveal herself to her family she would make sure she got a duvet as well. It wouldn't do to live in the past.

The old computer still sat on the table in the corner of her side of the room, large and beige with the chunky monitor, not like the modern one downstairs in the study with its sleek flat screen. She preferred the study one and used it when the house was empty, like it was now. There were times she'd nearly been caught when Emma came back unexpectedly, and she often wished she could stay around to witness Emma's puzzlement.

She wandered through the house touching things, finding out their secrets, the things they hid from each other. Like Ryan's silk pyjamas and undies, she could imagine him wearing them. But he'd always been on the effeminate side, although he usually managed to hide it.

When the doorbell rang, Jade debated whether to answer it, or whether she should return to her hiding place, but what did she have to lose. She swung the door open before she had a change of heart.

When she saw the policeman standing on the doorstep, her eyes narrowed. Bill Murphy his name was, and he had a thing for her mother. She didn't like that, and she didn't like him. Her mother needed protecting, because all men were predators. Maybe her day wasn't going to be wasted after all.

Bill smiled. 'Is your mother in, Emma?'

Jade smiled back. 'No, but she won't be long. You can wait if you like.' She stood back to allow Bill to enter. 'I was about to put the kettle on if you fancy a cuppa.'

'That would go down a treat.' Bill followed her to the kitchen.

She flicked the light switch, the kitchen was always in

semi-darkness because of the large tree outside the window, then she smiled again and nodded at the table. 'Sit down and I'll get it.' Her fingers closed on the two jade beads in her pocket and the pill nestled beside them.

'I wanted to talk to you anyway, Emma.'

'Oh, and what would that be about?'

'I wanted to ask about your father. How you got on with him? When you last saw him? That kind of thing.'

Jade's hand tightened on the kettle's handle. 'I have no interest in him, and I haven't seen him since he left.' She poured hot water into two mugs, each containing a teabag and one of them with the added pill.

'What about your mother? I understand she went to see him.'

'I don't know anything about that.' She laid a mug in front of him. 'Why would she want to go and see him?'

'I don't know, Emma. You tell me.'

She watched him sip the tea.

'Ryan's the one who missed him. Maybe you should talk to him.'

'Oh, I intend to. But we need to talk to your mother first, because she was seen outside your father's flat.'

Jade shrugged. 'She went to ask him about Jade. She thought he'd know where she was.'

Bill nodded.

Jade noticed his eyes were unfocused. It wouldn't be long now.

His hand slipped on the cup's handle and he seemed to be having trouble holding it.

'Something the matter?' She removed the cup from his hand. 'Better put that down before you spill it.'

'That's better.' She sat on the chair opposite and studied him. She had plenty of time to do the needful. Her mother was at work and Ryan had said he'd wait for her to finish before he returned. It would be hours before they came back.

Bill slumped further down in the chair. His eyes had a puzzled expression but they seemed to bore into her, and she didn't like it.

'Time for your injection.' She patted his arm. 'I won't be a moment.'

She left the kitchen, went to the hiding place where she kept her stash, and selected a syringe and a packet of the pure white heroin that had cost her so much. The white was better than the rough brown stuff the druggies used, because she could mix it with water and didn't need citric acid.

Returning to the kitchen, she put the heroin and water in a spoon, flicked her lighter on and held the flame under the spoon. It was a moment before it bubbled and reached the constituency she wanted. She flicked the lighter off and replaced it in her pocket. 'It won't be long now,' she said, avoiding Bill's eyes.

While she filled the syringe she hummed a tune her mother used to sing to her when she was a child.

'Ready now?' She walked over to Bill. 'We'll need to get your arm out of the jacket though.' She lifted the arm and pulled it out of the sleeve, unbuttoned his shirt cuff and rolled the sleeve up. 'That's better. You won't feel a thing.' She plunged the syringe into his arm. 'There, that wasn't so bad, was it?'

36

Phil nudged Ryan's back with his shoe. 'That's your initiation over, mate,' he said. He grinned at Gus who was adjusting his trousers. 'Time to celebrate.' He slung his arm round the younger man's shoulders, and the two of them left the gents washroom, leaving Ryan on his own.

Ryan didn't move. He lay face down on the floor with the smell of disinfectant so strong in his nostrils he wanted to puke. The marble tiles sent chills coursing through him, and he struggled to pull his trousers up to hide his shame. Pain burned in his nether regions, increasing as he pulled his knees up to his chest. He felt sticky and unclean and was shaking all over. How could he ever face anyone again. He wanted to die.

All those romantic notions he'd had, the curl of desire in the pit of his stomach when he saw Phil, and it had ended like this. A grotty assault in a men's loo, an ordeal he'd thought was never going to end. A tear trickled down his cheek and he started to cry, quietly at first, until the sobs increased in intensity to match the shuddering of his body.

A hand touched his shoulder. It felt red hot against his skin. He recoiled, thinking Phil and Gus had come back.

'It's all right, they've gone. I was worried about you, and when I saw them leave I thought I'd better check.'

Ryan struggled to get his sobbing under control and looked up.

It was the girl from behind the bar. The one who didn't make him feel inferior. The one who had tried to warn him about Phil. He wished now he'd listened to her. He could see her eyes taking in the situation, but there was no condemnation in them.

'Are you OK?'

Was he OK? Of course he wasn't OK. He felt like shit, but no way was he going to tell her that. He looked away from her and nodded, afraid to speak in case he broke down again.

Her hand tightened on his shoulder and she seemed to hesitate before she said, 'Let's get you out of here in case they come back.' She held out her hand to him.

A surge of panic overtook him and he started to shake again. The thought of the two men returning spurred him into grasping her hand, and he stood up. The suddenness of the movement made his head swim and he clutched one of the sinks, leaning over it in case he was sick. He ran the cold tap and splashed water in his face. The dizziness and nausea abated, although it didn't make him feel any cleaner.

'My laptop.' He looked around and saw it lying against a cubicle door.

'I'll get it,' she said. 'Now come on, let's get out of here.'

She took him by the hand and led him out of the washroom, over to the bar, and into a small room behind it. She placed his laptop bag on one of the chairs, pointed to another one, and said, 'Sit, and I'll get you a drink.' She left the room, quickly reappearing with a glass in her hand. 'Drink this, you'll feel better.'

Ryan sipped the liquid. It burned all the way down to his stomach. 'I don't drink whisky,' he said. 'In fact I don't drink much at all, maybe wine with a meal, sometimes.'

'Drink it,' she said. 'It'll make you feel better.'

Her eyes seemed to have increased in intensity, and Ryan wasn't sure whether they were green or grey, but they had these amazing flecks of brown in them. They had a hypnotic effect and he raised his glass and swallowed. She was right, though, he did feel better after he'd finished it. He leaned back in the chair and closed his eyes, maybe another one would deaden the memory of what Phil and Gus had done to him. He held the glass out to her.

'I told you it would help.' Her voice seemed to come from a distance.

He opened his eyes. 'Thanks, you were right.'

She took the glass from him. 'My stint here is finished until later tonight. If you want to clean up and have a shower you could do it at my flat.'

Ryan studied her, not sure whether he was being propositioned. She seemed embarrassed by his stare and shook her brown hair with its amazing crimson streaks, so that it fell over her face. He usually felt intimidated by women, who all seemed to be taller than he was, but Kara was small and slim, not much bigger than him, and she was attractive. However, Ryan wasn't interested in women or girls, although he was no longer sure he was interested in men either.

'My mother,' Ryan said, 'she'll expect me to drive her home.' The thought of facing his mother after what had happened, and in his present condition caused a shudder of humiliation to vibrate through his body.

'She's already gone,' Kara said. 'One of the doormen came up to tell me she'd left you the car, that's why I came looking for you. I should have interrupted what was going on, but I couldn't. I knew Phil and Gus were in there with you, but I've had a run in with them before and they scare me.' She shivered. 'But the offer is there if you want it, and it would let you get cleaned up before you drive home.'

'OK,' he said, not sure what he was getting into.

Kara slung Ryan's laptop bag over her shoulder and he followed her out of the club, and down the stairs.

The back door swished shut behind them. Ryan paused a moment to breathe in the fresh air. It was good to be outside again after the claustrophobic feeling of the night club. The weather had changed since he'd entered it a few hours previously, the sky had darkened with a thundery look, and spits of rain pricked his face. The car still sat where he'd parked it.

'My flat's in the next street. We don't have far to go.'

The flat was up two flights of stairs in an old tenement, they wound upwards inside a turret shaped stairwell attached to the rear of the building. A large window halfway up barely illuminated the stairs because the glass was dirty, and a smell of cats and rotting rubbish hung in the air. Kara stopped outside a door that looked as if it hadn't seen a paint brush for many years. She unlocked it and led him inside.

'We're here,' she said. 'It's not much and it's only temporary until I get something better.'

Ryan nodded. It wasn't as clean as his mother's house, but nothing could be that clean.

'The shower's in there.' She pointed at a door. 'There's clean towels on the rail.'

The shower room was small, not much bigger than a cupboard, but the water was hot and Ryan let it flow over him until all the dirt and grime washed away. However, it did nothing for his inner feelings of uncleanliness, which he thought would be with him forever. He wasn't sure how long he'd been in the shower when he heard the tap on the door.

'I've made tea,' Kara's voice was muffled. 'And I've sponged some of the marks off your clothes. They don't look so bad now, although they may be damp in places.'

He turned the water off. 'Thanks, I'll be out in a minute.'

The bath towel was large and he knotted it round his waist before exiting the shower room.

'Feel better now?'

He nodded. Heat rose from his neck into his face and he wondered if he was blushing. What did Kara expect from him? 'Look, I'm not . . . I can't . . . '

Kara laughed. 'Don't worry, I'm not coming on to you. I only wanted to help. I've been in a tight spot with Phil and Gus before and I know what it feels like. By the way, if you're thinking of involving the police, you need to know Phil's a killer. He wouldn't think twice about topping you.'

'Police!' Ryan hadn't even considered it. 'The last thing I need is cops knowing about what happened and making snide comments behind my back.'

'Good thinking. Now get your clothes on while I go into the kitchen and pour the tea.'

Ignoring the drips from his hair, Ryan dressed as fast as he could. He was towelling his hair when Kara returned.

'Hot and sweet, get it down you before you go.'

The tea was sickeningly sweet but Kara indicated it was good for shock, so he swallowed it before taking his leave.

It didn't take him long to drive home after collecting the car from Teasers' car park. Once he got there, though, he was reluctant to get out, the shame from what had happened burnt too fiercely within him. He sat, breathing deeply until his nerves felt less frazzled. He couldn't sit there forever. It was time to face his family and act as if nothing had happened.

The house was quiet and at first he thought no one was in, however a light shone in the kitchen, his mother had probably returned home. The door slammed behind him. He'd meant to close it quietly but it slipped out of his fingers. He hesitated, then ran up the stairs. He would shower again before he faced his mother and Emma.

37

The fog in Bill's brain increased as he tried to puzzle out what Emma was up to and what was happening to him. He wanted to ask her but couldn't get his mouth to work, even his arms and legs no longer seemed to belong to him. She must have slipped something into the tea. But why would she do that?

The effort to think was becoming too great, all he could do was watch her.

He'd first noticed the paralysis creeping over him when she removed the cup from his hand and sat down to study him. She'd had a strange expression on her face that made her look less like Emma. Funny, he hadn't noticed it when she'd invited him in to the house.

Was it possible this was Jade? She and Emma were identical twins after all.

The syringe wasn't a surprise, because why else would she have drugged him. It was how she operated. It was her signature.

The injection when it came was merely a pin prick, but when she depressed the plunger he could feel the warmth of the heroin travelling along his veins. Was this what the junkies meant by feeling a rush?

It was pleasurable and soon he floated above himself, lapsing into a drug induced coma where all he wanted to do was sleep.

The sound of a door slamming drifted to him from somewhere far away, but he didn't even think of rescue, he was in such a pleasurable state. Neither did he notice Jade's momentary alarm, nor did he see her slipping out the back door.

The sound of feet running up the stairs, so quiet it could

have been rain pattering on the leaves of the tree outside, barely impacted on his consciousness.

Sleep came, and gradually the dark enveloped him.

A waft of air drifted across the team room. Kate turned, thinking it might be Murphy returning, but groaned under her breath when she saw the imposing figure of Superintendent Logan marching across the room. He was accompanied by a tall, slim, unsmiling blonde woman of indeterminate age.

'Ah, Detective Inspector Rawlings, Miss Christensen informs me you haven't yet met.'

'That's correct,' the woman said, holding out her hand for Kate to shake. 'Astrid Christensen, procurator fiscal. It's a wonder we haven't met at the crime scenes.'

Kate detected a note of reproof in the woman's voice.

Damn! She'd clean forgotten to contact the fiscal's office about the murders.

It wouldn't have been so bad if there'd only been one, but now there were two, there was no excuse. She should have remembered it was the fiscal's job to be present at every crime scene, so she could weigh up the evidence and decide whether a prosecution should go ahead.

Kate realized she'd committed the unforgivable sin of keeping the fiscal out of the loop.

'I understand you are new to the department.'

Now the woman's tone was condescending, and Kate watched her exchange a tight-lipped smile with Superintendent Logan.

'Yes,' Kate said, trying hard not to sound undermined.

'If you can update me on the progress of the investigation, that would be helpful.'

'Of course.' Kate looked over the room to where Sue was gathering up her belongings in preparation for her task of bringing Diane Carnegie in for questioning. 'Sue, can you spare a minute,' she said. 'The procurator fiscal requires to be updated on our investigation.'

Kate led the way over to the whiteboard. 'As you can see there are several strands in the investigation, some more obvious than others.

'Firstly, we have two bodies, both men with no apparent connection to each other, and each one murdered by a drug overdose within the past few days.

'The first one, John Gregson, a known paedophile from the Manchester area was found on Monday the 12th of March, but had apparently been killed on the Friday before.

'The second body, that of Paul Carnegie, was found today, which is less than a week since the first murder was committed.

'On the face of it these seem to be two isolated murders, but the thing tying them together is the jade beads which were pressed into each man's eyes, and of course, the method of killing, plus the fact we now have reason to believe Paul Carnegie was a paedophile as well.'

The procurator fiscal studied the board intently. 'What leads do you have?'

'The whole investigation keeps coming back to the Carnegie family. Paul Carnegie's ex-wife, Diane Carnegie, her daughter Emma, and son Ryan. There is also the question as to whether their other daughter, Jade, has returned from the dead.'

The fiscal raised her eyebrows but said nothing.

'Jade was Emma's twin, and she went missing five years ago when she was thirteen. It was presumed she was dead, but now there is some doubt. Diane, the mother, went through a mental breakdown after Jade's disappearance, and still has mental health issues. She was also witnessed visiting Paul Carnegie's flat yesterday evening. We are currently pursuing a plan to bring her in for questioning.'

'How reliable is this witness?'

'Not the most reliable. She's the mother of a missing schoolgirl, Megan Fraser. She was the one who found Paul Carnegie's body. She believes he abducted Megan and claims to have seen a photograph of her daughter on the murdered man's computer.'

'If that is the case, is it not possible she might have killed Paul Carnegie?'

'That is a possibility, although I can't see how it ties in with the previous murder.'

'The missing child. What is happening there?'

'A search of the area was instigated when she went missing, plus a door to door, plus press coverage. However, this is a child who has a history of running off and staying with friends or acquaintances, and we had no reason to think differently until Mrs Fraser said she saw her daughter on the victim's computer.'

'I see, and what are your plans now?'

'DC Cartwright is currently examining all the photographs on Paul Carnegie's computer to see if that gives us any leads to her whereabouts. But we do have another avenue I want to explore, and that's Paul's mother. He apparently had close contact with her and there is a possibility he might have a bolt hole on her estate. However, I'd need a search warrant to take that forward, and at the moment there's insufficient evidence for that because we only have Mrs Fraser's word there are photographs of her daughter in the computer, and as I said before, she's not the most reliable witness. That's why we need to find the photographs of the child first.'

Astrid Christensen turned to the superintendent who was perched on the edge of a desk and swinging his leg. 'I've heard enough for the time being, Nigel, but I trust I'll be kept informed.'

'Of course.' He smiled at her before turning towards Kate. 'Make sure it happens.'

'Yes, sir.' Kate gritted her teeth and hoped it didn't show through her smile.

'Oh, by the way. I'd think twice before bringing a woman who has mental issues in for questioning. Particularly as the evidence is thin.' With that parting remark, Astrid Christensen left the room.

'Well, you heard her,' Kate said to Sue. 'We'd better hang fire on bringing Diane Carnegie in for questioning.

We'll do the softly, softly approach tomorrow, and maybe by that time Murphy will have graced us with his presence.'

Megan's head was fuzzy and she wasn't thinking straight, maybe this was what dying felt like. The dark was as intense as ever and she was stiff and sore.

She dreamed of being in her mother's arms, with her face pressed into her mum's bosom, and it had felt all soft and warm. She relaxed, the past few hours had been a nightmare and she was safe, and she vowed never to take her mother for granted again.

Then she woke, back in the dark nightmare.

The sound of the lock, clattering against the wood of the door, aroused Megan out of her stupor.

He was back!

She tried to think of all the things she'd rehearsed to say to him, but her brain was full of cotton wool, and all she could focus on was the fear.

The dark shape in the doorway stood for a moment before approaching her. A hand reached out. Megan tried to shrink back into the corner, but there was nowhere for her to go.

The hand grasped her arm, and a woman's voice said, 'Don't be afraid. I've come to help you.'

Megan relaxed. She felt the cold steel of scissors snipping the rope round her wrists, and then her feet.

'Can you stand?'

Megan struggled, pushing her arms on the wooden box at her side to give her leverage. 'I think so,' she said, but the words wouldn't come through her parched lips and turned into a moan.

'Good.'

The woman put an arm round her and helped her stagger to the door.

'Now you must get as far away from here as you can.' She released her hold.

Megan turned to where she could see a light shining through the trees.

'No, not that way,' the woman said, 'he'll find you if you go that way.'

She turned Megan to face the other way, where no light showed.

'Go quickly,' she said, 'and if you hear any sounds following you, hide.'

Megan stumbled off into the darkness of the wood. She had to get as far away as possible. She mustn't let him find her.

38

Jade paused. She listened for a moment with her hand on the open back door, expecting to hear footsteps approaching the kitchen. When they clattered upstairs she considered returning inside and finishing the job, but it was too risky. With one final backward glance at the comatose body of Bill, she slipped outside, easing the door shut behind her.

She'd taken a chance with Bill, although she hadn't expected to be disturbed so early. But it had been satisfying to dupe him into thinking she was Emma. It had all been going well until the front door opened. Now, sliding along the rear wall of the house, she couldn't resist one final look through the kitchen window, to enjoy a fleeting moment of exhilaration because the policeman had succumbed. The drugs had done their work, there would be no coming back from the dark place he had lapsed into. Pity about the jade beads though, she would have liked to include the final touch, her message she'd been there. Still, it couldn't be helped, and now she'd done her job, her mother would be safe from his vile intentions.

Men, they were all the same, preying on women and girls for their own needs. They needed to be punished.

She stepped onto the grassy area where her mother hung the washing to dry. She was in the open here, and she glanced around to ensure no prying eyes peered out of any of the windows. The ankle length grass was wet from the earlier rainfall and by the time she reached the bushes her feet were soaked. Pushing aside the wet branches to reach the fence, the smell of wet foliage and loamy earth increased. Beyond the bushes was the boundary fence and more back gardens. It wasn't the easiest of routes but it was safer than being recognized leaving the house.

It was time for her to go into hiding again. It wasn't yet time to reveal herself.

Diane huddled into a seat at the rear of the bus. She had been on the point of ending it all when she'd looked up from the water and saw, over to her right, a children's playground. It had brought back pleasant memories of an earlier time when she'd taken all three children for a day's outing to this place which she now realized was Broughty Ferry. Why she hadn't recognized the place earlier, was beyond her. Maybe it was because she'd been so tied into her misery it obliterated everything else.

Now she knew where she was, she walked to the beach beyond the castle and remembered the happier times. Running on the sand, throwing sticks for the dog, and Jade whooping with delight. Even Emma had seemed to enjoy herself.

It was then she knew she owed it to Jade to be there for her when she was ready to come home. And she wouldn't let her down.

She walked back to the main street to catch the bus home, not noticing the rain, nor how wet she was.

The bus was empty but she continued down the aisle to a seat at the back. She sat down, scrunching herself into the corner, ignoring the dampness round her legs where the edges of the coat touched, and pushing her hair back, over her collar to prevent drips rolling down her neck. Most people chose the front seats so she hoped she'd be left in peace. It would give her time to reflect on her life and what was happening to her, and why she'd nearly ended it all. Of course it was all tied up with Jade's reappearance, she knew that. But finding Jade had become such an obsession with her, and now when Jade seemed so near, she couldn't understand why she was unreachable.

Maybe Jade's reappearance was only in her mind, a figment of her imagination fuelled by her obsession. Maybe the family were right. Maybe it was time to consult the doctor again.

It seemed no time before the bus arrived in Caird Avenue, pulling up behind another one. Diane got off, almost colliding with Emma who must have been on the bus in front.

'Mum!' Emma frowned at her. 'You're sopping wet. Where's the car?'

'I wasn't in the mood for working, and I left it for Ryan.' Diane felt a slight irritation at Emma's concern. It felt as if her daughter were keeping tabs on her.

'But you wouldn't have got as wet as that just coming home in the bus.'

'No!' Diane's irritation increased. 'I guess not. But I needed time to think.'

'Where have you been?'

'Broughty Ferry. I used to take you all there when you were little.' Diane looked at Emma and sighed. Why did Emma always have this effect on her. After all, Emma was her daughter as well, and she was so like Jade, yet could never take her place. Emma didn't have that extra spark of life Jade had. But that didn't excuse her rejection of her daughter. The only daughter she had left, unless of course, Jade really had returned.

'In this weather?' Emma frowned, and seemed about to say something else, but instead compressed her lips and shook her head.

'Let's go home, Emma.' Diane forced an unnatural warmth into her voice, and she smiled at her daughter. She had the feeling they'd been on the point of an argument and didn't feel up to it.

As soon as he reached his bedroom, Ryan tore his clothes off and heaved them into the corner. He turned his face away from them unable to bear looking at what had once been his favourite shirt, jacket and trousers. It had taken him a long time, saving every spare pound he had, before he was able to afford to buy them at Harvey Nick's in Edinburgh. But now, after what had happened he would never wear them again and would get rid of them at the first opportunity.

The memory of what Phil and Gus had done to him, flooded back. He shuddered. The smell of puke, urine and shit, mixed in with disinfectant, would never leave him. It was stamped on his body for all time and he was sure it would be obvious to anyone who looked at him.

He listened for a moment in case his mother was coming upstairs to check on him, but when he heard no sound he bolted for the bathroom, locked himself in and set the shower to hot. Standing under the shower head, he let the water stream over his head and body. Then, grabbing a coarse, exfoliating sponge, he rubbed and scrubbed at every area of his flesh.

Ryan wasn't sure how long he was under the shower, scrubbing himself, before he heard the front door open and someone come in. But still he didn't get out from under the hot water. He wasn't clean yet.

It was the scream reverberating through the house that finally made him screw off the water, jump out of the shower, grab a towel, and hurry downstairs.

Emma's thoughts were in turmoil as she walked up the street with her mother. She wanted to say so much but choked it back. It wouldn't help, and she feared her mother was on the point of a breakdown.

She didn't believe for one moment Jade had returned. There were too many unexplained factors. Like where Jade had been for five years. A thirteen year old couldn't vanish and live another life somewhere else. Someone would have noticed. It would have been different if Jade had been an adult, then it might have been feasible, but not a thirteen year old, it simply wasn't possible.

Emma glanced at her mother, but Diane's face gave nothing away, and she seemed intent on reaching the house.

They turned the corner from Caird Avenue into Johnstone Avenue. Home was within sight, and she could see a light on in Ryan's room. Good, she would talk to Ryan about her concerns. Maybe if they presented a unified front to Diane they would be able to persuade her to go for treatment.

'I'll use my key,' she said, 'it'll save you hunting for yours.' But when she placed her key in the lock the door swung open. That wasn't like Ryan. He was usually fastidious about locking the front door.

She hesitated on the doorstep. There had been a lot of burglaries in the surrounding area over the past few months. If it was a burglar he might be violent, and her mother was in no state to handle a confrontation, but neither was she. However, someone had to investigate and she was younger and fitter than Diane.

'You wait here,' she said to Diane. 'I want to have a look around first.'

'Why?' Diane shrugged her coat off.

'The door is open, that's why. We don't know who might be here.'

'I don't know why you're fussing. It'll only be Ryan.'

'Ryan would have locked the door after he came in.' Emma struggled to hide her exasperation. 'Wait here and I'll have a look around. Better safe than sorry.'

The stair light was on, as well as the kitchen light. She stood for a moment considering her options. If she investigated upstairs first that would leave Diane vulnerable if the burglar was downstairs, but the same applied to a downstairs search. Making her mind up she tiptoed up the hall passage towards the kitchen light. She pushed the door with the tips of her fingers, slowly opening it.

The kitchen was empty, except for the body of a man slumped over the kitchen table.

Emma didn't know what she'd expected, but certainly not this. She stood looking at him and was vaguely aware of Diane padding along the hall to join her. Her mother's scream jolted her into action, and she walked over to the table to examine the body.

Footsteps thudded down the stairs.

'What's up?' Ryan stood in the kitchen doorway. He was

barefoot and had a bath towel tied round his middle.

'What does it look like,' Emma snapped.

'Shit, he's not dead, is he?'

'He's lying here with a dirty big syringe stuck in his arm, and he's not moving. What do you think?'

'Who is it?'

'You tell me, you were in the house with him.'

'I went straight upstairs when I came in. I thought Mum was in the kitchen.'

Diane walked over to Emma. 'Who is it?'

Emma tried to block her view. 'It's that copper. The one you said was helping you find Jade.'

Diane pushed past her. 'Oh, no! It can't be.'

'What's he doing here?' Ryan adjusted the towel round his middle.

'I don't know, but we've got to do something. Phone the police, I suppose, they'll have to be informed.'

Diane reached out and removed the syringe from Bill's arm. 'We have to help him. He might not be dead.'

'I'll call an ambulance, although it's probably a waste of time.' Emma walked back to the hall to get the phone. 'Then I'll call the police.'

39

It was a mess. Kate sat at her desk and stared into space. Two dead bodies, a missing schoolgirl, a dysfunctional family she desperately wanted to pull in, and no evidence to support it. And where was bloody Bill Murphy? Her first impressions had been right, the man was a walking disaster and nobody ever seemed to know where he was or what he was doing. And if all that wasn't enough she'd managed to annoy the procurator fiscal, and the super was probably convinced he'd made a mistake appointing her to this job.

She tightened her lips and frowned. Doing things by the book wasn't working. The longer she sat here twiddling her thumbs, the longer that child remained at risk, wherever she was. At least she could restart the search for her.

Standing up and thrusting her chair back with such force it clattered off the filing cabinets behind her, she strode to her office door.

'Sue! Who was that inspector in the Greenfield office the one Murphy was working with on the door to doors?'

Sue, who had been looking over Jenny's shoulder as she scrolled through the computer, looked up. 'Inspector Mason, ma'am.'

'Thanks.'

Kate hurried back into her office, checked the list of office numbers, lifted the phone and dialled.

'Inspector Mason's not available,' the voice said. 'Can I put you through to Sergeant Forbes instead?'

'Yes.'

'Detective Inspector Rawlings, it's Sergeant Forbes here, what can I help you with?'

'It's in relation to the incident in your area today. The murder. We have reason to believe the victim abducted a child, Megan Fraser, before he was killed and I need you to organize a search party in your area. We need to find her before she comes to further harm.'

'Ah, yes. I remember Megan, we've had search parties out for her in the past, but she always turns up.'

'This time it's different,' Kate snapped. 'We have evidence that Paul Carnegie was involved in Megan's disappearance, and it would appear it's not the first time this man's done something like this.'

'Evidence, you say?'

'Yes, we're examining his computer and there's definitely evidence he was involved.' Kate crossed her fingers, they hadn't found the images yet.

'I'll get the search organized right away, ma'am.'

Kate detected a note of reluctance in his voice but she didn't care.

She'd just hung the phone up when Sue popped her head round the door. 'We've found the photos of Megan, ma'am.'

Kate joined her at Jenny's desk.

'They took a bit of finding,' the detective constable said. 'They were in hidden files buried deep in the computer, and there's more girls than Megan in the files. I've also found a file named Jade. DS Murphy asked me to look out for her name as well.'

'Let's concentrate on Megan for the time being.' Kate's finger itched to grab the mouse and scroll through the photos faster, but she restrained herself. 'There's a lot. He must have been watching her for some time.'

'Yes, ma'am. But here's where it gets interesting.'

Kate hissed breath through her lips. These photos were different. They were of a girl lying in the corner of what looked like a shed or outhouse, with her hands tied in front of her. The girl's eyes were closed and Kate couldn't decide whether she was looking at a drugged girl, or whether it was a body.

'Right, that's it. We need to search Patricia Carnegie's house and grounds. Get that organized, Sue.'

Sue turned away from the monitor and looked at Kate.

'I've met Patricia Carnegie and I'd think there's no way she'll allow us to search her property without a warrant?'

'Well, we can't waste any time. You look up the list of sheriffs, and justices of the peace. See who's on call and I'll get the forms filled in.'

Kate stamped off to her office. Blasted forms, blasted paperwork. It always got in the way.

Sue became increasingly frustrated as she worked through the list of sheriffs, phoning each one in turn. Either there was no answer, or an apologetic voice at the end of the phone explaining why he wasn't available.

'Damn,' said Sue to no one in particular, 'you'd think at least one sheriff would be available to grant a warrant.'

Blair grinned at her from his position, perched on the edge of her desk. 'What about the JPs, any of them available?'

'I'm about to start working down the list,' Sue snapped. Did he think she was an idiot?

Several phone calls later she manage to locate one justice of the peace who was available and she made arrangements to take the warrant out to her immediately.

The JP, Mrs Barrington, lived in a bungalow in Cairnie Street. Sue parked at the kerb and, followed by Blair, walked up the path to the door. It was opened at her first knock by a little grey-haired lady.

'Come in, my dears,' she said. She led them into a living room with chintz-covered chairs. 'Now sit down and tell me all about it.'

Sue perched on the edge of an armchair, while Blair stood in the doorway.

The woman sat down and smiled at Sue. 'You are sure I can do this,' she said, 'it's been a few years since I presided over a District Court.'

'Your name's on the list of available JPs, ma'am.' Sue wasn't entirely sure herself, the woman looked old and not her idea of what a justice of the peace should look like. But her name was on the list of approved JPs.

'Oh well, I suppose you'd better explain it all to me before I decide whether to sign your warrant.'

Sue explained the case in detail, before saying, 'You can see how important it is for us to find this girl, and we have reason to suspect she might be hidden on Mrs Carnegie's estate.'

'Oh dear,' Mrs Barrington said, 'I can quite see that. Let me borrow your pen and I'll sign the warrant.'

Sue handed her the pen and the form to sign.

'I do hope you find her,' Mrs Barrington said as they left.

Sue strode to the car, closely followed by Blair.

'Are you sure the warrant the old biddy signed will be OK?' Blair subsided into the passenger seat.

Sue switched on the ignition and pressed hard on the accelerator. 'I don't give a damn how old she was or whether or not she's still practising as a JP. Her name was on the list and that's all that matters.'

Kate breathed a sigh of relief when Sue returned, waving the warrant in the air.

'Right, Sue, you're with me. Jenny, you stay here and keep digging into that computer.' Kate grabbed her jacket and shoulder bag. 'I've got a police search party lined up. They're waiting for us to serve the warrant and give them the nod to get started. Let's go.'

The rush hour was over but it still took them 20 minutes to reach Patricia Carnegie's house. Police cars lined the road outside the gates and Kate swung past them giving a flash of her lights and a toot on the horn when she entered the tree-lined drive. The cars followed her in.

'This is it,' she said to Sue as the car crunched to a halt in front of the door and, taking a deep breath to quell the fluttering feeling in her chest, she got out, marched up to the door and raised her hand to knock.

The door opened before her fist struck the wood. Patricia Carnegie peered out at them.

'I heard you coming,' she said, her eyes flicking over the line of police cars in the driveway. 'What's all this about?'

'We have a warrant to search your property, ma'am.' Kate showed her the document.

Patricia Carnegie took it but her eyes didn't move away from the cars.

'Why would you want to do that? And what are you looking for?' She sounded genuinely puzzled.

'We have reason to believe a child may be hidden on your property.' Kate kept her voice official with a tone of severity.

'You won't find any children here.' Mrs Carnegie's voice was strident. 'What on earth made you think you would?' She turned away from them and made a vain attempt to close the door.

'We have the warrant, ma'am.' Kate's foot was firmly in place so the door couldn't close. 'You are legally bound to allow the search.'

'Oh, well, if you insist, but you'll find no child here so you're wasting your time.' Patricia Carnegie gave them a thin-lipped smile.

Kate beckoned to the police sergeant who had emerged from the first car. 'Get two of your men to search the house,' she said. 'The rest of them can start with the grounds.'

Patricia Carnegie glared at her. 'They'd better not make a mess,' she hissed through clenched teeth. She stamped back into the house.

'That was easier than I anticipated.' Sue's voice was thoughtful.

'Shouldn't we be glad of that?' Kate had been happy about how easy everything had been, but she picked up on the doubt Sue seemed to be feeling.

'I don't know. This lady's a wildcat when it comes to her son. I would have expected her to be kicking and screaming.'

'Maybe she knows more than she's saying about what her son got up to.' Kate left Sue and walked into the house to the gleaming kitchen where Patricia Carnegie was fussing over an espresso machine.

Sue was right, the woman was too calm and accepting of what was going on, despite her initial half-hearted objection.

Megan stumbled through the wood, tripping on roots and slipping on dead leaves. Her blouse and skirt were sodden, and her hair clung in wet strands to her neck. She stopped to catch her breath, leaning on a tree trunk, and staring into the darkness. She could no longer see the light from the house at her back and she didn't know how far she'd come, nor how far the trees stretched. But the trees couldn't go on for ever. Surely there would be houses, or a road she could follow. There had to be something.

She heard the noise of a car in the distance, but it was coming from the direction of the house, and the woman had said it wasn't safe there. Her heart thumped in her chest and she shuddered. It meant he had returned and would be looking for her. She had to get further away.

She cast a fearful glance back the way she had come, but all she saw was darkness and trees. And in front of her, more darkness and trees, but that was the way she would have to go, she couldn't risk staying here in case he caught her again.

Suppressing a sob, she stumbled deeper into the wood where the trees were thicker and darker, and more menacing.

40

'I don't know, I couldn't feel a pulse. I think he might be dead.' Emma's hand ached, it was gripping the phone so hard.

She listened to the mechanical voice at the other end of the line.

'Of course I'm sure it's an overdose, he had this blasted big needle sticking out of his arm.'

She listened again. 'I don't know what he's taken, all I know is he had a needle in his arm.' Her voice got higher in pitch, until she was screaming. 'Just get the damned ambulance here, because if he's not dead, he soon will be.'

She rammed the phone onto its cradle and leaned against the wall, taking deep breaths until the panic in her chest subsided.

A green and yellow checkered car with a flashing blue light on top screeched to a halt outside the house, and a paramedic carrying a bag, erupted from the passenger side. This was closely followed by a police car which drew up behind the ambulance car. A policeman got out of the passenger side and followed the paramedic to the door.

'Where's the ambulance?' Emma demanded, glaring at the man in the green coverall suit.

'We're first responders, love. Now where is he?'

The policeman stood back to allow a second paramedic past.

'In there.' Emma pointed down the corridor to the kitchen. 'He's in a bad way . . . I don't know if he's still alive.'

The paramedics pushed past her. 'We don't have time to waste, love.'

They ran down the corridor. Emma followed close

behind.

Diane was sitting in a chair in the kitchen. She seemed dazed, but her eyes were fixed on Bill's prone body.

'I'll have to ask you to leave, we need room to work,' the first paramedic said to her, while feeling Bill's neck with his fingers.

'Might be a flicker there. We need to get the Naloxone into him right away if he's to have any chance.'

Emma stood in the doorway, feeling helpless. She wanted to reach out to her mother, who still sat immobile on the kitchen chair, but to do that she'd have to step over the paramedic's legs, and he'd already indicated he needed room to work.

The paramedic rummaged in his bag until he found what he was looking for, an oblong shaped pack. He twisted the ends off the pack and produced a syringe. Looking up, he spotted the policeman. 'Can you get them out of here. I'm going to have to get this into him and get him into the recovery position. I'll need room to do it.'

'You heard the man,' the policeman said, 'he wants you all out of the way so he can work.'

Emma glanced despairingly at Diane who gave no indication of having heard. She wanted to move away but not without her mother.

'I said everyone out, and I meant it. So get out now.'

Emma backed away but didn't take her eyes off Diane.

'Now,' he snapped, 'I'm not going to say it again.'

At last Diane looked up, and Emma beckoned to her. 'Come on, Mum. We can't do anything here, and we need to get out of the way.'

Diane followed her down the passage and into the lounge, where she slumped onto the settee and looked blankly at the door.

Emma sat down beside her and put her arm round Diane's shoulders. 'It'll be all right, Mum.'

But she didn't think it would be all right, and thoughts scurried round her brain.

What was the detective doing here anyway? And how

come he chose their kitchen to take an overdose? And why didn't Ryan see him when he came home? Too many questions and no answers.

Patricia Carnegie ignored Kate and lifted the cup of Espresso to her lips while she stared out of the kitchen window to where lights bobbed and flickered, indicating the start of the search.

'They won't find anything, you know.' She sounded smug.

'Nevertheless, we have to search, when it concerns a missing child.' The smell of the coffee annoyed Kate. She hadn't eaten anything since lunch time, and she didn't know when she would get the opportunity to grab a bite.

One of the policemen entered the kitchen. 'Nothing here, ma'am.'

Kate nodded. 'You'd better join the search outside.'

'Yes, ma'am.'

'I hate to say it, but I told you so.' Patricia Carnegie took a sip of her coffee and turned her gaze back to the window.

'We're not finished yet. Don't go anywhere.' Kate resisted the temptation to whack the woman across her smug face, and marched to the door. What was it about this case that had her emotions getting out of hand? She was usually better at controlling herself than this.

The rain was heavier now, and she didn't have a waterproof. She was tempted to sit in the car, but that wouldn't look good to the men doing the searching. If they could put up with the rain, so could she.

She looked around for Sue, but the policewoman was nowhere to be seen. She must have joined the search.

Sighing, Kate trudged to the edge of the wood, listening to the men moving forward in a line searching the undergrowth.

'Ma'am.' Sue appeared at her side. 'We've found a shed, they're cutting the lock off now. I thought you might want to be there when it's opened.'

'Thanks, Sue.' Kate followed her into the wood.

The shed door gaped open, and one of the men was shining his torch inside. 'Nothing here, ma'am. But it looks as if someone has been here.' He picked up a length of rope. 'This has been cut, looks like it was used to tie something up.'

'I think this is the place in the photos.' Sue's voice was hushed.

'What's in the wooden chest over there?' Kate's pulse raced, surely the girl couldn't be inside, but it was big enough to contain her.

'It's padlocked, ma'am, but we'll soon get that off.'

Kate held her breath when the padlock bounced off and hit the ground. If the girl was inside, there was no way she'd still be alive.

'Oh, shit.' The constable turned away from the chest, clamping his hand over his mouth.

Kate closed her eyes. Her head swam and she didn't feel good. They'd found her, and they were too late.

'Ma'am.' Sue's voice penetrated the fog in her brain. 'It's not Megan. It's something a lot older than that.'

Kate forced her eyes open and walked over to the chest to look. She didn't know what she'd been expecting, but certainly not a skeleton lying on an ancient velvet cushion.

A faint rumble of voices from the kitchen seeped up the corridor and into the lounge like sibilant whispers. Emma strained to hear but could distinguish nothing. Diane sat beside her on the settee, her fingers restlessly stroking and picking at the arm of the chair. Other than that, she seemed oblivious to what was going on. Ryan was nowhere to be seen. Did that mean he had something to do with what had happened? Emma's mind was too confused to try and work it out.

A siren, announcing the arrival of the ambulance, jolted her out of her thoughts. It parked at the kerbside behind the paramedics green and yellow checkered car. The ambulance driver and another paramedic got out and hurried up the path to the house, their feet thumping on the hallway floor, as they rushed to join their colleagues in the kitchen. The sound of voices increased but nothing else happened, making her wonder what they were doing.

At last, after what seemed a lifetime to Emma, two of them stretchered Bill's body down the hallway. Rising from her seat to look out the window, she watched as they loaded Bill into the ambulance.

'Is he going to be all right?' She turned to face the policeman entering the room. A policewoman stood guard at the door.

'We don't know, miss. He's being taken to the hospital now. But in the meantime I need to ask you some questions.'

Emma returned to the settee and grasped Diane's hand.

'First of all I need all your names, dates of birth, that kind of thing. We'll get that out of the way first.'

Emma supplied the information, although she wondered what it had to do with anything. But the policeman had said it was procedure so she thought she'd better not argue.

The door opened and Ryan entered fully clad.

'And you are, sir?'

Ryan collapsed into an armchair. 'Ryan Carnegie,' he said. 'I live here.'

'Right.' The policeman scribbled in his pad as Ryan gave him all his details. 'Now we'll get on with what happened here tonight. First of all I want to know who our overdose victim is.'

Emma shrugged. 'He's a detective who has been investigating my sister's disappearance.'

The policeman looked up. 'Have you got a name for this detective?'

Emma looked over at Diane. 'Mum, you know more about him than me.'

Diane's fingers stopped rubbing the chair arm. 'His name's Detective Sergeant Bill Murphy, and he's with the CID.' Her voice was flat, as if she were reciting from a book.

The policeman looked over to his colleague.

'Get on to HQ and check it out.'

The policewoman reached for her airwave set, nodded and left the room. No doubt to report in without the family hearing.

'Tell me about your sister and her disappearance.'

Emma sighed. 'It's old news. She vanished five years ago, but they've reopened the case.'

'I see.'

'What was DS Murphy doing here, and how come he's overdosed in your kitchen?'

Emma shrugged. 'None of us know the answer to that. We'd only just come in and there he was.'

'I don't think he was a drug user.' Diane's voice was quiet, but penetrating. 'He was a nice man who was trying to help.'

The policewoman came back into the room. 'I got through to CID, they're sending someone over and we've to protect the scene until they get here.'

The policeman tucked his notebook into his pocket. 'We'd better leave the rest of the questioning to them.' Turning to the family he said, 'I want you all to stay here. Nobody is to leave the room.'

41

Kate thought she'd never get the picture of that grinning skull and skeletal frame out of her mind. She swallowed hard before she said, 'Well it's not Megan Fraser, that's for sure.'

'No, ma'am, but I think she might have been here.' The officer held up a piece of material that looked like a rosette.

'What is it?'

Sue peered at it. 'It looks like a ponytail scrunchie, one of those fancy ones with frills. I think Megan was wearing one when she disappeared.'

'You'd better bag it,' Kate said.

'Try not to handle it too much, while I pop back to the car to fetch an evidence bag,' Sue said.

She was back in moments, Kate reckoned she must have run all the way there and back, and the scrunchie was safely bagged.

Sue handed one of the officers a roll of blue and white tape. 'I brought this as well,' she said, 'we can get this taped off as a crime scene. One of you will have to stand guard until we can get the SOCOs here.'

Kate backed out of the shed. 'We'll need dogs,' she said, 'because if she's not here, she must be out in the wood somewhere.' Or dead and buried, Kate thought, although she didn't say it.

Kate plodded back to the house over the sodden ground. She could see the glimmer of light from the windows, and behind her lights flashed between the trees, as the searchers moved deeper into the wood.

Inspector Mason stood by the bonnet of his car instructing a new batch of searchers. Kate beckoned to him and he finished what he was saying before turning his attention to her.

'We've found evidence Megan was held in a shed which is a few yards inside the wood. I thought we might get the dogs involved in the search.'

'I'll get on to it right away,' Mason said. 'I'll get someone to contact her mother for a piece of clothing as well.'

Behind her, Kate heard Sue give a muffled laugh that was quickly turned into a cough.

The inspector looked at her but didn't say anything. He was already talking into his airwave set while they walked towards the house.

Kate hid a smile. The inspector's beat covered the Greenfield estate, so no doubt he knew May Fraser better than they did.

'Come on, Sue,' she said, increasing her pace, 'we need to have another word with Mrs Carnegie. That lady has some explaining to do.'

Patricia Carnegie sprawled on the white leather sofa in the lounge, a glass in her hand. She looked up when Kate and Sue entered the room. 'Well, what is it now? Don't you think you've upset me enough?'

'We've found the shed,' Kate said in a grim voice.

'Well what of it? It's only a garden shed. It's where Paul keeps . . . kept his tools.' She sipped her drink.

'I think it's more than that.' Kate marched over to the sofa and looked down on Patricia. The woman pulled back as if she felt threatened.

'What do you mean?'

'We opened the wooden chest in the shed and found skeletal remains inside.'

Patricia's eyes widened. 'You're lying.'

'No, and what's more we found evidence Megan Fraser had been there, but she's not there now.'

'That's impossible.' Patricia laid her glass on the coffee table. 'I would have known about it.'

'We think you did know about it. And I want to know where Megan is now.'

'Well, she's not here, you've searched.'

'But you know where she is.'

'How would I know that, when I didn't even know she was there?'

Kate turned to Sue. 'This is getting us nowhere. We're going to have to take her into custody.'

'You can't do that, I don't know anything. Maybe she is in the wood, but you're searching there, so you're bound to find her.' Patricia smirked. It was as if she were taunting them.

'Where does the wood lead?' Kate demanded, and turning to Sue, she added. 'We can start searching from the other side. That way we're bound to find her.'

Patricia picked up her glass again. 'That might be difficult. You see there's a large, water-filled quarry at the far side of the wood. Anyone approaching it in the dark might not even see it until it was too late.'

Kate had never felt more like hitting someone than she did now, but she bit her lip, and glared at Patricia who studied her drink as if she'd never seen it before.

'We need to alert the searchers,' Kate said to Sue, turning her back on Patricia. She marched to the door, opened it and shouted to the constable outside. 'I want you to stay on guard at this door,' she said, when he hurried over to her, 'and don't let Mrs Carnegie out of your sight.' And without a backward glance at Patricia Carnegie, she marched down the hallway to the front door.

Kate and Sue stood on the doorstep. Over in the wood, flickering lights relieved the darkness, pinpointing where the searchers were. The rain had turned sleety, and the chill in the air was reminiscent of winter, rather than the approach of spring. Kate pulled her collar up, but it didn't relieve the chill that had swept over her when she heard about the quarry.

'If I find out Patricia Carnegie sent that child in the direction of the quarry, I'll have her guts for garters,' she hissed.

Sue said nothing, but the expression on her face indicated she felt the same.

Kate gave herself a shake. Standing here brooding about what she might or might not do wasn't helping to find Megan. She had to alert Inspector Mason to the dangers the quarry represented to both Megan and the searchers.

Inspector Mason stood at the edge of the wood, his point to point airwave set in his hand. He turned at Kate's approach. 'A dog is on its way, in fact, I think the dog van's arrived.'

Kate followed the line of his eyes and watched a police van crunch to a halt in a space that looked hardly big enough to take it. The police handler got out, opened the rear door of the van, and after reaching in to grab the dog's leash, a large German Shepherd, jumped to the ground.

Inspector Mason turned away from Kate to walk over to the handler.

She grabbed his arm, forcing him to stop. 'The searchers need to be alerted . . . ' Kate kept watching the dog.

Mason stopped and turned.

'There's a quarry at the far side of the wood and it's not visible in the dark. The searchers need to be aware it's there.'

'Damn!' He marched over to the dog handler. 'The child's mother is in that car.' He pointed to the far side of the semi-circular area in front of the house. 'She's got an item of clothing for the dog to get the scent.'

He turned abruptly, and with his airwave set at his ear, he strode into the wood.

Kate watched him until the trees swallowed him up, then she turned her attention to the dog handler who was now at the far side of the parking area. A woman got out of the police car and handed him something, and even from where she stood, Kate recognized the bulky form and wild hair of May Fraser.

She groaned. 'That's all we need,' she said to Sue, who stood beside her. 'Try to keep her away from the searchers.'

The gravel crunched beneath her feet as she strode over to join them. She forced a smile to her lips, and said, 'There was no need for you to come here, Mrs Fraser. You might have been better to wait at home.'

May Fraser snorted. 'It's my lassie out there,' she said, 'and what kind of mother would I be if I didn't come along to help.'

The dog handler knelt beside the dog to allow him to sniff the blouse Mrs Fraser had handed him.

'He's got the scent.' He stood up and allowed the dog to sniff around the area, but after a few minutes it was obvious, even to Kate, the dog had not picked up the scent.

'He might have carried her to the hut,' she said, 'maybe we should start there.'

'Right, where is this hut?'

'Follow me,' she said.

May Fraser tagged on behind.

'Sue, maybe you could take a statement from Mrs Fraser,' Kate said. 'There's no need for her to come into the wood, it's not the nicest place, and she'll be far warmer in the car.'

Sue led a reluctant May Fraser to the car while Kate accompanied the dog handler and his dog to the hut in the wood.

Kate watched the dog pick up the scent. At least that confirmed Megan had been here. But where was she now? She could only hope the dog would track her down before she reached the quarry. A cold shiver of fear engulfed her.

Megan stopped to catch her breath. It rasped from her chest and up through her throat, sounding like a death rattle. She was so cold and so wet, she thought she'd never be warm again.

Her head was swimming now and she kept thinking of her mum, aching to be enclosed in her arms. She wouldn't even mind the swearing she would get for not coming home.

She slid down the tree she was leaning on, and sat on the damp moss at its base. If only she could go to sleep and wake up back home, but that was a dream, and her life had become a nightmare.

She heard a dog in the distance, and saw a flickering light. He was looking for her. But he mustn't find her.

Grasping the tree trunk, she hauled herself up onto her feet and stumbled on.

42

Jenny stared at the silent phone and bit her lip. She was near to tears. She liked Bill, and the caller's information was vague about whether Bill had survived the overdose.

Someone would have to attend the scene but there was no one in the office except for herself, and she'd never attended a crime scene on her own before. But first things first, she would have to let her DI know. Kate wouldn't be pleased if she wasn't kept informed.

Kate answered the phone immediately. 'What is it?' She sounded testy.

Jenny struggled to keep her voice steady. 'It's DS Murphy, ma'am.'

'Oh, he's turned up has he. It's not before time.'

'No, ma'am. It's a lot more serious than that.' Jenny tightened her grip on the phone. She had difficulty controlling her hand as well as her voice. She explained the situation while Kate listened.

'Right,' Kate said. 'You need to refer this to the SOCOs and get over to the Carnegie house. Make sure the scene is protected until they get there, gather the family together, and I'll join you as soon as I can get away.'

'Yes, ma'am.'

'Hold it together until I arrive.'

Jenny laid the phone on the desk, aware she'd given Kate a garbled account of the situation. She cursed herself for allowing Kate's terse reply to throw her. Oh well, it couldn't be helped. She hoped Kate wouldn't think she was an idiot.

Kate kept walking out of the wood towards the large semi-circular area outside the house, where all the cars were parked. She could no longer feel the fingers holding the phone to her ear, and as she listened to the voice, her eyes grew bleaker, and the feeling of despair that had swept over her when Patricia Carnegie told her about the quarry, intensified a hundredfold.

She had never felt so alone as she did now, walking through the trees with their waving branches scattering rain over everything. The darkness was intense, although the flickering lights from the torches behind her pierced the darkness like stars in an overcast sky. She could only imagine what Megan must be feeling if she was out there.

Reaching the parked cars, she thrust the phone into her pocket and scanned the area, looking for Sue. She located her at the far side and approached her. 'We've got a situation, I'm going to have to attend another scene. I'll leave you in charge here. I'll be on the end of my phone if you need me,' she hesitated, 'or if you find anything.'

'What is it?' Sue's face showed concern.

'Bill's on his way to hospital, apparently he's in a bad way.' Kate looked out into the darkness. 'Tell me something, did Bill ever take drugs?'

'No, he didn't even dabble.'

'I thought not.'

Sue gave Kate's arm a shake. 'What's happened?'

'He was found in the Carnegie family's kitchen with a needle in his arm. It's an overdose.'

'An overdose of what?'

'I don't know but I fear our killer may have got to him.'

'Why would the killer target him?'

'Maybe he was getting too near the truth. But I have to see for myself before I decide. You'll have to hold things together here while I go and investigate what's happened.'

'Keep me posted.' Sue wrapped her arms round her body. She looked as miserable as Kate felt.

'Of course.' Kate headed for the car. It was squeezed between two police cars and it took all of Kate's driving skills to extricate it from the space. But at last she was free and had it facing the right way, but she still had to drive carefully down the drive which was lined with police cars and vans. One large van forced her onto the grass verge and she prayed it wasn't bordered by a ditch. But once she reached the main road she put her foot down, anxious to get to the Carnegie house as soon as possible.

Sue watched Kate drive off until the car was out of sight. She could hear the searchers beating their slow way through the wood. A search was always slow because it had to be thorough, no bush or thicket could be ignored and it all took time. Maybe the dog would speed things up, provided it retained the scent of the missing girl.

The thought of a water-filled quarry, somewhere out there at the end of the tree line, nagged at Sue, and she knew time was running out. She stared into the wood, imagining Megan running between the trees, while the searchers moved forward at a snails pace.

Turning her collar up and digging her hands into her pockets, she strode towards the trees. She couldn't remain back from the search while a child was missing.

It was darker underneath the dripping branches, the torch lights were further away, and she felt as if she were being swallowed up. She soon reached the hut which was now cordoned off by a ribbon of blue police tape. She nodded at the officer left guarding it until the SOCOs arrived, and continued to plunge further into the wood.

The ground beneath her feet was soggy, The tree branches swayed, and an unending pelt of rain battered through the foliage. The damp and the wet seeped through her clothes, chilling her. It would be easy to get lost here.

Up ahead she heard the searchers, and she was glad of the odd flicker of light piercing the darkness. But she couldn't see or hear the dog and his handler. She hoped the dog would produce results.

She stopped, and stared ahead, trying to put herself in Megan's shoes. What would the girl be likely to do? She wouldn't know the searchers were police and it would be safe to be found by them. She might think it was her captor pursuing her. But what would she do? Would she hide? Or would she run? And if she ran, sooner or later she would reach the quarry.

Sue shivered, and started to walk in the direction of the flickering lights, hoping they would find Megan before the child plunged over the edge of the quarry.

Emma glanced at the clock on the mantel. They seemed to have been sitting in the living room for hours, but it was only 20 minutes since she'd last looked at it. Thoughts whizzed round her head, questions which had no answers. The mystery of why the detective had been in their house. Who had let him in? Why had he overdosed here? If he intended to overdose why not do it somewhere else? She glanced over at Ryan, sitting in a brooding silence in one of the armchairs. Was Ryan involved in this? And if he was, why?

She grasped her mother's hand. It was cold and still, no longer twisting frantically at the material of her skirt, nor rubbing the arm of the settee. It wasn't like Diane. She was too calm, almost as if she were in a trance.

'You feeling OK, Mum?'

Diane's gaze was fixed on the doorway where the policewoman stood guard, and she gave no indication she'd heard Emma.

Ryan shifted uneasily in the armchair at the other side of the room. He had a look on his face Emma had never seen before. Was it fear? Or was it embarrassment? Emma wondered again if he'd had a hand in what had happened to the detective.

The front door opened and a cold breeze wafted round the room. A white clad man walked past the living room door. He looked like something out of a science fiction film, or an operating theatre.

Emma rose and walked over to the policewoman, reaching her in time to see another white suited man walk up the hallway.

'Who are they?' She stared after the man – at least she thought it was a man – watching as he vanished out of sight into the kitchen.

The trace of a smile hovered on the policewoman's lips as she said, 'They're SOCO.'

'What the heck's SOCO?' It seemed to Emma the policewoman was talking a different language.

'Sorry, I should have explained. They're the scene of the crime officers. They need to examine the kitchen where the body was found.'

Emma shuddered. Body? Did that mean the detective was dead? But she was afraid to ask.

'Why do they have to do that?'

'Forensics,' the policewoman said. 'They always do that when a crime's been committed.'

Emma stared at her. She felt her chest tighten and it was difficult to breathe. 'So it's a crime. I thought he'd overdosed.' Her voice sounded strange, even to her.

'That's what we're trying to find out.' The policewoman looked embarrassed. She was probably wondering if she'd said too much.

'What happens now?' Emma wasn't sure why she felt scared.

'CID will want to question you. We're waiting for them to get here.'

'But we've told you all we know already.' Emma took a deep breath. There was no reason for her to feel scared, so she pushed the feeling away, replacing it with annoyance.

'Well you're going to have to tell them as well.'

'I see.' Emma walked back to the settee, subsiding into it with a disgusted sigh. What a damn pain in the neck. All this bloody hassle because that damned detective decided to overdose in their kitchen. She grasped her mother's hand again, stroking it, and wondering how Diane would survive all the upheaval.

43

Kate couldn't help thinking about Megan, stumbling about in the wood in the dark and the rain. The girl must be terrified and Kate was unable to help because she was on her way to another crime scene. She could only hope the searchers would find her before she reached the quarry. She shuddered at the thought. But thinking about it wasn't doing her any good, she had another crime scene to attend, and it was important they nail this sicko who was killing men with lethal injections.

She forced herself to concentrate on her driving, watching the windscreen wipers swish the rain from the windscreen, and trying to avoid staring into approaching headlights which masked the massive puddles forming at the side of the road.

Thoughts rolled round her head while she drove. Why had Murphy been targeted? He wasn't a paedophile. At least she didn't think he was. And why was he in the Carnegie house in the first place? He hadn't told her he was going there. But did Murphy ever tell anyone what he was up to? She was still thinking when she pulled up in front of the house.

Light shone from the front window and the occupants could easily be seen from the street, perhaps it was intentional, or perhaps so much was going on they hadn't thought of it.

She got out of the car and stood for a moment looking around. It was a habit of hers, sizing up her surroundings before she entered a building.

The gate and front door to the house were open, and a policeman was on guard at the door. Well at least they'd got that right. The street, however, was quiet, and with a start

Kate realised it was after nine o'clock and most people would be ensconced in front of their televisions.

A curtain twitched at the house next door. There was always one in every street, a neighbour who knew everything that was going on. Kate made a mental note to speak to the person hiding behind the curtain.

She checked her shoulder bag to ensure she had a notepad and pen, fished out her warrant card, then walked up the path to the front door. She held up the card to the constable, who nodded and stood aside to allow her to enter.

DC Jenny Cartwright met her in the hallway. 'DS Murphy has been taken to hospital, the SOCOs are working in the kitchen, and the Carnegie family are in the living room. PC Fraser,' Jenny indicated with a nod of her head to the constable at the front door, 'along with WPC Cameron took a statement from the family. They're saying they found DS Murphy unconscious in the kitchen when they returned home. They claim to have no idea how he came to be there.'

'Are there any witnesses to confirm their statements?'

'I checked if they'd done a door to door, to see if any of the neighbours saw anything, but apparently they weren't able to get any other officers to the scene, and they needed to protect it.'

'I see.' Kate looked towards the kitchen where two white clad figures were dusting surfaces.

'The needle and syringe were still there, as well as the cup he'd been drinking from. The SOCOs already have them bagged for examination in the lab. There was something else,' Jenny's voice grew more thoughtful, 'two green beads lying on the table. They were like the ones Murphy had me enlarge on the computer. They matched the photo of the beads from the Carnegie file.'

Kate remembered. Murphy had produced the photograph of the necklace that had belonged to Jade Carnegie. The necklace her mother said she'd never be parted from. The beads in it were a direct match to the ones found in the eyes of two different men, and now it seemed they'd been intended for Murphy's eyes as well.

'Good work, Jenny.' Kate smiled at the young officer. Despite Jenny's outward appearance of ineptitude, she'd proved to be an efficient investigator.

Jenny's eyes behind her owlish spectacles glowed with pleasure, but all she said was, 'Thank you, ma'am.'

'Do we know what's happening with DS Murphy?'

'I phoned the hospital. He's still in Accident and Emergency, and they'll be moving him to a ward later. They said the Naloxone should have kicked in by now, but they think there's something else in his system so they're running tests. They said he wouldn't be available to question until they've counteracted everything.'

'Did they give any indication how long that would take?'

'They weren't specific, but they said to check tomorrow.'

Kate mulled over the information, sorting it out in her mind into levels of priority. Murphy's condition would have to be checked. His evidence would be of prime importance. She'd need to talk to the SOCOs, and of course, interview the family. Ideally she'd like to see each one individually but that might not be possible here, and she wasn't sure if she had enough evidence to take them in to Headquarters to interview. If she did that, they might be there most of the night and she was aware of the fragility of Diane Carnegie's mental state. On the other hand, the house was a crime scene, so she couldn't allow them to have the run of it until the SOCOs were finished, and even after that it might be better to preserve the scene for a time.

Coming to a decision, she decided to interview the family together before making her mind up, and to be safe, she'd run it past the procurator fiscal. But if she was going to do that, she'd need all the evidence available, which included anything that neighbours might have seen.

'DC Cartwright, I want you to do the door to door while I interview the family. Take the WPC with you, I'm afraid I can't recall her name . . . '

'It's WPC Cameron, ma'am.'

'Yes, well take her with you and find out if any of the neighbours saw anything. For example, if they have any information on when each one of the Carnegie family arrived home, or if they saw anyone in the house or leaving the house before that. You might find the house on this side,' Kate pointed, 'of particular value. I saw a curtain twitch when I arrived.'

'Yes, ma'am.'

Jenny grabbed her duffle coat from the end of the banister. She walked over to the WPC standing guard at the living room door, shrugging the coat on as she went, then the pair of them left the house. The wind and rain caught Jenny and she pulled her hood over her head. Both of them hunched their shoulders and scurried in the direction of the house Kate had indicated.

Kate remained standing in the hallway watching them, but her mind was on Megan, out there in the dark, the howling wind and the rain. There had been no word from Sue, and she had no idea how the search was proceeding, and whether they would find the girl before she reached the quarry.

Megan couldn't feel her hands or feet, but she continued to run. She could hear sounds behind her and they were closer now. He wasn't alone. She'd heard of rings of men who grabbed girls off the street and did all sorts of horrible things to them. Her breath caught at the back of her throat and she tried to run faster, but the soggy ground clutched at her feet slowing her progress. The trees were thinner here. Maybe she would reach a road, or a house, or something. Anything that would get her out of the clutches of these men.

A root grabbed her foot and she pitched head first onto the ground, wildly flailing her arms in a vain attempt to break her fall. She hit the ground with a thump that winded her. Her face and nose thudded into a muddy patch. She lifted her head and snorted to clear the mud, and that was when she saw a light in the distance. There must be a house or building over there, but it seemed far away and the sounds of the search were getting ever nearer.

She was tired, her arms and legs ached, she couldn't feel her feet and she had an overwhelming desire to give up, to lie there until the men found her. Maybe they wouldn't see her if she lay still, or maybe she could crawl under a bush and hide. But she knew that was impossible, because they had a dog, and even if they didn't find her, the dog would. And if they found her what would they do to her? She shuddered.

The distant light seemed to wink at her and she struggled into a sitting position. She looked back over her shoulder and could see torches blinking through the trees, which meant her hunters were getting nearer. But if she could get to the house before the men reached her, she should be all right because a lighted house meant people. It took all of her strength to scrabble to her feet, but once she was up she had a sudden surge of extra strength and started to run, towards the light and safety.

The trees thinned, and suddenly she was out in the open with grass beneath her feet. The wind whipped at her sodden clothes and hair. The rain battered down on her. But she continued to run, battling through the storm, away from the hunters and towards safety. She had to get there before the hunters reached her.

At that moment the earth vanished beneath her feet and she was unable to suppress the scream, that burst from her lips, when she felt herself falling.

44

'You do the knocking and introduction, and I'll follow up with the questioning,' Jenny said to WPC Cameron.

Walking from the Carnegie house to the neighbouring one Kate had indicated, had been enough time for Jenny to find out the young officer's name was Alison, she had recently graduated from Tulliallan, the Scottish Police College, and this was the first time she'd been involved with a crime of this seriousness.

Before Alison's hand made contact with the door, it swung open.

'I saw you coming.' The man was old and stooped, but his eyes were alert. 'Come in, come in.' He ushered them into a living room cluttered with magazines and newspapers on every available surface, as well as the floor beside an armchair which was obviously where he sat. He collapsed into it and nodding to them, said, 'Take the weight off your feet, the sofa's quite comfortable.'

The sofa was a patterned moquette with sagging cushions and Jenny perched on the edge, fearing it might swallow her if she leaned back. Alison wasn't so careful and had to struggle to regain her balance.

'What a to-do this is,' the man said, his eyes gleaming. 'Never had so much excitement in the street before.'

Jenny glanced at Alison, but the young officer was still struggling out of the depths of the sofa and had obviously forgotten she'd agreed to make the introductions.

Jenny smiled at the man. 'I'm Detective Constable Cartwright, and this is Police Constable Cameron, and we'd like to ask you a few questions.'

'Of course.' The man clasped his hands in his lap, the action making the blue veins on the back more prominent on the parchment-like skin. 'I'd be glad to do anything to help.'

Jenny fished in her shoulder bag for her notebook and a pencil. 'First of all we'd better have your name, and date of birth.'

'Dennis Fisher, and I was born on Christmas day in 1928.'

Jenny scribbled in her notebook. 'That makes you eighty-one. I must say you're remarkably alert for your age.'

Dennis smiled. 'I try to keep active and interested in what's going on.'

'What can you tell us about tonight?'

'I saw it all you know. I saw them all come home and I heard the scream. I stayed at the window, saw the ambulance car, and the ambulance arrive. Saw you lot arrive as well.' He nodded at Alison.

Jenny scribbled more notes. 'That's fine, now did you see anything before they all came home?'

'There was a man. I'd seen him at the house a couple of times. He knocked at the door and someone let him in.'

'What time was that?'

'It was a good while before the news came on the telly. I'd guess about half-past-five, or a quarter-to-six.'

'That was before the family came home?'

'Yes.'

'Did you see who let him into the house?'

'No, I'm afraid not.' He fidgeted in his chair. 'Did he do something? Did he hurt someone? I saw them carry someone out to the ambulance, and I did think he looked a suspicious character.'

'I'm afraid I can't go into details about what happened in the house. But I'm sure the newspapers will report it as soon as they are able.' Jenny paused. 'Now let's get back to what you saw. After the man entered the house, did you see anyone leave?'

'No, I'm afraid not.'

'And it was after that the family came home?'

'That's right. First the lad came home, then about half an hour later Mrs Carnegie and the lass came home. That's when I heard the scream.'

'What time did the son come home?'

'I was watching the BBC News, although the Scottish News hadn't started, it must have been about quarter or twenty-past six.'

'And what time did Mrs Carnegie and her daughter get home?'

'Ah, the Scottish News had just finished so it would be seven o'clock, or maybe five minutes after.'

Jenny scribbled the arrival times in her notebook.

'That's a great help,' she said. 'But after the scream, what did you do?'

'I did think about going out to see if I could help. But I'm not young any more and didn't think it might be a sensible thing to do.' He scratched his chin with long blackened fingernails. 'Anyway, I didn't want to get involved.'

'Did you phone the police? Anything like that?'

He shifted in his chair as if it had suddenly become uncomfortable. 'No,' he said with a note of aggression in his voice, 'as I said, I didn't want to get involved.'

'I see.' Jenny snapped the notebook shut. 'Well, thank you for your time, you've been very helpful.'

Jenny looked over her shoulder when they reached the street, but Mr Fisher's door was closed, although she detected a slight movement in the curtains.

'Come on,' she said to Alison, 'let's get the rest of the neighbours questioned, although I doubt if we'll get anymore than we got here.'

Kate peered into the kitchen. 'Colin?'

One of the white-suited SOCOs looked up. Kate hadn't been entirely sure it was Colin because only the men's eyes showed behind the all encompassing hood and face mask. But something about the way he moved and held himself led her to believe it was him.

'Found anything interesting?' She leaned against the door-frame and waited for him to approach her.

He lowered his face mask and nodded. 'We found the syringe on the table, but it's been touched by Diane Carnegie. Apparently she pulled it out of his arm when they found him here, so I'm not sure whether we'll find any useful prints on it. We may be lucky though. I've also bagged the cup he drank from, it'll need to be fingerprinted and analysed to see if anything was in it.'

Kate nodded. 'I expect there will be, because that's the way this killer works. Drugs them first, then injects them.'

'I've also bagged the green beads we found on the table. If I'm not mistaken they'll be a match for the ones we found in our previous two victims' eyes.' He reached into his evidence case, pulled a bag out, and held it before her. 'What d'you think? Are they the same?'

Kate peered at the beads through the bag covering. 'They certainly seem to be.' She sighed. 'I'll need the house gone over to see if there's any drug paraphernalia as well as more of these beads.'

'Looks like we're going to be here most of the night, I'd better get a move on.' Colin grimaced, pulled his face mask up and turned back to the task in hand.

Kate walked down the hall to the living room, where she could hear the murmur of voices. As soon as she opened the door, it went quiet. Diane sat on the sofa, white and drawn, as silent and still as a statue. Emma, who was sitting beside her, looked up but said nothing, although Kate noticed her hand tighten on her mother's. Ryan was slumped in an armchair with his eyes closed and gave the appearance he hadn't heard her come into the room.

She pulled a chair over from the side of the room and sat. She had no intention of putting herself at a disadvantage by sitting on the sofa beside the two women, nor was she going to risk sitting in an armchair. She needed to maintain a dominant position.

'I'm Detective Inspector Rawlings, and I need to ask you some questions about what happened tonight.'

'We've already told the other police officers all we know.' Emma's voice was belligerent, although her body language reflected weariness.

'Well, you're going to have to tell me all over again, and if you don't do it here, I can easily arrange for you to come to the police station.'

Emma shrugged, but her face reflected what she thought.

Kate dug a notebook and pencil out of her shoulder bag. 'First of all I want to know how Detective Sergeant Murphy came to be here.'

'How should we know? He was here when we arrived.' No doubt the family had already compared notes and Emma seemed to have taken it on herself to be spokesperson.

'Were you the first one home?' Kate deliberately made her voice formal and challenging.

'No, Ryan was. He was here when we got back.'

'Then maybe Ryan can answer the question.'

Ryan opened his eyes. 'I didn't even know he was here until they found him.' He nodded at his mother and sister.

'Someone must have let him in?'

'Well it wasn't me.' Ryan looked as if he was on the point of crying. 'Oh, I know I'm going to get the blame because I was the first one home. But I went straight upstairs because I wanted to shower.'

'It wasn't us either. He was here when we got in.' Emma leaned forward in her chair and glared at Ryan.

'Let me get the facts. You arrived home, when?' Kate addressed the question to Ryan.

'I don't know, it must have been after seven o'clock, but I went straight upstairs and showered.'

Kate wondered if he knew he was repeating himself. 'You were alone?'

'Yes, but I was with someone before I came home, her name's Kara and she works at the club. She could tell you what time I left to come back. And my mum and Emma came in just after me. I wouldn't have had time to do anything.'

Kate turned to Emma. 'And you, what time did you get home?'

'I didn't look at the clock, but it must have been about

half-past sevenish. I was with Mum, we arrived together.'

'Had you been together all evening?'

'No, we bumped into each other at the bus stop. I was coming back from uni and Mum had been at Broughty Ferry. We walked up the road together.'

'Can anyone verify this?'

'Maybe the bus driver, but they're always so busy it's doubtful they'd remember.'

'I expect someone from the university can verify what time you left?'

'I suppose. I was in a lecture. A lot of folk were there, although I wasn't sitting beside anyone I knew.'

'Mrs Carnegie? Is there anyone who can vouch for you at Broughty Ferry?'

At first Kate thought Diane hadn't heard her and was getting ready to repeat her question. But then Diane stirred, and looked at Kate with a blank expression in her eyes.

'No,' she said. 'I was just walking. I saw a group of young folk who gave me cheek but I don't know who they were.'

'I see.' Kate consulted her notes. 'When you got home you went upstairs and showered. Is that right, Ryan?'

'Yes.'

'Did you go anywhere near the kitchen?'

'I've already told you that. I didn't go into the kitchen, nor anywhere else. Just upstairs and into the shower.'

'So, Emma, maybe you can tell me what happened after you walked up the road from the bus, and got to the house.'

'I put my key in the lock but the door swung open, which was unusual, and I thought maybe we had a burglar. I told my mum to wait while I went in, but she followed me. I went into the kitchen and that was where we found him. He was sitting on a chair and was slumped forward on the table, and he had a needle sticking out of his arm.'

'You're sure the needle was still in his arm.'

Diane looked up. 'I removed it,' she whispered. 'I know I shouldn't have touched it, but I was afraid if it was left in it would hurt him further. He was a nice man, he didn't deserve that.'

Kate closed her notebook. 'I think that will do for now. But I'll want to question you again after I've got all the other details.'

'When will be able to leave the living room? I think Mum needs to get to bed, she's exhausted.'

Kate had been wondering, ever since she arrived, what she was going to do. She didn't think it would be appropriate to take them to the station at this time of night, but on the other hand she couldn't allow them the run of the house while forensics were still involved.

'Leave it with me, I'll see if I can arrange somewhere for you to stay.'

Emma stared at her. 'Does that mean we can't have the use of our own house?'

'Not until forensics are finished with it, I'm afraid.'

Kate left the room before Emma had time to argue.

45

The scream echoed through the wood and Sue knew, instinctively, they were too late. Megan had plunged into the quarry. There could be no other reason for the scream.

The light from the torches held by the searchers flickered in front of her and she hurried in their direction. She wanted to run but the trees held her back. However, they didn't seem so thick here, and all of a sudden she was in open ground, the trees behind her and soggy grass embracing her ankles.

Megan must have started to run when she reached this open ground which would be why she hadn't seen the edge of the quarry.

The searchers had now stopped, their torches trained on something below them. Sue heard the murmur of voices as they talked together and shone their torches into the stygian depths. She thought she saw the glint of water, far below.

'She won't stand much chance if she's gone into that,' Sue heard one of the officers say.

'Wait,' she heard another say. 'What's that down there, I saw something white.'

'Where?'

'Over to your right, about a quarter of the way down.'

'I see it. D'you think it could be her?'

'Not sure, but there's something there.'

Sue felt like grabbing one of their torches, but instead, she ordered, 'Everyone move nearer to that area and shine all the torches in that direction so we can get a larger beam of light.'

She moved along with them, and when they were above the section of the quarry where they thought Megan might be, she leaned forward and shouted, 'Are you down there, Megan?'

A faint cry echoed upwards. 'She's there,' Sue said, 'but we'll never get her out of the quarry ourselves.' Without looking up, she snapped, 'Radio it in and get mountain rescue out here, we'll need them. And tell them we'll need a helicopter as well. And tell them to be damn quick, she might fall from whatever she's perched on.'

She waited a moment until she saw one of the officers on his airwave set carrying out her instructions, then she leaned over and shouted down, 'Hang on Megan, we're sending for help and we'll get you out of there as fast as we can.'

Kate listened in silence to Jenny's report. The two officers had been shaking the drips off their wet coats when she emerged from the living room.

'I see,' she said, 'so the neighbours are in agreement DS Murphy was admitted to the house before any of the family came home. That complicates things.' She had been sure Bill's attacker was sitting in the living room, but if the information given was correct that seemed to rule them out. It was possible one of them could have been here, left the house and doubled back. She would have to check their alibis, but in the meantime she had insufficient evidence to hold them further.

'Wait here until I make a couple of phone calls,' she said, 'then I'll tell you what I want you to do.'

Her phone discussion with the procurator fiscal was brief. She reported the stage the investigation had reached, and what she planned to do. The PF agreed with her, and that was that. She had anticipated objections and arguments because they'd got off on the wrong foot, but they hadn't arisen, so when she clicked the phone off it was with a sigh of relief.

Megan and the search party had never been far from her thoughts since she'd left Sue in charge at the search site. It was time to check out what was happening.

'It's Kate,' she said when Sue answered the phone. 'What's happening at your end?'

She listened while Sue made her report, her initial feeling of elation at being told Megan had been found was quickly dampened when the child's situation, perched on a ledge, half-way down the quarry face, was explained to her.

'I'm coming back,' she said. 'I think I've done all I can here.' She clicked off her phone.

She stood considering for a moment, and then turned to Jenny who had been murmuring with Alison in the hall. 'Jenny, I'm going back to the other scene,' she said, 'but there's still work to be done here. I'm going to make you liaison officer with the family for the time being. That means you provide them with support, but it's also important you are careful how you react with them and what you say to them. We don't want them to think we believe in their innocence, because we don't know at this stage that they are. Be supportive but be careful how you phrase your answers to their questions. Can I trust you to do that?'

'Yes, ma'am.'

'The first thing you need to do is find somewhere they can stay the night. Check out with them if they have any friends or relatives. Failing that, get onto the Housing Department's Homeless Section, they might be able to place them in one of their Homeless Units on a temporary basis. And make sure they know we'll want to speak to them again tomorrow.'

'Yes, ma'am.'

Kate grabbed her coat and rushed out of the house, hoping against hope the helicopter and mountain rescue team had arrived at the quarry.

Tears trickled down Megan's face, mixing with the rain. She was frightened and miserable. The ledge had only broken her fall because of the bush growing out from it, and the bush was slipping under her weight. If it gave way, she wasn't sure she would be able to stay on the ledge because there would be nothing for her hands to hang on to. She'd already explored the rock face with her fingers, but it was smooth with no cracks anywhere. All she had to grasp were the branches of the bush.

At first she hadn't been sure what was worse, falling from the ledge or being chased by the men. But it had been a woman who shouted down to her, and she now knew the men looking for her were the police, not the nasty men she had envisaged.

The woman had said help was on its way, but the bush didn't feel secure, and she prayed they would hurry up.

The bush moved again, and she squealed.

46

Kate, clutching her coat, stumbled as she hurried out of the house. She thrust her free hand out in an attempt to grasp the door-frame, missed and found herself holding onto the police constable's arm instead.

'You all right, ma'am,' he said.

Hiding her embarrassment behind a smile, she said, 'Thank you, I'm fine now,' and hurried down the path.

A vicious gust of wind caught her, blasting rain into her face, when she emerged onto the pavement, and she battled down the road to where she'd parked her car. She threw her coat onto the passenger seat, silently cursing herself for not pulling it on before she left the house. But it was too late now, and she was soaked.

She drove fast, reaching Patricia Carnegie's property earlier than she'd anticipated because there was less traffic on the road than there had been previously, and she realized with a start, it was almost midnight. Where had the hours gone?

A helicopter passed overhead as she parked the car, splashing light on the ground, illuminating the trees. She said a prayer under her breath, hoping they would reach Megan before it was too late.

'What's happening?' The woman who accosted her when she got out of the car looked like a witch with her red hair whipping in the wind. 'Nobody's telling me anything.'

'Everything's going to be all right, Mrs Fraser.' Kate tried to sound soothing, which was difficult because she was every bit as anxious as May Fraser.

'That's all right for you to say, but it's not your daughter out there.'

'We're all as concerned as you are to ensure your

daughter's safety.'

'I want to see her.'

'You must have patience and let the rescuers do their job.'

'She's dead, isn't she?' May's voice reached screaming pitch. 'And nobody's telling me.'

'That's not the case,' Kate said, while at the same time hoping the helicopter would be able to winch Megan out of the quarry without mishap.

The helicopter was hovering now, and Kate guessed the rescue operation would have commenced. She wanted to be there to join them, but she couldn't leave May Fraser while she was in such a distressed state.

'What are they doing?' May Fraser whispered.

Kate debated with herself how much she should reveal to Megan's mother, coming to the decision the woman needed to know and she had no right to keep the information from her.

'The helicopter is there to winch Megan up from the place she's fallen.' Kate didn't want to say quarry. 'She's perched on a ledge that's difficult to reach, that's why we need the helicopter. Once they've got her off the ledge, they'll take her to hospital to be checked out.'

'She's not dead then, but she's maybe hurt.'

'Maybe.' Kate put a hand on the woman's shoulder.

May Fraser shuddered. 'I'll want to go with her to the hospital, mind.'

'I'll make sure you're taken there. Now, come on, let's get you sitting in that police car again. It's far too wet to be standing out here.'

The light underneath the circling helicopter flashed down on them illuminating everything in its harsh beam. As it swung over the quarry, Sue saw the black water far below, rippling in the helicopter's down-draft. The position of the child looked even more precarious than Sue had thought. The ledge was small, barely a protuberance on the quarry wall, and the only thing that seemed to be preventing Megan slipping off was a bush, growing from the side of the quarry.

'Hang on, Megan,' Sue shouted down. 'We're going to get you out of there.'

A rope ladder dangled from the circling helicopter, but the wind, which had increased to gale force over the past hour, buffeted the helicopter, and the ladder swung wildly below it.

'They're never going to get her out that way,' a voice muttered behind her.

Sue shivered, because she knew they were right.

A shape appeared on the ladder, but still it swung wildly, and the helicopter was forced to circle away before the man smashed into the quarry wall. The down-draft was fiercer now it was hovering above the group of searchers, and flying low enough for the man to jump to the ground.

He strode over to the group. 'We're not going to be able to winch her out,' he said, 'the wind's too strong.'

'So what now?' Sue shouted over the sound of the helicopter. 'She's not going to be able to hold on much longer.'

'We're going to have to scale down the quarry wall to get her. My mates are bringing down the equipment.'

'Can you do that?' The noise and the wind from the blades had increased and Sue had to shout even louder.

He looked over the edge. 'It's an old sandstone quarry but it shouldn't give us any problems. We'll need somewhere to secure a rope though to haul her out, and this ground's soggy.'

'The trees are back there, will your rope be able to reach them?'

'Sure, no problems.'

By this time the helicopter was a few feet from the ground. It looked bigger now it was lower, a yellow monster with RAF Rescue written on the side. It hovered, the blades still beating furiously, gradually they reduced speed and the fierce wind they'd generated died down. Men loaded with equipment and coiled ropes jumped out.

Sue hurried back to the quarry edge and shouted down to Megan. 'Keep hanging on, Megan. We're sending climbers down to hoist you out, it won't be long now.'

The down-draft from the helicopter blades whipped round Megan, first flattening her against the quarry wall, then threatening to tear her off it. The bush swayed in the wind and she felt it slipping under her weight. She tried hard not to move in case it gave way altogether, but this was increasingly difficult under the force of the wind.

She had a horrible feeling she was never going to get out of here, and only the voice of the woman shouting down to her, gave her hope.

She'd looked down when the helicopter flew overhead, even though the wind from it almost made her lose her grasp, and she could see the ladder was never going to work. It kept hitting the quarry wall. But what was worse, it lit up what was below her. It looked black and horrible, and she was sure it was water because of the ripples on the surface where the wind from the helicopter blades hit it. She knew in her heart she wouldn't survive if the bush gave way.

Her whole body was shivering with the cold and the wet, her hair was plastered to her head dripping huge drops of water down her neck, face and back. It was like being in a cold shower, but worse. Tears streamed down her cheeks, and she desperately wanted her mother. In her mind, she prayed to God, although she didn't believe in him, and she promised to be good from now on. Never again would she defy her mother, nor would she think she knew better and adults were stupid.

The helicopter flew away from the top of the quarry, and the wind stopped buffeting her. She was glad of that, although she didn't want them to go away, because that meant they weren't trying to reach her. She looked up, but all she could see was the wall of rock rising above her and the floodlight from the helicopter flickering at the top.

A voice echoed down to her. 'Keep hanging on, Megan.

We're sending climbers down to hoist you out, it won't be long now.'

The bush creaked, and shifted again.

'Hurry up,' she whispered.

47

As soon as the last man jumped from the helicopter it rose again and headed for the quarry, hovering above it so the searchlight illuminated everything.

'You'll need to clear this area,' one of the rescuers said. 'We'll need room to work.'

'I'll see to it.'

Sue turned to the nearest police officer. 'Get several officers together and clear this area. Send the officers we don't need back to the car park at the house to await further orders, and keep a core group here.'

'Yes, ma'am.' The officer started issuing orders to those nearest to him and gradually the searchers retreated to the wood.

Meanwhile the team of mountain rescuers were attaching ropes to trees, bringing them back like the strands of a spider's web to join up with a curious metal plate with multiple holes. Once these multiple ropes were secured to the joining plate, two thick ropes were attached to feed out the other side. They did this all over again so they now had two sets of rescue ropes.

None of the men stopped working long enough to speak to Sue, and she stayed back, out of their way.

'That's it,' the man in charge said, 'we're almost ready to go, but we'd better take a cradle down because we don't know what kind of state she'll be in.'

Two of the men who had been busy strapping harnesses to their bodies, fastened the ropes to it with massive metal clips, before striding to the edge of the quarry. They lowered themselves over the edge and started the descent, the rope gradually playing out as they went.

'We're on our way down, Megan,' one of them said, 'it

won't be long now until we get you out, hang on tight.'

The first officer to emerge from the wood was the police dog handler, but the flickering lights among the trees indicated others following him.

May Fraser who had been on the point of stepping into the police car, turned to Kate. 'They're coming back, they must have got her.'

Before Kate could stop her the woman ran across the car park to the officers coming out of the wood.

'Have you got her? Where is she?' May Fraser's voice shrieked at one officer.

Kate, who had been hurrying to catch up with the woman, could see the officer's startled face.

'It's all right, Mrs Fraser. I'll find out what's happening,' she said. 'You go back to the car while I talk to the officers.'

'I'm not going nowhere, until I see my Megan.' The woman's voice was obstinate.

Kate turned to the officer. 'What's happening. As you can see, Megan's mother is desperate for news.'

'The rescue team are there, ma'am. We were sent back here to give them more room to work.'

'I want to go to her,' May Fraser said. 'She'll be scared, and kids need their mums when they're scared.'

'It's better if we wait here.' Kate put an arm round the woman's shoulder. 'You heard the officer. The rescue team needs room to work.' Kate led her back to the car. 'I'll wait here with you, and I'll see you're the first to know any developments.'

Kate would have preferred to go through the wood to the rescue site, but she daren't leave Megan's mother. She had no way of knowing what the woman would do if left to her own devices.

The helicopter was back, its light shining into the depths of the quarry. Wind from the blades buffeted her and made the bush sway. Megan could no longer feel her hands or feet, and wasn't sure how long she could remain clinging to the bush.

A man's voice shouted, 'We're on our way down, it won't be long now until we get you out, hang on tight.'

'Please hurry,' she whispered through chattering teeth.

She looked up and could see two shapes scaling down the wall of the cliff to her. One of them held something bulky, which clattered every now and again against the quarry wall.

The bush slid further down the cliff face, and she closed her eyes, praying it would hold until the men reached her.

'You OK, love?'

The voice was next to her ear. She opened her eyes and found a man on either side of her.

She nodded. The bush slipped further, but an arm circled her waist.

'My name's Joe, and we're not going to let you fall, love.'

She nodded again.

'How are your feet and hands? Can you help us climb to the top?'

'Can't feel them,' she whispered.

'OK. I'll tell you what we're going to do. We're going to get you into this cradle and winch you to the top, but you have to trust us, and don't struggle.'

'Yes,' she whispered, anything was better than clinging onto this bush.

The cradle, which looked like a hospital stretcher was positioned between the two men. They carefully lifted her away from the cliff face, laid her in it, and fastened straps round her, so she couldn't move.

'You OK?' Joe said.

She nodded.

'When I give the signal they'll start pulling you to the top. It'll be bumpy but you'll be safe. Try not to wriggle.'

'OK,' she said, her voice barely above a whisper.

'You ready?'

She nodded.

'OK,' he shouted up the cliff face, 'pull her up.'

Megan stifled the scream that bubbled up inside her. Joe had said the cradle was safe and she had to be brave. But each time the cradle banged against the quarry wall Megan imagined it tossing her out, into the depths below. She closed her eyes and prayed.

The buzz of the helicopter reverberated through the wood, although Kate couldn't see it. Then it appeared, rising in the air, shaking the trees. A whirlwind, whipping the leaves in its path, battered the officers standing in the car park as it passed overhead. Kate closed her eyes against the stinging bombardment of gravel.

May Fraser leaned out of the police car and looked up. 'Where's the helicopter going? Does that mean my Megan's OK?'

'Stay here. I'll check,' Kate said.

She strode to the edge of the wood, but there was nothing to be seen yet. Then she saw it, the flicker of a torch, followed by another and another. It wasn't long before the searchers emerged from between the trees, most of them had a bedraggled appearance and seemed glad to have returned from their mission, although a few strode purposefully into the car parking area close to the house. Sue, deep in conversation with Inspector Mason, was one of them.

'Well, did you find out what's happening?'

Kate hadn't heard May Fraser come up behind her.

'I thought I told you to stay in the car.'

'If you think I'm going to bleeding well stay there, you've another think coming,' May Fraser snapped. 'It's my Megan they've been looking for, and I want to know what's happening.'

The woman had a crazed look on her face, emphasized by her fiery hair whipping round her face and head in the wind. She looked like a medieval witch.

'OK,' Kate sighed. 'We'll check it out with my sergeant.'

'Which one's he?'

'She's the one who's just come out of the wood.'

'What you waiting for then?'

Kate sighed and walked over to Sue and Inspector Mason. 'Mrs Fraser's anxious to find out what's happened with Megan.'

The inspector and Sue exchanged glances, obviously deciding who was going to speak. The inspector nodded his consent to Sue, saying, 'I need to see to my officers, I'll catch you in a minute.'

Sue turned to face May Fraser. 'Megan is all right. She'd fallen over the edge of a quarry but the mountain rescue team soon got her out, and they've taken her to Ninewells Hospital to be checked.'

'Is she OK? She's not hurt, or anything?' May Fraser pushed her hair back off her face.

'She's not hurt, although she's very cold and needs to be checked at the hospital.'

'I want to see her. You said I could go with her once she was found.'

Sue placed a restraining hand on the woman's shoulder. 'We thought it best if we got her to hospital quickly, that's why we used the helicopter, but I'll make sure one of the police cars takes you there.'

The police officers had started to disperse to their cars, and Sue beckoned one of them over.

'Can you arrange for Mrs Fraser to be taken to Ninewells Hospital to be with her daughter?'

'Yes, ma'am.' The police officer turned to May Fraser. 'If you come with me we'll get you there right away.'

May Fraser walked off with him without a backward glance, or word of thanks, to Kate and Sue.

'Thanks, Sue, you handled that well,' Kate said. 'I was getting to the end of my tether with that woman.'

'I don't suppose you can blame her,' Sue said. 'It is her daughter after all.'

Inspector Mason joined them. 'Sue's kept me up to speed on your investigation and I've left two men on guard at the hut. I'll also leave a car here to keep an eye on Mrs

Carnegie. I don't trust that woman, and I think she played a part in what went on here.'

'Thank you,' Kate said. 'Your help is most welcome.'

'I've been in touch with SOCO, but they thought it would be best to wait for daylight to start investigating the hut and the surrounding area. In your absence, I agreed. I hope you don't mind?' There was an anxious look on Sue's face.

'No, I don't mind,' Kate said, 'and now, I think you should go home and get some sleep. You've had a pretty exhaustive time here tonight, and there's not much else we can do until morning.'

'Yes, ma'am. I hope you're going to do the same.'

'I'll do a phone check with Jenny first to make sure everything's tied up at that end.'

'Goodnight, ma'am.'

'Team meeting at 9am,' Kate said, and then dialled Jenny's number on her phone.

48

Diane paced the floor, her hands picked at her skirt, and her hair flopped damply against her neck. Jade watched her with a worried frown on her face. Her mother seemed to be disintegrating in front of her eyes.

From the time the police had arrived at the house, Jade had remained in the shadows watching. Ryan seemed to have slid into a world of his own, sitting with a faraway look on his face, while Emma had simply been pathetic. She'd clung to her mother's hand, supposedly to give her support, but it had seemed to Jade, that Emma needed more support for herself than she was able to give Diane.

Jade had itched to take over, but she'd waited her time until the detective with the owl-like specs had driven them to this bed and breakfast place. During the chaos of the move it had been easy to replace Emma, who seemed to have lapsed into an apathetic state. And now she was here, Jade wasn't sure what to do for the best.

She'd thought she was helping Diane by disposing of the detective. What she hadn't reckoned on was the depth of feeling her mother had for him, and watching her mother pace, she grew more and more disturbed. Maybe it would have been better to have allowed Emma to remain in charge, but now she was here she was unwilling to allow Emma back in.

'Why don't you get in the bed? You'll feel better after a sleep.'

Diane stopped pacing momentarily. 'I can't sleep in that bed,' she said. 'Other people have slept there.' She twisted her hands together in a washing motion. 'There's no way it can be clean.'

'Of course it's clean, mum. These places change the

sheets daily.'

Diane made a snorting noise. 'That's what they say, but I don't believe it.'

Jade stared out the window, watching the wind whip the trees in the garden, and the rain spatter off the patio.

'So what are you going to do? You can't pace the floor all night. You'll be a wreck by morning, and that detective said they'll want to question us again. You'll be in no condition to be questioned.'

Diane gave no indication of hearing her, but she joined her daughter at the window. 'Why would anyone want to harm Bill? He was a good man, and he was trying to help us. He said he'd find Jade and I believed him.'

Jade gripped her mother's hand. She opened her mouth to tell Diane she was here, but choked the words back. It wasn't the time. Diane wouldn't understand and it was better to let her think it was Emma in the room with her.

'I don't think he was a good man. I think he was a risk to you. I could see him trying to weasel his way into your affections.' Jade drew breath. 'All he wanted was to get into your pants.'

'Emma!' Diane took a step backwards. 'I've never heard you talk that way before.' Both her tone of voice and the expression on her face indicated the level of shock she felt. 'In any case I don't believe it. He was a nice man.'

Jade clenched her teeth, she'd almost given herself away. She should have known that was something her sister would never say. It was going to be a long night.

It was three in the morning before Kate staggered upstairs. She'd driven home in a trance-like state, it was as well the roads had been quiet. Gavin moved when she slid under the duvet.

'You didn't phone,' he mumbled.

'Sorry,' she said.

She remembered when they were first married he used to wait up for her, worrying about her, and scolding her for not phoning. Over the years, though, he seemed to have grown accustomed to it, probably knowing that once engrossed in a case, nothing else impinged on her consciousness, and the last thing she ever thought about was phoning to let him know she would be late.

She pulled the pillow up round her ears and closed her eyes. But sleep evaded her and she lost count of the number of times she raised her head to look at the clock to find the hands had only moved five or ten minutes.

Outside the wind howled and the rain battered off the windows, and she played over and over in her mind, her vision of what Megan must have felt trapped in the quarry. She stumbled through the wood with her, felt her misery and fear, and wondered if the child's experience would scar her for life.

It was a relief when the hands of the clock indicated seven, and she could throw back the duvet and slide her feet out of the bed. Her head felt woozy, but that would soon clear after she'd had a cup of coffee, and her usual slice of toast. It was all she would have time for if she was to be back in the office by half-past-eight.

A hand gripped Bill's wrist. 'Ah, I see you're awake,' a voice said. 'We're going to take blood for testing.'

Bill turned his head in the direction of the voice, his eyes focusing on the needle and syringe, and he jerked away, trying to get out of Emma's range. Her face loomed over him, familiar and yet not familiar.

'It's all right,' the voice said, 'a slight prick, and it's over.'

'I think he's hallucinating,' another voice said.

All Bill could see was the needle and syringe and Emma's face, although he wasn't sure it was Emma's face. But he knew he couldn't let her stick the needle into him.

'Mr Murphy, you're in hospital now. You're safe. But we do need to take blood. It's the only way we can be sure what else is in your system.' It was a different voice, and Bill turned his head towards it.

When the sharp pain of the needle punctured his flesh, he screamed, 'No!'

A hand grasped his. 'There's nothing to worry about,' the voice said. 'Go back to sleep now until the effects of the drugs wear off.'

Nightmares bedevilled Bill for the rest of the night, and a lot of the time he was unable to distinguish between dreams and reality. He kept seeing Emma slide the needle into his arm and, although he tried to fight it, he was unable to move. Gradually he regained a grip on his senses, but was unable to make his body do what he wanted.

The night seemed to last forever. But when daylight crept through the window at the end of the bed bay, his brain was becoming more functional. He tried to puzzle it out, coming to the conclusion he had been suffering the effects of whatever drug Emma had put in his tea, because heroin would not have had the paralysing effects he'd been experiencing. If it was rohypnol, as he suspected, it would take at least eight hours to wear off. He looked at the clock, but was unable to calculate whether or not the eight hours were up.

The man in the bed opposite was shouting and cursing, and Bill wasn't sure whether he was awake or asleep. Further down, the curtains were drawn round another bed, and Bill could hear the murmur of voices. He lay watching the clock and listening to the curses, and wondering why he was still here. Surely the effects of whatever was in his system would have worn off by now.

He decided it was time he did something about it, so he wiggled his toes, moved his arms and then his legs. Everything seemed to be working. But now came the critical test. Would he be able to stand up? He looked round the ward, but couldn't see any nurses, and guessed they were all busy behind the curtains further down the bed bay. He slid his legs out of the bed and stood, holding on to the side of it for a moment before letting go. So far so good. He took a few steps, swaying slightly, but although his balance wasn't as good as it should be, it was OK.

Now where were his clothes? Locating them inside his bedside locker, he pulled them out and dressed.

At that moment a nurse appeared round the end of the bed bay. 'What are you doing?'

'I'm taking myself out of here.' Bill stared her out.

'But the doctor needs to see you before you can be discharged.'

'Tough,' Bill said, 'because I'm discharging myself. I'm quite at liberty to do that, you know.'

The nurse looked flustered, and Bill felt sorry for her.

'Look,' he continued, 'I don't want to get you in trouble, but I'm going. If you have any papers I need to sign to say I'm discharging myself, get them for me.'

'You shouldn't, you know. You need to be seen first.'

'Just get the papers for me to sign.'

She vanished round the corner of the bed bay, returning a moment later with a bundle of forms.

Bill scribbled his signature where she pointed out it should go, then strode towards the way out.

'We can't be held responsible for anything that happens to you.' The nurse's voice echoed up the ward after him.

49

The ward door swung closed behind Bill. He hesitated for a moment looking at the stairs and the lift doors, and decided on the lift. It rose slowly, transporting Bill from level five to level seven, and freedom.

Bill always found the layout of the hospital strange with most of the wards on lower levels than the main entrance, and miles of corridors to traverse to get anywhere. And now he had to walk an endless corridor before he could leave.

The concourse, when he reached it, was quiet. The shops were shuttered and the only sign of life was the electronic noticeboard suspended from the roof, indicating the times of the next buses. A sleepy receptionist behind the main desk didn't bother raising his head as Bill passed by. Meanwhile, automatic doors swung open on his approach, and he quickened his pace, anxious to leave the hospital behind him.

A blast of bitterly cold air hit him when he stepped outside the centrally heated building. He felt in his pockets for his wallet. It was still there, so he headed for the solitary taxi sitting in the stance, ignoring the bus idling its engine at the bus stop.

Bill paid off the taxi outside police headquarters. Wearily climbing the steps to the entrance doors, he walked through them into a deserted reception area. A policeman on duty nodded to him through the glass division, he nodded back, walked to the lift, pressed the buttons for the entry code, and headed upwards to the team room.

The room was empty, and he collapsed into his chair, glad no one could see him.

Since waking up in the hospital, his brain felt as if it had been through a meat grinder. Thoughts and flashbacks were jumbled together, until he was unsure what was fantasy and what was reality. He tried to concentrate on the previous evening's events. He had gone to Diane's house, but he wasn't sure why. He forced himself to think back to when he got out of the car and walked to the door. So far, so good. In his mind, he raised his hand to knock, and the door opened. Good, he was getting events into some kind of order. He closed his eyes and tried to visualize the person who answered his knock, opening them when he realized it was Emma.

Sadness engulfed him. Emma was such a quiet and self effacing girl, it was difficult to imagine her with a murderous streak.

He closed his eyes again and followed her up the hallway into the kitchen. That was when the flashback kicked in, and all he could see was Jade advancing towards him with the needle and syringe. He tried to move, but his limbs wouldn't do what he wanted, and all he could do was watch.

His eyes snapped open in an effort to dispel the horror, but it was a few moments before he was able to breathe easily again.

So was it Emma, or Jade, who had tried to kill him? Or were they both the same person?

After shaking his head in an effort to clear it, he got up, went to the filing cabinet and brought out the Carnegie file. When he'd looked at it previously he'd concentrated on the police investigation and what happened, but all sorts of meetings had been held. He'd leafed through those, thinking they were unimportant for the current investigation. But maybe it was time he studied them in more depth.

The file was a thick one. He opened it and moved to the section containing the case conference minutes. The Social Work Department had been involved because Emma and Ryan had been children at the time, and there had been concerns because of Diane's fragile mental state. And one thing social workers seemed to delight in was a multitude of meetings. Although, he couldn't blame them for wanting to document everything, considering how much mud was slung at them when things went wrong.

He skimmed the bureaucratic stuff, who was present and how they were involved, and concentrated on what was written about Diane and her children.

Screeds had been written on Diane's mental state, her suicidal thoughts, and whether the children should be taken into care. Ryan was assessed as being young for his age, with no friends, which wasn't surprising, because he didn't like football or anything that resembled rough and tumble activities. He preferred reading, dressing up games, and computers. Emma, on the other hand, was something of a mystery. No one seemed to know her likes or dislikes and she was described as having lived in the shadow of her twin sister.

After the disappearance of her sister, Emma had lapsed into a catatonic state. She spoke very little and the only people she seemed to recognize were her mother and father, and Ryan. At one point consideration was given to admitting her to a mental hospital, but her mother resisted this and insisted she stay at home. However, she did see a psychologist on a regular basis. During her treatment, the psychologist reported times when Emma did not seem to know who she was, and insisted she was Jade. No psychiatric diagnosis was ever given, and Bill got the impression that when Emma recovered from whatever had been ailing her, everyone heaved a sigh of relief.

It was noted in the reports Emma did not know she had suffered a mental breakdown, and was convinced she was the mainstay and support of her family.

Bill closed the file, leaned back in his chair and closed his eyes, while he concentrated on the information he'd read in the file. He'd heard of cases where more than one person resided in the same body. Wasn't there a book called Sybil? Or something like that? Where one person had multiple personalities? The psychologists and psychiatrists gave it a fancy medical name he couldn't remember. He had always thought it a lot of rubbish and put it down to attention seeking, but maybe there was something in it after all. And

266

now, after reading the file, it seemed possible Emma was more disturbed by the disappearance of her sister than anyone had realized, and that over the years she'd settled into the persona of the quieter twin. But if that was the case, who was she? Was she Emma, or was she Jade? On the other hand, maybe there were two of them.

Bill's thoughts went round and round in circles, and he put his head in his hands and groaned. This case had turned out a lot more complex than he'd anticipated.

Jade eventually fell asleep. She'd become frustrated because she couldn't persuade her mother to settle down. She had always been the strongest twin, both physically and emotionally, but now she was forced to admit Emma might have been better in this situation. That admission riled her, she was used to thinking Emma was helpless and hopeless. She spent a restless night, tossing and turning, before deciding to go back into hiding and let Emma take over.

The sheets tangled round Emma's body while she slept and when she woke the wind had dropped taking the rain with it. However the light filtering through the window was grey, bringing the promise of another miserable day.

The room was empty except for her mother pacing it, from door to window and back again. Jade had departed while she was asleep, and Emma had no recollection of her sister's presence in the room.

Emma untangled the sheets from round her legs, and sat up. 'Haven't you slept?'

Diane didn't stop pacing. 'How could I?' Her voice was little more than a murmur. 'I can't stop thinking about Bill Murphy and what happened to him in our house.' Her fingers tightened on the material of her blouse.

'But he's nothing to us. It's not as if he were family or anything.'

'Maybe not, but he was a nice man and he was trying to help.' Diane removed her fingers from her blouse and tugged at her hair. 'It's all my fault.'

'Why is it your fault?'

'If I hadn't asked him to help, all this would never have happened. And now he might be dead because of me.' Diane tugged harder at her hair, pulling a clump out.

Emma sprang out of the bed and grabbed her mother's arm. 'Stop it, Mum. You're hurting yourself.'

'I don't deserve to live.' Diane glared at Emma.

Such was the force of the glare that Emma took a step back and loosened her grip. Her mother had lost it. She had a manic look in her eyes. Without Emma's hand to stop her, Diane returned to tugging her hair. Emma decided that, whether or not her mother approved, it was time to call for medical help.

She rummaged in her pockets for her phone, but it was dead. In all the upheaval she'd forgotten to put it on charge.

'Damn,' she said. She grabbed her clothes, pulled them on, let herself out of the room, closed the door behind her, and hurried along the corridor to tap on Ryan's door.

'What is it?' Ryan was wearing black silk pyjamas that in other circumstances Emma might have thought glamorous.

'I need to borrow your phone.'

'What's wrong with yours?' Ryan started to close the door.

'I need it, Ryan. It's Mum, she's completely lost it, and she's pulling her hair out by the roots. We need to get help for her.'

'Damn, that's all we need. Give me a minute to get clothes on and I'll be right with you.'

Ryan closed his bedroom door and a few moments later reopened it. 'Let me have a word with Mum first,' he said as they ran along the corridor. 'You know how she is about seeing doctors.'

'OK, but we need to hurry. I'm afraid she's going to hurt herself.'

Emma opened the door to the room, but Diane wasn't there.

50

The first thing Kate saw when she strode into the team room was Bill slumped at his desk, with his head resting on his hands.

'Should you be out of hospital?' Her voice was more strident than she meant it to be.

Bill raised his head. 'There's nothing wrong with me. Besides, I can't stand hospitals.'

Kate snorted. 'I'm told that last night you didn't look as if you'd make it until morning. Anyway, I suppose it will save me a journey, because the first thing on my agenda today, was questioning you.'

'I reckoned you might want to do that, so I've been studying the file in order to make sense of what happened.'

'Someone tried to kill you . . . that's what happened.' Kate pulled a chair over to Bill's desk and sat. 'All I need is a name, so I can make an arrest.'

Bill sighed. 'It's not as simple as that.'

'You must know who stuck you full of heroin. Surely it hasn't scrambled your brain that much.'

'That's the bit that doesn't make sense.' Bill tapped the pencil he was holding on the cover of the file. 'That's why I needed to study this.'

Kate felt like strangling Bill, and she didn't disguise the exasperation in her voice. 'Just tell me who.'

'That's it, you see. I'm not sure.'

'Why?'

'Well, I thought it was Emma who let me into the house, she looked like her. But when she came at me with the needle and syringe, it didn't look like Emma at all. It was as if she'd changed into someone else,' Bill hesitated, 'and I wondered if it was Jade.'

'If you're right that means Jade must still be alive.'

Kate thought of the skeletal remains they'd found in the hut on Patricia Carnegie's property. She'd been convinced it must have been Jade in that trunk, but maybe not, maybe it was a different child altogether. They wouldn't know until forensic tests were completed.

'Not necessarily.'

Kate groaned. 'Make up your mind. Either it was Jade or it wasn't.'

Bill opened the file. 'That's why I was reading the case conference reports in the file. Did you know Emma was seen on a regular basis by a psychologist after her sister disappeared?'

'Go on.'

'The notes are full, but what caught my eye were the ones where the psychologist reported times when Emma didn't know who she was and insisted she was Jade. The psychologist put this down to guilt because her sister was no longer there, and she was.'

'Are you saying that Emma may not be Emma? That she's Jade.'

'That's one possibility.'

Bill lapsed into thought. 'The other possibility is Emma is more disturbed than we realized, and both she and her sister are living within the same body. I think there's a medical term for it.'

'You think she's suffering from Multiple Personality Disorder.'

'It's a possibility, because the person who injected me was nothing like the girl who let me into the house.'

'They could be working together.'

'I suppose so, but it doesn't seem likely.'

Kate leaned back in the chair. Why was nothing easy?

If Bill was right, they needed a psychiatrist to assess Emma, or Jade, or whoever the heck she was. If Bill was wrong, and there were two of them, they could end up arresting the wrong girl.

Whatever she decided to do it had all the makings of

being a disaster, and Kate could see her career vanishing down the tubes.

Diane's head ached where she'd torn her hair out. She hadn't meant to tug so hard, but everything was piling up and getting on top of her, and she was tired after pacing the room all night. Her thoughts were jumbled and she couldn't make sense of anything that had happened. How on earth had Bill got into her house? And who had done that dreadful thing to him? She had to get out of here, maybe if she had some fresh air she'd be able to make sense of the whole thing.

She knew Emma would try to stop her leaving so she continued to pace until Emma eventually left the room to consult with Ryan. And Diane knew what they would be discussing. They would be plotting and planning to bring in a doctor to see her. She didn't want anything to do with doctors; she'd had enough the last time.

Emma was hardly out the door before Diane grabbed her coat and handbag. She eased the bedroom door open and waited until after Emma rapped on Ryan's door, and while her daughter's back was turned, she slipped down the stairs and out the front door.

It wasn't far to walk back to her house. Blue police tape stretched between the gateposts and a policeman stood beside the front door. She hesitated for a moment because the car was parked right in front of him, and that was what she'd come back for. However, the police hadn't impounded the car, so there was nothing to stop her taking it.

She took a deep breath and continued to walk. Reaching the car she inserted the key in the lock, nodded at the policeman, and drove off. She was turning the corner at the top of the road before she breathed freely again.

Kate picked up the file from Bill's desk. 'You can't continue with this case, I'll take the file,' she said.

'But it's my case,' Bill protested.

'Not any longer. Don't you see, the minute you became a victim, you also became a witness. There's no way you can remain involved with Diane Carnegie and her family.'

Kate watched Bill's shoulders slump. She knew he had an investment in solving the case, but she couldn't allow him to jeopardize the prosecution by remaining involved.

She laid a hand on his shoulder. 'I'll take responsibility for this case from now on, Bill.' She had never used his first name before when addressing him, but somehow it seemed appropriate on this occasion.

'You're right, of course.' Bill's smile was forced. 'I've marked the relevant passages.'

Kate retreated to her office and opened the file, following Bill's markers to the parts he'd indicated. It made interesting reading and she made a note of the psychologist's name and where she was based. It was too early to phone, but it would be the first thing she did once the team meeting finished.

A tap on her office door interrupted her thoughts. 'Come,' she said, closing the file.

'Everyone's here, ma'am.'

'Thank you, Sue. We'd better get started.'

She rose from her chair, buttoned her jacket, and joined the team where they were gathered at the end of the room, in front of the whiteboard.

'Coffee, ma'am?'

'No, I won't bother for now, let's get on with it. Sue, will you mark up the board?'

Sue lifted a marker. 'Yes, ma'am.'

'Right, let's start with the Carnegie investigation. Jenny, where are we with that?'

Jenny adjusted her spectacles. 'The forensic team finished examining the kitchen where the assault took place before I left last night. They intend to return today to examine the rest of the house. I contacted the Housing Department, but they had no room in any of their Homeless Units, so they placed the family in a bed and breakfast establishment nearby. I've informed them we will have to talk to them again today, and I've added the address of the

B&B to the board.'

'What are they saying, so far?'

'They claim to have no knowledge of what happened in their house, and appear mystified. Diane Carnegie, the mother, claims to have arrived home with her daughter, Emma, and says that was when they found the body,' Jenny looked apologetically at Bill, 'in the kitchen of their home. Furthermore, Diane Carnegie claims she had just returned from Broughty Ferry, where apparently she'd been walking in the vicinity of the beach and castle. Emma Carnegie claims to have been at a lecture at the university, and she returned home by bus. She met her mother at the bus stop and they walked home together. Ryan Carnegie arrived home before his mother and sister, but said he went straight upstairs to shower. He saw a light on in the kitchen and assumed it would be his mother or sister. He did not look in the kitchen.'

Sue marked the information on the whiteboard. 'Ryan arrived home first? Do we have approximate times?'

'None of them are sure, but they all think it was round about 7pm. However, one of the neighbours has given us fairly accurate times. According to him, Ryan arrived home sometime between 18.15 and 18.20 hours. Mrs Carnegie and Emma arrived at 19.00 hours.'

Kate frowned. 'Any possibility one of them could have been in the house earlier, left and then returned?'

'It's possible. Ryan claims to have been with a friend, Kara Ferguson, up until a few minutes before he arrived home. Emma, claims to have been at a university lecture, but couldn't give the name of anyone who saw her. While Mrs Carnegie doesn't seem to have an alibi at all.'

'The alibis need to be checked.' Kate stood and walked to the board to study it more closely. 'We also have DS Murphy with us. I'm sure we're all pleased he's returned from the dead, so to speak. So we have an eye witness to what happened. Unfortunately for Bill, he can no longer be involved in the murder investigation because he is now a witness. I'll speak for him. I've interviewed him and there is confusion in his mind about who assaulted him. He thinks it was Emma who let him into the house, but is not convinced it was Emma who committed the assault. Whoever it was, she looked like Emma, but there were significant differences in manner, and he thinks it may have been Jade who attacked him. However, he has an interesting theory that Emma may be suffering from multiple personality disorder. I'm not totally convinced of that, but I'll be speaking to the psychologist who treated her five years ago.'

Kate studied the board. 'Now for the update on the Megan Fraser case. Sue, would you like to talk it through? Jenny can mark up the board.'

Sue handed the marker to Jenny.

'After an examination of Paul Carnegie's computer it became apparent he had some involvement with Megan Fraser's disappearance. Images of girls were found on his hard drive, and among them were images of Megan. There were also images of his daughter, Jade, who supposedly went missing five years ago. On examining the images it was detected Megan was trussed up in what looked like a garden shed. On the balance of probabilities we obtained a search warrant for Patricia Carnegie's house and grounds. A search was set in motion and we found the shed where Megan had been held, however she was no longer there. During an interview with Mrs Carnegie, we had reason to believe she might have set Megan free and directed her to run to the other side of the wood where she knew there was a quarry. By the time we reached Megan she'd fallen into the quarry and had to be rescued by the RAF mountain rescue team. She was taken to Ninewells Hospital. There are other developments in relation to this case which are not directly linked to Megan, although they are linked to Paul Carnegie. A search of the shed revealed evidence of Megan having been there, but it also led to the finding of skeletal remains enclosed in a large wooden trunk. Forensics intend to examine the scene this morning.'

'Thank you, Sue.' Kate faced the team. 'With reference to the assault on DS Murphy, I want Jenny and Blair to check out the alibis for the Carnegie family. Check the university for anyone who saw Emma at the lecture, and also check in Broughty Ferry to see if anyone saw Diane Carnegie. Get the local uniforms to do a door to door in the area. Find out which bus drivers were on both routes and see if they remember anything. And question Ryan Carnegie's lady friend. I'll talk to the psychologist in relation to Emma, and we wait until all the information is gathered before we do anything.'

Kate drew breath. 'Bill and I will work the Megan Fraser case. Sue, I want you to take charge of the Carnegie case. But first I want you to talk to Megan, find out what she remembers, and find out who helped her get out of the shed and what was said. If I'm not mistaken, Patricia Carnegie had a hand in that, and if that proves to be the case I want her arrested as an accessory. Jenny and Blair, you will report back to Sue. Bill, you're with me.'

51

Kate drummed her fingers on the desk as she waited for the phone to be picked up at the other end. It seemed to be taking forever.

'How can I help you?'

Kate stopped drumming her fingers. 'This is Detective Inspector Rawlings. Can I speak to Dr Murdoch, please?'

'I'll see if she's available.'

Kate couldn't place the music playing while she waited. She wasn't in the mood for soothing music, although her fingers tapped in time with it.

'Dr Murdoch, speaking.' The voice was soft, polite and female.

'I'm Detective Inspector Rawlings, Dr Murdoch, and I'm phoning in relation to Emma Carnegie. I believe you treated her a few years ago.'

There was a short silence. 'I haven't seen Emma for several years, but you must know I cannot give you details concerning a client.'

Kate struggled to keep her voice pleasant, even though she wanted to demand the doctor tell her what she wanted to know. 'Yes,' she said, 'but I wouldn't dream of asking you to disclose anything that wasn't already a matter of record. I've got the file on the investigation of Emma's sister Jade, in front of me, and I wanted to check out one or two things from the case conference minutes at the time.'

'I see.'

'Some of the statements you made at the time you were treating Emma, referred to times when she was confused about who she was, there are also references to times when she claimed to be Jade. I wondered about that.'

'This is typical survivor guilt.' Dr Murdoch's voice was

guarded.

'I understand that, but it did make me wonder whether it might be Multiple Personality Disorder.'

'Hmm, an interesting supposition. It did cross my mind at the time, but the episode did not last long, and Emma lapsed back into her own persona. I had no reason to label her with a Dissociative Personality Disorder label, or as you prefer to call it MPD.'

'Thank you,' Kate said. It was evident no more was to be obtained from Dr Murdoch, but it was enough.

'May I ask why you are requesting this information?'

Kate was tempted to play the doctor at her own game by saying she could not disclose details, however, that would get her nowhere. 'We have an ongoing murder enquiry with a survivor who claims to have been attacked by either Emma or Jade, and we are investigating the possibility Jade has made a reappearance, or that Emma has assumed Jade's persona.'

'I see.'

'I don't suppose there's a possibility you could see Emma on a professional basis?'

'Only if the family, or their GP request it, I'm afraid.' There was a brief silence. 'However, if the court were to request a report I would have to supply it.'

Kate replaced the phone after thanking Dr Murdoch for her help, then leaned back in her chair to consider what her next option would be.

'Damn!' Emma bit her lip. 'I should have watched her. There's no knowing what she'll do in her present frame of mind.'

'Maybe she felt cooped up and stepped out for a breath of fresh air.'

Emma snorted. 'The way she was talking? It's more likely she's headed for the Tay Bridge.'

'You don't think . . . '

'You didn't hear her. You weren't in our room this

morning.' Emma breathed hard, fighting to keep the tears at bay. 'Why do you think I want a doctor to see her? And now it's too late. She's gone.'

Ryan grabbed her arm and shook it. 'We have to find her. She can't be long gone. It only took me a few minutes to throw my clothes on.'

'You're right. If we hurry we might catch her. I bet she's gone home.'

Ryan let go of her arm and ran down the stairs. 'Come on, then.'

Emma grabbed her coat from the clothes rail which served as the room's wardrobe, and hurried after him, not bothering to shut the door behind her.

The street outside was deserted, except for Ryan who was running along it. Emma, who had one arm in the sleeve of her coat, hurriedly thrust the other one in and ran after him.

It didn't take them long to reach their home, but they were dismayed to see the car was gone.

'We're too late,' Ryan said, stopping several houses away from their own.

'Maybe the policeman saw her take it. D'you think we should ask him?'

'I don't know, we were supposed to stay at the bed and breakfast place until the police came back to question us.'

'They didn't actually say that, they said they'd question us again today. It's not as if we're under arrest or anything.' Emma could see Ryan wasn't convinced. 'OK, if you want to be a scaredy cat stay here and I'll go ask him.'

Emma strode towards the policeman. 'I'm looking for my mother,' she said, smiling up at him, 'and I wondered if she'd come back and taken the car. It was parked here last night.'

'Yes, miss. A woman drove off in it about five minutes ago. She headed that way.' He nodded in the direction of Clepington Road.

'Thank you, officer.' Emma smiled at him again, before returning to where Ryan stood shuffling his feet.

'She's gone.'

'What do we do now?'

'Look for her of course.'

'But where do we start?'

Where indeed, thought Emma. But she wouldn't rest until she found her mother and knew she was safe.

Noise in the office was part of everyday life, voices talking and laughing, chair legs scraping along the floor, hurrying feet, the jangle of phones, the gurgle of the coffee machine dispensing its sludge, even Kate issuing her orders – so the sudden silence once the team left, jangled Bill's nerves. Everyone had something to do, apart from him. He walked the length of the room and stood in front of the whiteboard, noting the new details that had been added.

The bed and breakfast establishment where the Carnegie family had been placed was one of the good ones and he was glad of that, knowing Diane's fetish for cleanliness. However, he couldn't help wondering how she had settled, and how all this was affecting her. It would be worse when they arrested Emma, and that would only be a matter of time. Diane would need support and Bill wasn't sure whether Ryan would be up to it.

He wandered back to his desk and sat down, but he was restless and couldn't sit still. He wanted to be out following the investigation, but Kate had shackled him to the office and he didn't like it. He moved papers round on his desk, lined up his pens and pencils, played with the computer mouse, and pondered whether he should defy her and go. However, there had been an edge to her voice that made him wary.

He hadn't smoked for over two years but the sudden urge for a fag was irresistible. He glared at the line of pencils, chose one roughly the size of a cigarette, stuck the end in his mouth and sucked. The taste of wood and lead stuck to his tongue, no replacement for the smoke he desired, and he crunched his teeth on it in disgust.

The sound of Kate's office door opening made him look

up, and he listened to the clack of her heels as she walked towards him. He laid the pencil he'd been chewing on the desk.

'The psychologist wasn't much help, although she more or less confirmed your theory about MPD. Says she can't assess Emma without a referral from the GP, or a court order.'

'The PF could ask for a court report.' Bill discreetly removed a piece of wood stuck to his tongue.

'We'd have to arrest her first. And who do we arrest? Emma or Jade? I'll need to think about it. Meantime there's something I want you to see. Get your jacket.'

The park bench was wet but Diane didn't feel it, nor did she feel the coldness of the wind whipping the edges of her coat. She had driven here in a daze to this place she had always come to with Jade, Emma and Ryan. It was a place with happy memories, a place where they had been a family. She could remember their squeals of delight as they tackled the equipment in the adventure playground, and after they tired of that she'd run races with them on the grassy area overlooked by Camperdown House, but without fail they had always ended up here beside the pond.

Today the water in the pond was grey, not blue as she remembered it, and the surface was choppy with ripples. But it didn't matter, this was a place of peace, a place where she could think. And she had so much to think about. Her brain ached with it.

One of her family had attacked Bill Murphy, of that she was certain. Someone let him into their home and tried to murder him, maybe they had murdered him, because she didn't know if he was alive or dead. A tear coursed down her cheek. She'd liked him, and she thought he liked her. There had been something in his eyes, and it was more than concern. But if he were alive, how could she face him, when someone from her family had tried to kill him.

She tried hard to think of Ryan and Emma. Which one of

them was capable of this? But no matter how hard she thought, she couldn't imagine either of them doing it.

There was only one thing for it, she would have to find out if Bill Murphy had survived the attack, and if he had, she would ask him who did it.

52

The large white forensics van was parked at the edge of the wood. Kate drew up behind it and rammed the brake on. She got out of the car and gestured to Bill to follow her.

'Why are we here?' Bill swung the car door open and levered himself out of the passenger seat.

He had spent the journey trying to puzzle out what Kate was up to, but he hadn't wanted to prod, and she hadn't been forthcoming. Now they had arrived he was even more puzzled, considering she had instructed him to have no more involvement with the Carnegie case.

'I want your opinion on the remains we found.'

She strode round the front of the white van and out of sight.

Bill slammed the car door shut. The house looked the same as it had when they'd interviewed Patricia Carnegie, but there was no sign of her today. It had a deserted feel, except for the policeman on guard at the door, and the car parked on the gravel area. The grass bordering it was a churned up mess of mud, the only signs of last night's activity. He should have been part of the search and rescue, but Emma Carnegie had put paid to that.

He walked round the van and stood on the edge of the wood. The trees, clustering closely together, with their branches weighed down by last night's rain, added to the darkness beneath the canopy of leaves, giving it an eerie feel. Bill shivered, imagining what it would feel like to be lost in there.

There was no visible path between the trees and Bill stared into the gloom, reluctant to set foot in this alien territory. Give him the tenements and the sink estates any day, he was out of his depth here.

Kate hadn't hesitated though, she'd plunged into the wood without a second thought, and he felt too embarrassed not to follow her. Sounds of her moving among the trees drifted back to him, although he couldn't see her.

Taking a deep breath he stepped off the grass and into the wood and followed the sounds.

The ground felt different under the trees. It had a spongy feel and his feet kept sinking into the moss. It was no longer raining, it had stopped sometime during the night, but the ground was still soggy and the trees dripped. Bill stumbled on and was soaked through by the time he reached the shed.

One white-clad figure was examining the ground outside, and inside were two others in white boiler suits. One of them bent over the wooden chest at the rear wall of the shed and pointed something out to Kate.

Bill joined them. 'What was it you wanted my opinion on?'

'I wanted you to view the remains before they're taken away for forensic examination,' Kate said. 'The skeleton is as we found it, and seems to have been arranged with care. There are fragments of her clothing and a necklace round the neck. I'm not sure but I think we may have found the missing Carnegie girl.'

Bill knelt down and stared at the small sized skeleton arranged on the red velvet cushion. The clothes looked like part of a school uniform, and the necklace was coral. He rummaged in his pocket for his iPhone and snapped a photograph of the necklace.

'I think you may be right,' he said, returning the phone to his pocket.

'Diane Carnegie told me she gave each twin a necklace on their eleventh birthday. Jade was given a jade necklace and Emma got a coral one. Diane Carnegie is the only person who can confirm if this was Emma's necklace.'

'If it is,' Kate said, 'that means the body could be that of Emma Carnegie, not Jade, and the girl we think of as Emma is actually Jade.'

'On the other hand, the girls were known to swap

identities from time to time, to confuse their teachers.'

Kate's shoulders slumped. 'There's nothing easy about this case, and it's not getting any better.'

The white-clad SOCO who had been quiet up to now, leaned over and said, 'I'll get an evidence bag for the necklace. It won't be needed for the forensic examination of the body.'

He went over to his crime scene kit box, selected an evidence bag, returned to the body and gently removed the coral necklace. He bagged it and handed it to Kate.

'Thanks,' she said, and stood up. 'I reckon we need to get Diane Carnegie to look at this. We'll do it when the Carnegie family are brought in for questioning.'

'What about Patricia Carnegie?' Bill nodded towards the house as they left the wood.

'As soon as we hear what Megan has to say I'll be issuing a warrant for her arrest, but I'll get the local officers to bring her in.'

Diane had no idea how long she sat on the park bench, watching the ripples of water on the pond, her thoughts going round and round in circles and always coming to the same conclusion.

The dampness from the bench had seeped through her coat, her hands and feet were frozen, and her body was chilled. She struggled up, aware her limbs were stiff and aching, and hobbled back to the car.

Her fingers were numb and it took a few minutes to unlock the car and ease herself into the driving seat. Then she couldn't start the car until her shivering stopped. But eventually she drove off, heading for Dundee Police Headquarters. Someone would be able to tell her what had happened to Bill Murphy.

The parking area was full, but she managed to squeeze into a tiny space at the top, partially blocking the vehicle next to her. She switched off the engine then slumped back in the seat, biting her lips and wringing her hands, reluctant to leave the car.

Panic overwhelmed her. She could hardly breathe. What if he was dead?

But she'd watched them put him in the ambulance last night and his head hadn't been covered. Surely that meant he wasn't dead. And if he wasn't dead, what did that mean for her family? And did she really want to find out? But maybe he was dead. He could have died at the hospital or on the way there.

Her fingers reached for her hair and she pulled it. She didn't want him to be dead. She liked him, and she thought he liked her. But what did that matter when her family were at risk.

She groaned and pulled her head down onto the steering wheel, tugging and pulling at her hair. Her thoughts were whirling again, so fast she couldn't think straight.

'Oh, God,' she said, 'tell me what to do.'

Bill slumped into his chair. He wasn't feeling his normal bouncy self, probably the drugs working their way out of his system.

Sue laid her coffee cup on the desk and looked over to him. 'You feeling OK?'

His head felt too heavy for his shoulders, but he risked a nod. 'Disorientated, that's all.'

'Hmm.'

It was evident Sue didn't believe him, but she returned to writing what Bill guessed was her report on Megan's interview. He had a problem with paperwork but Sue liked to keep on top of it.

Kate strode over to Sue's desk. 'Did you manage to interview Megan?'

Sue grinned. 'I had to do battle with her mother and one of the doctors first,' she said. 'But Megan seemed recovered and was able to give me the details. I've written it up for you.' She gestured to the paper on her desk. 'It's in longhand, I'm afraid, haven't had time to put it into the computer yet.'

Kate picked up the piece of paper and started reading. 'Did she say anything about Patricia Carnegie?'

'She said a woman let her out of the shed and told her to run in the opposite direction to the house, but unfortunately she couldn't see her face and didn't think she could identify her.'

'Damn,' Kate said. 'I don't think that will be enough for the PF to authorize an arrest, and if I run with it without her approval I'll get my fingers slapped again.'

Bill hid a grin. He'd have been tempted to arrest Patricia Carnegie anyway, although he agreed with Kate, the PF would probably refuse to prosecute her.

The phone rang. Kate and Sue were still discussing the report so Bill picked up the receiver.

'Someone at reception wanting to talk to Bill Murphy.'

'It's Bill here. What's it about?'

'Sorry, don't know. She wouldn't give her name or anything, but she looks pretty distressed.'

'OK, I'll come down.'

Bill left the room, muttering to Kate. 'Someone at reception. I'll take it.'

Kate nodded, and Bill hurried out of the room before she asked who it was. In any case he didn't know, although he thought it might be Diane.

'Well, where is she?' Bill asked when he got to reception.

'Outside.' The officer nodded at the doors. 'After she asked for you, she ran off.'

Bill hurried outside and stood at the top of the steps surveying the parked cars. It only took him a moment to spot Diane, walking with her head down and shoulders slumped.

He ran down the steps and along the pavement until he caught up with her, but she seemed oblivious to him.

'Diane,' he said, hoping she would stop, but she kept on walking.

'Stop, Diane. I need to speak to you.' He reached out, grasped her arm and turned her to face him. She looked even more haggard than usual. Tears streamed down her cheeks and her eyes seemed to have sunk into her head. He could feel her pain and wanted to pull her into his arms and hug her, until all the hurt she was feeling went away. But he knew he couldn't do that, not yet anyway, and maybe never.

'Thank goodness, you're alive,' she whispered. 'I am sorry, it's all my fault.'

He gave her a small shake, 'It's not your fault. It could never be your fault.'

He stood for a moment, looking into her eyes. 'You asked to see me.'

'I wanted to know you were safe.' She looked away from him. 'It should never have happened and it's all my fault.'

'I told you before, it's not your fault. You can't be held responsible for what someone else does.'

'Tell me one thing.' Diane hesitated, her eyes bleak. 'Which of my children was it?'

'You're shivering,' Bill said, 'we'll talk in the car, out of this cold wind.'

Once they were seated in the car, Diane looked at him. 'You didn't answer my question. I want to know which one of them was responsible for . . . ' her voice tailed off.

Bill reached over and grasped her hand. 'Emma,' he said, 'although she changed and I started to think she might be Jade.'

'Oh!' Diane stared out of the windscreen, but her eyes shone with tears and Bill was sure she wasn't seeing anything.

'It won't be long before Emma is arrested.' His hand tightened on hers. 'It's inevitable.'

'But you said it might not be Emma,' she paused, 'I always said Jade had returned.'

'But you don't want it to be Jade either.'

'No,' she said. 'I don't want it to be any of my children.' She pulled her hand from his grasp and raised it to her face. The tears were falling now, and she brushed at them with the back of her hand.

Bill hesitated before he spoke again, unwilling to add to her heartbreak, but he couldn't put it off any longer.

'Whether it was Emma or Jade, I don't know, but we're not talking about two people here.'

'What do you mean?'

'We've found the remains of a body, which we're pretty sure is your daughter, although we still have to wait for forensics to confirm it.'

Diane moaned and shrank back in her seat, giving the impression she'd grown smaller.

'I have something I want you to look at.' Bill took his iPhone out of his pocket. 'I took a photograph of this and I wanted to know if you recognize it.'

He switched the display on, found the photograph he was looking for, and held it out to her.

Diane stared at the picture of the coral necklace, then took the phone from him and cradled it to her breast, hunching over it and crying.

'Where did you find her?'

'The remains were in a cabin trunk, in a shed on Patricia Carnegie's property. We think your ex-husband was responsible.'

'Bloody Paul. I always suspected he knew more than he was telling.'

'I need you to tell me if you recognize it, Diane.' Bill cringed, feeling like a complete bastard.

'It's Emma's necklace.' Diane's face showed the depths of her misery and confusion. 'But how can that be? It was Jade who went missing, not Emma.'

'I don't know. All I know is that this necklace was round her neck.'

'When they do the forensic testing, will they be able to tell who it is?'

'They'll do DNA, so they'll be able to confirm the identity. But Emma and Jade are identical twins so they share the same DNA. I don't know if they'll be able to distinguish between them.'

'I see.' She sat up straight in the seat and handed him his phone. 'You've told me all I wanted to know, please leave me now. I need to go home.'

'I'll drive you.'

'No, I need to be on my own now.'

Bill got out of the car and watched her drive off. Worry nagged at him, and he hoped she wouldn't do anything rash. However, there was nothing more he could do. He hunched his shoulders and returned to the office.

53

Diane slammed on the brakes, she'd almost driven through a red light. The car stopped, marginally over the stop line, and she slumped back in her seat and closed her eyes. What was she going to do? Emma was her daughter and she did love her, even though she'd had problems relating to her following Jade's disappearance. Now she didn't even know whether Emma was Emma, or whether she'd been Jade all along.

The car behind her honked and she caught a glimpse of a furious face in her rear mirror. The traffic lights had turned to green and she hadn't noticed. She rammed the car into gear and drove off.

Reaching the bed and breakfast place, she drove up the narrow entry lane at the side and parked the car in the tiny car park at the rear of the building.

Her room was empty. She wandered along the corridor to Ryan's room, but that was empty as well. Her breathing quickened. Maybe they'd already been taken away by the police to be interrogated. Maybe she was too late and Emma was already languishing in a police cell.

Her thoughts ran riot and she started to pace again, backwards and forwards in Ryan's room, then several times along the length of the corridor.

She heard feet on the stairs and hurried to the top, but it wasn't her son or daughter, just a young girl who looked as if she should have been at school, pulling a toddler along by the hand. The girl avoided Diane's eyes, but turned round to stare at her before she entered one of the rooms.

Diane cringed. There had been fear in the girl's eyes. She went into her own room and looked at herself in the floor length mirror on the back of the door. She wasn't a pretty picture. Her clothes were wet and stained, her hair stuck out from her head where she'd been tugging it, and her face was white and haggard, with inset eyes staring back at her with a manic look. No wonder the girl had been afraid.

She pulled a chair over to the window and slumped into it, there was nothing she could do until Emma came back, or she had information where to find her.

Kate replaced the phone with a sigh. It was as she thought. The procurator fiscal was against arresting Patricia Carnegie. 'There's not enough evidence to stand up in court,' she'd said. 'We'll never get a conviction so it would be uneconomic to prosecute, and it would be another charge the public purse would have to bear.'

'Damn,' Kate said, leaning back in the chair. Her eyes felt full of grit, and she closed them, opening them again when she felt sleep threatening to overcome her. She stood up, because she knew if she remained seated she would give in to the desire to sleep, and walked to the door of her office. Bill was back, sitting at his desk. He had the dejected look and demeanour of a much older man. The drug overdose had evidently left its mark on him.

She walked over to his desk. 'You should go home,' she said. 'You look terrible.'

Sue looked up. 'I've already told him, but he's a stubborn blighter.'

Bill shrugged. 'What's to go home for? I'm better off here.'

Kate couldn't help feeling sympathy for Bill, he had such a pathetic look on his face. Realizing she didn't know anything about him other than he was an officer in her team, she wondered if her initial disapproval of his sloppy appearance had got them off to a bad start. She would have to rectify that, find out more about him, and maybe they might find some common ground.

'What happens now?' Bill fiddled with the pencils on his desk.

'The PF says we don't have enough evidence to charge Patricia Carnegie, and she wants us to wait until the information on the alibis comes back before we arrest Emma. She wants a watertight case against her.'

'Isn't there enough already?'

'There's enough, but it's this confusion between Emma and Jade that's worrying her. I suggested she commission a report from the psychologist, and she's thinking about it. In the meantime she wants a full report with all evidence detailed before we make a move.'

Emma and Ryan walked up the street.

'We've done all we can. We've looked all over and she's nowhere to be found.' Emma had difficulty keeping the tremor out of her voice.

Ryan shrugged.

The bed and breakfast place looked like a small hotel or an old fashioned boarding house. They walked up the path, went in and climbed the stairs. Ryan kept on walking along the corridor as Emma opened the door to the room she shared with her mother.

'She's here.'

Ryan stopped and came back.

'Thank goodness you're safe,' he said. 'We were worried.'

Diane looked at him with the glimmer of a smile. 'Of course I'm safe, but I need a word with Emma, in private. D'you mind?'

'That's OK, I'll be in my room if you need me.' Ryan closed the door behind him.

Diane sighed. 'Sit down, we need to talk.'

Emma dragged a chair over and sat. Her mother looked dreadful. She looked older than her years. Her hair was a mess, her complexion had an unnatural pallor, and her eyes were sunk into her head and dark-rimmed.

'What is it? What's wrong?'

'You expect me to believe you don't know what's

wrong?'

'I haven't a clue.'

'You were the one who attacked Bill Murphy, and left him for dead.' Diane's voice was flat.

'That's not true.' Emma stared at her mother, a look of horror on her face. 'I was at a lecture, I met you off the bus.' Diane didn't look at her.

'Are you sure about that?' Diane's eyes brimmed with tears. 'When you were thirteen, after Jade vanished, you had an episode where you acted like a zombie. You wouldn't speak to anyone, or do anything. All you did was lie in your bed and stare at something no one else could see. Do you remember?'

'No, that's not what happened. I was the one who supported everyone else.'

'No, Emma, that's what you've always thought, but what I'm telling you is the truth about what actually happened.' Diane brushed tears away from her face with the back of her hand. 'There were also times when you told me you were Jade, and I believed you, because you weren't Emma any more. You really were Jade. And after a time,' Diane's voice broke and she struggled to continue speaking, 'you became Emma again, and you didn't remember being Jade. I didn't tell you at the time because I liked it when Jade came back.'

Emma's mind whirled. What her mother was saying couldn't possibly be true. She would have remembered if she'd ever acted like Jade. They'd done it often enough when they were smaller, pretending to be each other.

'That's not true. It can't be true.' Emma couldn't keep the anguish out of her voice.

'I'm afraid it is.' Diane's shoulders shook. 'And now you've done this terrible thing.'

'I didn't, I couldn't. I was at the lecture.' Her voice tailed off as the memory of the lecture returned. She'd gone to the lecture theatre and taken her seat in the middle of the row, but she'd felt funny and had pushed past the others in the row to get out. After that she couldn't remember anything until she met her mother at the bus stop. There was a gap.

She remembered now, the lecture had started at four o'clock. It had been seven when she met her mother, and her feet had been so wet they squelched in her shoes.

There had been other gaps as well. Sometimes she lost an hour or two, and occasionally a whole afternoon. Then there were the times when she returned home to find her computer on when she was sure it should have been switched off.

She shuddered. Memories flickered in and out of her brain. Strange memories. Memories that didn't belong to her.

'It's not true, it's not, it's not.'

'But it is true. And the police know because Bill Murphy survived and was able to remember your attack on him.'

Emma stared at her mother. The feeling of horror creeping up on her intensified.

'They'll be coming to arrest you soon.'

'What can I do?'

'Take the car keys, get as far away from here as possible.' Diane thrust the keys into her hand. 'Don't tell Ryan, just go.'

The keys bit into the palm of Emma's hand. 'I don't want to go.'

'You must, it's that or spend the rest of your life in prison.'

Emma swallowed. She struggled for breath, her pulse beat loudly in her ears, and she thought she was going to pass out. She pulled herself together with an effort, and stood up.

'Go, go now,' her mother said.

She left the room without a backward glance, although she thought she heard a faint, 'I love you,' as she rushed down the stairs and out of the building.

54

Kate gathered the papers in front of her and listed the evidence in bullet points on a spare piece of paper before keying it in to her computer. She needed to make her report to the PF as tight as possible, but when she looked at it she wondered if she had enough.

The crucial pieces of evidence were the alibis and Bill's testimony. The problem was Bill wasn't entirely sure whether it was Emma or Jade who had attacked him. His theory of Multiple Personality Disorder looked like the ramblings of someone affected by drugs, which he had been. It would need a report from the psychologist to make that stand up in court.

The alibis were also vague. No one had seen Diane at Broughty Ferry and none of the bus drivers on that route could remember her. Ryan's alibi seemed to stand up, but a good prosecutor could easily make short work of that, and no witnesses were able to verify Emma's attendance at a late lecture, although several people had seen her at an earlier one.

'Damn,' Kate muttered, but no matter how she shuffled the reports the team had done for her, or rephrased her own report, she couldn't make it any better. 'It'll have to do.' She added her recommendation and pressed print, hoping the PF would see things the way she did.

Gathering up the sheets of paper, she stuck them in an envelope, scrawled the PFs name and address on it and took it out to the team.

'Blair,' she said. 'Will you deliver this to the PFs office. I need her decision as soon as possible.'

Blair grabbed his jacket. 'Yes, ma'am.'

Kate nodded and walked to the coffee machine. The

liquid sludge it delivered was awful, but she'd been fighting the urge to sleep all day and it was better than nothing.

Sue joined her. 'Are we bringing the Carnegies in for questioning?'

'I'd like to, but I reckon we'd better wait for the PF's take on our case.'

'Damned bureaucracy,' Bill muttered behind her.

'I agree,' Kate said, 'but I've already had my fingers rapped about not keeping her in the loop, and I don't want them rapped again.'

'But surely we have a good enough case.' Sue filled a paper cup with coffee.

'I think so, but whether the PF thinks so is another matter. She's the one who will have to prosecute and it depends on how much of a risk taker she is.'

Emma's mind whirled as she ran down the stairs and jumped in the car. She threw her shoulder bag in the passenger seat, fastened her seat belt and turned the key in the ignition.

Her mother's voice echoed in her mind. 'You must go, or spend the rest of your life in prison.'

She pressed her foot harder on the accelerator, then eased it off again. It wouldn't do to be stopped for speeding, and she didn't want to draw attention to herself.

She drove around for ages, unaware of where she was or where she was going. Twice she saw a police car, and on each occasion her heart pounded in her chest and her palms exuded sweat.

It was dark now, and as the hours passed the traffic thinned. The clock on the dashboard read ten past three and she hadn't seen another car for some time.

She drove onto the Tay Bridge and stopped the car in the middle, got out and leaned over the railing.

The water below looked black and bottomless, moonlight glinted off the waves, otherwise she might not have known there was any water there.

She hoisted herself up and swung her feet over so she

was sitting on the rail, looking down at the water. It had a hypnotic effect, seeming to call her, while a voice in her head taunted. 'You're too weak. You don't have the guts.'

Her hold on reality weakened and, for the first time, she was aware of Jade trying to gain control. She fought it. 'I am Emma,' she muttered. 'I am not Jade.'

The flash of headlights approached, and the car slowed when it reached her. She looked over her shoulder, smiled at the driver, leaned forward, and she was gone.

It was morning before the police came to tell Diane that Emma had been seen jumping off the Tay Bridge, but as yet no body had been found. They located her shoulder bag in the car.

'I'm so sorry for your loss,' the policewoman said before she left.

Diane nodded and clutched Ryan's arm. Now she had lost both daughters and Ryan was all she had left.

'Why would she do that?' Ryan's voice was troubled. 'She seemed all right, earlier on.'

'I should have told you.'

Diane didn't know where to start. How to explain things to Ryan when she herself didn't understand what was going on in Emma's mind. Maybe if she'd paid more attention to her daughter she could have prevented what happened. If she hadn't been so tied up in her search for Jade, she might have seen signs, and things wouldn't have escalated the way they did.

'Told me what?'

'The police were going to charge her with the assault on the policeman. And maybe other things as well.'

'Emma! I don't believe it. She was such a mouse.'

'They have proof.' Diane let go of Ryan's arm and walked to the window, staring out with unseeing eyes. 'Bill Murphy survived, and he told me it was Emma who attacked him.'

'The state he was in, it's a wonder he can remember

anything.'

'Emma's death is my fault, because I confronted her with it and told her to go before she was arrested.'

Ryan joined her at the window and wrapped his arms round her.

'Oh, Mum! It's not your fault. Emma made her own decisions, she always did. You can't blame yourself.'

'But I do, and now she's gone, and there's only you and me.'

Ryan's arms tightened round her. 'We have each other,' he said, 'and I'll look after you.'

Diane nodded, but she wasn't convinced. She would always blame herself, and she would have to live with it.

55

Two months later
Bill placed his report on Kate's desk.
She looked up and smiled at him. 'It's seven o'clock, we're both mad to be still working,' she said.

'I suppose, but I knew you needed this before your meeting with the PF tomorrow.' A wry smile twisted Bill's lips. Not so long ago he'd have made it a point not to do the report simply because Kate had been such a bitch. But she'd mellowed over the past two months and, although they'd never be bosom buddies, their relationship had improved.

'You should go home now.' Kate clipped Bill's report onto the back of her own.

Bill shrugged. 'There's not much waiting for me at home. An empty flat, a bit of hard cheese in the fridge . . . '

'No mates you can go and have a pint with?'

'Not really. Before Andy had his heart attack we'd go for a quick one when we finished up here, but he's still recovering so that's gone down the tubes for now.'

'Fancy a pint with me?'

'Sure, why not.'

'Only a quick one mind, because I'll need to get home at a reasonable time.'

A blast of music hit them when they entered the pub. 'I forgot,' Bill said, 'they always have a group playing on a Friday night. If it's too noisy . . . '

'It's fine, I don't mind.'

They sat in a companionable silence, nursing their pints.

'That Carnegie affair was a rum do,' Kate said.

Bill nodded. 'Pity it ended the way it did. I would have liked to see what a court made of it.'

His mind drifted to Diane, and he wondered how she was

299

coping. He should have gone to see her after everything was wrapped up, but the problem was, that even with Emma's death there was still so much to do to wind up the case.

'I would have liked to charge Patricia Carnegie as an accessory to the abduction if nothing else, but the PF wouldn't wear it. Not enough evidence she said.'

'That's bureaucracy for you. The old ways of policing have gone, and we're all turning into bloody pen-pushers.'

Kate shrugged. 'The higher you go in the profession the worse it gets. Give thanks you're still a sergeant.'

'I guess you're right. I wouldn't like your job. Too many people you have to kow-tow to.'

Kate gulped the rest of her lager. 'Got to go. See you in the morning.'

Bill sat on, looking into the dregs of his pint. He should go home, at least he had a bed there, if nothing else. However, he didn't want to do that, but he didn't want to stay in the pub either.

He closed his eyes and thought about Diane. It was time he went to see her.

Ryan stood in the doorway watching his mother. She had been badly affected by Emma's death. It seemed to have had the effect of making her calmer, but she brooded more, although she didn't clean obsessively the way she used to and she had given up her job as a cleaner. Ryan wasn't sure if that was a good or a bad thing.

'I'm going out tonight,' he said.

Diane turned to look at him. 'About time. I thought you were going to stay cooped up in the house forever.'

Ryan didn't answer her. He closed the door quietly, and left the house.

His mother had no idea the effort it had taken him to decide to go out.

Too much had happened over the previous few months, culminating in Emma's death. By the end, when everything was coming to a head, it had felt as if he were sliding into a deep, black pit. And now, after forcing himself to leave the house, he wasn't sure it was the right decision. He was tempted to run back in and up the stairs, and close the door on the world outside.

He took a deep breath and told himself not to be a coward, that was no way to live life.

The club was fairly new, it had been open a few months, but he'd heard on the grapevine it was the place to go if you wanted some action. He wasn't sure if he wanted action, but he was sure he wanted to check it out.

What had happened with Phil and Gus, in Teasers' toilet, had been brutal and degrading. It made him doubt himself and his urges. But he was still drawn to attractive men in the same way others were attracted to beautiful women.

Ryan stood hesitantly in the doorway listening to the music seeping out from the bar into the street. He wore tight white trousers, and a silky black shirt, open at the neck to display a thick gold chain. His face was perfectly made up, but not overstated. His skin looked flawless with a dusting of face powder, his eyebrows had been plucked and pencilled, his mascara was discreet, and his lips were coloured with the merest touch of pink lipstick. While his hair, normally tied back in a ponytail, flowed over his shoulders and down his back in silky waves. His arm still ached from brushing it.

Pushing the thought of Phil out of his head, he opened the door and walked in. The pulse of music was louder inside, and the bar resounded with voices and laughter. Male couples and female couples swayed to the music on the tiny dance floor. Others propped up the bar or sat at tables over to the side of the room.

Ryan breathed a sigh of contentment. He knew, instinctively, this was a place where he fitted in, a place where he could be himself instead of hiding away. And maybe, just maybe, he might find a kindred spirit here.

The house felt empty after Ryan left. Diane wished she'd commented on how nice he looked, but she hadn't wanted to embarrass him. Poor Ryan, he'd experienced so much trouble coming to terms with how he was. She knew he'd taken Emma's death badly, just as badly as he'd taken Jade's disappearance, and she regretted not having given him more of her time.

She still hadn't got over Emma. When she'd told her to go, she had no idea Emma would do something so extreme. But at least she was at peace now, although Diane had no daughters left.

The doorbell startled her out of her reverie, and she was surprised to see Bill Murphy on the doorstep.

'What is it you want?' She debated in her mind whether to invite him in, but decided not to.

'I wondered how you were.' His voice was hesitant. 'I should have come to see you before . . . ' He shuffled his feet. 'If there's anything I can do to help . . . '

'I'm sorry,' she said. 'But there's nothing you can do to help me. Please don't come back.'

She closed the door, walked down the hall, and into the living room. She meant to sit down and forget he'd been here, but something drew her to the window.

He was still standing at the door where she'd left him, but as she watched, he turned and walked down the path. The dejected droop of his shoulders increased her sadness, and she was unable to move away from the window until he drove off.

He'd been a nice man, she'd liked him and, although there had never been anything more between them, there had always been that slight frisson of electricity. The merest suggestion they could have built a relationship.

With tears in her eyes, she turned away from the window. It was time to scrub the kitchen floor.

CHRIS LONGMUIR

Chris is an award winning novelist and has published three novels in her Dundee Crime Series. Night Watcher, the first book in the series, won the Scottish Association of Writers' Pitlochry Award, and the sequel, Dead Wood, won the Dundee International Book Prize, as well as the Pitlochry Award. Missing Believed Dead is the third book in the series.

Chris also publishes a historical crime series, the Kirsty Campbell Mysteries, featuring one of Britain's first policewomen.

Her crime novels are set in Dundee, Scotland, and have been described as atmospheric page turners. Chris also writes historical sagas, short stories and historical articles which have been published in America and Britain. She confesses to being a bit of a techno-geek, and builds computers in her spare time.

Chris is a member of the Society of Authors, the Crime Writers Association, and the Scottish Association of Writers.

www.chrislongmuir.co.uk

Also by Chris Longmuir

DUNDEE CRIME SERIES

Night Watcher

Dead Wood

Missing Believed Dead

THE KIRSTY CAMPBELL MYSTERIES

Devil's Porridge

The Death Game

HISTORICAL SAGAS

A Salt Splashed Cradle

NONFICTION

Nuts & Bolts of Self-Publishing